Having previously worked as a journalist and then a psychotherapist, Caroline Dunford enjoyed many years helping other people shape their personal life stories before taking the plunge and writing her own stories. She has now published almost thirty books in genres ranging from historical crime to thrillers and romance, including her much-loved Euphemia Martins mysteries and a new series set around WWII featuring Euphemia's perceptive daughter Hope Stapleford. Caroline also teaches creative writing courses part-time at the University of Edinburgh.

Praise for Caroline Dunford:

'A sparkling and witty crime debut with a female protagonist to challenge Miss Marple' Lin Anderson

'Impeccable historical detail with a light touch' Lesley Cookman

'Euphemia Martins is feisty, funny and completely adorable' Colette McCormick

'A rattlingly good dose of Edwardian country house intrigue with plenty of twists and turns and clues to puzzle through' Booklore.co.uk

HOPE
TO
SURVIVE

Caroline Dunford

ACCENT

First published in 2021 by Headline Accent
An imprint of HEADLINE PUBLISHING GROUP

1

Cataloguing in Publication Data is available from the British Library

ISBN 978 1 4722 7665 0

Typeset in 10.5/13pt Bembo Std by Jouve (UK), Milton Keynes

Printed and bound in Great Britain by Clays Ltd, Elcograf S.p.A.

MIX
Paper from
responsible sources
FSC® C104740

Headline's policy is to use papers that are natural, renewable and recyclable
products and made from wood grown in well-managed forests and other
controlled sources. The logging and manufacturing processes are expected
to conform to the environmental regulations of the country of origin.

HEADLINE PUBLISHING GROUP
An Hachette UK Company
Carmelite House
50 Victoria Embankment
London EC4Y 0DZ

www.headline.co.uk
www.hachette.co.uk

I write about the two world wars because my family and I are bound up in the events of WWI and WWII. My two grandfathers served in both the wars, and my parents survived the Blitz as children in the heart of London. Echoes of what my grandfathers and their wives went through have reached down to my generation and on to my children. Those two wars changed everything and everyone. If certain psychologists and biologists are to be believed, some of those memories are even locked within our generational DNA. I cannot imagine enduring what they went through. But then I am sure neither could my grandparents. They were ordinary people in a time of great crisis. They did what they did because to do otherwise was unthinkable. I suspect this is the heart of warfare, the very ordinary doing the extraordinary because they must. I will never praise war, but my undying gratitude and admiration goes out to those who fought to defend their families, their country and their way of life.

In particular, I'd like to mention Edward Dunford, my paternal grandfather, who commanded two fire engines on the London Docks during the worst of the Blitz. His career as a firefighter ended when he was blown from the top of the tallest ladder into the fire he was attempting to extinguish. Amazingly, he survived.

Chapter One

August 1939, London

We were sitting in one of the offices my godfather didn't have.
The room was neat, business-like and only slightly bigger than
his huge leather-topped desk. It was situated on the fourth floor
of a Georgian building which had a lovely view over the park.
My godfather, Fitzroy, sat in one of those rotating captain's chairs
and swivelled slightly from side to side. By the window was a lea-
ther wing-backed chair, angled to make the best of the view, and
by the fire was a medium-sized dog basket with a white puppy
snoozing in it. Bernie and I sat in front of the desk in two upright
wooden chairs, clearly chosen for their lack of comfort. Bernie,
wearing a ridiculously short skirt that practically showed her
stocking tops, was sitting with her legs crossed, swinging the
uppermost one annoyingly and repetitively. My godfather passed
her a newspaper and a pen.

'What do you expect me to do with this?'

'The crossword,' said my godfather, and ignored her from that
point on. He picked up the papers I had given him and then
dropped them on his desk again. 'None of these will do, Hope.'

'We *have* looked,' I said.

Without glancing up, Bernie said, 'Hope doesn't want a large
apartment. She thinks I would hold parties.'

My godfather raised an eyebrow at me. I shrugged somewhat
helplessly.

'So, money isn't the issue?' he asked.

I leant over and took back one of the papers. On it I wrote an

1

amount with *Bernie's Budget* written above it. It was neither a small sum nor an outrageously large sum. In fact, it seemed to me to be the perfect amount for a half-share of a two-bedroomed flat somewhere respectable. Currently, Bernie was outstaying her welcome at the American Embassy where her father had been Ambassador, and I was staying at my club, The Forum. The real reason we were not yet ensconced in a nice little flat was because my godfather hadn't approved of anything we had found.

While Bernie was not related to my godfather, I wouldn't have put it past him to cause her some trouble if he felt she was leading me astray. However, I had my own more than adequate resources. I could do whatever I liked. In fact, my father would have strongly approved of my ignoring Fitzroy's advice. Except I knew he generally gave very good advice. Even if it didn't always look like the wisest course, his nudges, in the case of my investments and other aspects of my life, had always proved acutely provident. But then I knew that Fitzroy was a senior member of the British Intelligence Service. And I knew this because he had recently recruited me.

'I suppose you could try this one?' he said, opening a drawer and passing me a property listing. I scanned through the details and recognised it was perfect in every way. Two bedrooms, a social area, a well-equipped kitchen so we could cook if we had to, a decent bathroom, and even a small balcony off the living space. It was in Pimlico, Belgravia Road, on the edge of Warwick Square. One of those nice, white-brick, terraced buildings that had once been townhouses but had, over time, been carved up into separate flats. The moment I saw it I knew it was the place he had intended us to have all along. I passed the paper to Bernie, who dropped the newspaper on the floor.

'Ooh!' she said. 'Sunset cocktails on the balcony!'

Fitzroy's expression grew somewhat pained and he shifted in his chair, focusing his attention on me so that Bernie was only on the very periphery of his vision. 'What do you think?'

'Perfect,' I said. 'How very clever of you to find exactly what we wanted.'

The lines around his eyes crinkled slightly and he gave an almost imperceptible nod.

'Is there a telephone number to call?' I asked. 'Perhaps we could give them a quick ring and see if we could visit later today. Bernie? There's a telephone in the lobby of that little hotel we passed on the way here, the one you wanted to go into for a quick cocktail when you thought we were much too early?'

'Oh, good idea,' said Bernie, standing. 'Thank you ever so much . . .' She floundered, and offered her hand to Fitzroy. 'Well . . . I'll see you in the cocktail bar, Hope.'

A short period of time after she had closed the door behind her, we saw her in the street, hurrying along as fast as she could in her tight skirt. I sat back down in my chair and relaxed. 'You know she has no idea how to address you,' I said.

Fitzroy gave me a half-smile. He turned and opened the cupboard behind him. 'A small brandy?' he said, pouring me one before I could protest. 'You do know, don't you, that the whole idea behind cocktails was to disguise the taste of the awful liquor they used during Prohibition? Mucky stuff. Do you like this office? The view is excellent.' He remained by the window, watching Bernie wiggling her way along the street. 'It isn't mine, but I'm thinking of keeping it for a while.'

'Bernie,' I said, in an attempt to bring the conversation back on track. 'I have to tell her something. Should she refer to you by your military rank? Should she call you Eric, like Mother does? Or should she call you Fitzroy?'

'She knows I'm your godfather, that should be enough. If she wants to address to me directly, which I am disinclined to encourage, she can address me by the rank I am wearing at the time.'

'Which will change?'

'On occasion.'

'Along with the uniform, no doubt,' I said, 'and I will be able to offer no explanation. She is more observant than you think.'

Fitzroy gave a slight snort.

I sighed and took a small sip of brandy. It was excellent, so

3

smooth it felt honey-like. 'You had that property in mind all along, didn't you?'

'Of course. It had to be properly assessed and vetted. But your little friend needs to believe I came across it by accident. You can make up some story – the property of a great-aunt of mine, or some such thing.'

'Do you have a great-aunt?'

'No, you're probably right. I'm too old for a great-aunt. Keep forgetting my age. You can make it an aunt. And yes, I believe I do still have some of those.'

'Have you really become Bernie's guardian?'

Fitzroy winced. 'No, not exactly. I have made an agreement with her parents that I have a . . . err . . . "watching brief". I don't believe they would have left her behind otherwise, and you certainly can't live on your own.'

'So, I owe you another debt of thanks?'

'My dear Hope, you owe me nothing. I am simply doing my best to be a decent godfather to you.'

'I think my father thought that your involvement would entail little more than postal orders and Christmas cards.'

Fitzroy finished his brandy with a flourish and set down his glass lightly. His skin didn't flush. My mother had told me he had a head for spirits. (What she had actually said was, 'For heaven's sake, never try to out-drink your godfather. You'll end up under the table and he'll hold it over you for ever.')

Fitzroy coughed. 'Yes, well, your father, decent fellow that he is, has never exactly been a close acquaintance of mine. He's often misjudged me.' He cast his eyes down at that, in mock sadness. I half suppressed a giggle. When he looked up, all trace of humour was gone. 'Are you sure, Hope, that you want to come and work for me? It's going to be damned difficult.'

'I thought we had already agreed?'

'Your mother didn't believe me either when I warned her. She found out the hard way. I'm conflicted about watching you go through the same process.'

4

'I can never predict what you will say next.'

'Thank you,' said Fitzroy. 'I appreciate that.' He took a deep breath. 'You came in to see me today as my goddaughter, and I have treated you as such. When you attend me as one of my people, I will behave very differently.'

'Of course. I don't expect special treatment,' I said.

'Good. I couldn't give it to you, even if I wanted to. We probably won't meet here. I'll let you know where and when. I'd like to have had some time, privately, to get you up to speed on the various sections, but I doubt Herr Hitler will afford me the courtesy. You're as well skilled, if not more so, than many of the recent recruits, but you haven't exactly been trained through official channels. People will want to test you. You'll have a rough time of it.'

'My mother coped, didn't she?'

'Admirably, but it was a different time, and her personality, well, it's . . .'

'More robust than mine?' I finished.

'More passionate,' corrected my godfather. 'You are more like me, a watcher and a schemer.'

'You seem to have done all right.'

'I, my dear, am a man, and have all the advantages thereto pertaining. There are precious few of us who appreciate and value how much women can offer the Service.'

There didn't seem to be much I could say in response to this. I waited a while to see what Fitzroy would say next. He put his glass on the side. When he sat back down at the desk, he leant forward, resting on his elbows and steepling his fingers. I waited while he watched me. Despite having spent a lot of my early childhood sitting on his lap and, I am told, tugging at his moustache, I found the figure before me daunting. I knew better than to look away, and eventually I gave in and spoke

'How's Jack Junior?' I asked, glancing down at the puppy, glad to have an excuse to avoid the scrutiny of his gaze.

'Just Jack,' said Fitzroy, snapping my attention back to him.

'I'm sorry.'

Fitzroy made a sound halfway between clearing his throat and a cough. It was the closest he came these days to expressing emotion. 'Do you think you'll be all right living with Bernie? She's a very noisy cover for you, but then, I suspect, if she sees or hears anything she shouldn't, you'll be able to tell her she was drunk and imagined it.'

'You make her sound awful.'

'I don't believe she's currently doing herself any favours. I'm hardly running with the younger set, but even I'm hearing things . . .' He trailed off, leaving it to my imagination to finish the sentence.

'You hear everything,' I said, earning myself a fleeting smile. Then my godfather sat further forward and put his arms on the desk.

'Hope, my dear, I am very proud of you, and always will be.'

This time it was my turn to deflect. I looked down at the sleeping dog. 'Are you really going to keep this office? It's rather small.'

'Yes, but officially it won't exist. There are a lot of changes happening within the Service at present. A lot of people carving out their personal domains. Even I've been promoted.'

'To?'

He frowned, as if trying to recall. 'Lieutenant-Colonel,' he said. 'Makes me feel as if I should grow a bigger, bushier moustache and make noises like an ageing bear. At least that's how I remember them from my youth.'

'Congratulations.'

Fitzroy shrugged. 'As long as I'm allowed to do my job, I don't much care what they call me. Maybe don't mention it to your mother, though. It's all still a bit iffy when it comes to ranking females in the Service.'

'I thought you said my mother had retired?'

Fitzroy shook his head. 'She mostly withdrew from field work, but she never stopped working for, or rather with, me. In the current circumstances, she's back on the team. One of my, I mean

6

our, most experienced officers. I hope to keep her out of the field. She'll be adding being a handler to her other duties. Don't worry, I won't put you two together. I'm aware you don't have the smoothest of relationships. However, she could be in London a fair bit. It might give you two an opportunity to bond.'

'But where would she stay? Do you mean she would be staying with me?' I could feel my heart begin to race at the thought.

Fitzroy shook his head. 'No, she has her own flat.'

'What?'

He frowned. 'You didn't know? Your mother bought it a long time ago, when we were working together during the Great War. It gave her a base here to operate from.'

'But I thought she . . . I mean, I didn't . . . I don't think my father knows.' I felt myself blush for the first time. Only my mother, I thought. 'It's . . .'

'You didn't think she stayed with me, did you?' said my god-father. 'That would hardly have been proper.'

'No, of course not. She's never spoken much about that time. Before I was born. I knew she was involved . . .'

'Very much so. Your mother is a first-class spy. Euphemia has spent her life in the service of others. Only thing the poor girl ever got to do that she enjoyed was active service.'

I got up. Unsaid between us was the knowledge that my mother had only ceased field work because of me. 'I should go and meet Bernie.'

My godfather stood and came around the desk. I looked up at him. 'You admire my mother, don't you?'

He put a hand on my shoulder. 'I am very fond of you both. Be careful, Hope. I won't be around as much as I'd like over the next few months. All kinds of new shifts afoot.' He handed me a business card with a single telephone number on the front. I turned it over and saw a short list of names and places. 'Learn them, then burn it.' He gave me a lop-sided smile. 'It's what you might con-sider my answering service on the one side. The other is . . . well, if I'm unavailable, those are contacts who'll go to extreme lengths to help you, if need be, no questions asked. I sincerely hope you will never have to use them, but if you get yourself into a tight corner, do. But,' he said, putting his other hand on my other shoulder so I could feel the weight of both, 'only use them with caution, as a near-last resort.'

'Near-last?'

'Last resort is often too late, in my experience. If you still think the situation can be salvaged. I feel as if I am leaving you untethered. I'm not. You're skilled, even if you're coming in as a new recruit. It's simply damned hard for me to remember you're a capable young woman and not a child any more. I suspect I may be becoming sentimental in my old age. Definitely something I shall have to address.' He lifted his hands away from me. 'As well as what's coming, I have family business to attend to, at exactly the wrong time. Typical of my father to make life as inconvenient as possible.'

It took me a moment to work out what he was saying. 'Your father? Oh, I'm so sorry.'

Fitzroy shrugged. 'Don't be. It has raised certain complications that I must deal with, but other than that I am not affected. We were never close, and I have found myself profoundly unmoved, unless my grief is masking itself as irritation.'

I tried in vain to think of a response, failed, and bent to pick up the newspaper Bernie had dropped on the floor. I handed it to him. He glanced at it and his eyes widened. 'Well, I'll be blowed.'

I peered over. 'Bernie's very good at crosswords. She does them when she's bored, which is often.'

'Hmm?' said my godfather, frowning and clearly not listening to me. 'I shall have to tell them to make it harder . . . unless . . . no, that seems quite unlikely.' He focused his attention on me as if waiting for me to supply an answer to the unspoken question. Again, the moment passed as I failed to find anything to say. 'You should check in on your asset, Harvey. I've already had to quash one report of him acting outside the lines of the law. Tell him to get himself in order or he's burned as an asset.'

He opened the door, effectively closing down the conversation. I stood on tiptoe and kissed him briefly on the right cheek. His face softened slightly, but he nodded towards the door. I was out on the street before I realised. I'd been so lost in thought, I hadn't had a chance to meet Jack properly. Still, if my godfather was leaving town, maybe he would leave the puppy with us, if he considered the apartment suitable. I had a sneaking suspicion that the criteria for Jack's accommodation would be stricter than his criteria for that of Bernie and me. And why had my mother never told my father or me about her London flat? If it was meant to be a secret, Fitzroy had given it away awfully casually. And he never gave away secrets. Did she still use it? When she said she was paying a short visit to relatives, was she actually coming here? And if she *was*, what was she doing?

Chapter Two

In the small hours of the morning on 1st September, the telephone burst into life.

RING! RING!

Bleary-eyed, I sat up. Bernie would probably sleep through the angels sounding the last trumpet on Judgement Day. Our aptly named charwoman, Mrs Spring, wouldn't turn up for a considerable number of hours yet.

RING! RING!

With enormous reluctance I crawled from the warmth of my bed.

RING! RING!

Could it actually be getting louder? Where were my slippers?

RING! RING!

I brushed under my bed with my hand but found only a cocktail glass. I pulled it out and looked at it, trying to remember how it might have got there.

RING! RING!

I padded in my bare feet across the cold marble floor of our foyer in Belgravia Road.

RING! RING!

The telephone vibrated angrily atop the small marquetry table upon which it sat.

RING! RING!

How annoying. How persistent. Likely one of Bernie's suitors.

RING! RING!

'Hello?' said my godfather when I picked up the receiver. I felt positively discombobulated. All I could manage in my befuddled state was a sleepy greeting, which came out as, 'Haaa-ooo.'

'What's wrong?' he snapped. 'Why did it take you so long to answer my call? Did you have to run all the way down from White Orchards?'

'I was asleep.'

'Asleep?' Astonishment and reproach sounded in his voice.

I blinked and shook my head. 'You sound shocked. Would you rather I was out at some seedy nightclub snorting cocaine?'

'Frankly, I would find that more understandable for someone of your age and social status at this time of the morning. However, you've always been a sensible girl.' Again, I heard that tone of reproach.

'Is that a—'

'Now listen. I need you to come in.'

'This morning?'

'No, Hope. Now. Germany has invaded Poland. This is how it'll all kick off. God knows, we're not prepared for any of it.'

He gave me a street name, no number, then rang off.

This then was my godfather in spymaster mode. My mother had always claimed, contrary to my experience, that Fitzroy was horribly bad-tempered, and this must have been what she meant.

I staggered, literally leaning on one wall, then the other, of our hallway as I made my way to the bathroom. The electric light gave my skin an unpleasantly sallow effect. I turned on the cold tap, which spluttered a bit, but finally delivered a decent stream. I splashed my face with water – it was stunningly cold, like slivers of ice penetrating my brain. It did the trick and I finally woke up. Fitzroy had said Germany was invading Poland. He'd said we were not prepared, and he would know. For the first time I wondered if I could handle what was coming. I felt bile rising inside me. I leant over the loo just in time and expelled last night's

11

supper. As Bernie had been the one who cooked it, it tasted slightly better on the way back up. I straightened and washed my flushed face, rinsed out my mouth and told myself not to be a fool.

Ten minutes later, I was writing a note to Bernie on the pad by the telephone:

Been called away. Aim to be back by dinner. If not, don't worry – as if you would!
 Have a sober day? Think of your liver.
 Love H

A quarter of an hour later, due to my good fortune in catching a cab driver still on shift, I turned up outside a block of very non-descript offices. The building looked so thoroughly innocuous that I knew it had to be the right place.

I jumped out, paid the cabbie, and ran in through the rust-coloured double doors. Inside I found a small vestibule. An older man in a smart suit sat in a tiny office behind a window, sipping a cup of tea. 'Hope Stapleford,' I said, hoping this was enough.

'You're late,' growled the man in a surprisingly deep voice. 'ID card?' He spoke with the clipped voice of an army man, but he was in civilian clothing. I felt very much like asking him who he was, but common sense prevailed. I was already late.

I went to hand it through the little letterbox-like grille at the bottom of the window, but he didn't release the latch. 'Up against the glass, please.'

I did as I was told. 'Through those doors and up to the third floor. Room 345. Report to the Commander.'

I took the lift, which was poky and smelled of stale cigarette smoke, and it creaked and shuddered its way up to the third floor. I found room 345 easily enough. From it came the sound of male laughter and one singular basso voice. 'Now, now, lads. We should give her a chance.'

I gritted my teeth before opening the door. I had the distinct feeling that, other than a few secretaries, there weren't many

12

females in this building so, the odds were, they meant I was the 'her' to be given a chance.

I knocked and entered. A barrage of eyes met mine. It took me a moment to separate out the individuals, but I sensed immediately that my godfather was not there.

'Apologies for my lateness,' I said, knowing better than to offer an excuse. 'I am Hope Stapleford. I was told to report to this room.'

'Miss Stapleford, who is also out of uniform,' said the basso voice.

'I'm sorry, Captain, but I have yet to be issued with a uniform.'

'Look, miss, you have come to the right room, haven't you?' said a younger man, with a sergeant's stripe. 'We're all regular army here. Don't normally include women, unless you're making a tea run.'

I surveyed the room quickly. It looked as if both the furniture and the men had been hastily assembled. The chairs were only similar in that they all looked office-like and uncomfortable. As well as those, an assortment of small desks and slightly larger tables filled the room. Of the men present, the Captain, tall, slightly overweight, and skirting middle age, was the only man standing. The other man who had addressed me sat on a chair, rocking backwards. He had a cheeky face, tight red curls, and as many freckles as a leopard has spots. Two men sat on the edges of desks. At the very back of the room, out of direct light, I could see the silhouette of another man leaning against the wall with his arms folded. He struck me as the figure most worthy of notice because of all of them he was the one most at ease. The others, even the Captain, displayed signs of tenseness. Jaws were set too firmly, eyes blinked too rapidly, and the two men sitting on the desks were clearly trying too hard to telegraph relaxed postures. I wanted to ask what made them all so uneasy, but I kept my thoughts to myself.

'No, I am quite sure I am meant to be here,' I said to the

13

Sergeant. 'I received a phone call from someone I trust completely, telling me to report here. Besides, I wouldn't have even known this was an Army building without having been given the directions.'

'Still seems a bit of a rum do,' said the Second Lieutenant sitting on the desk. Despite a weak chin, he had a well-built physique and a fitting upper-crust accent. 'What do you think, Captain Max?'

'I had been told to expect a Cadet Stapleford,' said the captain, 'but I had no idea you would turn out to be a *woman*.'

I bristled at this comment, knowing from what I had overheard it was a lie, but I brought to mind my godfather's stern warning about the regular army and respect for hierarchy.

'Is this a problem, sir? Is there a particular reason why you require male recruits?' I did my best to sound polite.

'We're an ideas group,' said the chirpy red-haired sergeant. 'We'll be talking about logistics and stuff. Nothing to interest a woman.'

'I have a degree in mathematics from Oxford,' I said. 'I may be of some use.'

The Captain rubbed his chin. He was still standing. A heavy frown creased his forehead. 'Well, I suppose you might be of help with the adding-up, but we're a high-security group. Can't say I'm keen on having a female present. No offence, my dear, but ladies do tend to gab on a bit, don't they?'

A number of retorts came into my head, but none of them were suitable for a so-called superior officer. Why the hell had Fitzroy sent me here, and why had he put me in as a lowly cadet? Surely I was better than that?

'Who gave you your orders?' asked the Captain. 'You said you trusted them.'

Only at this point did it occur to me that Fitzroy might have sent me in as one of his people to monitor this unit, or someone within it.

'Come on, girl. Spit it out,' said the Captain. He looked more

14

relaxed now. I could already picture him on his telephone afterwards, calling up someone and saying, 'You'll never believe this, but we've been sent . . .'

Fitzroy hadn't said if I could mention his name, but common sense dictated I refrained from doing so. Besides, I only had one of his code names. I realised with growing astonishment my godfather had kept me ignorant of his real name – other than his Christian name, Eric – the whole of my life.

'I can't say,' I said.

'What!' blurted the Captain. 'You may be a new recruit, so I'll overlook your insolence this one time, but you've been asked a question by a senior officer. Reply, or I'll put you on a charge! How would you like that?'

The man at the back of the room stepped into the light. Middle-aged, but clearly fit, he had short greying black hair, dark blue eyes, and was wearing unmarked fatigues. 'She's all right,' he said.

The room turned as one to look at him.

The Captain spluttered, 'You mean you know her, Cole?'

'I know who she is,' said Cole. 'You brought me in as a consultant, Max. Trust me on this. She's all right. You'd be a fool to leave her making the tea,' he added.

All eyes turned back to me with renewed interest. 'Well, that's quite a recommendation,' said the Captain, sitting down again. 'Cole tends to be rather scant when it comes to praise.'

I took this as an invitation to stay and edged further into the room. One of the men on the desks turned a chair around for me. I sat on it, my hands folded in my lap, and waited. As I did so, I mentally assessed the men in the room.

My gaze didn't go unnoticed by Cole, who suddenly spoke. 'Before we go any further, Cadet, give me an appraisal of the men in this room.'

I looked at the Captain, who nodded.

I started with the red-haired Sergeant. 'You have a slight Irish lilt to your voice,' I said. 'You're wiry rather than heavily muscled. I haven't seen you move, but I would hazard that you can hold your own in a scrum. Your formal instruction goes back no further than basic training. You're bright and alert, but your background and class have held promotion back. I could beat you in a fight.'

The Sergeant laughed and held out his hand. 'Lewis Bradshaw. People don't normally detect the Irish in me. My grandpappy came across decades ago. You're welcome to challenge me any time, darlin'. I'll be gentle.'

I gave a slight, insincere smile. 'The Second Lieutenant is the fittest man in this room, but his arm strength is greater than that of his legs. I suspect he is a sportsman. Oxford rowing blue? Only recently joined up.'

'Martin Wiseman,' said the man in question. 'Spot on. Good parlour trick.'

I didn't smile. 'The Lieutenant is harder to assess. Both he and Second Lieutenant Wiseman have spent some time studying – acting, I think. They have unusually good deportment, and have been overly careful not to turn their backs on the room. Probably at college together. Clearly old friends, but the Lieutenant is not a rower. He might be more of a reader. Until I see him move, I can't comment on his physical prowess. He's not a boxer. On the other hand, there are some fighting disciplines that leave less of a tell-tale influence on the body.'

'Charles Merryworth,' said the man, nodding to me.

'And me?' said Cole.

'You, sir? With respect, I'd go a long way not to make an enemy of you.'

He laughed. 'See why they sent her to you now, Max? She's Alice's daughter. Probably been in training all her life.'

Chapter Three

The Captain registered who my mother was, but no one else did. I could see them fizzing with questions, but Captain Max moved things along.

In what was little more than an old office, smelling faintly of dust and polish, he told us the likely fate of the nation. 'We've got a bit of a job on, lads.' He coughed, 'And lady.'

Everyone looked at me again. I felt like saying, please, ignore my gender, but I doubted it would have a dampening effect. If anything, it would have made things even more awkward. There were other women in the Army, mostly secretarial and nursing, but presumably none were quite as jumped-up as me.

'Ahem, as I was saying, it's going to be a bit of work this time to beat the Boche back into his lair. I don't like speaking ill of our gentlemen in Westminster, but it has to be said, they have miscalculated. Now, that's between you and me. It's not to leave this room. I hope we're clear on that.'

His eyes sought mine. I nodded slightly in an attempt to stop him drawing even more attention to me. He coughed again. 'Many of us who were in the last show came to believe that the Great War would indeed end all wars. The loss of life was beyond anything you young men could imagine. Absolutely staggering. The better part of a whole generation wiped out. Hardly a family in the country hadn't lost a father, a son, or a brother. Often more than one. The men of whole estates went off to war together and died together. Even those from the best schools, Eton, Harrow,

Rugby, wiped off the face of the earth. We had no idea how we'd ever recover. Terrible time. Terrible.' He heaved a big sigh. 'But we got back on the ruddy horse. Pulled the country back together and we vowed, on both sides, never again. Seems this Hitler chappie didn't get the memo. So, when Mr Chamberlain announces, "peace in our time", most of the people in power are of the opinion that is exactly what we've got. Except it isn't. Only goes to prove you can never trust the Boche. Sneaky devils. Didn't mean a word of it. Hitler is still coming, and now we're on the back foot. That won't do. That won't do at all.'

The three young soldiers made various supportive noises. 'Can you explain what you mean by on the back foot?' I asked.

'Do I have to spell it out to you, Miss Stapleton?' said the Captain, getting my name wrong and clearly not expecting a reply.

'I would find that helpful, sir,' I said.

The Captain wiped his hand across his forehead. 'Do any of you other chaps have an idea of what I mean?' he asked hopefully.

'We're not in a place to face Hitler's armies yet,' said Bradshaw. 'We need to start getting men overseas as fast as we can. Drop men into Norway before the Germans reach it. We need to get the BEF to dig in on the French Eastern Border. Get the trenches in. We need to think about Poland too.'

'Excellent,' said the Captain. 'I can see you read your briefing thoroughly, Bradshaw.' What briefing, I thought, and determined to telephone my godfather when I got home. Something was amiss here. 'Trouble is, we're not ready for the show.'

'How so, sir?' I asked again.

'I think he's made it clear enough, Stapleford,' said Merryworth. 'We're a bit late to the party, but we can make that up, sir, can't we?'

'We thrashed them once,' said Wiseman, 'we can do it again. Obviously, it won't be easy, but warfare has moved on. We've better methods at our disposal. It doesn't have to be as bloody as last time. We need to hit them hard and hit them fast. Show them that Britain won't stand for this kind of over-reaching German ambition.'

The Captain ceased his pacing to face us. He shifted his weight slightly from side to side. It wasn't much, but it telegraphed his uneasiness to me. 'There's more, isn't there, sir?' I pushed.

'They need to know, Max,' said Cole. 'You wanted my opinion, and my opinion is there's no point having this think tank if it doesn't base itself on the utter truth.'

The Captain coughed again. 'Very well. Now, this will be hard to hear, chaps.' I think by this point he had forgotten I existed. His eyes were on some horizon only he could see. 'Great Britain, I regret to inform you, is far from ready to fight. We are recruiting manpower, but we lack weaponry, machinery, planes, tanks, and trained soldiers.'

There were audible gasps in the room as his words sank in.

I got the distinct impression that the Captain was even more worried than he was letting on. He paced around the room, throwing looks at Cole, who didn't open his mouth again, though he nodded a couple of times when the Captain outlined how tactics and strategy had worked during the last war. Then he opened up the debate.

Wiseman, Merryworth and Bradshaw proved to be as eager as schoolboys competing to win merits for their house. It seemed the purpose of our little group was to think about how warfare could be conducted in modern times – and this I took to mean, with the current limitations we had. The Great War had been one of attrition. Two great armies facing each other across no man's land, taking it in turns to sacrifice soldiers in the hope of gaining a few inches of ground. This time Herr Hitler hadn't bothered with any of that and had marched forth and taken what he wanted.

'It's clear this whole affair is going to be nothing like the Great War,' said Captain Max. 'We've got to think about things in an entirely different way – like the Boche are, but better. We need young minds and new ideas. That's where you come in.'

19

I almost got interested before we were told that our particular area of focus was on developing food and supply lines. Of course, I was aware these are crucial for military advancement, but from the way our situation had been described I wasn't at all sure we were even going to get to the stage of marching men across Europe. Besides, Napoleon had used a grocer as his quartermaster, and it seemed a sensible idea to use someone who knew about food and not simply how to eat it. Also, it was clear to me that we needed to start thinking how we were going to feed the British Isles if Hitler continued his march across Europe.

'What is the state of our Navy?' I asked. 'You've suggested that we are a little under-prepared, sir, but do we still control the seas around us?'

'That's classified.'

I stopped asking anything after that. If he wasn't prepared to give us the relevant information we needed, what was the point of being there at all?

The meeting eventually broke for tea and sandwiches. I was left feeling no more comfortable than when I entered.

Cole caught up with me on the steps down to the cafeteria. 'It's remarkable how like your mother you look,' he said. His voice was calm and deep, and he walked quietly, despite wearing boots, placing each foot down with quick grace, like a cat picking its way over difficult ground.

'So I've been told,' I said. 'Though we're very different in temperament.'

The edge of Cole's mouth twitched. 'I can tell,' he said. 'Your mother would have been all over those men.'

I stopped on the step. 'I don't know what you mean.'

Cole stopped too. Fortunately, we had been the last to leave the room. 'I meant she would have verbally torn them apart,' he paused. 'Let's just say she wouldn't have taken any nonsense from them.'

'She can be confrontational,' I said. 'Do you know her well?'

Cole nodded and gestured at me to go forward. 'Better than

most in the Service, with the exception of your commanding officer, Fitzroy. He isn't one for rules and regs, for the most part, so he let her have her head. I'm glad to see you have more sense. Things have moved on. No one can behave in the regular army like she used to.'

'A difficult remark to respond to,' I said. 'I didn't get the impression you were part of this – what? Strategy group?'

'No, the Captain brought me in as a consultant, but as you have no doubt realised, and I have confirmed, there's nothing much for me to do here. Or you, for that matter.'

'You don't think discussing new ways to move supplies is going to cut it, do you?'

We'd reached the bottom of the steps now. I could see the rest of them, except for the Captain, who had gone off elsewhere, disappearing through the double doors to the cafeteria beyond. 'There'll be a lot of box-checking going on,' said Cole. 'I doubt this particular group will come to anything much. Max is all right, but he's out of date. He's just as much on the back foot as he claims the country is. Who attached you to this unit?'

I shrugged. 'I was told to report to this building and the man at the desk told me which room to go to. I don't know any more than that. I don't have a uniform, and I'm not aware that I'm officially attached anywhere.'

'Hmm,' said Cole. 'I suppose it's possible he doesn't know what to do with you.'

'You're referring to my godfather,' I said.

This earned me a smile. 'Good for you,' he said. 'Straight at it.'

I took a deep breath and prepared to step off the cliff. 'I don't know,' I said. 'Before the war there were certain things I was going to do for him, but they sounded more like police work than anything military. I wasn't given a rank. Can you be enlisted in the army without knowing?'

Cole raised an eyebrow, in a manner uncannily like my godfather. 'If there's a way of doing that, then I imagine Fitzroy would know how.'

Chapter Four

I didn't get home until late that night. I found Bernie draped over
the balcony, cocktail glass in hand, wearing an entirely inappropriate evening gown. She waved at me as I walked up the street.
'Hello, Hope,' she called. 'You're just in time for a drinky-poo!
Simon had to go home, or report to someone or something, so I
have a whole jug of freshly made cocktail left. Isn't that simply
divine?'

I put my head down and walked faster.

'Hope! Hope, darling! Look up.' She leant further over the balcony. Far too far. She slipped and almost went over. A glass sailed
through the air and smashed on the pavement beside me. I barely
darted out of the way in time. 'Oopsie!' said Bernie. 'I've done a
smash-smash. Second one today. What a fumble-fingers I am.'

'Get back in the flat!' I hissed.

'What? What did you say?' said Bernie in the voice of someone
whose hearing had been damped by more than a few glasses of
whatever it was she was drinking.

I unlocked the front door and raced up the stairs. I yanked
open the door of the flat, which Bernie or whoever Simon was
had left unbolted, and charged into the front room. I pulled
Bernie back into the flat by the back of her dress, turning her and
pushing her hard towards the settee, so she landed face down. As
she scrabbled to right herself, I closed the doors to the balcony
and bolted them shut. Inside, I was fizzing with anger, but I knew
there was little point talking to her tonight. It wasn't that Bernie

made a habit of drinking, but the few times I'd seen her like this at college, the next morning she always claimed to have no knowledge of anything that had happened.

Our telephone rang loudly. Bernie pulled herself up to a sitting position. 'Well, that's jolly rude, don't you think? Ringing that thing at this time of the night. It'll wake up the neighbours and they will blame us.' She looked regally indignant, right up until the moment she fell off the couch.

I went to the hall and answered the telephone. I kept my voice curt. If it was a neighbour wishing to complain, hopefully this would put them off.

'Glad to hear it's only your friend in that disgraceful state,' said my godfather's voice. 'I sent you a package, but my delivery chap has only just got back. Apparently, Bernie plied him with cocktails.'

'And he drank them?'

'I believe he found it impolite to refuse.'

'That was probably more to do with the dress that Bernie is almost wearing,' I said.

'Quite possibly,' said Fitzroy. 'I really have no further interest in the matter. Said chap is no longer with us.'

I assumed he meant he had returned the soldier to his outfit, rather than anything more sinister. However, I decided to leave the point without clarification. Fitzroy did not sound in a good mood.

'I'll check for the package,' I said. 'And I'll let you know if there is a problem. I have only this moment arrived.'

'I realised. I need to talk to you. There's a lot to discuss, but it looks like I'll be elsewhere for a while. Give your mother a call, will you? It sounds like your father isn't doing too well. Chin up, dear girl.' Then, before I could ask him anything else, he rang off.

I put the receiver gently back on its hook. My godfather had been unquestionably irritated and also, in all likelihood, had someone spying on me, but his absence made me feel very alone. Bernie lay on the floor, hiccupping softly, her eyes closed and a

23

silly smile on her face. I understood, for the first time, why my godfather kept a dog as his only permanent companion.

I went across to remove the choker Bernie was wearing, in case it did what its name suggested. She was now completely fast asleep on the floor, but she flopped obligingly back and forth like a fish out of water while I undid the neat bejewelled catch. I took it through to her bedroom and placed the sparkling thing on her dressing table. It was heavy. It might even have been real diamonds. Diamonds she had been openly displaying to any passing felon.

I sighed. Since our adventure with the undercover Nazis, she had changed, and not for the better. I took a blanket off her bed and returned to what the estate agent had called 'the drawing room', but which was really a nondescript space between the hall and the kitchen where we'd positioned two settees. I threw the blanket over her. It half covered her face and she made a whiffling noise, akin to the noises Jack's predecessor had made in his old age. I relented and pulled it away from her face, then I went and found the package the unfortunate Simon had been sent to deliver. It was a cadet's uniform, in that particular Army shade that resembled mud. I had hoped both my education and my class would have merited me a lieutenantship – even a second lieutenantship. Was I to be the lowest of the low, despite the supposedly lifelong training I had received? I examined the uniform for any other markings. Nothing. It appeared I was not so special after all.

I checked the time, and decided it was too late to call my mother. She and my father kept country hours. Maybe I could call her at luncheon tomorrow if I skipped going to the cafeteria. I'd noticed there was a telephone box on the street corner, opposite the main entrance.

I awoke next morning to the ringing of my alarm clock and the smell of freshly made coffee. The uniform hung on the back of my door in all its unappealing brownness. It was also, I

24

discovered, rather prickly. Accordingly, I put on my best silk underwear – which would cheer me up – and shrugged my way into it.

I found Bernie in the kitchen. She handed me a cup of coffee. I saw that bacon, eggs, lard and a frying pan had been neatly set out, along with a loaf of bread, a bread knife, the butter dish and a butter knife.

'I thought you'd rather I didn't attempt cooking,' said my flatmate in a very soft voice. 'I seem to recall you know what to do with these things.'

'I learnt to cook on an open fire in a field when I was six,' I said.

'Really?' said Bernie, perching herself on a high stool. 'How very strange of your mother.'

'It wasn't she who taught me,' I said, adding a touch of lard to the pan and turning the heat to low. 'Although she approved. She said learning to feed oneself was a basic life skill.'

'Goodness,' said Bernie. 'How thoroughly modern.'

I cracked an egg into the pan and heard Bernie gasp as if I had performed a magic trick. Sadly, I knew she wasn't being sarcastic. 'You're going to need to learn to fend for yourself,' I said as I added the bacon. 'I expect I'll be out a lot.' I turned and looked at her. 'Working.'

'Oh, how harsh. I suppose it's your duty, or some such thing. It isn't mine, is it?'

I shrugged. 'I expect we'll all have to do our bit. If I were you, I'd choose what you want to do before . . .'

'I'm pushed? I thought we were going to be nurses together?'

'It seems not,' I said, sliding breakfast on to my plate. 'I didn't make you anything. I don't have time and I doubt you'd be able to keep it down.'

'I did something terrible last night, didn't I?'

'Oh, more than one thing,' I said, starting to eat, standing up. A glance at my wristwatch told me I needed to leave now.

'I'm frightfully sorry, Hope.'

I rolled up the last piece of bacon with my fingers and popped it into my mouth. Bernie watched me in horror. 'You always are,' I said after I'd swallowed. 'You need to get yourself in order, B. If I can help, I will, but you seem determined to mess up.'

'Not sure that's entirely fair—' began Bernie, but I'd had enough and, taking a leaf out of Fitzroy's book, I merely walked out of the front door.

Warm and brightly sunny, it seemed as if no one had sent Nature a memo declaring that we were at war. I passed several people in light summer coats on the street who nodded and smiled at me in my uniform. I couldn't help but feel that war was still a long way off so far as the civilian population was concerned.

At the discreet Army building, I held my ID up to the grumpy old man on reception and went straight to the room we'd previously met in, noting by my wristwatch that I was five minutes early. It felt as if I, at least, was getting on with business, even if I wasn't entirely sure what that business was. My best guess was that Fitzroy had sent me here to be some kind of observer. 'Chin up' had been our code when I was a child for keeping my eyes and ears open. Clearly this department was not attached to my godfather's and he wanted to know what was going on. As far as I could tell, it was nothing but a lot of hot air. I don't count myself as particularly good at mathematics, despite my degree, which I earned with more sweat than skill, but even I realised that without actual data to work with, there was very little we could do.

I put my hand on the doorknob, and hesitated. Should I knock? Then from inside I heard Captain Max's voice.

'So, what do you think of them?'

'Difficult to say,' answered Cole's deeper tones. 'Hasn't been a lot to judge them on.'

'I suppose you'd rather have them climbing trees and jumping off cliffs,' said the Captain, his tone making clear what he thought of such ridiculous exploits.

'It would test their grit,' said Cole. 'Only one I've seen

anything in is the girl. Holding her own against the men can't have been easy. But she'll have been raised that way – to think she's superior to most, like her father.'

'No idea if she has the gumption to back it up?'

'She clearly has skills, but I don't know how reliable she might be. Other outfits might suit her better,' said Cole. He sounded thoughtful rather than unkind. I hovered, wondering what to do. I'd rather like to be sent to another outfit. The chaps I'd met so far clearly didn't think much of women and had already closed ranks against me. I could make an effort to win them over, but I already knew my heart wouldn't be in it – unless the Captain or Cole provided me with a good enough reason to do so.

There was a pause in the conversation. Immediately I opened the door and put on my best startled expression. 'Oh, I'm sorry, sirs,' I said. 'I didn't realise anyone was here. I'll wait outside.'

'No need,' said Cole. 'I was about to leave.' He nodded at Max. 'Captain, you know where to find me if you need me.' I stood back to let him past. He paused for a fraction of a second as he passed me and looked me in the eye. I had no doubt that he knew I had been listening.

As soon as he had passed, I entered the room. Max gestured to me to take a seat, which I did.

The room had been reorganised with plain wooden chairs in a circle, and just one desk behind these. The Captain sat at the desk and began to read through some papers. I was completely ignored. In other circumstances I might have got up and walked around the room, examining the faint diagrams I could see pinned to the back wall. However, a senior officer had told me to take a seat and I was fairly certain this meant I had to remain sitting. Fitzroy had warned me about obedience in the regular army. In an outfit like my godfather's, I suspected things were far less formal. Fitzroy hated inactivity almost as much as he hated wasted time. My impression of Captain Max was that he valued respect and obedience to the letter. I could almost hear the scream forming at the back of my mind.

Ten minutes passed. The Captain barely moved, except to turn a page every few minutes. He had to be an exceptionally slow reader. I gritted my teeth. Where on earth were the others? Fitzroy had got me to report here, and while I accepted the cogs of a large entity such as the army might move slowly, I expected some signs of activity.

Half an hour passed. Mentally, I reviewed the ways I had been taught to move silently through various terrains that could be found in England. After an hour, I gathered this had to be some kind of test. But whether it was a test of patience or initiative I had no idea.

No one else had appeared when an hour and a half after my arrival, the Captain, who had been shifting slightly in his seat, and who I suspected had imbibed a touch too much coffee for his ageing bladder, spoke.

'Thank you, Stapleford. Take this and report to the basement.' He held out a piece of paper. I rose, took it and smartly saluted him. I didn't read it until I had closed the door behind me. It was an order to report to the typewriter training room.

This room was situated two levels lower than the cafeteria and entirely subterranean. The lighting was underpowered and flickered and the walls changed from painted ones to being covered in square tiles of a dull off-white ceramic, and the stairs were stone rather than wood. A mythologically minded individual might have been reminded of entering the underworld.

My descent ended when I came to heavy, wooden, double doors. I pushed one open. Beyond was a small room with a desk and behind the desk, a single door that was closed. Sitting at the desk was a female sergeant with tight curls, a beaky nose and no discernible lips. She looked like she could give Cerberus a run for his money.

'Papers!'

I handed over the single sheet from Captain Max and opened my ID to show her. I didn't make the mistake again of trying to hand it over. She gave a short snort and stood up. 'Follow me,' she barked. She rose and taking a key from her pocket, which remained attached to her uniform with a short chain, she opened the door, ushered me through, and locked it behind us.

The first thing I noticed was the noise. We were in a cavernous room with a barrelled ceiling which must have been the cellar of a much earlier and older building. The room was lined with desks and at each one sat a young woman with a typewriter. I counted thirty-one and noticed another two women patrolling the room. All the desks faced the far wall, which was completely blank. The room was much brighter than the corridor, having rows of naked bulbs threaded across the ceiling, no doubt in an attempt to fight the gloom of the windowless vault. Even so, the gloom was winning.

I was directed to an unoccupied desk, then handed a manual on how to operate a typewriter and a sheaf of papers. 'When you feel you are sufficiently advanced, signal one of the instructors and your speed and efficiency will be assessed. You will not be released to any department until you are competent. Until then you will report here daily. There are breaks at 11 a.m. and 2.30 p.m. Lunch is between 12 noon and 1 p.m. Outwith these times you may not leave the room. Your day starts at 9 a.m. and finishes at 5 p.m. If you are unwell you will need a signed letter from an Army doctor when you return.' With that she turned on her heels and left me.

At this point it dawned on me that sitting still and waiting for orders had obviously not been the right response to Captain Max's ambiguous test. However, I suspected that I had been set up to fail, and whatever I had done would have led to me being removed from his creative 'think tank'. In retrospect, what struck me as particularly strange was that Cole not only knew my father but thought him egotistical. Bertram Stapleford was one of the kindest and most generous men anyone could ever hope to meet.

Chapter Five

When I was a child my godfather had spent considerable time on ensuring that my fine motor skills were up to scratch. Accordingly, within a few days of typing I had progressed at a fast-enough rate to receive a smile from the beaky Sergeant when I arrived for work. 'I fear we will be losing you soon, Stapleford,' she said. 'It's a pleasant change to have a young woman who does what is asked of her quietly and obediently. Well done.'

I smiled back and wondered if I could possibly get Bernie recruited here as a form of mind-numbing revenge for her recent behaviour. She and I hadn't spoken since the morning after the balcony incident. In fact, she'd been discreetly absent from the flat. An occasional newspaper, full ashtray or burnt pot of coffee were the only signs that she was still alive. I was finding the typing room training as tiring as it was dull and I had little energy to seek her out. Come to think of it, I hadn't seen Bernie for a couple of weeks and I knew I should make an effort to catch up with her. I reminded myself that Bernie had abandoned her family to stay in London with me and, while she knew lots of people, I remained her only true friend.

I took my seat, mulling over Beaky's comment. Quiet and obedient were not words I would use to describe me. If this was what Captain Max had wanted me to prove, I'd certainly shown I was not egotistical, I didn't consider myself superior and I could obey orders (even if they were given by idiots of limited intellect).

I finished my latest report on the nutritional value of cheese, collected the papers, lined up their edges, placed them in the correctly labelled folder and handed them to the instructor with a carefully primed smile that suggested only a minor hint of pride and a strong desire to please. She clicked her stopwatch and motioned to her colleague to come over, gesturing with one of her overly manicured hands.

One of the most difficult things for me was that no one spoke. The typewriters, when they were all going at once, made a jolly racket that echoed loudly due to the acoustics of 'the vault', as the girls referred to our room at break time.

The girls had proved to be a vacuous lot, manicuring their nails between typing sessions, bemoaning split ends and comparing notes on the romantic natures, or lack of the same, of their boyfriends. When I tentatively suggested that if their boyfriends were so bad, they should be thrown over, I was told 'didn't I know there was a war on' and something about 'supporting our boys'. I'd stopped listening by then and returned to thinking about my own plight. I realised the hardest part for me was being locked in. I tried very hard not to imagine fires or floods, but I hated that Beaky appeared to hold the only key. It was only after I'd spent some time surreptitiously examining the door between exercises, and had reassured myself that I could force it open if absolutely necessary, that I'd been able to settle down to my tasks.

To my surprise, the second instructor pulled me from my reverie. 'Yes, I agree she is ready for the next stage.'

She motioned me to follow her. The second instructor led me across the room to the blank wall. I'd never had an opportunity to get close to it before, as papers and instruction booklets had been handed out to us by the instructors. At the very back of the room, hidden by the sloping descent of the vault, was another door. This discovery, along with the fact the instructor didn't take a key from her pocket to open it, but merely turned the handle, struck me as near magical.

I took a deep breath and prepared to step over the threshold into a top-secret operation.

Across that threshold I found around twenty women, all seated at very familiar-looking desks with typewriters, though none of them were using the typewriters at that particular moment. Instead, a female instructor, who even Beaky could have beaten in a beauty contest, was dictating a letter. She was like a vulture hovering over dying prey. All the women were frantically scribbling on notepads. I looked over the shoulder of one of them and saw the page was covered in incomprehensible squiggles.

'Pitman shorthand,' said my escort in my ear. She gestured to an empty desk, and then winked at me in the manner of someone initiating me into the inner sanctum of a secret society.

Another instructor handed me a booklet and notepad and whispered that I was to go about learning simple words for now as I was very much behind the others. Personally, I didn't care if I was a thousand leagues behind the others. It had become evident that my top-secret training was to enable me to become a confidential secretary. I could think of few things more depressing.

I arrived home that evening in a foul mood. I considered telephoning Fitzroy as soon as I got in, but a moment's consideration led me to the conclusion that not being given a job that I liked was no reason to bother him. I had kept up with events in the outside world enough to know that all sorts of things were happening overseas. The girls I was training with thought this was all some kind of strange game. For them, the relentless advance of the Nazi war machine was secondary to them being able to go out with men in uniform on Friday nights. They were perfect confidential secretaries, uninterested in anything except for their own tiny little worlds. All the top-secret documents dictated to them would go in through their ears and come out of their fingers, with very little notice taken of the actual content. Unless, of course, there was a shocking report on a lack of face powder.

The best I could hope for was that Fitzroy thought my acquiring these skills would be useful for a later operation. My mother said he always had a plethora of schemes running at once, and I had to have faith that in one of them I would be called to do something useful – and perhaps even slightly interesting.

I opened the front door. 'If you've drunk all the gin, Bernadette,' I called, 'you're damn well going out and buying more.' Even as the words came out of my mouth, I regretted them. This was hardly in the spirit of greeting my friend and flatmate.

Bernie surprised me by coming out of her room, fully dressed in elegant evening wear, and looking rather glamorous. I closed the door behind me and paused in mock surprise. 'Is this the same girl who lies drunkenly around the flat? Has a fairy godmother been? Should I be checking for golden carriages outside?'

It was a bit mean, but she looked beautiful and happy. I was thoroughly fed up and covered in ink and dust. My hair hadn't seen a brush in hours.

'I'll have you know,' said my flatmate, lighting her cigarette with an elegant gold lighter engraved with a large *B*, 'that I haven't been drunk *once* since that appalling night. I blame the jug the cocktail was mixed in, must have been something wrong with it.'

While I stood bemused at this nonsensical statement, Bernie wandered further into the room. She walked with a definite swish of her hips and blew smoke delicately into the air. Whatever she'd been up to, it had agreed with her much more than all the wretched notepads and typewriters did with me. I felt myself grow more annoyed and did my best to push the jealousy down. I had agreed to work for Fitzroy's Department, and in so doing, agreed to do whatever came of that. The fact that my best friend seemed to have been having a whale of a time while I'd been enduring endless boredom was hardly her fault.

'So, I take it you're dressed up like that for a jolly night out with the girls? Am I invited?'

'You, Hope?' said Bernie. 'A night on the town? Not your scene, surely? No, I'm being escorted out by a respectable gentleman. I shall be perfectly safe.'

I felt a funny kind of tension in the air. 'Am I missing something,' I said. 'Do I know this remarkable man?'

'It's your godfather,' said Bernie, drawing herself up to her full height, and looking down her nose at me.

For some reason she clearly felt I would challenge such a statement. Instead I laughed. 'First time I've heard Fitzroy referred to as respectable,' I said. 'My mother says he doesn't even like being called a gentleman.'

Bernie pulled a face.

'You're going out to dinner with my godfather? Why?'

'He's very handsome, you know.'

'He's more than twice your age, and he's sworn to be a bachelor.'

'Well, now he's inherited a title, he might be thinking differently. His family was positively decimated due to the last war and that terrible Spanish influenza. They've had rather a bad run of luck generally.'

I blinked. I knew my godfather was sometimes referred to as 'my lord'. I had also assumed that 'Lord Milton' was just another of his aliases – at least that's what my mother had said. I was inclined to trust information from her rather than him. We may not always get along easily, but my mother and I don't lie to one another. Fitzroy, on the other hand, lies as easily as he breathes.

'So, he's wooing you?' I struggled to keep the mockery from my voice.

Bernie's gaze flickered downwards. 'I don't know that you'd call it wooing. Tonight's the first time he's taken me out to dinner. We normally meet for luncheon. He's been frightfully busy.'

'What do you talk about?' I was still trying to fathom the angle my godfather was playing. Whatever else was going on, I knew there was no way he would marry anyone as flighty as Bernie.

'If you *must* know, he's been giving me crosswords to do,' said Bernie. 'I'm hoping for a Christmas proposal!'

'Goodness,' I said, and suddenly I had the strangest sensation of falling, even though I knew I was sitting perfectly still. 'Goodness,' I repeated.

'You've gone quite white,' said Bernie, hurrying over to me

34

and kneeling down as best as her dress allowed. I'm sure I heard a couple of stitches tear, but she wasn't paying any attention. 'I haven't got anyone,' she said. 'My family is back in the States. I don't regret staying here, but you're so busy. I really thought we'd spend more time together. I thought we were going to be nurses together. I've been ever so lonely.'

'Is being lonely a reason to get married?' As I said the words, I realised that in Bernie's world it most certainly was. 'Oh, dear,' I said. 'Are you sure you want to marry Fitzroy? I know he can be charming, but he's actually rather serious in private.'

She smiled a little too brightly. 'Maybe I'll bring out the fun side of him.'

I had the sense to keep any further thoughts to myself. 'Well, whatever happens, I hope you'll be happy.'

I meant that I hoped she would be happy, regardless, but Bernie took it differently. She jumped up, leaned over and embraced me. 'Oh, thank you, Hope! I was worried you'd be upset, after all, he's been a member of your family since before you were born.' She straightened up and stepped back. 'And now I'll be a member too! What will that make us? Will you be my step-goddaughter?'

'No,' I said, standing up. 'It doesn't work like that.'

The bell rang. 'That'll be him! Shall I bring him up so you can let him know you're OK with this? I mean, subtly. He hasn't asked me yet. I don't want to ruin the moment.' And with that she ran off to answer the door.

I took a deep breath and stood, waiting for the pair of them to return.

Chapter Six

Fitzroy walked through the front door looking particularly resplendent in evening wear. His hair was dark and brushed to a high shine. He had a moustache again, small, neat, extremely fashionable. Both were, as only I and a few others knew, dyed. He saw me watching him and frowned.

'Where's Bernie?'

'I put her in the car,' he said. 'She was being rather excitable, and I wanted to talk to you.' He closed the door behind him and took off his hat. I reached out to take it, but he shook his head. 'Can't stay,' he said. He looked towards the closed door. 'She won't touch anything, will she? I mean, she won't try and drive it?'

I shrugged. 'You never know with Bernie. Is Jack in the car?'

'No, strangest thing. This one hates her. But then he is a puppy and she does keep trying to pick him up as if he is a pet.'

I raised an eyebrow at him. He gave a quick, wry smile. 'Yes, I know. I prefer to think of him as a companion animal. He's well-treated, but not fawned over like some child substitute.' He paused. 'What's the matter with you? You looked quite pale when I came in and now you've gone even whiter. Your uniform is in a shocking state. If it was anyone else, I'd report them.'

'Bernie thinks you're going to propose. Are you?'

My godfather's jaw dropped slightly. I watched in fascination as he struggled for words. I'd never seen Fitzroy wrong-footed. It didn't last long, but the darker side of me couldn't help relishing the moment of revenge for all the times he had thrown me off guard.

'Am I what!' he roared.

'She just told me that you're romantically involved.'

'And you believed her?' said Fitzroy. 'Good grief, Hope, have you no sense? You know how I work. I assess people. I need to get to know them in order to work out how to use them. Why on earth did you encourage the girl to think in this way?'

'Me, encourage her?' I fired back. Inside I was feeling much calmer, but I didn't care to show it. 'Have you looked in the mirror?'

Fitzroy turned and looked in my hall mirror. 'I do scrub up rather well,' he said, tweaking his scarf slightly.

'What exactly are you assessing Bernie for?'

'Hmm,' said my godfather. 'Can't tell you exactly, but I will tell you that, despite appearances, the girl has a remarkable mind. Of course, it's never been trained properly, but I think she could be quite useful in covert signals – that kind of thing. I doubt we could ever deploy her anywhere, but there's still . . . well, I've said quite enough. Have I reassured you that I am not going to marry your flighty best friend?'

'It isn't any of my business,' I said.

My godfather, who never fails to surprise me, stepped forward and hugged me tightly, just as he used to when I was younger. 'Don't be silly, Hope. You're family. You and yours come first. I don't have the time or the inclination to involve myself with anyone else in the longer term. You and your mother are quite enough trouble as it is.'

He stepped back. 'Oh, good heavens. You're all dusty. Get me a brush!'

I ran off. When I came back, he was battering at his coat with his gloves. 'Thank you,' he said, taking it and beginning to meticulously restore his appearance. 'Now, the reason I came up was not to announce my upcoming nuptials, but to say I have arranged a pass for you to go home for a few days this Christmas. It will be coming through shortly. I've done it on compassionate grounds. Your father is still unwell. I'll try and get there myself during the season, but I don't know if I will make it. Your mother is having a much smaller than usual party. Quiet, but still festive. Be nice to her. She's under a lot of strain.'

'You're not coming for Christmas? You always come to White Orchards for Christmas!'

Fitzroy returned the brush, taking the opportunity to kiss me quickly on the top of my head. 'Things are changing, my dear Hope. You need to prepare yourself.'

Then, before I could ask what this cryptic comment meant, the door was already closing behind him. I didn't bother going after him. He'd said what he came to say, and I knew from long experience that further questioning would gain me no traction. Instead, I went off to see if Bernie had left me any hot water. I was badly in need of a bath.

Bernie returned to the flat that night, unengaged, and went straight to bed. I was pretty sure I could hear her crying herself to sleep. I did think about knocking on the door, but I'm not good at the comforting thing. Besides, I suspected that her pride had been hurt more than her heart. I could all too easily see her getting more and more upset and spiralling into a rage, her anger directed at me either for not warning her, or for being smug about her failure, or some other equally inaccurate thing. I do very much hate confrontation. I decided the best thing to do was to give her time to recover. However, to show I was thinking of her, I started to swipe the odd biscuit or small cake from the canteen at work. None of the women I worked with appeared particularly observant. There was no challenge in sneaking all the best biscuits out from under their noses. It was far too easy. Each night, I'd leave them for Bernie, and every morning when I went off to work all that remained would be crumbs. It was rather like living with a benevolent but hungry ghost.

My pass came through for Christmas. I sent my mother a

telegram telling her when I would be home and asking her if I could bring Bernie as she had nowhere to go. I received a very short reply by return telling me that I could. However, the tone of the note was so terse I knew this was Mother trying to do the right thing rather than actually wanting Bernie present. This was most unlike her. Ever since I could remember, Christmas and New Year at our house had always been two weeks of parties, with people coming and going over the fortnight. The house was always full of life, joy and laughter. Only Christmas Eve was kept for family, which naturally included Fitzroy. It would be a real shock to both my parents if he were to forsake this tradition.

At work I carried on learning shorthand. I found it very much like learning a foreign language. My mother had told me that my grandfather was a polyglot. My mother herself reads Ancient Greek and Latin, and I had recently become aware that she had learnt German. My father is half French, and I have picked up a decent amount of that. It's a secret between us. As my mother never bothered to learn it, we've never told anyone else. But, generally, I find learning languages about as easy as I would attending Bernie's endless cocktail evenings – dull, pointless and a severe pain in the liver.

However, after the debacle with my godfather, Bernie appeared to be turning over a new leaf. My offerings of biscuits finally coaxed her out of her room, and we started spending the evenings together. We took it in turns to cook. Fitzroy had ensured I could cook on an open fire but had never actually schooled me in the arts of the kitchen (I can imagine our cook's face if he'd tried). I had slightly more of an idea than Bernie, so between us we generally came up with something edible, and certainly nothing that a cocktail on the side couldn't help.

'It's the gin in it that kills the poison in our cooking,' Bernie joked.

We acquired a couple of basic cookbooks and it wasn't long before Bernie had fast overtaken me. She spent her days at home making bread, jam, cakes, and sumptuous evening meals. One evening not long before Christmas I came home to the sweet smell of onions, tomatoes, and something meaty and yeasty. 'Where on earth do you get all this?' I asked.

'Well, some of it comes from friends,' said Bernie. She was standing over the cooker stirring something. Her hair had gone slightly frizzy in the heat. She wasn't wearing any make-up, but she was wearing a gingham apron. I had never seen her look younger or prettier. 'Some of it comes from Mummy, and some of it is cheats that I've learnt. I bet you think you can smell meat?'

I nodded and approached the pan. It looked like a hearty stew. The dumplings on top must have been added recently. They were beginning to swell and expand.

'There isn't any meat in it,' said Bernie triumphantly. 'But even when you eat it you won't believe me.'

She dipped in a fresh teaspoon and gave it to me to taste. After a day in the dark confines of the basement, battering my head with silly symbols, and the long, frosty walk home, it was like swallowing a piece of heaven. 'That is marvellous,' I said.

Bernie beamed in delight. 'You really think so?'

I nodded and went to dip my spoon in again. 'No double dipping,' said Bernie. 'Go and get changed. Food will be on the table in fifteen minutes and you need to brush the dust out of your hair.'

I obediently went and did what she asked. I never did see the dust falling on my desk. I presumed it came from the ceiling, but by the end of each day the basement was thick with the stuff and so was I.

I came back in good time to see Bernie ladling out the food. 'Bernie,' I said carefully, 'when you said you got stuff from friends you didn't mean the black market, did you?'

Bernie carried the plates over and set them down. 'No, I didn't. I can't swear to where my friends get their goods, but I wouldn't know how to go about contacting the black market even if I wanted to.'

'Good,' I said. 'Fitzroy keeps . . .' I hesitated. In the past my godfather had always watched over me himself, but it would be

40

foolish to think he had time to do that now it was wartime, and I was an adult. But he did have a way of hearing things. 'An eye on me,' I said in compromise. 'He'd react very badly to us having such dealings.'

Bernie took off her apron and sat down. 'He certainly has his fingers in a lot of pies.' Then unaccountably she giggled.

I paused with my laden fork halfway to my mouth. 'Ooh,' I said. 'What have you done now?'

'I haven't done anything but cook,' said Bernie. The corners of her mouth twitched in that way she has when she knows something you don't.

I pushed back my chair, resisting eating the food in front me. Damned hard though it was. 'Spill,' I said. 'If you've got yourself into something, I'd rather know sooner than later.' A thought struck me that completely vanquished my appetite. 'It wasn't a hoax, was it? You and Fitzroy pretending you weren't engaged? You're not about to marry my godfather, are you?'

'Would it be so very bad?'

'Yes,' I said. 'Awful. I know you both. You wouldn't suit.'

'I happen to disagree,' said Bernie, 'but no, it wasn't a hoax. I'm not engaged. Although I haven't given up the hunt just yet.'

'You've been hunting him under your bed? Or in the wardrobe?'

Bernie shook her head. 'I admit I was rather down for a while. And I was cross with you. If you hadn't told him I don't think it would have ever occurred to him what I was up to – not until it was too late.'

'Fitzroy told you that?' I said. It was utterly unlike my godfather to give away a source, let alone drop me in it with my best friend.

'Yes, when he came out of that flat that night. It put a real downer on the evening, I can tell you. I didn't know where to look. What on earth were you thinking?'

'What on earth was my godfather thinking? Was he trying to wreck our friendship?' I countered.

41

'It did seem a bit odd at the time. He came out. Started the car, got in, and said as casually as you please, "Hope says you're hoping we'll marry. I can tell you now, young lady, that is not a possibility. I'm far too busy for a wife, and even if I wasn't you would never be a consideration for me."'

'Gosh, that was rude,' I said. I was genuinely taken aback. Fitzroy could be blunt, but he was always civil, and treated women, of all ranks, with an old-fashioned courtesy.

'I know,' said Bernie. 'I could feel the heat in my face. I must have looked like a tomato! I seriously considered jumping from the car.'

'What did he say next?'

'Nothing. He drove me to the restaurant without another word. When we got there, he started talking about all sorts of things, as if the conversation had never happened.'

'What did you do?'

'I played along. What else could I do? Then when I got home, I vowed I'd never see him again.'

'Probably wisest,' I said. I pulled my chair back in and started to eat. At least Bernie didn't appear angry. If anything, she was the happiest I'd seen her.

'Only you know what he's like,' she continued. I swallowed quickly, burning my throat. 'Everything is on his terms. About a week later, he got back in touch. Didn't mention that evening or the conversation but took me out to luncheon and offered me a job.'

I shifted in my seat, doing my best to hide my jealously. 'Oh, really,' I said as lightly as I could manage. 'What as?'

'Doing this,' said Bernie, gesturing with both hands to the table.

'Feeding me?'

'Don't frown so. Not everything is about you! No, cooking. He said a lot of people would have to cook more if the war went on for a while, and with fewer and fewer ingredients. So, as I hadn't a clue how to cook, but was "reasonably bright" – and yes, he did actually say, "reasonably bright" – I would make a good test subject. Only it's been going so well they might use some of my recipes in a little book!'

'Gosh!'

'It would all be strictly hush-hush. Incognito, but telling you doesn't count, does it?'

'Er, well, probably not in this case,' I said carefully. It was nice to see Bernie so happy and I didn't want to ruin her good mood. 'But you mustn't assume it's safe to tell me. Unlike Fitzroy, I'm not important. You can tell him just about anything, and he'll be cleared for it. Me, not so much.'

Bernie nodded. 'I see. Your godfather has told me a number of times to keep my mouth shut. Don't look so shocked. He says it far more politely than that, but I know what he means.'

'So does this mean I can look forward to more delicious meals?'

'Sorry,' said Bernie. 'I'm writing up my final report tonight. No more special parcels for me. But I can keep on cooking if you want? I suppose I ought to learn how to shop.'

'You haven't been shopping?' I asked. 'But you . . .'

'I pretended. Never been inside a grocer's in my life. Before I started the project, I merely ordered from Fortnum's!'

I could help laughing. 'I see Fitzroy's point. If you can cook, then anyone with a brain can.'

'Yes, and he said that most of the recipes are aimed at people who have some cooking skills, so it worked out rather well. At least I think it did. I hand it in tomorrow, and he's going to get back to me.' She cringed and grinned at me. 'I do hope he's pleased.'

'I'm happy to give a reference as to how yummy your food is,' I said.

'Maybe something a bit more . . . a bit less nursery?'

I grinned. 'I'll tell my godfather you've become an excellent chef in only a few weeks. That will impress him.'

Bernie tried to smile modestly and failed. 'What department is he in?' she asked.

'Diplomatic liaison. You remember how he used to show up at the Embassy? But he helps out with other stuff.'

Bernie nodded. 'He's mentioned the idea of sending me on some kind of top-secret course. That can't be to do with cooking, can it?'

At this point I knew I should remind Bernie she shouldn't tell me such things, but I wanted to know, and I knew Fitzroy wouldn't tell me a thing. 'I can't imagine what that would be.'

'I wonder what else he thinks I can do?' said Bernie tilting her head to one side. 'But then I'd never have imagined I'd be any help with this recipe book. You know, I think your godfather sees hidden talents in me.'

'This is really, *really* good,' I said, tucking into my food. I had no idea what else he might see in her, but I had a bad feeling. More importantly, why was Fitzroy developing Bernie's skills, and leaving me to rot in a dusty basement? It was hard not to feel peeved.

Chapter Seven

As December came in not only the weather, but the public feeling, grew colder. The cries of 'It'll be over by Christmas' faded and people began to talk of the 'phoney war'. Fitzroy, who I met in my hallway again, collecting Bernie from the flat, commented, 'It damn well isn't phoney for the Poles. The Norwegians are getting fretful too – and so they should be.' His gaze focused in on me with sudden intensity. 'You know you can't repeat anything I might say to you, don't you? I'm so used to talking freely to your mother I sometimes forget you're not the same . . . you look so damn like she used to. Uncanny.' He frowned ferociously at me.

'I'm sorry,' I said hesitantly.

The frown vanished. 'I'm cross with myself, not you,' he said. 'I don't usually roll over for a pretty face. Thank goodness I'd already sent Bernie down to the car. That girl's mouth is wider than the Channel. You'd have thought living in one embassy or other for most of her life she'd have learned to keep her mouth shut. Far from it! Every rumour I've dropped in her hearing has been repeated back to me at the Club as if it was gospel. She's certainly well rooted in the British upper classes. But currently she's only good for spreading *dis*information, and we've pretty well got that covered.'

'Why are you taking such a strong interest in her?' I asked as casually as I could.

Fitzroy gave me a wry smile. 'Feeling jealous, are we, Hope? You've had me training you since you could walk. Long enough, don't you think?'

'I only know a fraction of what you know,' I said, meaning to add I would be happy to learn more, but Fitzroy interrupted me.

'Well, thank God you realise that,' he said. He must have seen the disappointment in my face because he sighed. 'Hope, I am inordinately busy . . .'

I bit my tongue, so I didn't comment on him having time to escort Bernie here, there and everywhere.

He waited to see if I was going to voice my objection and nodded when I had the sense not to test him. 'I honestly am. If I am with Bernie, you can be assured that I am doing several other things at the same time. She's not as observant as you. I could pitch the package for a dead drop on her foot and all she'd notice is whether or not her shoe had been scratched.'

I smiled slightly at that.

'You're not good enough at the skills I currently need for me to use you without putting you into a great deal of danger. And besides the risks of being eviscerated by your mother, I don't want to see you come to harm. There's only so much I can shield you from during a war, but I can at least not throw you into matters way out of your depth. I rather suspect that there will come a time when I need your particular skills, but not yet. For now, I'd rather you were stationed somewhere safe. At least that's one thing I can take off my plate.'

'Is my mother in danger?'

Fitzroy's eyes opened wider for a moment. 'No more than most of us, and a lot less than others. She won't go into the field while your father is so ill. She is doing analysis for me as usual, and she's running a number of agents for me. Most of the time she's up in the Fens. Totally safe. And that is far more than I have officially told you.' He paused. 'She worries about you a lot. Keeps asking me to check in on you. Part of the reason I started using Bernie as cover – got her doing something useful rather than making mischief for you. Neither of us want attention drawn to you. Then of course there was that crossword that got me thinking. I'm going to get her to sit some signals tests shortly, so don't be surprised if she starts talking about ciphers out of the blue. She's not fallen in with the wrong crowd – again.' He gave a somewhat deeper sigh, which I found myself echoing. Bernie had been of great use in breaking into a foreign spy network before the war began. Unfortunately, she'd had no idea she was doing that, and the spy who we'd turned had only been uncovered through their affair. 'Her taste in men has always been awful,' I said.

'And to think she wanted to marry me,' said my godfather. 'I am insulted.'

'I'm sure it was for your looks rather than your personality,' I said. 'After all, she barely knows you.'

'Hmph,' said Fitzroy. 'Keep yourself out of trouble until I call on you, young Hope.' And he left. I followed him out into the stairwell

'Could have been your car,' I called after him, but he didn't even look up as he briskly descended the stairs.

And so the days dragged on. I read the newspapers, looking between the lines for what was actually happening in the world. I thought of ringing up my mother, who would have a much better understanding of how things stood, but the tension of my inviting Bernie for Christmas still hung between us. I could have tried to ring up and only speak to my father. That would be difficult, but not impossible – but on the other hand, if what I suspected was true, I didn't want to worry him.

What I saw and felt was an ominous lack of concern for the machinations of Herr Hitler. The complacency of our local greengrocer – who had fought in the last war, losing a leg, and thought that there was no possible way Germany and England would risk direct conflict again after the hideousness of the last one – seemed to me to be reflected in politics. The campaign for 'Peace in our Time' flourished, while all around us Europe was beginning to burn.

I longed for Britain to draw a proper line in the sand. We had said we were at war, but I wasn't hearing much about any fighting happening. I now saw my godfather too fleetingly for decent conversation, but he wore a perpetual scowl, worse even than his normal frown. Without a doubt he felt things weren't going the right way. But he made no time to speak to me.

We were at war, but we weren't at war. The Pact of Steel between Italy and Germany, which had so rattled the nation back in May before we even declared war, seemed now to be regarded by most as something 'them foreigners are up to', as the girls learning shorthand put it. Of course, our boys were shipping overseas, but there was still a whiff of romance about this.

I couldn't decide if the truth was being hidden from us, or if our government led by Neville Chamberlain, the erstwhile peace-seeker who had thought he could bargain with Hitler, was still expecting a diplomatic resolution for Britain.

Meanwhile I was transposing recordings that spoke at unusual speed about the manufacture of cheese. It was thrilling.

Then one morning, the night after Bernie had decorated the flat with holly and greenery that had made me sneeze all night, when I came into the basement in a terrific temper, tired out of my wits, I was told to report to the senior instructor. 'You're being put forward for your test today,' said my vulture-faced teacher. 'I'd pass if I were you. Next test is scheduled for end of February or later, depending on what happens.'

I cursed Bernie inwardly. I cursed myself for being allergic to some unknown plant, but not to dust. A decent allergy like that would have got me out of this place weeks, no, months ago. This morning my head was thick with disgusting stuff, my brain was foggy, and I kept sneezing violently. My eyes, which had been red-rimmed in the bathroom mirror, now felt itchy, and my vision was blurry.

By the time I was taken into a small room that might well have been a cupboard before the basement became a clerical hellhole, I was fizzing with annoyance. Two people awaited me. A very stiff-looking woman in a blue military uniform I didn't immediately recognise and an Army Captain. Infantry, I think. Neither

48

introduced themselves. The woman told me to sit down and get ready. I sat down behind a little desk that held a typewriter, paper and a notepad. No pencil. I took one from behind my ear without thinking, earning a nod from the Captain. Evidently having basic equipment to hand was thought part of the test. I suppressed the 'Bah!' that threatened to break out from between my lips. Fortunately, my taciturnity was taken for performance anxiety.

'Bright girl. Passed our first little test,' he said. He turned to his companion. 'Doubt she has anything to be nervous about.'

I'd never seen Fitzroy in uniform. His Department didn't seem to care much about such things, and he hadn't bothered to teach me about them. He had, however, warned me of taking the kind of liberties he did with authority. 'I get away with it,' he'd told me when I was much younger, 'because I get things done. I'm much more of your seek forgiveness afterwards rather than ask permission type. I do not encourage you to follow my example. You need to be an expert in your field before you can hint that you know your superiors are no more intelligent than the average kipper. Of course, there are always good chaps, but heaven knows after the last show they are few and far between.' I was definitely in front of a 'kipper'.

The woman dictated a letter. I dutifully noted it down in shorthand and then typed it up. It was about sending supplies to an army barracks that was lacking potatoes and also a special type of ammo cartridge. It meant making up some stuff phonetically as I was going along, but it was hardly challenging. I found it just the right side of awkward to enable me to stay awake. When I had finished typing the letter, the woman held out her hand for it. She then passed it to the Captain, who glanced through it and nodded.

'Again,' said the female examiner and began to dictate a longer letter on issues with struts in aircraft.

After this process had been repeated five times, a stopwatch appearing from the third trial onwards, I hadn't the faintest idea how I had been doing. Certainly, all my letters made sense, and no one had asked to see my actual shorthand. 'It's the material that matters,' the woman had said when I offered her my notebook. The Captain, who by now was hiding a yawn behind his hands as he rested his elbows on the table, took each letter and compared it to one in front of him. By the end of the fifth try the most interesting sound in the room was his stomach rumbling. The woman, if anything, appeared to be growing more and more frustrated. If I was lucky I had done badly enough they would throw me out. I had managed not to sneeze, but only by dint of pulling faces, and I was constantly sniffling. I couldn't imagine how anyone would want me as an addition to their office.

The Captain looked up from perusing my last letter. 'Capital! Capital! Young lady, you've positively aced it despite Miss Simmons' attempts to unseat you.' The woman gave a thin smile like a curl of lemon rind. He opened a manila folder and glanced through it. 'And that high a security clearance! It's like all our Christmases have come at once. We can certainly use you, Miss Stapleford. Not often we get such a bright girl in our clerical pool.'

The bright girl felt her heart sink lower than her boots. My only hope was that the war would take a turn in such a way that Fitzroy required my skills. But as I suspected that would mean things got much worse I couldn't in good conscience really wish for this. As it was, I was sent to the outer desk of an aged colonel, who slept in his office and asked me to type up letters to his club about the infractions of younger members. 'Just keep 'em in the "top secret" file until they go out,' he said. 'Our little secret, my dear. Perhaps you'd like to come to luncheon with me in the club?' He was standing by the side of my desk, looking over my shoulder, when he said this. I didn't, as I easily could have, pick up my pencil, turn quickly, and insert it into the fleshy part of his thigh. Instead I said, 'My godfather is a member. He takes me to dinner there on Ladies' Night. It's lovely.' I paused. 'Lieutenant-Colonel Fitzroy.'

'Huh,' said the aged Colonel, drawing back slightly.

'The only thing is I often work through luncheon, so I think I will have to decline your kind invitation.'

'What-er-um. Probably best.'

He disappeared back into his office. I had no doubt he was phoning the clerical pool for a prettier and certainly less well-connected typist. This suspicion was confirmed the next day when I arrived only to be directed back to a typing pool. At least this one wasn't in the cellar. All thirty of the women here were fully qualified. An armed guard stood outside the double doors and all materials were kept under very tight control. I had sight of sensitive, and yet still very boring, material. We weren't allowed to talk, but the clatter of all the typewriters going off at once was unpleasant. I mainly typed letters about supplies and supply lines. The actual place names were coded, but I suppose I could have made a good guess at what they were if I had wanted to. Which I didn't. Such information was dangerous and of no use to me. And as for Fitzroy, if he'd wanted to know any of it, he would have simply picked up the phone and asked for it to be sent to him with an armed escort. However, I suspected a lot of the supply lines might well have been worked out by him or my mother. Certainly, Fitzroy knew the French countryside very well, as well as the harbours on both sides. I assumed this meant my mother likely knew them too. Over the years I had pieced together more and more information about their working relationship, and if I hadn't known she adored my father, even I might have thought it a bit dubious. But for all his womanising ways, Fitzroy appeared to have a sibling-like relationship with my mother. I could see that, but I couldn't for the life of me understand how it had come about. As he said himself, Fitzroy was used to wrapping women round his little finger, not the other way around, and yet my mother had an almost witch-like hold over him.

That day after I'd been sent to the clerical pool, I came home to find Bernie weeping on the settee. She was completely bent double and sobbing her heart out. I dropped my things in the hall and ran in.

'What on earth is the matter?' I cried. I dropped down onto my knees on the floor beside her.

Bernie sat up, showing me blue eyes, blurred with tears, that still looked beautiful. Even the drops trickled artfully down her face. 'Jack bit me!' she wailed.

'Jack?' I was lost for a moment. 'Jack Hayward? Or Jack Bellway?' I asked summoning the only two males of her acquaintance I could think of named Jack. 'Why would they bite you? Have you called the police?'

'No, the dog!' said Bernie. 'I wouldn't mind if one of *them* tried to bite me.'

'Do you need me to take you to the doctor?'

Bernie shook her head. 'No, your godfather patched me. He did it rather well.' She showed me a neat bandage that ran over the back of one her hands. 'He was so *cross*,' she said. The last word rose into a wail and she gave a huge sob.

'I should damn well think so,' I said. 'His dog should be better trained than to bite people. Even if it is only a puppy. Was it very sore?'

Bernie shook her head as the next major sob was marginally adverted. 'Not really. He's only got little puppy teeth. Barely a scratch, but Fitzroy insisted I needed it disinfected and kept clean. But you don't understand, he was cross with *me*!'

'You? I don't understand. Did you do something to make Jack bite you?'

'I was tapping out a . . . a *thing* with my pencil. It's easier to do that than try to do it in your head. But Jack didn't like the tap-tap-tapping, and he jumped up and bit me.'

'You've lost me. Why were you tapping a pencil? I didn't even know you owned a pencil.' I associated pencils with work, and imagining Bernie doing any sort of work was very hard to do.

'I was doing a test at his flat. He said he didn't want me to do it in his office, because he didn't want anyone to know I was doing it . . .' Even as she said this, her hand flew to her mouth, and her eyes opened comically wide.

52

'I'm not going to tell anyone,' I assured her. 'So, the dog probably jumped for the moving pencil, but missed and bit you?'

Bernie frowned. 'I suppose that could have been it, but Fitzroy said I had been teasing his dog. I tried to explain why I had been tapping but he called it a damn poor excuse and said if I needed to tap things out I was no good to man nor beast. Then he put me in a taxi and sent me home. I think I've failed!' This produced quieter, and to my mind, more genuine sobs.

'I know he can be bad-tempered, but my godfather is a fair-minded man. He'll realise you didn't mean to distract the dog. Maybe if you practise you'll get past needing to tap for whatever reason you needed to.' I knew full well he must have been testing her on Morse code. 'Listen, this will cheer you up! I hadn't had a chance to mention it before, but Mother's invited you for Christmas. We'll get to spend it together. Won't that be fun?'

Bernie's expression drooped further. 'I don't know if I can. If he does pass me there's some hush-hush course I'm being sent on over Christmas.'

'Really,' I said, sitting back on my ankles. All I could think of was Fitzroy saying he didn't know if he'd make it to White Orchards for Christmas, and now I knew why. A course! Fitzroy might have no intention of getting married, but he still had an eye for a pretty girl. Clearly Bernie had been charmed into not perceiving the danger of going off alone for Christmas with Fitzroy. I opened my mouth, and then closed it again. If teaching Bernie to do Morse code was about getting her alone somewhere for Christmas, Fitzroy was going to an awful lot of faff when he was supposed to be very busy. Besides, I knew, despite the fact he could infuriate me, my godfather wasn't the kind of man to seduce an innocent girl. An eager, willing and experienced girl might not pass his attention by, nor would a targeted foreign female spy, but Bernie? The problem was, she always led people on to believe she was much 'faster' than she actually was. But surely Fitzroy was old enough and clever enough not to be taken in by her silly games?

Bernie read at least some of what I was thinking. 'It's not like that,' she said. 'It's in Scotland. I have to go by train. He isn't coming with me.' Then she realised she had given me privileged information yet again. Honestly, if they let Bernie near anything top secret, I thought, they'd have to lock her up. She simply wasn't capable of keeping her mouth shut.

Chapter Eight

I had four days off for Christmas, which was longer than anyone else I knew. I kept the knowledge to myself. I'd also out of the blue received extra petrol coupons, so I would be able to test my night driving.

I arrived home mid-afternoon on Christmas Eve. The sun hovered on the edge of the horizon as I drove up to White Orchards. The last rays of the day skittered over the road making it glitter like fairy dust. The house loomed up before me, still slightly crooked after the re-jigging of the foundations to drain the marsh from beneath it but, rather than a dark and imposing shadow, I only saw a welcoming shelter. Giles, looking somewhat snowy on top himself, opened the door as I parked the car. I got out carefully. The ground was slick underfoot.

'I'll get Mannings to bring your things in, Miss Hope,' said Giles.

'Thank you, Giles,' I called, as I picked my way towards him. 'Merry Christmas!' When I reached the door, I handed him the bottle I had been carrying. 'Home-made eggnog,' I said. 'Keep out the chill of the Fens.'

'Thank you, Miss Hope. The staff will appreciate it.'

'No, that's for you. I've other things for the staff. Nothing big, I'm afraid. Even in London there's not a lot about at the moment.'

'I'm sure whatever you have chosen, miss, will be more than adequate,' said Giles, carefully slipping the bottle into a niche by the door. 'Welcome home. As ever, it is a delight to see you.'

'Oh, for heaven's sake,' cried my mother's voice. 'Close that door, man. The child will freeze and Mr Stapleford has only just got over his winter cold. We don't want him to have another one.'

Giles's expression shifted to the neutral look of slight disdain he always wears in the presence of my mother.

I went forward and hugged her. 'Goodness, you're thin, Hope,' said my mother. 'I never thought to say that to you. Are they not feeding you in London?'

'I've been busy working, Mother,' I said.

'You're positively fading away. We shall have to feed you up before you go back. How many days have you got?'

'Four,' I said. 'More than most.'

My mother nodded. 'Makes me extra glad dear Bernie isn't coming. I do like the girl, Hope, but it's just this Christmas is liable to be rather special.' Her eyes shone for a moment. She blinked rapidly. She released me from the hug and held me by my shoulders, reminding me very much of how Fitzroy behaved when he had serious things to tell me. 'You haven't been back for a while, dear . . .'

'I'm sorry, I—'

'No,' said my mother, 'I do understand. It's simply that you haven't seen your father in a while. Please don't let it show if his appearance surprises you.'

I frowned and shook my head slightly.

'This winter has been very hard on him. Not only the cold, but the new war. We . . . we gave so much in the last war – especially your father. It cost him much of what was left . . .' she paused and swallowed. 'Much of what was left of his health, so to think it was all for nothing . . . It's destroying him.'

She let go of my shoulders. 'Still, seeing you will cheer him enormously. He's missed you so much, and he's very proud of you.' She hesitated, then added in a low voice, 'If you happened to let slip you're not working with your godfather I think he'd be very relieved. He knows how dangerous that work is.'

We began to walk further into the house, leaving Giles behind.

'I'm not,' I said. 'At least not yet. He said he didn't have need of my skill set at present.'

My mother nodded, all at once the professional. 'He's quite right. Thank goodness he doesn't know you speak French fluently.'

I stopped in my tracks. 'I thought you didn't know! I thought it was a secret between Daddy and me.'

My mother carried on walking. 'Oh, he still thinks it is.' She stopped, looked back at me and beckoned me on. 'My dear girl, I was trained by one of the best, did you really think you could keep that kind of secret from me?' She gave me a small smile. 'I don't suppose you've heard from him?'

I shook my head. 'I thought you were in regular contact,' I said.

'In the usual way of things,' she said calmly. 'But not at present. Talking of presents, your father is very proud of what he's found for your gift, so please, even if you hate it, pretend you love it. Do you want to know what it is?'

'No,' I said. 'I like the surprise.'

'Really,' said my mother. 'I always prefer to know what people are giving me. Thank you, by the way, for the stationery set you're going to give me. It's exactly what I need to write to your grandmother and uncle. Usually I only ever have official paper in the house and I can hardly write to them on that.'

'You're welcome,' I said, slightly stunned. 'Have you always known what you were getting from Daddy and me?'

We were outside the library now. My mother nodded. 'Ever since your father bought me that green hat for my birthday. The one that bore more resemblance to a dissected frog than millinery. He was so disappointed I didn't like it. But to be fair to the man there have only been one or two misfires in over twenty years of marriage. That's far more than most wives can say.'

She opened the library door and went in. I followed, my mind churning with new information. I stopped in my tracks when she moved to the side and I saw my father.

My chubby white owl of a father was thin. Not rake-thin, but thinner than I ever remembered him being. His face had long lines running down it and into his snowy wreath of a beard. His eyes still sparkled, but the words that flashed into my mind were 'frail' and 'old'. My father had often been unwell during my childhood, but always he had emerged from the bout of whatever ailed him with renewed vigour. 'I've escaped death's clutches again, Hope,' he would cry and ask me to go riding with him or hunting or some such outdoor pursuit. It always tired him, but he took extreme pride in showing me he was on top of things. The man before me looked unlikely to be able to make it to the door unaided.

'Hello, Daddy,' I cried, running forward, and dropping to my knees to hug him round his much thinner waist. 'You're looking in remarkable fettle for an old owl!' I stretched up and kissed him on the cheek.

'Old! Old!' cried my father. 'I'm younger than your godfather!'

'Oh, he's positively decrepit nowadays,' I said.

My father brightened considerably. 'You hear that, Euphemia? Sounds like the devil has finally caught up with the old boy.'

My mother calmly took a seat. 'It was only a matter of time,' she said. 'Whisky, Hope? That drive must have been very cold.'

I struggled out of my coat. Giles appeared behind me and took it away. 'I've left everything in the car. Giles said he would have it brought in. It's like an ice-rink outside.'

'Well, you're here now,' said my father. 'We can batten down the hatches and enjoy our Christmas. There's no one else turning up till Boxing Day, is there, dear?'

My mother shook her head. 'No. Just family. Some old friends are due on Boxing Day, and my brother said he'd come down for the Duck Shoot if it's still on.'

'I don't see why not,' said my father. 'Besides, duck hunt or no, he should want to come and see his sister!'

'Actually, we should probably go up there,' said Euphemia. 'He has much more of an estate to contend with, but I heard a rumour that my mother and the Bishop might be there.'

'Dear God, no,' said my father. 'The Bish I don't mind. A bit loose in the belfry now, but as charming as ever, even if he doesn't know what year let alone what day it is. But your mother! If ever there was . . . well . . . I mean . . . she's scarier than ever. Even *that man* is scared of her. Admitted it himself last year. Said we should license her as a weapon. Her tongue was sharper than any knife he'd ever met.'

'He never did,' said my mother, laughing.

'I swear to you. Positively terrified of her. Apparently, she cornered him in a tearoom, and he couldn't get away. Says he still has nightmares about it.' My father waggled his finger at my mother. 'You don't know everything, you know. Men talk. Even *that man* and I.'

My mother laughed again. 'Take your whisky with you and get changed, Hope. Your father has planned a feast for tonight, and carol singers. We'll dress the tree before dinner. Your father is determined to make it the best Christmas Eve ever. I do believe you may even find a stocking at the end of your bed tomorrow morning. Just like the old days.'

'Father Christmas won't forget you either, my dear,' said Father. 'He's been a busy old bee this year.' He smiled at me. 'It's going to be a great Christmas, Hope!'

I smiled back, but it felt like a dagger through my heart. I realised now my mother had been trying to warn me. My father thought this would be his last Christmas, and from the look of him it might well be.

I dressed quickly for dinner. Bernie had given me a sparkling dark green evening dress, 'because you need to have something decent for Christmas', as a present. I stood looking at my reflection. I had kept my hair down, and the dress made my eyes sparkle. I thought I looked rather nice and that my father would like it.

I checked my wristwatch. I might just have time to slip along and see my mother before it was time to go down. I hurried along the corridor, tapped on my her door and opened it. She was standing in front of a mirror holding up a necklace. I gasped. Our eyes met in the mirror. She turned and pulled me into the room.

'The potatoes must be doing well!' I said. 'That necklace is amazing.' I indicated the diamond star that hung on the end of a gold chain. The star was a good inch and a half in diameter and would have cost a fortune.

My mother looked at me a little oddly for a moment then returned to her dressing table. She put the necklace back into its box. 'No, your father didn't buy it for me. It's an inherited piece.'

'You're not wearing it?'

She shook her head. 'No, I don't think it would go well with this dress,' she indicated the V-necked rose silk evening dress she wore. It was simple, sleek, and timelessly elegant.

'It would.'

'But I wouldn't want to upset your father. I've never worn it since I got it. You may find it silly, but sometimes I like to hold it up and see how it might look. Vain of me, I know. It'll be yours one day.'

'So who gave it to you?'

'I inherited it,' repeated my mother. 'Your father doesn't know. It would make him feel bad that the only jewellery he was ever able to afford to buy me were my rings.'

'But he gave me diamond earrings for my twenty-first,' I said.

'And they look lovely on you,' said my mother. 'I don't have any need of sparkling things out here in the Fens. But you live in London. It's quite different.'

'He's never bought you any jewellery?'

'Hope, we had a house to rebuild. The original builders were terrible. I wouldn't have trusted them to make a mud pie. Then, of course, we had to get the estate going. Building a cottage school isn't cheap.' She held out a hand to me. 'I've never minded. I want the people who live here to have good lives, and as land-owners it is our responsibility to ensure that happens. The estate is in good shape now. Your father is proud he'll be handing it on to you in much better order than when he found it!'

'But that won't be soon, will it?'

My mother looked down for a moment. Then she blinked rapidly and raised her chin. 'I don't know, Hope. That's the truth. I have the sense that this new war has done him in. He can't see that all we did before needed to be done. He can't understand how any man can condone killing his fellows. He knows Hitler is bad and we will have to fight him, but I don't think he realises how evil the Fuhrer is. There's no need to tell him. This isn't his fight. I think what he fears more than anything is that this is your fight.'

'I'm not doing anything to help,' I said. 'I've learned to type.'

'But it is your fight, my dear. We of the old brigade will support you as best we can, but the true tragedy of war is that it is always fought by the young. At least, God willing, this won't be the slaughter of a generation as it was before.'

'But it will be bad, won't it?'

'Very,' said my mother. 'If I, or Fitzroy, ring you up and tell you to go, do it. Get out of London no matter what is happening. Pack yourself a bag and leave it by the flat door. Grab it if you can, but don't delay. If we say get out, get out. Head for here.'

Goose pimples ran up and down my skin. 'You're frightening me,' I said.

'Well, hopefully, it won't come to that. Let's go down and help your father set up the tree. I've told him he can direct us. We will be his elves.'

We managed to position the tree, place the candles, and light them without setting fire to anything else. As usual it stood in the wide front hall, so it could be seen as one entered and exited all the rooms and from the front door.

My father had placed the first candle, and then said, 'Spiral out from there, girls.' He then sat down in a chair and watched. Giles passed through the hallway several times. The final time he turned up we were about to light the candles. He tried to discreetly place the bucket of sand he had with him in the corner.

'You are not going to put these candles out until we are all in bed,' commanded my father.

'Yes, sir,' said Giles.

'What's more you will have them all lit by seven a.m. so they are burning when we come down for breakfast.'

'Be realistic, dear. I don't intend coming down on Christmas morning until ten at the earliest,' said my mother.

My father muttered a bit, and then said, 'Lit by nine a.m. then!'

'Of course, sir. I will station a boot boy to watch them.'

My father fumbled in his pocket and pulled out a shilling. 'Then you'd better give the poor boy this, and make sure he gets a decent Christmas dinner.'

'Indeed, sir,' said Giles, trying to suppress a smile. He doted on my father, who, he had once told me, was the 'best master' he had ever had. He was very proud that my father took such great care of the estate, which was quite unfair as I had learned as I grew older that my mother did most of the work. She happily fulfilled her husband's ideas of looking after their people, having been raised on the milk of noblesse oblige, but Giles totally failed to take this into account. Instead I had overheard him talking about the great articles my father wrote for the British newspapers on how all men regardless of station must be treated well. He was always at pains to explain that my father was not a socialist, and quite content with the social order, but that all those above had a duty to those below. Giles liked things neat and tidy. He thought my father collecting first editions was the perfect hobby for a gentleman. My mother horrified him with her comings and goings, and the special room, and even the special telephone, she had for her 'work'. He had no idea what she actually did, but as my mother had caught him trying to listen in on more than one occasion, she scattered clues for him – that she was a drugs seller, an arms runner, and, once, even a brothel owner. Of course, Giles grew more and more concerned, but could not cross the class divide and ask her what she was doing. They had been at silent war for decades.

My mother and I lit the tree, and my father switched off the electric light. There was a moment of darkness, broken only by the flickering flames on the tree, then we heard, very faintly, from outside the sound of carol singers. The voices rose merrily as the singers approached the house. My father roused himself to open the door, and the carol singers came in and grouped so neatly around the tree, I knew my father must have rehearsed them. Among them were several young men and women I'd shared my early years with at our tiny school. Many of them now had one or more small children hanging off their coat sleeves. Small tots with bright eyes, all dressed in neat woollen hats, scarves and mittens, a gift from the estate, gazed in awe at our tree, while their parents continued singing. They sang several carols, which I and my parents enthusiastically joined in with. At one point I thought I even caught the faintest ring of Giles's bass voice. My mother is a strong alto, but my father is a rather rough and ready tenor. Fortunately, he ran out of steam after the opening carol, and then sat back in his chair to enjoy the spectacle. Then the house servants appeared with trays of hot eggnog, mulled wine and steaming sausage rolls. Our carollers ate and drank their fill. Then each family was given a figgy pudding to take home for the next day. By the time we waved them off I was feeling happy but tired, as the length of my drive earlier was beginning to take its toll.

'Look to your daughter, Mrs Stapleford,' called my father. 'She is flagging and we've not even sat down to dinner yet. The young of today. No stamina.'

My mother took one of my arms and my father the other and we went in to dinner all three of us linked together.

Chapter Nine

I enjoyed Christmas Eve far more than I had expected to. My father was in the jolliest of spirits, and when I finally retired to bed, I was more than half drunk on the amount of brandy he had poured down my neck. This, after the special bottle of champagne he had insisted was entirely for me at dinner. I was most grateful for my mother admitting she too didn't mind the bubbly stuff, and helping me out.

All I can say is when they handed out livers for my parents' generation, they must have made them of iron. The next morning when I awoke, I felt extremely sorry for myself. My head was pounding, and my mouth felt like the sand of the Sahara on which several camels had left their unwanted and disgusting offerings.

A shy tapping at my door revealed a small maid, who must have only recently joined the household. 'Mr Giles said as you might like this, miss. He says your father swears by it.' She handed me a glass. I didn't even look at what it contained. I merely thanked her in the hope she and her foghorn-like voice would leave me in peace, and then gulped it down. It was disgusting and part of it was slimy. I placed the glass on my bedside table and lay back in bed waiting to meet my maker.

However, after some time had passed, I have no idea how long, I started gradually feeling better. At last I found I could open my eyes without the ludicrously bright light of day gouging chunks out of my brain. At this point I discovered my stocking. I felt as excited as a six-year-old. The parcels inside contained a lovely fountain pen (complete with my initials), a pretty compact of powder exactly my shade with a built-in lipstick, the latest in a pulp crime series my father had told me was excellent, and goodness knows how, but an actual small orange. I ate the orange and got up.

When I joined my parents at breakfast my mother called on me to admire her new earrings. Small, golden and set with topaz, they exactly matched her dark chestnut curls My father gazed on happily. 'Didn't do badly, did I?' he said. I went over and kissed his cheek. I was startled to find it cold and clammy.

'You did excellently,' I said. 'I loved everything Father Christmas brought me.'

'Course, your mother had to go and spoil it,' he said, still smiling.

'All I did,' said my mother, 'was remind Father Christmas that he shouldn't forget you. You were desperately in need of a new shaving set and some decent cologne.'

'Scared the willies out of me, Hope,' said my father as I sat down at the table. 'I saw the stocking at the end of the bed, I knew I hadn't put it there – and damn me if I didn't feel eight years old again. For a whole five minutes I must have been convinced Father Christmas was real. Somehow that's a much scarier thought when you're an adult. Some mad old coot breaking into people's houses and leaving presents or lumps of coal depending on how he thinks you're managing your life. Horrible feeling Like someone has been spying on you all the time.'

'How do you know he isn't real? I said.

'Oh, that was easy! I remembered I'd married your mother.'

'Slips his mind from time to time,' said my mother. 'You know, pleasant daydreams.'

They both laughed.

And so, the day progressed. We exchanged our more serious gifts. All were pleased with what they received. A proper picnic basket for the car was exactly what I needed. My father gave me another of his first editions, which I knew I would either have to leave at home or put in the bank. But the best part of the day was that my parents were so happy. I had never doubted they loved each other but over the years I had heard many a quarrel over money or politics, or even who the best writer of the day might be. All arguments were conducted with passion and seriousness, until finally one of them would yield. It was not unknown for arguments to last a week. It took me time as a child to understand how my father valued these spats. No longer the active man he had once been, he longed to still take part in the fight. He gave and expected no quarter. If he ever won, which was rare, he always seemed slightly disappointed. It was a long time before I understood that these quarrels had taken the place of other intimate activities they might have shared. Father had once told me that when I married, I should marry a man who not only adored me but had wit and charm.

'Generally, looks fade,' he had said. 'Not that your mother's have. I, mind you, have put on a touch of weight since my younger days, but I can still give your mother what for in a debate. Intellectual equals, that's what a decent marriage needs. Intellectual equals and respect. Everything else can go hang. And I mean everything. I was so glad you arrived when you did, Hope. I regret you never had any brothers or sisters. Nature didn't favour us that way. Your mother never seemed to have minded. Grand woman, your mother.'

I didn't fully understand what he had meant at the time and now, as a young woman, I tried very hard not to understand.

But on Christmas Day there wasn't a row in sight. Instead it was all jokes and reminiscences and displays of affection. We had a very happy celebration that included far too much food, slightly less alcohol than the night before, and various games, from hunt the slipper to charades. Admittedly, my father teamed up with me and directed me where to hunt, but he held his own at charades. We ended the day with a family tournament of chess, which to my surprise my father won. 'Always used to be rather good at this,' he said, smiling broadly.

When we were about to retire to bed there was a light dusting of snow outside. My father took me over to look out of the porch window. 'Lovely, isn't it?'

I looked up into the ebony sky with its scattering of tiny gems. There are so many more stars visible in the countryside. The night sky looked like the inside of a royal treasury all laid out on finest velvet with the moon, a giant pearl, its crowning glory. Everything outside was quiet, peaceful and at rest. 'Perfect,' I said, and he gave me the biggest hug and kissed both my cheeks before letting me go.

It was gone one a.m. when I heard a noise outside. I went to the window to see Fitzroy's car pull into the courtyard. I wondered if Giles was still awake or if I should go down and open the door. Then I saw a figure, wrapped in a shawl, running out across the white snow, leaving small footprints. Fitzroy got out of the car with some parcels in his hands but, on seeing the figure, he put them back inside. When my mother ran up to him, he caught her in an embrace and whirled her around, before setting her back on the ground. I gasped and wondered if he was under the influence. To my relief he didn't try and kiss her but handed her some of the parcels. They walked in together, their heads close as they talked.

Naturally, I needed to go down and ensure that everything was all right. I crept into the hall and retreated to a side passage where I should be able to listen to them. I heard Fitzroy knocking his boots against the stand.

'Shhh,' said my mother, 'you'll wake Bertram and Hope.'

'Wouldn't they be delighted to see me?' said Fitzroy in a teasing voice.

'Not in the middle of the night.'

'Middle of the night!' protested my godfather. 'It's barely dinner time.'

'Besides,' continued my mother, 'for all we know, Hope is spying on us now. I imagine it would be exactly the kind of thing you would have done as a child.'

'Well, you're wrong,' said Fitzroy. 'Could you hold this, please, while I take off my coat. It was freezing driving up. Almost as bad as that time in the Alps.'

'I don't believe that.'

'Well, it was cold enough. It would be good of you to offer me a whisky and light refreshment – say meat and three vegetables? A little gravy too would be nice. And if there's pudding going spare?'

'I don't know,' said my mother. 'Arriving in the middle of the night at a gentleman's house and purloining his vittles.'

'How is the old chap?' said Fitzroy, sounding suddenly serious.

'Not good,' said my mother. 'I tried to tell Hope I think this will be his last Christmas. I don't know if she understood, but I didn't want to ruin this time for her.'

'No,' said my godfather. 'Let her have this as a happy memory. Goodness knows we're all going to need them in the days to come.'

'Will it come to invasion?'

'I don't believe so – I can't believe so. But I think it will be a close-run thing.'

'I don't think Bertram could bear it if Germany invaded,' said my mother. 'It would break his heart.'

'Well, I, and a great deal of others, wouldn't be too happy either, you know. Don't worry, Alice. We'll keep the wolf from the door. We might not be as young as we were, but we have the knowledge and experience to guide those in our charge. We'll win the day.'

'She saw the star necklace.'

'Hmm? I do hope Jack isn't missing me.'

'Hope, she saw the Christmas Star.'

'Well, she's seen it before, hasn't she?'

'She doesn't remember. I told her I had inherited it but I could tell she wasn't convinced.'

'What would you expect? She's clever, our little Hope. I said from the start you should have told Bertram.'

'Tell him you'd given me a necklace that cost more than his car?'

'I didn't buy it for you. It was my mother's – who else would I give it to? Besides, you're only holding it until you pass it on to Hope. No one can find fault with me giving my goddaughter a gift.'

'I just don't want anyone to be upset this Christmas. I don't want anyone to think . . .'

'For heaven's sake, Alice, I have no one to spend my money on. At your request I've only ever given you and Hope fripperies to spare Bertram's feelings. It really isn't anyone's fault but his that he sunk all his money into White Orchards. How do you think I've felt watching you and Hope go without things I could have provided without turning a hair? But no, we had to protect Bertram's precious feelings. What about yours? What about Hope's? What about mine?'

'You don't have any feelings. You've always told me that,' said my mother in a lighter voice. I knew she wanted to leave this topic.

'I don't. Except where you and yours are concerned,' said Fitzroy. 'That and my duty to King and Country are all that have ever mattered to me.'

'Eric, please don't.' My mother's voice sounded broken. 'He has so little time left.'

'Yes, well. This was doubtless a discussion I should have had with your husband at a much earlier time. Don't worry, my dear, I won't ruin Christmas. I would have stayed away entirely, but – well, I'm going abroad in a little while and it might be a bit dicey. I wanted to see you and Hope before I went.'

'Don't you dare,' said my mother, her voice full of suppressed fury. 'Don't you dare not come back. I can't lose both of you. I can't.'

'The bloody politicos think as long as we have India, we'll be all right. They're worried about Russia, not Germany. I need to get proof we have to defend our own back yard. I'm as much of

69

an Empire man as anyone, but we cannot watch Europe burn and not lift a finger. We've done nothing. Nothing for the Poles, except declare war and march about at home. It's . . .'

'Catastrophic – or could be,' said my mother. 'Do you really think you have enough influence.'

'Alice,' said my godfather sharply. 'We should adjourn. I can hear a person breathing and I don't believe you have a ghost.'

I expected my mother to say something witty about ghosts not breathing, but there was only silence. I peeked round the edge of the passageway. They had melted away. The only sign anyone had ever been there was another coat hanging in the hall. I walked slowly back to my room. When I looked out of the window, I saw they had walked back over my mother's footsteps, so that all you could see in the snow were one set of scuffed tracks leading from the car. My mother was quite right when she said she had been taught by one of the best. He had been my instructor too, but I was beginning to realise that for their own reasons he and my mother had heavily restricted the skills I had learned. What I didn't know was why.

Chapter Ten

I had intended to drive back overnight. Fitzroy shook his head when I revealed my plan at luncheon. 'The moon's almost gone, and I don't doubt you know the area, Hope, but driving in pitch black without lights is no fun.'

'Indeed, I should think not,' said my father.

'But if I want to drive in daylight I'd need to leave almost immediately,' I said. Embarrassingly, I could feel a sob catching in my throat. Since overhearing the conversation last night, I had been focusing all my attention on my father. I constantly sought signs that my mother was wrong, and that his strength was actually returning. I flicked my gaze up towards him. He had his eyes closed as he sipped a glass of the wine that had been among the gifts Fitzroy traditionally brought the family at Christmas. He looked happy, but his raised chin revealed the crimped paper-like texture of his neck. The hand holding the glass had several large liver spots on it. Neither were a sign of illness, but it showed me very clearly that my father was ageing faster than most of his peers.

'We need you to be safe,' said my mother.

'Actually, if you agree,' said my godfather, looking at my parents. 'I'll take her back very early in the morning. It won't be light, but neither will it be pitch. I should have her back at post by the start of the day – and if I don't, I can always escort her in and smooth things over.'

'Do you mean she should follow you in her car?'

71

Fitzroy shook his head. 'No, she should leave it here. Petrol coupons are going to get even more scarce and, well, the car might be taken for scrap if it's in London. We're very short of materials. But out here, in a stable somewhere, it should be fine.'

My father nodded. 'Seems like a plan. Will you be able to get to work, Hope?'

I nodded. 'I don't need the car in town.'

'Good, well, that's settled,' said Fitzroy. 'You can spend the rest of the day with your parents and even get a few hours' shut-eye before we have to leave. If we wrap you up enough you can sleep in the car.'

'Does that mean we have to spend the rest of the day with you?' said my father to Fitzroy.

'Would you like me to go and sit in the coal cellar?'

'That would suit me perfectly,' said my father, 'but the girls would object.'

My godfather raised the back of his hand to his forehead, 'And to think I put two bottles of my very best brandy in the Christmas case I gave you. It makes the wine you are so enjoying look like soda water.'

'How can you be so horrible, Bertie?' said my mother.

'One of the few pleasures of ill health is that one dares to speak one's mind,' said my father. 'Where's the damn chess board. I'll thrash you yet, man. Won't go to my grave until I do.' My father rose unsteadily and tottered out of the room shouting for Giles.

'Don't pay any attention—' began my mother.

'Of course not,' said Fitzroy. 'Your husband and I have always conducted a faux war. What I need to know is whether I should let him win or not?'

'Almost let him win,' suggested my mother.

'So he wants to live and fight another day?' said Fitzroy. 'I can do that. But before I do, Hope, could you come out to the car with me. I have something for you.' My mother looked wary. 'It's so small Bertram won't even notice,' he assured her.

We got our coats from the hall and went out to the courtyard, only to find that the car had been moved into the garage. We crunched through the snow together.

'Old Merrit still around then,' said Fitzroy, taking the absence of his car with great calm. 'Poor Merry. I thought she'd be shot of him by now.'

I glanced at him in surprise. 'I thought they were a happy couple. They've been together since not long after Merry met Mother.'

'Hmm,' said Fitzroy.

'You have to tell me now,' I said tugging on his sleeve. He looked down at me, an expression of mild disapproval in his eyes. 'Surely I don't have to consider your rank when you're here. You're not on duty.'

Fitzroy tweaked his sleeve. 'I'm always on duty,' he said. 'But I think I have mentioned before that when we are alone, or with your family, as long as we aren't part of a serious and on-going situation, I won't stand on formality with you. To be honest, I rarely stand on formality with my people. I'd always rather they said what they thought – as long as they give me the respect I am due. And don't tug my coat out of shape, for example.'

I let go.

'I suppose I can tell you. Merry is very intelligent. She hasn't had much opportunity to learn, so it isn't obvious to everyone. Your mother spotted it at once. Probably what drew them together at that awful house. But Merry had very few cards in her favour. Then she compounded that by marrying a man of the lower classes, who was perfectly content with his station. Nothing wrong with Merrit. They were, I think, fond of each other. Probably still are, but Merry's life has been smaller than it could have been. She got a clear sight of that when Merrit went missing in the Great War. He was presumed dead, and Merry fell in love with someone else. Someone who could give her a better life, raise the class of her children, and who valued her intellect.'

'What happened?'

'Rather like a bad penny, Merrit turned up.' We were almost at the garage by now. Fitzroy stopped in the lee of the house. 'I'm being unfair. He's not a bad man. He's decent, honest and works hard to give Merry and Michael the best life he can. But if she had married more wisely and less quickly – or if Merrit hadn't come back – her life would have been different, fuller and more fulfilling. Of course, your father sponsored Michael up to Oxford, and that's a lot more than Merry would have hoped for. Your mother has always tried to look after her, but Merrit has a clear and finite sense of what he thinks he and his wife should do. He didn't want Michael to go to university, but Bertram had a serious chat with him and he let the boy go. Strange really,' said my godfather, 'so many men who experienced the classes living and dying alongside each other in the trenches came back with a greater concept of the equality of man – not communism, but more of an appreciation of what any man can achieve given a better start. Merrit it seems came back with a smaller outlook. But I can't say I ever got to know the man or wanted to.'

'But you know Merry?'

Fitzroy nodded. 'Quite well. She and your mother were close before Merry married, and very close when we thought him lost. He's never approved of their relationship. Idiot man. I do hate to see the potential of an intelligent woman held back because of a foolish choice in marriage. Please, Hope, be very certain of the man you intend to marry. I mean, obviously, I will check his background thoroughly, but even so . . .'

I laughed. 'Will anyone actually get through your screening? It's more likely I'll be a spinster than you'll like any of my beaus.'

'I will like any man, of any class, who loves you as you deserve. He will need to value your intelligence, independence, and integrity.'

'One of them on every street corner,' I said.

'I want at least one person I know to have a happy and fulfilling marriage,' said my godfather.

'But you know my parents,' I said.

'Of course. We should get moving again. I think rather than

feel that the wind is rising. I hope it doesn't bring sleet with it. That would make our journey back tiresome.'

'Was it you Merry fell in love with?'

Fitzroy laughed loudly and heartily. 'No. No. She has always, quite rightly, regarded me with suspicion. Now hurry along or your father will claim a win by default.'

The garage, which now took up half of the stables, smelled of wet wood and oil. I breathed in deeply. I found it comforting. Fitzroy got a package from inside the front of his car. It was small enough to fit inside his hand.

'Now, my dear. I don't usually give you valuable gifts. I'm very wary of displeasing your father. I don't know how much impression it has made on you, but I really do have a lot of money and no one to spend it on.'

'The Service pays you that well?'

Fitzroy grinned widely. 'Please don't set me off. When I was recruited it was as important to be of independent means as it was to be of the right background. The idea the Service pays anyone properly is almost indecently funny. No, I inherited money from my mother, who was an heiress in her own right – from America. I am actually half-American, but I would prefer you to keep that between us. I have also always invested wisely. Generally, I keep my riches under wraps. It hasn't earned me any friends and never will. Even your mother doesn't know the full extent of it – though I think she suspects. Anyway, I wanted to give you this. It belonged to my mother. It is platinum with rubies. In her days it would have been just another piece, possibly her own mother's, but today it is a rarity. You can wear it and it's also small enough to fit in a pocket. I've also included a chain so you can wear it round your neck underneath your uniform, if you wish. I don't believe it would in any way identify you. My mother never even wore it England when she was alive.'

I opened the small box to find a delicate ring lying on top of a gold chain. The shank was carved like bamboo and at three places

75

around this were trumpet-like flowers carved from rubies with a tiny dab of gold at their heart. It was exquisite.

'Bit old-fashioned, I suppose.'

'No, I love it,' I said, flinging my arms round his neck and kissing his cheek. He returned my embrace with one arm and made that noise that meant he was pleased but had no intention of being soppy enough to show it. I hugged him hard and then stepped away.

'The flowers should really be amethysts, I've always thought, but I assume the jeweller considered them inferior stones. Anyway, it's meant to be bamboo and morning glory. Most unlikely bedfellows, except they were considered lucky during the Victorian age.'

I picked the ring up and found it was already threaded onto the chain. Fitzroy helped me fasten it. He stood back and looked at me. 'Definitely suits you. Now tuck it inside and put the box in your pocket. I don't want to upset your father.'

We walked back towards the house. I thanked him again, but he waved my thanks away. 'I'm glad you have it and not one of my clutching relatives. None of them has any right to even a speck of my mother's possessions. Obviously, you and Euphemia get the main things in my will, but it's hard to make provision for every little thing. And I wanted to tell you about the link to luck with that. My mother always thought it brought her luck. Although I'm not usually superstitious . . .'

We had reached the front door. 'You talk as if you're dying. You may marry someday.'

'I doubt it,' said my godfather. He had his hand on the door-handle. I could see Giles approaching from the other side. He paused, saw Giles and smiled ruefully.

'I've learnt the hard way, Hope, that death is a sudden thief. He is quick and ruthless. One moment the person you love is alive, the next it is as if they never existed. Prepare yourself for that, my dear, as much as you can. Our most loved ones are stolen from us without warning.'

Then he wrenched the door open, so that Giles, reaching for

the door handle, stumbled forward. Fitzroy stepped adroitly aside, but Giles managed to right himself. It cost him some dignity and a startled gasp.

Fitzroy indicated for me to go in. He clapped Giles on the shoulder as he went past. To me he said, 'Just a game I play with old Giles. He'd ban me from house if he could, so I always like to get to the door before him – in case he bolts it one day.'

'He could have fallen and hurt himself,' I said.

'Nonsense. All butlers are required to have an excellent sense of balance. It's a British law. Now, where's your father and his dratted chess board.'

The day continued pleasantly and between us we kept my father in excellent spirits. My mother informed me that a maid had packed for me, so all I needed to do was be ready at the appointed hour to go back to London with Fitzroy. We decided I would say my goodbyes after dinner, rather than expect my parents to get up at dawn.

Fitzroy's warning to me was ringing uncomfortably loud in my ears when I bade them goodnight. I felt suddenly much younger than my years and I wanted nothing more than to stay at home until New Year at least. For the first time I felt the leash of my uniform and I didn't like it. I understood better than ever before why Fitzroy had always played the maverick. The ordinary way of things was choking – and yet many people comfortably succumbed to that yoke.

I crept downstairs at the first sign of light and discovered my bags had already been taken from the hallway. I let myself out of the front door. I didn't want to turn around and look back at the house. I didn't want to end this happy visit fearing it was the last of the best times.

When I got into the car my godfather said, 'I'm sorry I spooked you, Hope. But forewarning is your best armour. Even if it doesn't feel so at present.'

I smiled and nodded. I had been thinking about what he'd said and my mind was full of questions.

'Now, I suggest you get some rest. The moonlight is far fainter than I had hoped. I need to drive at a reasonable speed for us to get back to London in time, so I will need to concentrate completely to keep us out of the ditch. I certainly won't be able to indulge you in my usual witty repartee.'

I didn't believe this for a moment. Fitzroy was a daring driver, but a highly skilled one. I'd been with him when he'd torn along on nights worse than this while instructing me in the art of pick-pocketing – with even the occasional heart-stopping gesture. But I knew there was no point trying to get round him once he had decided on a course of action. Hopefully, I would wake up before we reached London, and being tired he might be more open to persuasion. Accordingly, I snuggled down.

'I'll try not to snore,' I said.

'Yes, do that,' said my godfather, grinning, 'and if you wake up to the sound of *me* snoring, give me a nudge, there's a good girl.'

Chapter Eleven

I awoke, fortunately not to the sound of snoring, but to my own teeth chattering. I sat up and tried to rub the circulation back into my arms.

'You're cold, aren't you?'

The thin light that comes as dawn struggles to rise outlined Fitzroy's face, casting the planes of it into darkness and light. Despite his age, his profile remained clear and unchanged since my earliest memories. Only his beard had varied over the years, with even, I half remembered, a rather scrubbing brush moustache at one time.

'Hope?'

'Yes,' I managed to say through my chattering teeth. I had several witty responses in mind, but my jaw was too jittery to get them out.

'Damn,' said my godfather.

He stopped the car and did a U-turn in the middle of the road, with all the ease of a ballet dancer spinning on the spot. 'I can't think of anywhere open right now, but we're reasonably close to a safe house of mine. I believe it's empty.' He drove at an alarming speed back up the road we had just come down, suddenly swerving into a field.

It turned out the field had a rough track across it, and obviously no livestock as it was open to the road. I peered out of the window into the shadows. I thought I could make out ruts in the dirt. Was some kind of crop sown here? The car rocked increasingly from side to side.

'Damn,' said Fitzroy again.

'I'm sorry,' I said, quietly, so he could pretend he hadn't heard. My godfather either welcomes apologies with open arms or loathes them. Much like the way he reacts to humanity in general, now I think of it.

'You can't help it,' said Fitzroy in a tone of voice that rather suggested he thought I should have been able to.

'I wore only warm things and more than one layer,' I said. 'I thought it would be enough with the blankets and the hot water bottles.'

'About time you got yourself a decent driving coat,' said Fitzroy.

'I left it in my car,' I said in a small voice.

'Why the devil would you do that?' snapped my godfather. He took a sharp left turn behind a tall hedgerow and we emerged suddenly on to gravel in front of a respectably sized house. It looked as if it might once have been the local vicarage or perhaps the home of a farm factor.

He shut off the engine and jumped out. 'Come on,' he said, striding up to the door.

The house was in complete darkness. All the windows were shuttered. Fitzroy pulled a key from his pocket and opened the door. Inside he lit a gas lamp and took me straight through to the kitchen. He lit the stove. 'Sit right next to it. It won't have time to get that warm, but we can get some hot coffee in you, and even this mausoleum is warmer than the car. Maybe you should walk around a bit, jump up and down. Get the blood flowing again.'

Rather self-consciously, I began to do as he suggested.

'Properly, Hope, not like a wounded pigeon,' was all he added as he brewed the coffee. It gave me a chance to see his driving coat. It was much heavier than mine, and was clearly weighed down with a multitude of filled pockets. I wondered what the chances were that he might lend it to me.

'Drink this,' he said, thrusting a cup into my hand. 'Sit by the fire, so you don't get cold again. I'll see what I can find.'

I was on my second cup of coffee by the time he returned. I

80

could feel most of my limbs if not my toes. He threw down a large blue coat over another chair. 'That should keep you warm. You'll have to take it off before you get out of the car. You could get court-martialled for wearing it.'

Several thoughts collided in my head at once. 'Is it an Air Force coat?' I asked. 'Why do you have it? Am I actually conscripted into the Army?'

Fitzroy helped himself to a little coffee. 'Don't drink too much,' he said, ignoring my questions. 'I'm going to have to drive like the clappers as it is. We won't have time for – what do the Americans call it? Comfort stops.'

I felt myself blushing, but I put down my cup unfinished. 'Well?' I asked in as non-hostile a voice as I could manage. 'And thank you for the use of the coat,' I added quickly.

The single oil lamp Fitzroy had lit made it difficult enough to see as it was, but he still turned away from me before answering my questions. Pointlessly, I thought. My mother was the only person who could read him clearly. I might pick up on the occasional expression, but generally he was far too stoic for me to read. Obviously, and interestingly, he didn't think so.

'I'm sure I put your papers through a while ago,' he said.

'Don't I have to sign something?'

'You have – and you signed the Official Secrets act too.'

'I did? I don't remember this.'

'You must have done,' said Fitzroy. 'I certainly have that piece of paper.'

I frowned. I couldn't think how . . . . He interrupted my thoughts. 'Yes, it's an airman's uniform, a Captain. Part of the dressing-up box I left here. Learnt to fly during the last show. Although that was all a bit string and sealing wax. I kept it up. Enough to be able to do the basics. Never had the time to learn properly. Always too busy. By the way, have you seen young Harvey recently? I understand he's veered from the straight and narrow yet again. Is he worth putting out a hand to save? Or shall I let him go under?'

81

'Harvey? In trouble? Oh dear. I had meant to go in search of him, but the typewriting course was wearing me out. Then Bernie started feeding me the results of her cookery for your friend's recipe project.'

'Mouth as wide as the Channel,' murmured Fitzroy. 'But honestly, Hope, if you take on assets it's your duty to keep an eye on them. You knew Harvey had a disreputable streak, and you still used him. I even went to considerable effort to clear his record.'

'You make it sound as if I'm working for you, but I've been sitting in a basement learning dictation.'

Fitzroy took of his driving cap and ran his hands through his hair. 'I thought this was obvious, but I must have been wrong. Hope, working in espionage is pretty much a life-long commitment. Now, I suppose you learned fairly early on in life that I was spy. I don't remember ever telling you . . .'

'It was Father.'

'It would be. The thing is, generally one does not in the usual way of things go around declaring oneself a spy.'

'I know that,' I said with ill-concealed scorn.

'So, you understand the concept of a cover?'

'Yes, you use one on a mission to explain your presence.'

Fitzroy sighed and ran his hand through his hair again. 'No, dear, you need one all the time. When you and Bernie came to talk to me about your flat, did you think you were in the office of Fitzroy, Spymaster?'

I nodded.

'No. I was then based in the Department of Works.'

'You mean there isn't a headquarters for espionage somewhere?'

'Yes, of course there is. We have various bases, and various offices, but I'm still, by the skin of my teeth, working in the field.' I must have looked puzzled, because he added, 'As opposed to solely driving a desk. Which I would find incredibly tedious. I like to be out and about. I don't mind letting the younger chaps do the running around, but I like to keep my hand in.'

'So you mean this secretarial business is a cover?'

'Can you think of an easier way to get you into a department where I believe there may be trouble? A lot of what I do is counter-espionage. I take it you know what that means?'

I didn't dare to do anything but nod.

'You're young, pretty, and no one would think twice about you being a secretarial assistant with a high clearance. You're more than capable. And before you say anything about being able to do other, more exciting things, espionage is rarely exciting, and when it is, it's usually the am–I–going–to–die–today exciting. As your career develops you will be put where you fit. So, shall I save Harvey or not?'

I blinked, bewildered. 'Yes,' I said. 'Save Harvey. Please.'

'Are you sure?'

I nodded.

'Well, he's not getting an easy ride a second time. I'll give him an option other than jail, but if he doesn't like it, he's not my problem.'

'But if I am working for you why haven't you told me? Or issued me any instructions?'

'You mean orders,' said Fitzroy. 'Because that isn't the way I work. A lot of my agents are out in the field gathering data. They come to me when they have results. I do task people, but that is when there are particular missions. A lot of the time my people have a watching brief. Do you understand?'

'I think so. I'm to keep my eyes and ears open and tell you if I see anything odd. But how do I get in touch with you?'

'You have my emergency number. Otherwise you can let your mother know if you need to talk. I will check in from time to time, but I am very busy at present. This war is most disruptive to my normal schedule.' He paused to grin at me. 'Oh, if anything happens to me, Griffin can direct you what to do next. I've left all the protocols in place. For the duration of the war, at least, your mother would take my place.'

'My mother?'

'Yes, she's first class. Pity about her lack of languages, but that's her only flaw. I may have massaged the truth when I first asked you to work for me. I thought if you knew how deeply your mother was in, you might say no. You're hardly on the best of terms.'

'We got on fine at Christmas,' I snapped. 'You lied to me!'

'I lie to everyone – except one person, and that isn't you,' said my godfather. 'Now, all my safe houses, and I mean mine not the Department's, have the same key. A copy will come to you if anything happens to me. You and your mother get my entire estate.'

'Don't you have other relatives?'

'Don't like 'em.' He chuckled to himself. 'It'll set the wolves among the sheep. I'll be sorry not to see the chaos. Your father will dislike me more than ever.'

'I thought you got on quite well.'

'We've only ever had one falling-out, but it's never been resolved. We are civil and sometimes we remember the times when we did enjoy each other's company.'

'What did he do?'

'Hope, I suggest you don't get tangled up in this. It all happened before you were born.'

I nodded slowly. 'As a child I never questioned it, but as I grew up it struck me . . .' I broke off, unsure if I would offend him.

'What?'

'The three of you have an unusual relationship.'

'Hmm.'

'I mean, you spend so much time together.'

'Hmm.'

'And if you don't even like Father . . .'

'Hmm,' said my godfather.

'Are you cross I'm asking?'

Fitzroy shook his head. 'No, they're natural questions. I have no answers for you. Have you finished with that coffee? I need to clean the cups.'

We left shortly afterwards. The coat was magnificently warm.

At the door as Fitzroy locked up he said, 'I'm glad we had this little bit of time together. It might be a while before I get to see you again.'

As we got into the car, I blurted out, 'But I don't want you to die!'

He flashed me a look of surprise as he started the car. Then he said, 'I would rather avoid death for as long as possible. Unfortunately, Fate can have other ideas. I don't intend to die, Hope, but it is my duty to make provisions.'

'You're about to go and do something terribly dangerous, aren't you?'

'This discussion is over – and that's an order.' He drove down the rutted lane and out on to the road.

I couldn't ever remember Fitzroy seriously telling me something was an order. I looked across at his profile. The light was increasing. I could see the outline now, but he appeared stony and expressionless. I'd had a slim hope he had been joking, but I doubted it. I decided silence was the better part of valour. I watched him drive for a while. If I paid attention to how quickly the countryside sped by, I felt sick. Eventually, he looked down at me and said, not unkindly, 'Try to get a little more sleep, my dear. I've no doubt you have a long day ahead of you.'

I opened my mouth to speak.

'Shhh,' said my godfather. 'When I need you, I know where to find you.'

Chapter Twelve

A hand on my shoulder woke me. I was outside the clerical building where I had previously worked, before the time with the amorous old colonel. 'You're being posted back here. They'll tell you inside. You're more or less on time. I'll leave your case back at the flat. Hurry now, before you get into trouble.'

I stumbled out only half awake. Fitzroy didn't move from the wheel. He raised a hand to me. 'Be careful, my dear,' he said and drove off. It took all my willpower not to run after him.

I turned and walked over to my old workplace. The irritable old man on the door merely nodded at me. I searched for my pass. 'Don't you need to see this?' I asked.

The man shook his head. 'Didn't know you were one of his people,' he said and nodded me through.

I assumed he meant working for Fitzroy and presumably that meant he was too. For the oddest reason I didn't feel as lonely as I had when my godfather drove away. As I trotted up the stairs, I realised that to be on the point of tears watching a relative, who lived in the same city as you, drive away was ridiculous for an adult woman. But then Fitzroy always made me feel like a child.

When I got to the top floor, I realised the doorman hadn't told me where to report. I'd automatically gone up the stairs, but perhaps I should have gone down to the basement? I retraced my steps and headed down. I'd rather make a mistake at a clerical level than walk into some secret meeting upstairs.

I found the usual receptionist lurking in her dark dungeon.

She nodded at me and pointed to a couple of chairs. I sat down. A feeling was beginning to grow inside me that everyone knew more of what was going on than me. I reminded myself I was a spy, working my cover, and sat up a little straighter.

I didn't have long to wait. The vulture-faced instructor appeared. I realised, apart from having internally named them *Beaky* and *the Vulture*, I had no idea of their names. 'Ma'am,' I said, standing as she came in. This earned me a grim little smile, and an invitation to sit. She pulled out a chair and sat opposite me. In her hands she had a manila folder. She opened this at an angle that prevented me from seeing the contents. She flickered through some papers.

'I see assisting the Colonel didn't work out.'

'No, ma'am.'

'The reason?'

'I don't believe I lived up to his expectations.'

Another grim little smile. 'Very discreetly put. It was always a risk putting a pretty girl with him, but you do have an unusually high security clearance.'

'Yes, ma'am,' I said.

'So discreet,' muttered the woman. 'Anyway, it appears your old colleagues want you back, and as they require a ridiculous security clearance, there really isn't any other choice. It seems a shame to put you there when we have excellent officers who are having to deal with mountains of critical paperwork, but under "requirements" they generally put "anyone with half a brain", whereas the think tanks are very picky about who they take. Really should be the other way around, but there, you didn't hear me say that. Report to the top floor. Room 103, Cadet Stapleford, and may God have mercy on your soul.'

She stood up and I did the same. I hadn't seen anyone saluting down here, so I didn't. I hadn't ever actually had to salute anyone, and the thought of it made me feel rather silly. I didn't exactly object, but I didn't want to get it wrong. Obviously, as a cadet, no one was going to salute me. I made my way back up the stairs, thinking that the Colonel was hardly writing important letters and wondering if I was really a cadet or if that was part of my cover. Ranks never seemed to make much impression on Fitzroy, including his own.

I opened the door and the first face I saw was the freckled visage of Sergeant Lewis Bradshaw. 'Hello, luv, welcome back.'

After a day of taking down the frankly idiotic ideas of Merryworth and Bradshaw I was ready for a hot bath and an early night. Both Cole and Captain Max appeared to have exited this 'think tank', and I could hardly blame them.

I opened the front door to the flat and for the first time it felt like coming home. White Orchards would always be my home, but the flat felt like a sanctuary of sorts. Suddenly, the length of my day and everything that had happened, hit me like a ton of bricks. I hung my coat on the rack and flopped onto the settee like a floundering fish. I heard a door open inside the flat. I hadn't realised Bernie would be back yet. I propped myself up on an elbow and saw her come in. Unusually, she wore a pretty but reserved dress with very high heels. She was twisting her hands together, pulling at the nails on her index fingers. I was used to seeing her take pains with her manicure.

'What's the matter?' I asked with some foreboding. 'What have you done?'

'I haven't yet,' she said. 'I only got back early this morning. They had us working on Christmas Day. Although we did have a nice turkey dinner and a glass of sherry. Not that I like sherry that much. It's too sweet. I can't drink much of it. That might have been the idea, I suppose. Oh, hell! I'm doing it already.'

She sat down in the spare chair and put her head in her hands. 'Why, oh why, did your wretched godfather get me into this? He must have known how it would be. Oh, I'm so unhappy I could eat mud.'

'I beg your pardon?'

'That's what you English say, isn't it? Go down the garden and eat mud?'

'Go and eat worms,' I corrected. 'It can't be that bad. Worms taste horrid. All gritty and slimy. And they wriggle while you're chewing.'

'You've eaten worms?'

'I spat them out. I was only three.'

'You always did have a strange sense of adventure,' said Bernie. 'Why didn't he send you?'

'Send me what?'

'On the wretched course!'

'I don't know,' I said. 'He seemed to think you had the kind of mind for it.'

'He told you?' Her face fairly shone with relief.

'Not all of it,' I said carefully. 'Oh, is this about you having a mouth as wide as the Channel?'

'Ouch, he told you he said that?'

I smiled. 'He doesn't tell me that much. Only bits and pieces. If it helps, I have signed the Official Secrets Act too. However, I don't think you can tell me all about what you've been doing. My security clearance is apparently unusually high for a cadet, but that's not saying a lot. I know you've been doing a Signals Intel course, but that's it. And I don't think you should tell me more than that.'

'That's something,' said Bernie. 'Everything feels so horrid. Don't you think? Only I've been told I'm not allowed to say that. It's negative on morale or some such thing.'

'I think you can say what you like to me about your mood,' I said. 'I'm not going to report you, but I'd be very careful about saying anything like that outside these walls.'

Bernie nodded. 'I just have the feeling that awful things are coming.'

'The Germans?'

'Well, obviously. But . . . oh, I don't know. People can call this a phoney war all they like, but the things I've heard that are happening in Poland on both the Russian and German sides are . . . are evil. I don't understand why we aren't doing more than patrolling the edges of France.'

'Well, I think we should have gone to Poland's aid,' I said, 'but between you and me I suspect we had neither the trained men nor the arms to spare. We're hideously under-prepared for what's coming. I know Fitzroy has been champing at the bit at the British inaction for a while now. Did he tell you about Poland?'

Bernie shook her head.

'Oh, Bernie, was that the kind of detail from your course you shouldn't have mentioned?'

'No,' said Bernie with an obvious sigh of relief. 'I heard this somewhere entirely different.'

'Where?' I said. I suddenly felt more awake.

'In bed,' said Bernie almost too quietly for me to hear.

'What!' I fairly shot up out of my seat at this. 'Have you been sleeping with my godfather!'

'No!' said Bernie hotly. 'I haven't. Why are you so territorial about him? He's a grown man, you can bet he's sleeping with someone.' She gave me an odd look. 'Unless you . . .'

'No, I do not,' I said angrily. 'He's like another father to me. You're trying to avoid telling me who you've been with, but I know you. You wouldn't have mentioned it at all if there wasn't a part of you that wanted to confess. So who is he? Please don't tell me this is another married man?'

Bernie sank back down into the chair. Slowly I retook my seat, my eyes not leaving her. I was enormously fond of Fitzroy when he wasn't annoying me, and perhaps I was a bit territorial about him, but I had never thought about him *that way*. I didn't want him to get mixed up with a walking disaster like Bernie, but then he'd told me he felt she was too hot to handle, as well as rather dull. I supposed he must have a love life, but he'd never mentioned any lady friends to me, and I certainly wasn't going to pry. He'd never brought anyone to White Orchards, and I took that as a clear signal that part of his life was off-limits. I was so lost in my own thoughts that I didn't realise Bernie was talking.

'So, it gets to Christmas Eve, and I admit I was feeling rather down. I missed Father and I missed you and all our London friends.'

'Your London friends,' I said, but she ignored me and carried on. I realised I must have missed the initial revelation of the name.

'There was a Christmas Eve dance, but I kept thinking how much nicer it would have been to go with you to White Orchards. I remember sitting in my room and moping. I heard music from somewhere outside, and I don't know, something in me just snapped. I got up, had a bit of a wash, put on one of my prettiest frocks and plastered myself in make-up. I got my hair to go right for once. If I say so myself, I looked like a goddamn movie star. I didn't have a partner, because I'd made such a song and dance about not going, so I went on my own. Only he was there, in his uniform – and he looked dreamy. Our eyes met across the dance floor and locked. We'd only ever kissed before, but we both thought he could get into awful trouble over it, so we weren't being – well, public about our attraction. So, I only gave the slightest of nods before walking onto the dance floor. I did not encourage him in the slightest. You have to believe me. I mean, I may have had the teensiest bit too much to drink, and I suppose I was rather flirting with some of the young men, but I didn't go across the dance floor. He came to me. He said, 'Miss, I do believe you may be feeling the effects of the evening. I think I should escort you back to your room. He pretended as if he didn't even know who I was. He's very clever. Then he put his arm through mine as standing was proving just a trifle tricky at that precise moment and took me back to his room.'

'You were drunk, and he took you to his room. That doesn't sound very gentlemanly to me.'

'Oh, no. He went back to the dance. He left me to sober up. But he had the loveliest squishy bed, so I settled down and went to sleep. I only woke up when he'd come back and was taking off my shoes. I was quite with things by then. I suppose I might still have been a bit over-excited, but I thought Bernie, old girl, why don't you give yourself a Christmas present? Mummy and Daddy hadn't sent me anything, and you were away, and there was no one else there who'd even been kind to me. And the course such

91

hard work, so tiring. I only meant it to be a few kisses and maybe a bit more, but things got rather out of hand for both of us. Don't misunderstand, I was totally in agreement with what we did at the time.'

'And now?'

'I like him an awful lot, and he's respectable enough. He seems to like me too, but I didn't fancy being – well you know. So, I said we mustn't do it again – and he proposed!' She held out her left hand. On the ring finger of her left hand was a middle-sized diamond. She turned it back and forth in the light, watching it twinkle. 'It's not awfully big, but it is pretty, isn't it?'

'Bernie, what have you got yourself into now?'

'Oh, his security clearance is far higher than mine. He's a what-do-they-call-it, top brass sort of chap. Navy, obviously.'

'Obviously,' I said. 'So, this was Christmas Eve and he's already proposed?'

'With breakfast in the morning. It was so romantic.'

I supposed it was possible Bernie looked lovely in the morning, all those curls tumbling everywhere. I looked a terrible fright. Any man I married was going to have to have a strong stomach when it came to breakfast in bed. 'Congratulations,' I said as convincingly as I could.

'I know what you're thinking,' said Bernie. 'But it looks like he'll be at sea again soon, and he said he learnt last time that taking your time over matters of the heart during war was unwise.'

'The last war? How old is he?'

'Early fifties,' said Bernie. 'A nice dependable man, with only a slight fleck of silver in his hair. He's a widower too, so he'll know all about being married.'

'Any children?'

'I don't know,' said Bernie.

'What's his favourite colour?'

'Oh, that's easy. The colour of my eyes – and navy blue. He's ever so proud of his rank.'

'Did he say why he proposed?'

'I told you. He said he might be in combat soon.' She shivered with barely concealed delight. 'My hero.'

'You're saying that with a straight face?'

'Oh yes, he got lots of medals last time. He's going to show them to me after we're married.'

'I take it I should start looking for a new flatmate?'

Bernie looked for a moment bereft.

'I take it he won't want to move in here?'

She laughed at this. 'Oh, no,' she said. 'He has his own London house. He's taking me to dinner tonight, I hope. He said if he got into town he would. He said he'd need to start introducing me to people, so the announcement of our engagement won't be such a shock.'

I stood up. 'I should get cleaned up. It will be a pleasure to meet him.'

'I haven't told him about you. Only that I have a female friend who shares with me.'

I waited for my invitation to meet him. It didn't come.

Bernie looked at her watch. 'I should go down and be ready. He likes things to be punctual – Navy man.' She threw her coat over her shoulders and hurried out. I watched her go without a word.

I waited until I heard the car outside, then I picked up the phone.

'Hope,' said my mother's voice. 'How lovely to hear from you so quickly. I do hope Eric didn't run you into a ditch.'

'No, everything is fine,' I said. 'I even got back in time to do a full day's work as a clerical assistant.'

'How tiresome,' said my mother. 'Hear anything interesting?'

'Not at all,' I said. 'How is Father?'

'Having a little lie down. He loved having you here, but I think he pushed himself a bit hard. He needs to rest up. I could get him to call you later, if you wish?'

'No, it's all right. I'm very tired and he'd hear it in my voice and worry. Please give him my love and tell him I miss him.'

'Certainly, dear. You do know you are ringing on the secure line, don't you?'

'Yes, I need to ask you about something, it's both personal and I suspect – well, I'm prying.'

'Oh, good!' said my mother. 'With your father asleep, and nothing much happening, I'm terribly bored.'

'Bernie's got herself engaged.'

'Oh, Lord! I should never have balked at having her here.'

'You didn't,' I reminded her. 'I knew you weren't happy, but . . .'

'It was only because I wanted to give your father a special time – with the three of us.'

'I know. And you know Bernie, she attracts trouble like a magnet attracts iron filings.'

'Very apt,' said my mother, 'who is he?'

'Well, apparently he's a senior Navy man, around fifty years of age.'

'That's a relief. I thought for a moment . . .'

'I did too . . .'

My mother chuckled. 'We should leave the poor man alone. His private life doesn't concern us. But Fitzroy and Bernie – if ever there was a match made in the underworld.'

'He told me he'd never consider her – or rather told her to her face.'

'Ouch,' said my mother, 'and I bet he had been flirting with her only moments earlier. He can be quite crushing. I thought he was making a mistake when he said he was going to use her as a foil, but he said she needed control, or she'd draw attention to you. I told him he should have found her a job somewhere. It turns out she is actually quite bright. A possible untapped mathematical genius.'

'She met the Navy chap at a course over Christmas.' I told my mother the story.

'Oh, that doesn't sound good,' she said. 'He took her to his room rather than hers. Sounds as if he planned that part all along. And she barely knew him before?'

94

'From what I can gather.'

'Hmm, that proposal sounds like the kind of thing a brass hat might do when he realises he seduced the American ambassador's daughter. Everyone knows we're trying to get them into this war. Goodness knows we need the help. He'd have been in a rare bind if he messed up Anglo-American relations over – well, Bernie.'

'I don't think he sounds nice or good for her,' I said.

'Can't say I think I'd take to him on the evidence provided so far. I take it you want me to do some digging? What course was she on?'

'I only know it was Sig Intel. Fitzroy got her on it.'

'Right. I'll get the details from him next time he calls. Shouldn't be too long.'

'Oh, I thought he was going off somewhere . . .'

'You know I can't talk about that sort of thing, even on this line. But I shouldn't worry about him. He has been a cat with nine lives, but he knows only too well he's spent quite a few.'

'I'm not sure if that makes me worry less or more.'

My mother laughed. 'I should go, dear. Your father will be missing me. Remember you can call anytime, but in general use the family phone. You might even get your father answering.'

She hung up. Her gentle reprimand stung. With needle-point precision she had found my weakness – my fear that I wasn't really a spy at all, and that she and Fitzroy were putting me places where they thought they could keep me safe.

Chapter Thirteen

I celebrated New Year with an early night. Bernie was out with her fiancé, and even if my work colleagues had invited me out (which they hadn't) I wouldn't have willing spent any of my free time with them. Not having the car meant there was no chance of paying a flying visit home. I did ring my parents up, on the family phone, to wish them Happy New Year, but that was as close as I came to celebration.

January marched on, and apart from the desecration of Poland, which was given no more than lip service by the majority of our elected officials, we were still waiting for battle to commence. British troops saw no action, and the phrase repeated more and more often on the lips of the public was 'phoney war'. I felt like a phoney myself. My mother and godfather claimed they had spent much of my childhood teaching me spycraft, but now Europe was slowly succumbing to the heel of the German jackboot, all I could offer my country was a little light typing. Perhaps if I had been noting down things of great importance, supporting those who were going to fight this war, it would have felt better. Instead I was left with three men who thought they were the answer to all Britain's planning issues, but would be hard pressed to find any location outwith central London.

But still, through my typing I learned things. I learned that a German plane had come down in Belgium and in it had been plans (code name: Fall Gelb) to invade the Low Countries. The

Low Countries began to mobilise. They informed Britain and France of their find and everyone started getting very busy.

I read the information passing over my desk and became increasingly confused. Fog banks happen, but not only had the German pilot got himself lost, he had then switched off the fuel line, supposedly by accident. The plane had crash-landed, its wings breaking off, but no one had been hurt. The pilot had had an officer on board with him, who was responsible for the plans. There had then followed a series of bizarre attempts by the officer to burn the papers. He tried to set fire to the plane, but his lighter wouldn't work. He piled up the papers and asked a local farmer for help, who gave him a single match. Then later, during inter-rogation, one of the two had tried to place the papers in a stove.

I hadn't any way of discovering if Fitzroy had been involved in any of this, but it was all so crazy I thought it likely. But then the dates mentioned in the folder passed without incident, all the senior officials of the countries involved breathed a collective sigh of relief, and things pretty much settled back down to normal. It was annoy-ing and depressing. I imagined my godfather, who was sure in his bones of the coming advance of Germany, brooding, drinking brandy somewhere and raining down curses on the heads of all politicians.

Even Bernie, who Fitzroy had had some secret hopes for, appeared to have given up on the real war happening any time soon. Instead she was often out at some dinner or dance when I came home. I had no idea how her fiancé had this much free time. He had to be a strictly eight a.m. to five p.m. sort of sailor. I held a slim hope she was still working on some secret project, but as she usually came back very late, wearing a ball gown, it seemed unlikely. If I did manage to catch up with her, she deflected my questions. I decided if she wasn't going to tell me, I wasn't going to ask.

Then in the middle of January my mother phoned and said, 'I don't suppose there's any chance Bernie has jilted her sailor, is there?'

'No,' I said. Whereupon my mother's tone became semi-formal.

'Shame. Eric's not as concerned as I am. He doesn't exactly approve, but he points out she isn't our family, and if her parents are fine with it, we have no right to interfere.' She paused for a moment. I had no idea she was merely gathering breath. Then she was off. I had no chance of interrupting as she offloaded information and opinions so fast I could barely keep pace.

'So, Hope, dear, if this girl is a good friend, interfere as much as you bloody well can. Eric's normally a good judge of character, but I think he's got this one wrong. I did a fair bit of digging and my instinct tells me there is something off about this man. It's all between the lines, but I swear it's there. Sadly, my instinct is currently not enough for Fitzroy to put a spanner in the works. He thinks it a great coup for Anglo-American relations. He's thinking about the bigger picture, not Bernie, so unless I come up with evidence as to why this is an awful thing for Bernie he won't, and I quote, "touch it with a seven-foot-long ruddy barge pole", which I thought was unnecessarily vulgar, but there, he's always saying he's not a gentleman. I'm afraid he did add that even if I had evidence, he wasn't sure he could move on it without incurring official wrath. Which he won't do as he's pushing several projects that are already getting him stern looks from the higher-ups. He said to say to you that he's sorry, but he has to spend his credit where it will do the most good, and not squander it on silly young women. He had the grace to say he was referring to Bernie, not you. He does so hate it when I slap him. Anyway, he applauded your loyalty to your friend, but said this wasn't his skirmish. From which I take it if you manage to sabotage the relationship, he will be very annoyed, but not incandescent. I think he's rather surprised that a middle-aged man of apparently serious disposition should be interested in Bernie and she in him. Obviously, it's a sex thing on this sailor's side, and while Fitzroy has always had an eye for beauty, he wouldn't understand how any man could contemplate a long-term relationship without being mentally in tune with his mate. As for Bernie, I suspect she is still looking for a father figure. Did you know she tried to throw herself at Eric? Frightened the life out of the poor man. Give him five men in a bar to tackle with no more than a teaspoon and he's happy, but one pretty, well-connected, predatory young woman and he's hiding behind my skirts. Silly thing.'

The last two words were said with amused affection, but also a strong inflection of the general inferiority of the male gender. My mother had been a suffragette, and while she had never told me the details, it was clear she had never left behind her belief that all men were generally a bit helpless and confused and needed strong women to help them. (I'm aware this was not the outlook of suffragettes in general, who were fighting for parity, but my mother was never one to follow the general line.)

'Hope? Are you still there?'

'Yes, Mother, I was thinking.'

'Just the kind of thing your father would say, only he'd have been asleep. Can I leave Project Bounce Bernie's Beau with you then? Not sure I have much pull with Amaranth. We write to each other and pretend we're friends, but secretly we dislike each other intensely. Well, I loathe her. Remember, call any time. Always nice to hear your voice.'

She hung up before I could reply.

This was quite the longest telephone interaction, I couldn't term it conversation, I could ever remember having had with my mother. Christmas had been very pleasant; could it be that we were moving forward in our relationship? I could never put my finger on what kept us always on edge with one another. I could ascribe it to keeping a lifetime of secrets, except my godfather and I had always got along, and he'd been in the business longer than she.

I decided to stay up and wait for Bernie. I assembled toasted cheese sandwiches, ready to heat when she got in. Even if I was fast asleep, I often heard Bernie come in, not by the sound of the door closing – she'd had plenty of practice closing doors silently for nefarious reasons – but rather the frantic ransacking of the kitchen when she got in. Toasted cheese was her weakness. Apparently, there's nothing like mature cheddar available in America, and Bernie was trying to make up for the eight or so years she'd spent in her home country away from decent cheese.

I'd fallen asleep on the settee when I suddenly woke with a start. The latch clicked, and in the darkness, I saw the outline of a female figure in a full skirt closing the door. I switched on the lamp next to me. Bernie leapt like a cat with its tail on fire and uttered pretty much the same noise as the cat would have made.

'Oh, my goodness, Hope! You scared the life out of me.' I noticed her American accent had become slightly more pronounced, and for some reason, Southern. I doubted she'd ever been to the southern states, her family certainly didn't come from there. No, her accent was more the kind of quaint thing a British man might imagine after watching a Hollywood movie. My morale level dropped a bit. Whatever was going on, Bernie was enjoying her role and playing it to the hilt.

'I've got toasted cheese under the grill, ready to go, if you want some?' Once I had her sitting down and eating she wouldn't be able to get away.

I got up and moved towards the kitchen. I waited to see if she would take the bait. I needn't have worried. No sooner were the words out of my mouth than I heard the swish of her coat dropping to the ground and quick tap-tap-tapping of her heels as she hurried after me. 'Oooh, Hope, you hero. I'm famished. How did you know?'

I turned on the grill. 'No idea. The fact I am woken most nights by you opening and closing every cupboard door while you rifle though the kitchen, never gave me a clue.'

Bernie threw herself down onto a stool and lit a cigarette. I stifled a sniff. I didn't smoke myself and didn't like my food tasting of it. But tonight was not the night for that talk. I checked the cheese under the grill, not yet melted, and then took in my friend.

Despite her make-up, and there was a lot of it, she had shadows under her eyes. Her lipstick was blood red, her eye shadow silver blending into gold. She looked beautiful in a certain way, but many years older than her real age. She saw me looking and set down her tiny handbag to take out a compact and dab with a powder puff at her nose. 'I know it's a lot, but the dinners I'm going to are always so dark. Cedric likes me to leave an impression. He says what someone thinks of you is often decided within the first minute of meeting, so it's very important to be visible.' She was wearing a pillar box red dress with a low-cut sweetheart neckline.

'You're certainly that,' I said. Then I added quickly, 'You do look lovely. Not a lot like the Bernie of our student days, but . . .'

'Heavens, she'd never have the time to put on this much make-up. Let alone take it off. I remember tumbling into bed and then practically tumbling out the other side again to get to a tutorial. In those days I could survive on four hours sleep or less!' She laughed as if this had been ten years ago, when it wasn't even three. Clearly, Cedric also liked her to play up to his age, rather than her own. At least that meant he might have the grace to be embarrassed about marrying a girl young enough to be his daughter. That was all very well after the last war, when there were hardly any young men around, but nowadays there were more than enough – for now.

'Hope!'

A faint wisp of smoke came from the grill. I pulled the toasted cheese out just in time.

'There you go, my lady. Welsh Rarebit for two!'

'Rabbit?'

'It's what it's called.'

'You Brits are so strange,' she said and pulled a piece of toast apart with her fingers. 'It's hot.'

'Surprising!'

'Oh, stop trying to sound like your godfather,' said Bernie. 'He can be such an ass at times.'

'What?' Something in my tone sobered her.

'That's unkind of me. He was only trying to be nice; I suppose. He asked me tonight if I was sure I wanted to marry Cedric. I mean, what a thing to say. He had his chance and he blew it!'

'I thought it was rather the other way around. Not that you had a chance, but rather you were keen, and he was not.'

Bernie's cheeks flushed slightly, but she waved my words away with a careless gesture. 'Cedric says I must be careful. He says that men are always after girls like me. Especially middle-aged ones. He says it doesn't matter what they say. I should never believe them. I'm so young and beautiful I can't help but bring out the hunter in the male sex.' She ate a bite of her rarebit. I hadn't touched mine. 'Wasn't that a nice thing to say? Don't you want your food? I could eat a horse. Apparently in France they do, Cedric says.'

'I don't think it was a kind or pleasant thing to say at all,' I said.

Bernie smiled. 'Well, you've nothing to worry about.'

I gasped slightly at this.

'No,' said Bernie quickly, and her Southern drawl disappeared for a moment, 'not like that, Hope. You're very pretty, but you're not one to dress up and paint your face, are you?'

'I think my commanding officer might object.' Although the truth was, I was expected to look neat and tidy. Some of the girls took that to mean they could wear simple make-up.

'I understand,' said Bernie. 'We're both doing our bit for the war effort in our own way. Cedric says these dinners, where *things* get discussed, always go much better when I'm there. He says it's essential for a number of reasons, not least that he and I represent an Anglo-American pact. He's hopeful that the more we're in the newspapers the more likely the American Government are to come in to support us. Apparently, Britain is shockingly under-resourced. If the Germans come knocking, the Brits are liable to go down like a set of ninepins.'

'I can't believe your Cedric said that,' I said, standing. 'It's forbidden to talk in a demoralising manner.'

'Well,' said Bernie, 'I mean . . . well, you know, how men talk to their women.'

'I know that kind of talk is treasonous, and from an officer!'

'Oh, don't be such a little cat, Hope. You'll catch your man one day.'

I put my plate down with a slam. 'I don't like this side of you, Bernie. Not at all. Whoever, whatever, your Cedric is, I don't like the sound of him either or how he wants you to behave. Just remember the last time you got involved with a wonderful man, not only was he married, but also in the pay of the Germans. It doesn't sound if this chap is much better.'

I stormed out of the kitchen. Behind me I heard, 'He's a widower,' but it was said in a dull sort of way rather than a defiant one.

We had a phoney war. Bernie had a phoney fiancé. And to all intents I seemed to have a phoney job. If things got any more jolly I'd have to seriously think about bearding my godfather in whatever lair he was currently lurking and demanding I be given something decent to do.

Chapter Fourteen

With the Soviet army having been driven out of Finland I thought I might see Fitzroy again. I didn't know of any official British involvement, but that was my best guess as to where he might have been going. However, after the Finns' success, the Soviet air force retaliated with massive air attacks. From what I heard, and I heard a surprising amount in our building, it had almost been an if-we-can't-have-it-then-no one-will kind of raid. It had certainly been a raid that targeted civilians as much as military personnel and installations. The whispers I managed to pick up made me feel sick. It's one thing for two armies to blast the hell out of each other, but to target civilians, women and children, I thought, changed the state of warfare considerably from what had happened in the Great War. This was a war that might be fought in a different manner, and not for the better.

My problem was that no one ever told me what was going on. In between typing for the idiots of the think tank, I could be suddenly returned to the typing pool and asked to type up documents from anywhere. My security clearance meant that I often saw the discussions that were going on between senior officers. I rarely saw the original reports. Very occasionally I overheard girls whisper about something their boy had told them – a lower rank who had happened to be on the spot of something odd.

Nobody bothered much what was said in my hearing. I was unsure if this was because I had the highest security level of the girls or if I had become invisible. Officers, almost always army officers, did venture into the typing pool, and some of the girls would flirt discreetly, or I'd see them stretch in their seats, opening out their arms, or moving their heads from side to side in a manner that could be arch, but could possibly be the result of leaning over their desks. The officers' eyes would flicker over the girls, even when they were speaking to our supervisor on urgent matters. Sometimes they lingered on one girl or another, but never me.

I kept my head down and did my job. This was enough to ensure I was left alone. What the people surrounding me never noticed was that I watched them. The body language of our supervisor, a crisply dressed blonde who wore the merest smattering of pink lipstick, and that of a certain Captain, who visited slightly more than necessary, convinced me that if they weren't already having an affair, they would be before the month was out. Betty, who sat next to me but one, was juggling two boyfriends, but thought no one else knew. Little Amy, who sat at the back, I was almost certain was in the early weeks of pregnancy. I had almost made up my mind to speak to her, but one morning she came in very cheerful, and I heard her say to her neighbour that 'Aunt Flo decided to visit after all.'

That little room with its constant pattering of typewriter keys on the roller, the 'bing' at the end of every line, the click of the lever that moved the page up a line, the low voices of women interposed with that of an occasional male visitor, the smell of ink, flattened by the sweetness of face powder and perfume, contained a world of human drama. Without even trying I had made myself into an observer that no one bothered unless they wanted work done. I might have been a piece of the furniture for all the general notice that was taken of me. Although a table would have been dusted from time to time.

Was this what Fitzroy had made me? Or was this who I always had been? I could read a letter and type it while my mind went entirely elsewhere. Of all of them I believe I was the only one who noticed the quiet despair that had begun to seep into the atmosphere like a new and unpleasant odour. It was this that made married men and women edge closer to adultery. It was this that caused some girls to run around with more than the usual fair share of men. They took risks in love, physical and emotional. Because the new odour was fear. Those outside might talk of the phoney war, but in little bits and pieces even the most dull-witted girl in the pool could see that Europe was in trouble, and if Europe was in trouble we would be next. At tea break there might be muttered comments that 'Hitler would never try his hand against England', but the certainty in those voices was wavering. Finland holding out was a great morale boost. Then, on the twenty-first of January, a German U-boat sank the British destroyer HMS *Exmouth* and all 135 souls on board were lost. It was the first great loss of life that registered with the British public. No one in my building doubted that Germany would now invade Denmark and Norway. And from what we saw in our typing pool Britain had no intention of intervening. It was like Poland all over again. We were leaving our allies to their fate.

I was depressed and ripe for a friend when Cole showed up at the typing pool. I heard his voice before I saw him and looked up. He was talking to the supervisor, but his eyes scanned the room. Unlike the other officers they didn't pause over the pretty girls, instead his gaze locked with mine. He nodded slightly and I gave a slight smile. Then I put my head down and went back to my work. I was about to turn the page, when a memo was placed over the paper. I looked up startled, but only to see Cole walking away.

I read the memo. *Lunch tomorrow? Noon. I'll clear it with your supervisor. Meet me in the café around the corner. C.* I picked up the note and slipped it into my pocket. I would have to destroy it before the end of the day. We were searched when we left to ensure we didn't take any documentation away with us. I assumed it had to be something to do with Fitzroy. I only hoped it wasn't bad news.

That evening I found Bernie at home at the flat. 'Cedric had

106

somewhere to go,' she said, when she saw my surprised face. 'After all, I can't live in his pocket, can I?'

I shook my head. We'd barely spoken since our last spat. 'Have you decided on a wedding date?'

Bernie kicked off her shoe in annoyance. It sailed across the room, barely missing the lit fire. I refrained from saying anything. She sighed, as only a girl who used to have servants and half a dozen security guards at her beck and call can, pulled herself up out of the chair, and retrieved her shoe. 'Sorry,' she said. 'I'm just so darn annoyed. One minute Cedric is all, *I should never have let my desire overcome me; we will be married as soon as I can arrange it. You are the only woman for me.* Then the next he's all, *for heaven's sake, Bernadette. Don't you know there's a war on? I can't be messing around with wedding cakes!* As if I had asked him to mess around! I'd left the tiniest of boxes on his desk and asked him to say which of the two cakes he preferred. It's jolly hard to plan a wedding all on your own.'

'Has he asked you to do that?'

She pouted. 'Well, no. He's given me an assistant and Mummy has been helping from abroad. She says there isn't much she can do from the States, but she seems to be doing too damn much if you ask me. She's booked me in with a dress designer. Apparently, she's sending over Grandmother's dress which can be adapted for me. If Grandmother's dress was so darn great why didn't she wear it for her wedding, that's what I want to know. It'll be some lace monstrosity that makes me look like an upholstered bolster, I know it!'

'Would you like something to eat?' I said. 'We've a couple of big spuds that would go nicely with some cheese.' I held up a potato when I saw her frown. She nodded. I doubted she would eat much, but it was a peace offering. From somewhere she found a bottle of wine and filled two glasses.

'I don't want to seem ungrateful,' said Bernie. 'I think Cedric is lovely and our one night of passion—'

'Oh,' I said involuntarily.

'Yes, he's closed the bedroom door until we are properly hitched. I don't get it. I mean, I'm not going to turn back into a virgin for my wedding night if he waits long enough.'

'Oh,' I said.

'I was, as it happens,' said Bernie, divining my thought accurately. 'The other chap I'd got involved with. The one that turned out to have unfortunate connections.'

'Being married?'

'I meant being a traitorous spy, but yes, him. We'd done everything but – I couldn't get myself to go over that finishing line. The consequence of going to Sunday school.'

'You?'

'I was expelled eventually when they found out I was reading the Old Testament not out of an excess of piety but because I wanted to summon demons like Solomon.'

'Why?'

'I wanted them to build me a little playhouse in the garden. I thought if they could do a ruddy great temple it would be no more than a snap . . .'

She stopped because I was laughing so hard. When I stopped, she said, 'This is nice, Hope. I don't want to lose this. I know I've been a bit of a prig lately, but I am ever so confused about Cedric.'

'Don't you love him anymore?'

'Well, I still think he's terribly handsome and I'm dying to go to bed with him again. Can't wait.'

'I understand. Can we move on to the problem?'

'You are such a prude! We're modern girls. We are allowed to fancy our husbands. In fact, it should be a requirement during the ceremony! "Do you fancy this man?"'

'He's been taking you out a lot.'

'He does it charmingly. That's the thing with older men. There's no fumbling at the coat check or when the wine tray gets passed around. He does everything with style and treats me like a princess.'

'That doesn't sound bad.'

Bernie took a sip of her wine. Then she looked down into the depths of the glass. 'You know, Hope, I always thought it would be rather fun to be a princess. When I'm with Cedric everyone treats me like royalty. They can't do enough. But no one talks to me! Even when we're having dinner together, he's so quiet. If I ask what he's thinking he either says he can't tell me as it's hush-hush or that I wouldn't understand. Then he asks me something about the dress I'm wearing or when and where I'm going to get my hairdo sorted.' She sighed. 'Cedric says these kinds of tumbling curls are fine while I'm a girl, but now I'm getting married I need to look more like a wife.' She lifted her chin and looked at me. 'Of course, it's this phoney war. It's getting to everyone. I sometimes wish the fighting would take off tomorrow. Which is horrid of me, because of course I don't want anyone to die, but it's the waiting that's getting to me.'

'Does Cedric think there will be a full-scale war?'

Bernie nodded. 'He doesn't like Chamberlain one bit. Says he's not a wartime prime minister.'

'It does sound as if he is caught up with work. But he does know you signed the Official Secrets Act, doesn't he? I mean, you must have a security level?'

'I asked him. We met somewhere I'm not allowed to talk about, even with you. He was on site for a different reason, but he had to know I'd signed the thing.'

'What did he say?'

'He said as I had declined to work there, they had rescinded my security status. In other words, I still can't talk about it, but I'm also not allowed to know anything else ever. He said it's a bit of a no-no backing out of intelligence work, and I should stay away from intelligence types. I haven't seen your godfather in ages.'

'Neither have I. That's not personal. He's busy. Did you say you didn't want to do whatever it was?'

Bernie shook her head. 'No, but Cedric said that they wouldn't want a married woman.'

109

I looked at her in disbelief. The timer on the cooker chimed. 'Oh goody, food,' said Bernie.

We sat down to eat together. I served. By the time we had finished I would have given good money never to hear the name 'Cedric' again. The more I learnt the more I disliked the man. It seemed to me he was keeping Bernie hanging around waiting for a wedding date, but at the same time his control over her was tightening. I'd never known a man to behave like this. I didn't know what to say to her. If my godfather wouldn't interfere himself, I determined I'd still catch him and ask what this kind of behaviour meant. Cedric sounded like an oddball to me.

Chapter Fifteen

I was still struggling with trying to get my head around Cedric and Bernie's relationship, when the time came around for my luncheon with Cole. He had used the word 'lunch', both very modern, and rather middle-class. But then for all my mother having come from the upper echelons I was just a girl who had grown up in the Fens.

I was working in the typing pool. My supervisor came up to tell me I could go for my meeting. It took me a few moments to realise that this was my meeting with Cole. I went to the café he had named. The double windows of the place he had chosen were fogged with steam. As soon as I entered, I hit a wall of sound. The place was packed with ordinary men and women, a few in uniform, eating egg and chips. I spotted Cole quickly. He was sitting near the back with his back to the corner. I went over to join him. He stood and pulled out the chair opposite.

'Thank you,' I said. 'But would you mind if I sat to your left?' It wasn't a prime position, but it gave me a three-quarters view of the room, rather than sitting with my back to everyone. He smiled slightly and pulled out the other chair. 'Now, is this because you want to be nearer to me or because you don't trust me to watch your back?'

I smiled politely. 'It's never a good idea to ask anyone to watch your back, is it?' I said.

Cole nodded as he sat down. 'Always better to rely on oneself,' he agreed. Then he added, 'I didn't think you'd be comfortable with me asking you out to dinner. We barely known each other.'

'This is fine. I know I'm seated all the time, but I find I get very hungry typing.'

He passed me the menu. 'I'd recommend the egg and chips. The ham here tastes odd.'

'I'll go with that then.'

The waitress came over, and he ordered for both of us. He added a request for tea, bread and butter, and water for each of us too. I thanked him. He shook his head slightly and sat watching me silently for long enough that I felt an intense desire to fidget. I didn't. Eventually I raised one eyebrow in query.

'Am I staring? I am sorry. It's simply that you're so like her.'

'My mother? Did you know her?'

He nodded again. 'I did indeed. Fiery, passionate woman, extremely intelligent. You're the image of her at this age, but a very different person, I think. I keep expecting you to say something Alice-like, but you don't.'

'I'm sorry if I am a disappointment,' I said, trying to keep my tone polite.

'Not at all. Alice and I may have worked together on occasion, but we never had the kind of relationship she had with your godfather. I think at that time he was the only one in the service who could keep her in line.'

'I don't understand.' Images of Cedric controlling Bernie passed through my mind.

'I mean only that your mother was an impulsive woman. We'd always thought he was a maverick, but there were times when she could rival him. Got the job done, though. He could cope with that kind of operation. I'm much more of a planning sort. I like to tie everything down before I go into action. Or as much as one can,' he said smiling. 'I mean, in our kind of work back then things went sideways all the time. It was all so new, and the kind of support there is now simply didn't exist.'

'Was it exciting?' I asked.

'Exciting. Terrifying. Awful. Glorious. All of those things. Except you had to keep your head. You had to push those emotions down. I, at least, couldn't let emotion distract me from the mission. I think your mother thought I was a bit of a cold fish. But really it was simply my way of coping. We all have to find a way to cope when life throws us into situations, we'd never have dreamed of being in. Don't you agree, Hope?'

'I haven't been in many situations like that,' I said with a smile. 'I'm definitely not so much in the back room, as in the utility room behind that.'

'That's a shame,' said Cole. 'It strikes me as a waste of talent.'

Our food arrived at this point, so I ducked replying. I could hardly agree that Fitzroy had left me out in the cold. He must have sensed he had pushed a bit too hard. He asked me about growing up in the Fens. The questions were straightforward enough, but I spotted enough to know he was appraising my skills. It was a subtle and gentle questioning and I deflected much of it. Whenever I did so he would retreat and come at me from another angle. I knew I would have to think over the conversation later when I had time to myself. I had given away that I had a flatmate and also that I had spoken to my mother recently. I had not given the location of my flat nor the details of what my mother and I had discussed.

I didn't feel at any point that Cole was hostile to me. It was a friendly conversation. He even laughed when I slipped up. It all felt like the kind of test Fitzroy might have given me when I was younger, but this was in a different vein. More like light interrogation between friends. I took it as a game. Albeit a game with a real assessment behind it.

Cole ordered jelly and ice cream, which came in little white bowls rather like the dessert at a children's party. We ate it with tiny plastic teaspoons. I giggled to see the implement in Cole's big and slightly hairy hand. He frowned at me and held up the spoon.

'I could kill a man with this.'

I must have paled because the frown turned into a grin. 'Got you there, little Hope.' He ate some of his pudding. 'I thought you'd be used to your godfather talking like that.'

I shook my head. 'No, he's never spoken to me about that side of things. I'll tell you before you ask that I chose to learn jujitsu while up at Oxford, but that was more about being a single woman out on her own.'

'Have you ever had to use your skills?'

'The jujitsu? A few times, but nothing serious. I've never maimed anyone, let alone killed a person.'

'Do you think you could?'

'I think in war we all have to do things that we might otherwise never consider. I only hope I'm brave enough to do whatever is asked of me. Though right now that is very little.'

'Feeling under-utilised?'

I shook my head. 'I shouldn't have said that. It's the waiting. It's affecting me the same as anyone else.'

'Except you have some idea of what is coming. I imagine your mother told you some of her tales.'

'No,' I said.

He smiled again. A different kind of smile I couldn't read. 'May be just as well. Anyway, Hope, you will need to get back to your desk. This has been most enjoyable. We must do this again.'

'Indeed, thank you. I've enjoyed this.'

He rose and held out his hand. 'Shall we say a fortnight's time if the world is still here?'

I stood and put out my hand to shake his, but he caught it up and kissed the back of it. Then he went to pay the bill. Unsure of what to do, I slipped out of the door.

I wasn't more than a few yards from the café when the hairs on the back of my neck rose. My instinct was to quicken my pace, but I suppressed it. For all I knew this was Cole testing me again. He struck me as man who had a dark sense of humour. I crossed the street and paused to look in the window of a bookshop. My eyes flickered over the latest offerings, but at the same time I checked the reflection of the street behind me.

As I did so I saw a man step into the doorway across the street. This wouldn't be unusual, except that as he did so, he tugged at the edge of his coat collar, ensuring the gap between that and the brim of his hat was minimal. My heart beat a little faster. I wasn't in the least frightened. If anything, I was excited, and I knew that the chemicals that produced my excitement can impart judgement. They can make you run faster, jump higher, give you the courage to engage an opponent, but not think clearer. I took some deep breaths while I pretended to admire the display of detective stories on offer. Once the blood pounding in my ears had quietened, I moved off briskly. Halfway down the street there was a haberdashery shop, and what could be more natural that a young woman, returning to a dull job, being distracted by whatever they had in stock?

As I drew level with this shop, I didn't have to feign interest as I suddenly saw some dove grey suede gloves that made my fingers itch with excitement. They were very much my thing. Ladylike, but also flexible enough to do most unladylike things while being worn. Such as picking locks. Modern gloves were so tight it was impossible to do much while wearing them except hold one's hands in a ladylike position. I paused at the window. My follower, with a remarkable lack of imagination, bent to tie his shoe. With his head down, his high collar, and his own sturdy gloves, I could make out little. I could now see he was taller than Cole and had a less stocky build. He also looked a bit, well, rigid as he tied his shoelaces. Either he felt too exposed or being in that position was uncomfortable for him. I now had to make a decision. Did I try and accost him, or did I go back to work? I thought it likely it was only some test set up by Cole, but I reasoned if it wasn't the chap wasn't likely to give up easily. I'd likely see him again, and I did need to be back at work, no matter how tempting the idea of an interception was.

Accordingly, I went down the two steps to the shop doorway and entered. The transaction of purchasing the gloves was quickly dealt with, but by the time I re-emerged onto the street

115

there was no sign of my stalker and his errant shoelace. I continued on my way to work, checking using the reflections in the surface of cars rather than windows to see if he popped up from anywhere, or if someone else took his place. For a while I thought a young woman with a pram might be a contender. She appeared to be wandering, taking the baby for an airing. She stopped to look in shop windows, and then had spurts of brisk walking. She followed me from behind and even led for short lengths. If she was my new stalker, she was highly skilled. Going in front and behind a target is difficult for even an experienced operator to both make look natural and not lose their mark. A pram offered the opportunity for hiding all sorts of weapons instead of a child.

I was almost at my place of work now, so I speeded up and crossed the road at an angle, apparently accidentally appearing beside her. My heart was in my mouth as I looked into the pram. A rather rotund little face looked cheekily up at me. 'Lovely child,' I said to the mother and hurried on.

It was only as I entered the lobby, I realised how foolish I had been. If she had been sent for me then she could have easily shot me, concealing the gun from view with the hood of the pram. I would have collapsed on the pavement and she would have moved away. Cole and I had taken a long time over lunch, and there were few people on the street. I had done something truly stupid because I wanted excitement. I could have been shot. The thought made me sick to my stomach. It would have killed my father, and my mother . . . I tried to pull myself together. I nodded at the doorman and headed to the typing pool.

I knew I wasn't an important target for anyone, but I was the goddaughter of a master spy, who had recently told me himself he specialised in counterintelligence. A German sympathiser, it didn't even have to be a professional spy, might have been sent to kill me either as a warning or to throw Fitzroy off his game. For the first time it sunk in that I was a liability to both my mother and Fitzroy. For them I was the most vulnerable piece on the board, and appreciating that now, I couldn't blame them for attempting to shield me in a desk job. Neither were currently in a position to use me as an operative, and I did them the courtesy of believing if there was something, I could do that would really help the war effort they would let me play my part. The problem was that although highly trained in some ways I didn't have experience. My abilities had just made me overplay my hand.

I decided I would phone Fitzroy tonight. He might not be there, but I could leave a message with Griffin saying I had a new-found appreciation of my situation, and his, and telling him about my stalker. Hopefully, that would be enough for him to leave me to handle the situation myself but notify me if he had any reason to believe he or my mother had enemies currently active on British soil. I was fairly certain that would be the case. Why, they'd even said before that they'd had enemies within their own department. Thank goodness the only person from their past to track me down was Cole, a friend of my mother's.

I scurried into the typing pool and sat down. My in-tray was empty. The supervisor came over. 'It seems the boys upstairs want you back, Stapleford. Quick now, don't keep them waiting.' I picked up my notepad and pencil. 'Room 103. There's a machine waiting for you.'

I went fast, but without running. I had no love for the freckled Sergeant Bradshaw and his cronies. And when I got there I found it was only the three of them, Bradshaw and the two officers, Wiseman and Merryworth. In the time since I had last seen them Wiseman had attempted to grow a beard to hide his weak chin. It was a scrappy sort of thing, and, I was fairly sure, against regulations. Merryworth had a fresh crop of spots and Bradshaw had what looked like a nasty sore on the side of his mouth. There was no sign of either Captain Max or Cole to restrain them.

'So, Stapleford, you finally decided to join us,' said Wiseman as I came into the room. 'I trust we haven't inconvenienced you too much. Not torn up your schedule much, what?' The other two sniggered. I sat down at my desk and opened my notepad.

'Nothing to say, Stapleford? Stand when you are addressed by a superior officer.'

I stood. 'Yes, sir, sorry sir,' I said. 'I think you mean senior.'

The look he gave me could have burnt off paint.

'What did you say, Stapleford?'

'My apologies, sir. I've spent a lot of time in the typing pool. Correcting grammar has become automatic. I meant no offence, sir.'

I was pretty sure my voice was subservient enough, but obviously I hadn't adequately schooled my features.

'You think you're something, don't you, Stapleford?' Wiseman moved close enough that I could smell his breath. Garlic at luncheon had not been a good choice. 'Don't you?' he repeated, much louder.

I didn't know what he was trying to do. Was he hoping I might cry? I've never been able to cry to order. Was he simply a bully? Had something happened with their little trio that he felt he needed to assert his alpha status? I had no idea. Which made it difficult to respond. I gave it my best shot.

'I think I'm an army cadet, sir.'

'Not some jumped-up little girl, whose daddy is an army bigwig? How could someone like you get that level of security clearance without a leg up from a relative. Or maybe it's a sugar daddy?'

I hadn't the faintest idea why my father's preference for sugar in his tea would make the slightest difference. This idiot kept speaking in riddles.

'What can I do for you, sir?' I tried to be placating.

'Say, "I'm a rude, insubordinate junior cadet with no skills", and I'll let this go. This time.'

The problem with a bully is they never stop. If I thought it would have ended there, I suppose I might have swallowed my pride – no, probably not – but I knew it wouldn't.

'I'm your high-security clerical support member of staff, sir. Rank, Cadet. Service, Army.'

After that things made a turn for the worse.

★

In retrospect, this confrontation had been fated from the time Captain Max had taken me out of this group. He'd relegated me to a lesser status for his own reasons and left three young men close together in rank without a clear leader or any real guidance. I imagined being called part of a think tank had bolstered their egos. It's true I wasn't always present to take notes, but whenever I did I can't say I heard anything of significance. If he'd asked me, or if I had been able to address them as equals, I would have said the boot was rather on the other foot, and that these men had no right to be in a think tank, and that it was only their connections that were keeping them out of harm's way. If I'm being generous, I might have added that between them there might have been a sense of guilt that they weren't going to end up in a war zone any time soon.

'Right, Stapleford. If you think you're Army, what about fighting me? How do you think you'd do in the real Army?'

This was my cue to back down, but I was growing tired of all this.

'I have no issue with fighting you, sir – providing you are giving me clearance to do so. After all, you are ranking officer.'

Wiseman stood several steps back and took off his jacket.

'Hey, wait a minute. You can't, she's only a girl!' This came from Bradshaw.

I gave him a tight smile. 'It's fine, Sergeant,' I said, 'I'm used to looking after myself.'

He turned to Merryworth for support. 'Charles, you're not going to let this happen, are you? You're a gentleman!'

'Silence, Sergeant,' said Merryworth. 'Remember your place. Or you'll be next.'

'Don't worry,' said Wiseman. 'I won't hurt her. Give a few bruises and sense of humility.' Then he ran at me.

I assume he meant to either charge me into the chair behind me or pick me up like a doll. I sidestepped him at the last minute and gave him a tiny extra shove into the chair. I suppose the floor was slippery, because he went down like a sack of coal. As well as

119

the smack of him landing headfirst in the chair, there was an audible sound of snapping bone. I had forgotten that some aristocratic noses break easily.

He put his right hand out on the wreckage of the chair and pushed himself to his feet. A red river poured down his face. I waited, out of range, to see what he did next. 'You saw that she tripped me!' he spluttered through the blood.

'Actually, sir, I didn't,' I said calmly. 'But if this is a real fight, as any Army personnel might expect to find themselves in in times of war, I should say it would have been perfectly all right for me to have tripped you. There are no Queensberry rules in war.'

Merryworth got to his feet. 'Go clean yourself up, Wiseman. We need to get on with some real work. Playtime's over.'

Merryworth outranked Wiseman, barely, so my bloodied opponent could use this excuse to quite properly step down.

'Sir,' he said, and left.

I moved back into my seat and opened my notebook. Bradshaw had reddened with embarrassment. 'Do I need to say,' said Merryworth to me, 'that what just happened is not to be mentioned beyond the four of us?'

'No, sir. Consider it already forgotten,' I said.

Merryworth studied me for a long moment. 'You're an odd kind of girl, aren't you?'

'So I'm told, sir.'

Merryworth marched over to the paper pinned to the wall. 'Right, now, we have to think of a different way to get supplies moving. Bloody Jerries have got the main roads all tied up. Stapleford, listen for now. It'll be your job to summarise what we end up with on the paper. So, Bradshaw, what might we do?'

'Air-drop them? We can do that.'

Merryworth wrote this down. 'But our problem is that there is a wide variation of how a package can land. Plus, if we are talking about everyday supplies we would need a helluva lot of planes. The Jerries have some tidy aircraft. We'd end up losing half of it during an air battle.'

120

'Yeah,' said Bradshaw, 'you couldn't get more than a sandwich in most of our fighter planes anyway.'

I stifled a smile at the thought of fleets of fighters dropping sandwiches for the troops.

'Yes, yes, it's ridiculous, Stapleford,' said Merryworth, 'but we need to think more imaginatively. We don't keep any idea to ourselves. We never know when someone else might make something of it.'

That sounded almost sensible. It also sounded a lot like an invitation to take part. I opened my mouth.

The door crashed open. Captain Max stood there. At his right hand was Wiseman, a cloth clutched to his face. 'That's her, sir. That's the cadet that struck a senior officer.'

Chapter Sixteen

I was let out of the lock-up in time to get home for dinner. A rather apologetic MP unlocked my cell. 'I've been told to send you home, Stapleford. Can I trust you on your own recognisance not to run?'

'Am I to report as usual tomorrow morning, do you know, sir?'

'No, Stapleford. You're to stay at your flat until the hearing is arranged.'

I made my way home without looking behind me at all. I wanted my stalker to attempt an attack. I had kept calm, even when I was arrested by the MPs. Inside I was incandescent with rage. I knew if the three of them decided to team up against me I could be facing a court-martial. And as we were at war the consequences of that could be dire. I knew I would have to phone Fitzroy and ask for help.

Fortunately, no one was home. I was about to lock myself in my bedroom to get myself in the right state to call my godfather when the telephone rang. I answered it. Of course it was him.

'I hear you broke a Lieutenant?' he said in a friendly voice by way of opening.

'Second Lieutenant,' I corrected. 'How much trouble am I in?'

'With me, none,' said Fitzroy, still cheery. 'I have no objection to ranking officers getting broken. I've done it a few times myself. Why don't you tell me the whole story?'

I did. I told him exactly what had happened and how.

'Not entirely sure why they've got you working with that lot, anyway,' said my godfather thoughtfully. 'You didn't ask to be assigned to one of the think tanks, did you?'

I told him about my original assignment and Captain Max.

'Oh, yes, I know him. Terrible misogynist. They should have known better than to assign a woman to him.'

He was silent for a bit. I waited. 'I suppose you're concerned the three of them might spin a yarn against you?'

'Yes.'

'Well, I can certainly stop them from doing that,' said my godfather as easily as if he had declared his intention to go and buy a bottle of milk. 'Or I could pull you out of the whole thing. Which would you rather?'

'Well, he wasn't there at the time, but I think Cole will speak up for me.'

'Cole,' Fitzroy made the one word sound like a rock sinking into icy water. 'What's Cole got to do with any of this?'

'Max asked him to come in and consult. He's there from time to time. I . . .' I was about to tell him about luncheon, but he interrupted me.

'Now, listen here, Hope,' he said in a deadly serious voice. 'You stay away from Cole. Don't listen to him, and above all don't trust him. Promise me.'

'I don't . . .'

'Hope, you will obey me on this. Promise.'

My godfather had never spoken to me like this. 'Yes, sir,' I said automatically. I'd never called him 'sir' before either. It came out without thought. And I wasn't being sarcastic in the slightest.

'Right, leave things with me. It's better if we let the investigation run its course. I don't want any more bright lights leading to my door. I'll ensure that the terrible threesome tell the truth. If it still goes sideways then I'll get you out. Better to play this by ear. Good girl.'

He rang off.

I had barely sat down in an attempt to collect my thoughts, when the front door opened and Bernie came in, followed by the man in the fedora. My stalker.

I jumped to my feet and yelled, 'Bernie, get away from him.' I dropped into a fighting stance.

'Why?' said Bernie, rather languidly considering my panic. 'Will I catch something?'

The man took off his hat. ' 'Ere, that's no way to speak about a mate. Here I was thinking you'd be glad to see me!'

I rushed over and threw my arms round his neck. 'Oh, you idiot, Harvey!'

Harvey rocked back slightly but regained his balance. 'Yeah, well, nice to see you too. I take it you thought I was someone else?'

I released him and went to peer round the edge of the curtain. A few people strolled along the pavement and there was more than one person sitting reading a newspaper in a car. For all I could tell the place was crawling with Fitzroy's people, or worse, someone else's. I didn't bother asking Harvey if he thought he'd been spotted. It was too damn busy out there for anyone to tell. Even I'd have a field day following someone this evening.

'How did you know it was Harvey?'

Bernie was pulling off her gloves, slowly and deliberately. 'Harvey has a distinctive gait,' she said, and gave him a dazzling smile. 'A hero's gait.'

This was perfectly true. Only a few months ago he'd dived in front of Bernie to stop her being shot, and taken a bullet to the leg. It had left him with a permanent limp, but for services rendered to us both, Fitzroy had cleaned up his police record and given him a fresh start. Which, if my godfather was to be believed, he'd already squandered.

'So what have you been up to, Harvey?' said Bernie waving her now exposed fingers around, and wafting her gloves.

Harvey raised an eyebrow at me. 'Could I take off my coat and have a bit of a sit down? Only I've been on me pegs all day.'

'Of course,' I took his hat and coat from him, and hung them up. 'Perhaps you'd like something to eat. I was about to make supper. It won't be anything exotic, but it will be filling.'

124

Harvey's eyes visibly brightened. 'I'd love a bit of whatever you're having. If you're sure you can spare it.'

'Chances are I might be court-martialled tomorrow,' I said, 'so I am determined to dine well tonight.'

I headed for the kitchen. Out of the corner of my eye, I saw Bernie still waltzing casually around in her coat waggling her fingers. Harvey had yet to notice. 'Why don't you get Harvey a drink, Bernie?' I suggested.

The next thing I heard was a crash and a smashing sound. I rushed back through. 'Bleedin' hell, girl, you almost had my eye out with that sparkler.' Bernie stood horror-struck in front of him with the better part of a martini down the front of her fine woollen coat. Harvey was hunched back in the chair, a smashed glass at his feet. Bernie gave a little cry and ran from the room. Her bedroom door slammed.

I bent down to help Harvey pick up the pieces of the glass. 'She almost shoved the bloody thing in my eye,' he said. 'I mean it's a lovely ring and all, but I didn't need to see it that close. Is she engaged, then? Anyone we know?'

I sat back on my heels. It's not a ladylike look but is surprisingly comfortable. 'Yes, she is. I was never sure how you two felt about each other . . .'

'You left the room so we could sort it out ourselves?' said Harvey. 'Well, she's not that fond of me if she never bothered to find me after the shooting, is she? Not that you did either.'

'I knew you were down by the sea. I thought you might need some time to think. I knew Fitzroy had seen you.'

'So you thought that meant I was all right?'

'I thought it meant he'd given you a clean slate, so you could choose what you did next.'

'Yeah, I know he meant that as a kindness – well, not kindness. 'E's not the sort of bloke people generally think of as kind, but I got it was a payback for helping you two out. Not that I asked for anything.'

I took the smashed pieces I had back to the kitchen and put

125

them down on some old newspapers that the potatoes had been wrapped in. Harvey added his pieces, waving my hands away as he neatly wrapped it all up, ready for the bin. 'So what happened?'

'Well, I've got a family, siblings I mean, and even with a clean slate most of the people in the area where I live know I'm – or was – a bit of a sly geezer. Most of them would happily buy me a pint in the pub, but they wouldn't trust me enough to hire me. Couldn't find work, could I? Couldn't enlist either. I tried, said I'd be a driver, anything, but no, due to the dodgy leg I was out on my ear. Then an old mate of mine comes around saying how 'e knows of some stuff coming in at the docks. Stuff nobody's gonna miss – you know the game. Only it turns out whoever owned the stuff was a mite more possessive than my mate 'ad realised. Never even got to see what it was. Instead I was treated to a runnin' tour of the docks courtesy of some ruddy police dogs as big as bleedin' donkeys, I swear. All hair and teeth they were!' He pulled a hideous face, making me laugh.

'I'm sorry I didn't try and find you. I think I assumed Fitzroy would put us back in touch.'

'Why?'

'Oh, because we're friends,' I said lightly. Fitzroy and I had discussed my running Harvey as an asset but decided not to tell him what we were doing for a while. In short, my godfather felt he was not a fully trustworthy character. He didn't particularly mind that, but he wasn't prepared to have Harvey officially on board until his loyalty to me was certain.

'Besides, I'm in the Army. That happened very quickly, I can tell you. I'm not doing anything in the least bit interesting, but they're certainly working me hard. Typing,' I added when he gave me an enquiring look. 'Typing, typing, and more typing.'

'So how come you're going to get court-martialled? Too many spelling mistakes?'

'I broke an officer's nose. He was being a pill, but you know – an officer and all that.'

'That sounds serious, Hope. I mean, can't they shoot you for that sort of thing in times of war?'

I turned back to threading the baking potatoes on to skewers for dinner. 'It is a bit concerning.'

'Blimey,' said Harvey. 'Some things never change. You might get shot and you're a "bit concerned". It's all coming back to me now.'

I stole a look up from under my lashes. Not my style at all, but I wanted to see his reaction. It wasn't what I hoped. He looked stern.

'And what's up with Bernie? She marrying a gangster or something? That diamond would feed an East End family for a year.'

I thought of making some comment about it not being very nutritious but thought better of it. His face, if anything, had gone darker.

'He's a senior officer in the Navy. First name Cedric. Widower. I haven't met him.'

'Hang on, you're living 'ere, and you've not met 'im?'

'He sends a car for her.'

'What do we know about 'im?'

I sighed. 'Nothing good. Nothing precisely bad either, but he seems very controlling. It's all Cedric this and Cedric that and Cedric thinks . . .'

'That could just be a girl bein' in love,' said Harvey.

'I don't know. I have a bad feeling about him.'

'But you've not met 'im. I better go and tap on her door. Make cooing noises over the ring. Maybe she'll tell me about 'im. Call us when food is ready.' He walked off but turned back at the door of the kitchen. 'I reckon we were fond of each other; you know. In a playful sort o' way. I mean, me being around didn't stop her getting caught up with that traitor, did it?'

'She was trying to get some attention from her parents,' I said.

'You think?' said Harvey. 'Well, that went well, didn't it. They buggered off and left her. I reckon our Bernie wants someone to look after her. This guy, middle-aged, is he?'

I nodded.

'Father figure,' said Harvey. 'He might be the right one for her.

She needs steadying, that girl. I mean, 'er and me, that wouldn't ever 'ave happened. Different classes, ain't we? About as far apart as you can get. It's a bit o' fun for 'er to run around with me for a while, but she's never going to be serious about the likes o' me. Besides, she hates it when I scold 'er.'

He disappeared into the corridor and I heard a faint knock. 'Hey, Bernadette, me girl. Give me an eyeful of that shiner!'

Later we all sat around together in the lounge picking at our extremely hot baked potatoes. The dining table only had two chairs.

'Ow, ow, ow,' said Bernie as she burned her fingers.

'Be a lady. Use your irons,' said Harvey.

Bernie smiled at him. 'Can't do that on my lap. Not built for it!'

Harvey had the grace to blush slightly. For a young, slender woman Bernie was fruitfully endowed.

'I'm going to eat off the floor,' I declared and plonked my plate down on the small table. I knelt in front it of it. This proved to be most satisfactory, and although decrying my decision, it wasn't long until the others joined me.

Sitting on the floor changed the group. Conversation became a lot easier and when Bernie lobbed a bit of potato skin at Harvey when he mocked her for not eating the best bit, he caught and ate it. I laughed for what felt like the first time in days.

'I've got beer,' said Bernie, jumping up. 'I just remembered. This lovely old sailor gave it to me.'

'That's no way to speak of your beloved,' said Harvey.

Bernie poked her tongue out at him. 'It's from Belgium and it says it's made with cherries.'

Harvey and I exchanged startled looks. Bernie returned with a larger than usual beer bottle with pictures of cherries on the front. Harvey took it from her.

'Look at that, fruit,' he said. He read the back. 'Made by monks. Do you have to be religious to drink it, cos I'm not. No more than most.'

There was a loud knock at the door. Both Bernie and I jumped. She looked at me.

'I'll get my gun,' I said softly.

'Girls, let's not do anything rash,' said Harvey sotto voce, 'might be some old man selling newspapers.'

'There's a lock on the front door, and a porter,' I said. 'No one should be able to get up to the landing without the desk downstairs signalling us.'

'What say we just pretend to whoever it is, we're not in?' said Harvey. 'If they didn't check with the porter, how do they know otherwise?'

We all sat very still and quiet. Silence. Then, a few moments later, another heavy thumping on the door. This time it startled Bernie so much she squeaked in alarm.

'Well, that's given the game away,' said Harvey.

'I'll get my gun,' I said. 'You get the door. Go slowly. I'll be right behind you.'

I was less than halfway to my room when the banging started again, but this time a loud male voice said, 'This is the police. Open up.'

'Oh, Lord,' I said to Bernie. 'I'll keep them talking, you open up the balcony doors for Harvey.'

Bernie got my meaning at once, proving she could be bright on occasion. I glanced behind to see Harvey standing like a startled hare in the middle of the lounge, still clutching Bernie's fruity foreign beer.

I ushered him with my hands towards the balcony and made my way to the door. 'Coming,' I said. 'Just a moment,' I made heavy weather of pretending to unchain the door, and then opened it a crack. 'Can I see your police cards, please?' I said.

A small card was thrust at me through the door. 'Inspector Freeman, ma'am. Could you let us in please?'

'Don't you need a warrant for that?' I asked.

'Not if we believe there to be a criminal on the premises,

129

ma'am. Please stand aside or I will be forced to arrest you for obstruction of the law.'

'I think you're making a mistake here, Inspector. I live here with my flatmate. There's no one else living here.'

'Please open the door, miss, or we will be obliged to use force.'

I stood back and opened the door. It had to have been long enough by now. Then I heard a shout from downstairs. The Inspector walked in. 'Good evening, miss,' he said, and introduced his sergeant, a small, sandy haired man called Colins. 'It's much better this way, you'll see.' He looked down at the beer and potatoes on the floor. 'Having a bit of a celebration, were we? Three places, I see.'

Bernie came over. She wasn't smiling. 'They got him, Hope. Grabbed him as he climbed over the balcony.' I could have slapped her. I knew Harvey well enough that he would have told a tale about us knowing nothing, and that he was a burglar or some such thing. He would have kept us out of it. But Bernie with her mouth 'as wide as the Channel' had dropped us in it up to our necks.

'I think we'd better all sit down and have a nice chat,' said Inspector Freeman in a cheerful voice. I watched the pulse point on his neck and thought how I had never stabbed anyone there.

It didn't take long to establish the facts. Harvey made it very clear we hadn't known where he was until he'd appeared beside Bernie when she was letting herself into the building. He said he'd only asked us for something to eat, and what's more we'd been trying to talk him into handing himself over to the police. He went on to say he had no idea what was in the crates at the docks and swore roundly he wished he'd never heard anything about the job. He offered to go with them freely if they'd leave us out of it. I could see Bernie dashing away a tear by the time he'd finished. I managed to keep her from contradicting Harvey's statement by pinching her discreetly whenever she opened her mouth.

When Harvey had finished the Sergeant put away his notebook. 'Well here's how I see it,' said the Inspector. 'You're not in any position to negotiate seeing how me and my men have got you fair and square.' He signalled to the Sergeant to put handcuffs on Harvey.

'I say, is that necessary,' said Bernie. 'My father's the previous American ambassador to England. I don't know what he'll think if a man is led out of my apartment in irons.'

'I imagine he'll think he shouldn't have left his little girl alone in London,' said the Inspector. 'I don't know what kind of ménage à trois you've got going on here—'

'Inspector, before you go any further,' I said, 'you should know that my friend here is engaged to a senior Naval officer and in the interests of public morale I think it would be better if you dealt with us all as discreetly as you can.' Bernie flourished her ring. The Inspector's eyebrows shot into his hairline when he saw the size of the stone. Obviously, I thought, a most unobservant man. 'You have already made a great deal of noise about this arrest. More noise, I would have thought, than the potential robbery of what was it – coal? Brass tacks? Packets of washing soda?'

'Boots. Boots for the army,' said the inspector.

Harvey and I exchanged glances. I could tell he'd had no idea he was being set up to steal from Army supplies. That changed things quite a bit. 'I don't believe my friend had any idea of what he was being asked to steal.'

The inspector grunted with authority. Or at least I think that's what he meant. To me and Bernie it sounded rather as if he was getting ready to spit. We both flinched backwards.

'My sergeant will take your names and details, ladies, and it will be decided in due course if we will bring prosecutions against you. It may be you only get a warning.'

'Oh, thank goodness,' said Bernie, looking at Harvey.

'Oh no,' said the Inspector, 'your fancy man here is going down. There's no doubt about that. Lucky if he gets off with ten years.'

Bernie, most unhelpfully, burst into tears.

131

Chapter Seventeen

I'd been waiting at home to be told my fate for over a week. For the seventh time Bernie accosted me at breakfast with her new plans of how to free Harvey. I listened to her latest scheme while I dipped my rather stale soldiers in my solitary egg.

'So, you see, they must have found out we were friends with Harvey and have been waiting outside. And the only people who knew about that were your godfather and his friends. Harvey has been set up. You need to talk to Fitzroy.'

I sighed and took a slurp of tea. 'I'm not exactly his favourite person at the moment. The police checked that I was working where I said, and this infraction has been added to my record. Consorting with criminals or some such thing.'

'Fitzroy rang you up?' Said Bernie bouncing excitedly in her seat. 'What did he say about – well, everything?'

'He didn't call me. The typing pool supervisor did to inform me it was going on my record. Fitzroy doesn't have to ring me up to let me know how annoyed he is with me. I already know. And he knows that.'

Bernie frowned heavily. 'You're wrinkling your forehead,' I told her. In a flash her hands were smoothing down the skin.

'It's because I can't get the skin cream I always use,' she muttered. 'Hope . . . no, never mind. You wouldn't understand.'

'I agree it's not the first thing on my mind.'

'Oh, your trouble at work? I wouldn't worry about that. Your godfather can sweep that under the carpet easily enough. Cedric

132

says he's really rather influential in some circles. Or, if you wanted, I could ask Cedric to help you out. He's an R.A., you know?'

'A fellow of the Royal Academy?' I asked, being deliberately dense. Before Bernie could inform me again of Cedric's many magnificent parts, the letterbox flapped. I got up to look. Bernie sat up straighter in her seat but didn't rise. Letters were getting rarer, and I knew how much Bernie hoped that her family would write to her. In particular she wanted to hear from her father, but her mother's infrequent letters, full of New York society parties, barely mentioned her father, except to say he was 'frightfully busy' and 'away most of the time.' I was rather hoping to hear from my mother, but it was a forlorn hope that she would put anything in writing. She was cautious that way.

But what I found on the doormat was a postcard that said simply, '*Egg and chips? 1pm.*'

'What is it,'? called Bernie.

'An invitation to dine,' I said and slipped the postcard in my pocket. I refused to say anything else.

Being kept on furlough at home had been a bit of a revelation. I had assumed Bernie, being something of a night owl, would sleep in, but actually she was up for breakfast almost every day. Then she mooched around the flat until it was time to meet Cedric, or failing that she let one of her old admirers buy her luncheon. I had detected the pattern that every time she did so, Cedric took her out for both luncheon and dinner for the next few days. It confirmed my suspicion he was possessive and controlling. I had, by now, taken a strong dislike of the man, despite the fact I had yet to meet him.

Bernie smoked cigarettes and read magazines this morning while she waited for Cedric's car to arrive. I had already pointed out that this indolent lifestyle would deaden her brain and make her grow fat. She worried about the fat bit for a while but did nothing to assert her mind. Compared to her brief stint helping me track down a traitor last year, she had slipped back a long way into being what my godfather would undoubtedly have called 'a waste of space'. She had never told me what she doing on the course Fitzroy had sent her on, but I got the impression that few people were accepted and dropping out to be with her Navy chap had put a black mark against her name as far as the security services were concerned. From one or two comments she made I gathered that Cedric, although somewhat of a genius strategy-wise, was not well liked, and prone to fits of temper with his staff. 'Although he's always absolutely darling with me,' she had said. Misgivings over the whole affair rang like several fire bells in my head, but with her parents apparently condoning the match all I could do was try to gently chip away at her infatuation. However, because I still didn't have a boyfriend, she often interpreted this as jealousy, and told me not to worry. 'Your man will come along!'

My godfather had always stressed, and my mother echoed, that a woman should never define herself by a relationship with a man. Fitzroy remained keen for me to marry someone worthy. My mother, I suspected, would rather I took long-term lovers than committed myself to one individual. She'd once said that unless I found someone as she had found my father, a soul mate, then she saw no reason for a woman to tie herself down to the whims of a single man. However, most men still controlled their family fortunes. I already had independence in terms of an income from my trust fund and had no need to marry for survival, unlike many of my peers, who even Bernie admitted were akin to brood mares. As yet, I hadn't met anyone. I liked Harvey, but not in a romantic sense. Anyway, I was fairly sure that he found me fright-ening. I hoped my godfather kept his word and helped him out a little. And speaking of keeping one's word, what was I to do about Cole? The man had been nothing but kind to me. Kind to me when no one else seemed to care.

'You've gone all frowny now.' Bernie broke in on my thoughts. 'You look like a walnut,' she said with a smug smile. In looks, Bernie was always competitive. Even with me when she had no cause to be. Blondes always attract more attention than brunettes.

'Yes, I bet I have. More on my mind than what cocktail dress to wear tonight.'

'Touché! I'm going to talk to Cedric about Harvey. It's time for him to show me he loves me without resulting to trinkets.'

'You are turning down jewellery?' I said in mock astonishment.

'A girl likes to be listened to now and then.'

'Good luck. In Naval Intelligence, is he?'

Bernie nodded. 'I believe so. Though I'm not sure what that means. Do you have underwater spies?'

'Even if I knew,' I said deadpan, 'I couldn't tell you.' I got up. 'I'll wash these. You always leave it too long, and plates stay greasy after they're cleaned.'

'One is used to having people to do that.'

'Yeah, well, one doesn't have people anymore, does one?'

'I positively cannot wait until I marry Cedric,' said Bernie, all trace of her American accent vanishing.

I left early for the café. I wanted to think on the way. The day was bright and fresh, and if things had been different it would have been the perfect day to go for a long spring walk. Now the streets were dotted with people in uniform. Despite the dull muddy colour of khaki, they stood out to me, as men and women hurried along with brisk steps. Civilians walked casually. Mothers with prams, girls and boys walking the family dog, people with their arms full of shopping. Most of them had cheerful expressions on their faces. It's difficult to be sad on a sunny day, and none of them had seen the reports that had come across my desk.

I had eventually promised Fitzroy that I would not trust Cole. That was easy. I trusted my mother and my father completely. I trusted my godfather completely to pull me out of danger, but I did not trust him when it came to telling the truth. He frequently admitted to me he rarely told the whole truth and that lying was part of his occupation. He'd claimed he only told the truth to one

135

person, who I assumed was whichever unfortunate individual he happened to report to as a commanding officer.

I opened the café door to see Cole sitting in his usual seat. I smiled in greeting and went to sit beside him. He pulled out my chair. 'Seeing as you're not in uniform,' he said with a quick smile.

'Oh, there's a whole story behind that,' I said, sitting and taking off my gloves. He watched me do so.

'I sometimes forget, but you are a lady, aren't you?'

I frowned. 'I don't have a title, if that's what you mean.'

He shook his head. 'I mean you have been brought up very well. Although I would expect no less of Alice. She always had that aristocratic touch. I imagine people often tell you that you're the image of her?'

I nodded, suppressing a sigh.

'Well, you're not. Your whole manner. The way you hold yourself. It's quite different. Alice, at your age at least, brimmed with energy. You always expected her to leap up out of her seat and be doing things. Every man in the room would have been watching her. She had a loud – vibrancy, I suppose you could call it.'

'Doesn't sound useful in her line of work,' I said, trying not to feel the lesser woman.

Cole shrugged. 'She could turn it off. Your godfather taught her how to be quiet, and unnoticed. Rather like he taught you. Except with you, it comes naturally. You're an observer by nature. I imagine you'd make an excellent strategist, probably you'd shine in propaganda too. You can look around this room and tell me what the people here do for a living, what mood they're in, possibly even what they're thinking about. You clocked all that when you walked in. Your godfather trained you every well. I suspect he concentrated on observation and evasion. Those are the strengths I see in you. Your mother was more – er, *action*-based. She fought side by side with him on occasion. Quite a pair of tigers, the two of them.'

'He told me I shouldn't trust you,' I said.

136

The waitress came over and Cole ordered egg and chips, bread and butter, and tea with toasted tea cakes for afters, without consulting me. When she had gone, he leaned back in his chair, watching me. 'Did he indeed. And do you?'

'I'm not sure I fully trust anyone!'

He laughed at that. 'Good girl,' he said. 'That's the best way. Generally, people disappoint. So, when did he say this?'

'He phoned me after I got sent home for . . .'

'Ah, yes, the Lieutenant.'

'Second Lieutenant,' I corrected.

'That makes all the difference.'

'I take it you have heard the story?'

He nodded. 'I've already spoken to your direct superior – in your favour, in case you hadn't guessed. Those three young men need much more leadership and guidance. They should be out in the field doing something useful. Which of them do you think is the best?'

'The Sergeant, Bradshaw,' I replied automatically. 'He thinks.'

'Crushing,' said Cole, still smiling. 'I agree. I think Bradshaw is the only one of them with potential.'

The food arrived and I ate my second egg of the day. I reminded myself that as the war went on, such supplies might well become limited and I should be grateful, but really, I've never been that keen on eggs. Growing up in the country I'd seen where they came from. I knew there were reasons, but it seemed typical to me that eggs, which I would have been happy to forgo, hadn't been rationed.

'Lost in thought?' said Cole.

'I'm sorry. I have a lot on my mind – but, I am sure, less than you do.'

'I don't tend to let things get to me much. I'm sorry though if you feel torn about being here. I'd rather thought our lunches could become one of the few things I actually enjoyed. I don't often come across people who remind me of myself.' He took a sip of his tea. 'I'm the quiet but deadly type too.'

137

'I only gave him the smallest shove. It's not my fault he's an uncoordinated oaf!'

'I wasn't talking about that,' said Cole, 'I mean you're good at jujitsu. There's a chap doing some training going around, Major Fairbairn. You should try and get to one of his classes. It would be perfect for you. I'm not sure they're letting women in yet, but they should. It's all about form, not strength. Fairbairn is a small man himself.'

'I work in a clerical pool,' I said. 'I don't think I'll see much fighting there.'

'Oh, you won't be there for long. I see your commanding officer quite frequently. We go way back. I mentioned we meet. I'm sure between the two of us we'll come up with something more fitting for you.'

I tried not to let my confusion show. I had thought Fitzroy my commanding officer, but I must have a different one as part of my cover. I tucked into some bread and butter to mask my confusion. Would Cole interfering, obviously, he thought, for the best, affect how my cover was being run. It was all much more complicated than I had thought. Fitzroy had told me not to trust Cole, so if he didn't know I was under cover as a typist then I couldn't tell him. The problem was, I knew what my cover was, but I didn't know what I *really* was. Was I a spy? I wished my godfather had been more forthcoming.

Cole stuffed a number of chips into his mouth. He didn't eat with his mouth open, but he wasn't going to win any competitions for table manners. He must have registered my expression, as he said through a mouthful of potato, 'In my line of work you tend to eat when you can and eat fast. Bad habit.'

'I thought you must be hungry.'

He grinned, and for a moment I realised he must have been quite a handsome man in his youth. He wasn't exactly old. I pegged him for around the same age as Fitzroy, but a lot more weathered. His skin had the rough deep tan of a man who spent much of his life outside. Icy blue eyes, very short greying black hair, of more than average height, and, really, wiry rather than stocky. I hadn't seen him grin before, but when he did his eyes lit up and he conveyed a mysterious charm – well, more of a dark mysterious charm. There was a certain saturnine aspect to him. It wasn't without its appeal, and in other circumstances I might have enjoyed practising my elementary flirting skills. Although what I might be prepared to do in a public café and what I would be prepared to do if we were alone was quite different. I recognised him for a dangerous man and was happy his earlier mention of taking me to dinner seemed to have been forgotten. Whatever he was, he was a link to the mysterious past of not only Fitzroy, but my mother as well.

'I can't say I'm entirely sure I know what you are,' I said, doing my best not to turn it into a question.

'No, I don't suppose you do,' he said. 'Has your godfather explained what he does?'

'Not exactly.'

'He's moved through a number of departments in his time. I'd say he has one core skill and a great many others required at an above average level.'

'You speak as if you like him,' I said.

Cole gave a thin smile. 'I respect him. He's a loyal servant of the Crown. He trained me – we share the same core skill.'

'Which of you is better?' I grinned as I said this to try and show no offence was meant.

Cole tilted his head to one side and frowned. 'I've never been entirely sure. He has more experience, but I'm the younger of us. Age slows you down. I imagine one day I'll find out.'

'Why do you think he told me not to trust you?'

'Do you trust me?'

I polished off my eggs with the remainder of my chips. Today they had been greasier, rather nasty slippery mouthfuls. I didn't care if I never saw another fried egg ever again. 'To be a loyal

139

servant of the Crown, of course,' I said. 'But personally, unless we'd been ordered to work together, I think not. I think you are someone who always bears watching.'

He did laugh at that. 'I'll take that as a compliment,' he said. 'Although generally, Hope, it's not wise to trust anyone in our business. With the work we do more often than not we have to be suspicious, to keep secrets, and to have our own back-up plans. The only two agents I ever knew who appeared to be completely open with each other were Fitzroy and your mother. And to be honest, I'm not sure she knew half of what he was up to. In fact, I'm fairly sure she didn't. Your mother has always been hampered by her sense of morality.'

'I'll take that as a compliment to her,' I said with a very tight smile.

'In the normal way of things, it would be,' He paused as if he was going to say something more. 'I do enjoy our chats. As well as being quite lovely, you have an interesting mind. Besides, we're graduates from the same school, aren't we?'

'You mean having been trained by—'

'Exactly, but I'm afraid time is tight for me today. Will you forgive me if we don't stop for pudding today? I'll buy you double next time – that is, if you're still interested in doing this?'

I nodded. Unsure of what to say. He put money on the table, pulled out my chair for me, and took my arm as we walked to the door. His touch was light, gentle even, but I found I both wanted him to let go and also, perversely, to hold my arm tighter. But more than anything what I felt was unease.

When we exited. he said, 'I'll walk with you a bit, if you don't mind?'

'Of course not,' I said, hoping I sounded sincere.

'It's all very well watching our words and talking in a crowded café, but some things can only be said away from others. For example, you asked what I do.' We were outside the bookshop. He turned me to face the window and drew closer to me. He bent down and breathed in my ear. 'I'm an assassin, Hope. Crown-sanctioned, naturally. Now, what do you think qualifies someone to train an assassin?'

I licked my lips. My mouth had gone dry. 'Being one themselves.'

'Exactly,' whispered Cole in my ear. 'Fitzroy isn't what you think he is, my dear. Not at all.'

Chapter Eighteen

By the time I got home it was mid-afternoon. Cole had walked me away from the window and talked about innocuous topics, while I stumbled through my responses. He talked about the crime books in the window and gave his opinion on which ones were the most believable, which the most entertaining, and which came close to being both. He said he had particularly liked March-Phillipps' *Aces High* and hoped that he would continue to write after the war was over.

I had barely got my racing thoughts under control when he made his excuses and released my arm. I wandered back to the flat in something of a daze. I stopped at a small local path and tried to force my thoughts into logical order, but I kept going around in circles.

Fitzroy hadn't had the time to explain why I shouldn't trust Cole, but I couldn't help thinking that he would say that if he didn't want me to believe anything Cole told me about their shared history. If Fitzroy's work had always primarily been as an assassin, I felt certain he wouldn't want me to realise this. We both, my godfather and I, knew I idolised him. In fact, until he had snapped at me on the phone, I don't think he had ever shown anger towards me. He had always been calm, supportive, and kind. Only as I grew into a young woman did his warm bear hugs stop. With my mother and I, he was charming, witty, and compassionate. Everything I would have imagined an assassin not to be. How much of it all had been an act? Did it make my mother an assassin too? From Cole's comment about her morality, I thought not. I thought, I hoped, the missions they had undertaken together had not been of that nature. I had no doubt my mother was stoic enough to kill if the situation required it, but I also knew – or rather hoped – she would do all in her power to avoid doing so.

Cole had something dark about him. I could see him as an assassin, could imagine him setting aside his humanity to get the job done. If I was honest with myself, I had known from the start there was something different about him, and although I recognised it as a darker aspect of his personality it didn't repel me in the same way it might others.

I thought of Harvey's horror when a man had died under interrogation by the man whom my godfather had supposedly sent to me as a live-in garage mechanic. Only on that fateful night it had turned out he had been a spotter in the Great War and had on more than on occasion captured an enemy soldier and extracted information. I hadn't wanted our prisoner to die, but when he did, I didn't see him as a sad loss to humanity, but rather an obstacle to be dealt with. My mechanic transpired to have more than adequate body-dumping skills.

That night didn't bother me. Harvey had been shaken by the event but equally by my calm reaction to it. And where had that reaction come from? From whom had I learnt to be so cool and detached in the face of death? I cannot recall any actual lessons where Fitzroy talked to me but about such matters, but our topics of conversation often wandered as we strolled through the lands of White Orchards. Taking me from my beloved father's side when he needed rest, my godfather spent years training me – little though I realised it then.

He came to stay at White Orchards for weeks at a time. Often this concerned analysis, or so I now believe, he was working on with my mother. I know my father put up with him because both he and my mother were working on the Crown's business, but my father had never taken an oath of office, unlike my mother, and generally only knew a little of what they were planning.

Standing back and trying to see the situation as an outsider might have done, I could see how glaringly strange it was that my father allowed another man to spend so much time with his wife, even to travel with her, and to stay for weeks at a time under his roof. Could Fitzroy really have found no better partner than my mother to work with? She was a country girl and not the product of a military family. She had never gone beyond home education by her father. I had never been told what had tipped her into Fitzroy's orbit.

I wondered, of course I wondered, how far the relationship between Fitzroy and my mother had gone. I had never seen them display more than a civil, if strong, friendship. But recently I had seen that most expensive diamond necklace that my mother kept hidden. I had seen Fitzroy pick her up and whirl her round on his arrival late at night, when he had no reason to think anyone else awake. Or was that simply his Christmas joviality spilling over? Certainly, he had been in high spirits the whole of the following day.

And all his personal wealth he was leaving to my mother and me. My father was not to be included. But then my father was an invalid. Perhaps he was merely being practical about our respective longevity?

As the thoughts whirled and danced in my head, two fears came back again and again. Had my godfather been training me all these years to be an assassin, and only the war had interrupted what would have been final induction? And had Fitzroy, who admittedly I still adored, been lying to me my whole life?

It left me wondering who I could believe and who I could trust. I could understand a natural rivalry between him and Cole. I could think of reasons Fitzroy would turn me away from Cole, but the main one remained that Cole knew the truth about the past. I could not see any motivation on Cole's part to lie to me. If anything, I suspected he wanted to support a fellow student of Fitzroy's, and I got the impression he had not been indifferent to my mother.

The revelatory conclusion I kept circling back towards was that

Cole, above all the people I had trusted my whole life, was the one who truly understood my situation and was trying to help me.

I could not have been said to be in the clearest of minds when I got back to the flat. I hung up my coat and made my way to the kitchen without noticing my environment. I ground coffee beans and filled the little metal jug with the grounds and water. My mother had brought the device back from a trip to Italy and it made the most excellent coffee. I hadn't even bothered to check if we had any milk. I hoped the shock of black coffee would do me good.

I sat down on a stool and listened to the water starting to bubble. Then for some unknown reason I felt an overwhelming compulsion to go and wash my face and hands. When I came back I found Bernie sitting in the kitchen. She wore the dress she had put on for luncheon, but she had removed all her make-up. 'Gosh, you look so much younger without all the stuff on your face,' I said. I patted her arm. 'Just as pretty, of course, but in quite another way.'

I had the strangest feeling that I was standing outside my body and watching myself talk. I heard myself ask her about her luncheon, and moan about having eaten eggs again. I teased her about probably having had lobster and oysters. She told me she had mostly eaten salad, which I responded was a great waste of a luncheon at the Navy's expense. I asked if she had been taken on to any of the ships yet.

Bernie shook her head. 'Cedric says that everyone has more than enough to do without running around after me. Apparently, they would on a boat. He says sailors always take visiting wives very seriously and treat them like princesses. He said I'd enjoy that.'

'Well, I suppose it's the next best thing to being royal,' I heard myself say.

'Yes, I don't think I ever had a shot there. Two princesses looking for husbands isn't going to leave many decent British nobles or even friendly European ones free.'

I frowned. 'They will only want one each,' I said.

'Of course,' said Bernie. 'How silly of me. That's what I meant. They'll take the cream of the crop. I will be very happy with Cedric.' She said the last sentence rather forcibly, as if waiting for me to challenge her.

I poured the thick black coffee into mugs. I left plenty of room for Bernie to add milk and sugar. Which was just as well, for the face she pulled from a single sip of the pure coffee could have turned a man to stone. 'You're not drinking it like that, are you?'

I shrugged. 'I rather like the bitter taste. I'm feeling a bit out of it this afternoon.'

'Must be catching,' said Bernie. 'I was almost asleep when you came in. In fact, I can't think why I'm drinking coffee.' She set it down and got up. 'I'm out again tonight, so I need my rest.'

'Of course. Cedric's running you ragged,' I hesitated for a moment, 'Bernie, I don't think you should ask him about Harvey. It doesn't seem right to ask an officer to help out a criminal – and Harvey has chosen to be one again. I mean it's different with Fitzroy. He's a bit of a maverick, but your fiancé is an officer and gentleman. Do you see what I mean?'

'I do actually,' said Bernie. 'Cedric said as much when I asked him.'

'Oh no,' I said, suddenly coming aback to myself. 'Did you row about it? He's not broken off the engagement, has he?'

'Oh, no,' said Bernie. 'That's not the kind of thing a gentleman would ever do. Jilting is only ever done by the lady. And, of course, your reputation is in tatters afterwards. No decent woman would ever consider it.'

'Well, that's all right then,' I said with a smile. 'I'm glad you still have your Cedric. I hope you'll be very happy together.'

'Thank you,' said Bernie. As she reached to put the stool back under the little kitchen table I saw a black and blue ring blossoming around her wrist.

'Ouch,' I said. 'That looks nasty.'

Bernie tugged her sleeve back down over her wrist. 'Oh, I'm

such a silly billy. I slipped on the gangplank. Cedric caught me in time before I showed my knickers to the Navy!' She gave me a broad smile. 'Now that might have been a reason to jilt me!'

'I thought you said you didn't eat aboard ship?'

Bernie looked at me blankly for a moment. 'Oh, no, we didn't. But I was so insistent about wanting to see one, Cedric took me across for a little peek. A sort of surprise inspection. A treat for me and something to keep his jolly old tars on their toes.'

'You certainly seem to be picking up the lingo,' I said.

Bernie shrugged. 'I imagine I will have to learn a lot of things as a Navy wife. I mean, did you know they don't go with them on the ships?'

'I did,' I said. 'Great Britain doesn't put women on the front line.'

'But they keep a cat,' said Bernie. 'I saw ever such a pretty little thing on the ship.' She stopped. 'Anyway, time for me to rest.' She walked towards the door but paused on the threshold and turned back to face me. 'You do know you're my best friend in the whole world, don't you, Hope?'

'I do,' I said laughing. 'Who else would put up with you?' I gave her a quick hug. 'You're mine too,' I said, although I wasn't entirely sure this was true.

Bernie went off to bed, and though I doubted I could tell him of my troubles, knowing I had a friend made my world seem a lot brighter. I decided I couldn't let myself be defined by the past. I had to make my own way, and not care about whatever my elders had got up to in their time. If it was important then I had to assume someone would tell me.

Chapter Nineteen

Of course, it's easy enough to make those kinds of resolution in the moment. Keeping them is far harder. I was finally called back into the office and exposed to what I can only term as a kind of internal trial.

A room had been set aside in the office building. It had wooden panels, large, rather dirty windows, and a thick red carpet. We sat on opposite sides of an enormous oval table which proved so highly polished that the papers laid on it constantly slithered away from their owners and picking up a sheet was an experiment in dexterity.

Considering we were at war, it all seemed rather overblown to me. I felt everyone involved, including myself, could have been more usefully occupied elsewhere. An old Colonel had been summoned up, probably from the corner of his club where he'd been dozing, to preside over matters. He sat at the centre of the top side of the table. His clerical assistant next to him. I sat at the left side, and the officer who was administering the trial and saying things like 'It is alleged' sat at the right side along with the three young officers. Captain Max was with them. Behind the table were two rows of chairs for, I presumed, witnesses or observers to use. There didn't appear to be anyone there on my behalf.

The Colonel, it was soon clear, didn't hear too well. He welcomed us all to the proceedings rather like an after-dinner speaker. He put his hands on the arms of his chair, obviously intending to rise, but then thought better of it and sat back in his seat. He said, 'Now, this is not like a normal court of law. Nor is it a court-martial. It may become so, depending on the outcome today. What we are here to do is determine what exactly happened, and if Cadet Stapleford has a charge to answer.' He paused to slurp at a glass of water. His moustache dripped when he put the glass down. I tried not to stare.

'I see my job here today,' he continued enthusiastically and with clear enjoyment of his own voice, 'as someone putting together an overview of what actually happened. Collating the whole story. Not unlike the director of a moving picture takes the parts of a script and the actions of the players and turns it into an understandable narrative. Now from what I have read, this young lady is in trouble due to you fine young lads, hmm?' he said, looking at Wiseman, Bradshaw, and Merryworth. 'All of you? Seems a bit of a stretch to me.'

'That isn't what happened, sir,' said Max. 'With respect, Cadet Stapleford took advantage of the goodwill of my young officer in what was clearly meant to be a harmless and playful situation!'

'You mean she's going to have a baby?' said the Colonel.

Everyone at the table said, 'No!' with my voice being one of the loudest. The clerical assistant set down her notebook, did her best to sort through the slithering papers in front of the Colonel, and passed him a manila file. He opened it. 'Oh, why didn't you say it was this one? Girl's obviously not right in the head. Struck a superior officer. Never should have let women into this building. Didn't have 'em in my day. Not unless you counted—'

'If I might explain, sir?' said Max.

'No, thank you,' said the Colonel. 'You, the boy with the funny-shaped nose. Tell me what happened.'

And then, quite remarkably, Wiseman told the whole story. He didn't say anything nice about me, but he didn't lie. Bradshaw and Merryworth confirmed all the details. Max broke in a few times, blustering about my 'ungentlemanly conduct,' until the Colonel finally said, 'But the point, my dear Captain, is that she is *not* a gentleman, and as she is not a gentleman you cannot expect her to abide by the rules of gentlemanly conduct. Would you care to explain your actions, Cadet Stapleford?'

'May I say, sir, that it was never my intention to inflict any injury upon the Second Lieutenant. I erroneously assumed that when I moved aside and gave him a slight forward incentive, he would have rolled out of the way of the furniture.'

'I'm an officer in the King's Army, not a ruddy acrobat!' snapped the man in question.

'I now see this was an ill-considered plan.'

'Bit of a stroke of luck that you got out of the way at all, I'd say,' said the Colonel. I was about to correct him, when out of the corner of my eye I caught movement. Cole moved along the row of chairs until he was fully in my eyeline. He shook his head slightly.

I took a deep breath. 'The whole situation I found somewhat unexpected and confusing,' I said.

'Still, I suppose you're a game girl for rising to these lads' mischief.' The Colonel let out a long 'hmmmmm'.

Then he said, 'Thing is, we can't have this kind of mischief in the regular army. It was different back in India in the old days. I mean, most nights Johnny Native was tucked up in his bolthole all nice and tidy for the night, and we officers could let our hair down. But this was during the course of a normal day, wasn't it? A normal day when one might reasonably expect members of His Majesty's Army to be comporting themselves with dignity and decorum. Hmmmmmm.'

He shuffled some papers in front of him. Then looked up. 'No need to drag this out. Send the girl back to the typing pool for now. The Sergeant seems to have done his best as an NCO to prevent unpleasantness. I suggest if he's useful in the think tanks you reassign him. You other two, however, are officers. Can't let that rest. I want both of them out on some kind of active duty. Good physical exercise and a lesson in the necessity of control and discipline in the Army. I feel confident Captain Max will find something suitable. I leave it in his hands. Although I shall require a full report on their relocation by the end of the week.' He stood. 'That is all, ladies and gentlemen. You are dismissed.'

I didn't hesitate. I got up from the table and made my way towards the door. Behind me I heard Max's voice raised in defence of his men. A loud crack echoed across the room. I dropped and turned in a half crouch, only to see the Colonel's cane lying across the desk. He had clearly felt it necessary to reinforce his point. His face was reddened, and he was talking in low, angry tones to all four men. I rose, hoping no one had noticed my reaction.

Cole came up beside me. 'Though it sounded like a gunshot myself,' he said. 'You need to learn to tell direction. Although I admit the acoustics are a bit muddy in this room. How do you feel after that?'

'Glad it's over,' I said.

'You were worried?' He raised a thin dark eyebrow.

I nodded.

He opened the door for me. 'You needn't have been, Hope. The Department had your back. You're one of us.' He placed a hand briefly on my shoulder. When I exited to the stairs, I turned to find he had disappeared elsewhere. I returned to the typing pool, where they didn't seem in the least surprised to see me. A number of papers lay in my in-tray. I sat down and started to work. After half an hour I found my hands had stopped shaking.

I continued to hope for reassignment somewhere more interesting, but the days came and went, and I found myself going through reams of paper, typing what seemed increasingly less important letters. The situation in Europe became worse and worse. Bernie, whom I might have discussed all this with, effectively disappeared. She still nominally resided at the flat, but I rarely saw her. I tried staying up late into the night to intercept her, but on the rare occasions I did see her, sometimes as late as three a.m., she pleaded tiredness and retired at once to bed.

'But you're getting so thin,' I said to her one three a.m.

Bernie shrugged. 'Brides are supposed to be thin.'

'You've got dark circles under your eyes, and you look, to be blunt, haggard!'

I expected this comment to evoke a torrent of ire. Instead, she merely shrugged. 'Cedric says with what is going on in the world, our small woes are of little concern.' She smiled briefly, and for once it touched her eyes. 'He talks to me about what is going on. He says that's the one good thing that came out of the – that venture Fitzroy enrolled me on. There's a lot of things he can speak about – it does him good to talk. Not everyone is seeing the situation like he is. It's his people who have to see our supplies get in by sea. He's the one who has to worry about the U-boats. He described them to me. They sound terrible.' Her expression changed to one of concern. 'All those men down in the darkness, practically at the sea bottom, the weight of the water on top of them, stacked with explosives. Living for weeks, months, in this tin tube waiting for the chance to send our people to the bottom of the sea. And they don't care who – men, women, children, drowning in the cold sea, crying out for rescue, but there's no one who can. The U-boat glides off to find another victim, leaving them to die. I think I'd rather get blown up at once than drown.'

'You sound as if you're as sorry for the Germans as for our people,' I said as gently as I could.

Bernie flung herself down on the settee. 'It's all so stupid. Such a waste of life. I bet half those men in the U-boats don't want to be there. They have to go into the Navy the same way our people do. It's such a waste.'

'Is that how Cedric feels?'

Bernie shook her head. 'No, Cedric would send all the U-boats to the bottom of the sea tomorrow, if he could. He hates the German down to the last infant.'

'And you?'

'Oh, I don't know,' said Bernie. She stood up. 'Don't worry, I have more sense than to show any sympathy for the other side to anyone but you. It's all so bloody. Cedric seems to think it's a grand adventure. He's desperate to get to sea, but they want him here. In charge of stuff.'

'At least you don't have to worry about him,' I said.

'No,' said Bernie, in an oddly flat tone. 'At least there's that. Goodnight, Hope.' She went to bed. I wondered if she realised that she would never have been more in sympathy with Fitzroy than at that moment. My godfather was utterly loyal to his country, but he hated the waste of any life. He loathed my father's duck hunts with a passion, describing it as a 'pointless slaughter of innocent wildfowl'. This adversity to death struck me as a very odd attribute for an assassin. But perhaps it was his unwillingness to kill unless absolutely necessary that made him a good one?

I followed Bernie's example and went to bed, my mind spinning with conflicting thoughts.

Weeks passed and Cole didn't invite me to luncheon. Bernie disappeared into her night life. Once I thought I heard her crying, but when I knocked on her door, she said she needed to sleep and asked me to leave her in peace. I thought of ringing up my mother, but the thought that she would badger me over not yet rescuing Bernie, or that she might tell me that my father was ailing again, prevented me. I knew I was burying my head in the sand, but I felt very much alone. I hadn't heard a thing about Harvey and had no idea of his fate. The police hadn't been back in touch with us, so I assumed we weren't required as witnesses. This made me hope that Harvey had struck some kind of a deal. His limp meant he couldn't go into any of the regular services, but maybe they would employ him as a quartermaster or something. Although the idea of putting Harvey in charge of a mountain of supplies was both amusing, and a very, very, bad idea. Much as I liked him. It seemed even with the best will in the world, a clean slate, and a helping hand from Fitzroy, Harvey couldn't help his fingers being sticky.

Of course, I thought of ringing up my godfather too. I lifted the receiver more than once, but I kept thinking of what Bernie had said, about our little woes not meaning much. I didn't want to come across as a spoiled child who asked him for better toys, or even simply for attention. He'd said he'd contact me when he needed me, and I had to be content with that.

And then I got a telegram. I closed the door and stood holding it. My legs trembled and I felt sick. All I could think of was that my father had died. I tried to tear it open, but my fingers wouldn't obey me. So, I got a knife from the kitchen, and sat down on the settee. I put the telegram on the little table, and as carefully as my shaking fingers allowed, slit it open.

My dear Hope,

Just to let you know I am off on holiday at last. Bit of a journey, so I may be out of contact for a while. Give my love to your mother, and remember, in case of emergency, ring the doctor.
E

I looked at this for a moment, as the meaning sank in. Fitzroy was off on a foreign mission that was serious enough he was informing me of his departure. Asking me to give my love to my mother was his way of saying she wasn't going with him. I puzzled over the doctor part longer than necessary, until I recalled my mother saying that Griffin, my godfather's man, had a medical background. I was to call him if things went sideways. 'E' was the easiest part. It was E for Eric.

I also knew that as he had sent this unencoded he hadn't had much, if any, warning that he was leaving. Normally, he wouldn't have sent something so blatant. But then for all I knew the telegram man had actually been one of his people under cover.

What it did mean was that, unless I counted Cole, I was completely without support. I liked Cole, and I trusted him enough for now. What I couldn't understand, and I needed to understand, was Fitzroy's antipathy towards the man. Should I continue to see him while Fitzroy was away? Was he dangerous to me? He'd warned me when not to speak to the judge. He'd told me the department was there for me. But he claimed Fitzroy was an assassin.

Weirdly, the idea Cole was an assassin, or that the Department employed such people, didn't bother me. I trusted that the Service rarely killed and only did so when absolutely necessary. This seemed of far less importance when the governments of the world were lining up men in their tens of thousands to go about the business of killing each other. A single assassin shooting a war-hungry politician might make all the difference. What was the death of one man when it might save the lives of millions?

I found it difficult that I agreed with this. I knew ethically I should be opposed to all death, especially that of innocents, but while I knew I would fight to the death for anyone I cared for, anyone who promoted war would get neither sympathy nor pro-tection from me. in Naturally, it would be preferable to kill one of those warmongers on the opposing side. The death of a leader, such as Mussolini, would throw their country into chaos. Could it be enough to stop the German war machine? Russia bubbled with unease. Could all eyes be directed there and away from Eur-ope? And the biggest question, and why I suspected the Crown had not taken this option: would it only make things worse? Power abhors a vacuum. You may remove one bad player only for a worse one to take his place. Though if half the things I had heard about Hitler were true, it was hard to imagine anyone worse.

When I started to imagine the playing pieces on the board, I knew I wasn't seeing the whole picture by a very long way. What truly worried me was whether anyone was seeing the whole picture.

Chapter Twenty

The weeks wore on, and spring edged into summer. Walking to work, coatless, in the golden mornings, hearing the sounds of children playing in nearby parks and gardens, the thought that violence raged in Europe was as incredible as it was repugnant. By now my dreams were overlaid with lines in type, as if I was narrating my own life. More and more frequently I stopped what I was doing at the flat, thinking something was wrong, only to realise I was missing the sound of all the typewriters in the typing pool clattering away.

I knew more than most people due to the papers that crossed my desk. Poland had been divided between the Germans and Soviets. The Polish Intelligence Service had managed to get some information out before any operatives left in the country were rounded up and exterminated. A few Polish airmen had managed to flee to Britain. They reported their country had been brutalised by both sides. Even more alarming came the whisper that the Nazis were segregating and rounding up Jews. Exactly why and what was happening to these people remained unclear, but the rumours that did reach us were horrific in the extreme. Unbelievably horrific.

I read more and more discussion about an officer, G, and the very mixed reception he was receiving. Some saw him as a visionary and others as a maverick risk taker. At first, I thought they were describing Fitzroy, but as the papers continued to flow through my typewriters, I realised whoever G was, he was a leader, as well as a visionary. Although Fitzroy ran, I guessed, a number of agents and involved himself in a variety of operations, often other people's, he was at heart a solo operator – as long as by solo one meant my mother and him. No this was someone completely different. I grew rather interested in his career as the war of words raged backwards and forwards. Apparently even the new Prime Minister had become engaged in the discussion, but I was not involved in typing papers from his office. One of the pool girls had come from his office and whispered over coffee and biscuits that he liked to dictate from his bath. I thought that utter nonsense.

I recognised I was becoming moodier and more withdrawn. The girls in the pool had tolerated, if not exactly welcomed, my presence reading a book at their table in the canteen at lunch. Now they actively moved to avoid me. I snapped at people my equal and barely kept my temper talking to my seniors. I ended up with three reprimands on my file.

The truth was I was desperately unhappy, and extremely lonely. Then one evening I came home and found Fitzroy on my settee. His hair was overgrown, and his red chin suggested he'd only just shaved.

'Hello, Hope,' he said, bounding up and coming to kiss me on the cheek.

I looked around confused. 'Is Bernie here?'

'No, why? Do you need her?' He stepped back and looked down at me affectionately. 'Oh, did you mean how did I get in? Honestly, Hope, do you even need to ask?'

'Do you often break into people's homes?'

'Not as much as I used to,' said my godfather. 'I have people to do that sort of thing for me now. Still, always worth keeping your hand in.'

He led me back towards the settee and pulled me down beside him, enveloping me in a hug. 'My little Hope!'

'Are you drunk?'

'Only on life, my dear. Do you have plans? Shall we go and find a decent dinner. I know just the place.'

157

'It's not eggs, is it?'

'Eggs are not a decent dinner. I've the car outside, and Jack will be delighted to see you. He's past the tiny puppy stage and on to the "I want to eat toes" stage. He's quite mischievous. He got into the pantry while I was away and made himself sick eating everything in sight. Griffin's had a terrible time with him.'

'You're suggesting we go to yours for dinner. Who's cooking?'

'I am.'

'Then I'm in.'

'Flatterer,' said Fitzroy, pulling me in and kissing me on the top of my head.

'You are in a good mood. Have we won the war, and no one told me?' I regretted the words as soon as they were out of my mouth.

'Sadly not,' said Fitzroy in a much more serious tone of voice. 'Trip to Norway was a right royal – well, never mind. I shouldn't have mentioned it. I wasn't commanding anyway. Observing, and only because I pulled all the favours I could to join them. Apart from a few dead German cyclists all we achieved was to get some poor little town bombed to hell and back. Shouldn't have told you that either.'

'Why did you want to go? You could have been killed,' I said. 'My mother would have been distraught.'

'Do you really think so?' said Fitzroy, brightening again. 'What about you?'

'Don't talk nonsense,' I said. 'Poor Jack might well have pined to death.'

Fitzroy gave me a look that I had rarely seen from him. It was so very rare I had to struggle a moment to decide what emotion his features were expressing. 'Ah, guilt!'

'Now, you're talking nonsense,' he said. 'All I will say is, as I have told you, I work largely in counter-intelligence and there were certain operatives I wanted to see in action. I thought – well, never mind that either. Tonight, I'm alive. I survived a

158

bloody awful experience and I'm glad about that. I'd like to celebrate life with my favourite goddaughter.'

'You only have one,' I said.

'Even if I had more, you'd still be my favourite!'

'Give me time to change?'

He nodded. 'I'll take a look around your kitchen while I wait, so I can suggest improvements. I need to keep busy.'

'Why?'

'No sleep in – no, I've lost count of the hours – can do that to you!'

I left him sorting through a kitchen cupboard, piling pots and pans behind him.

He did cook me a most excellent dinner, but his bright-eyed, over-jolly mood continued. Jack, sensing his master's state of mind and also over-excited by his return, dragged away one of my shoes, unobserved, that I had kicked off when I curled up in a chair for an after-dinner brandy, and more or less devoured it whole. If I had wanted to walk home, I would only have had one shoe and one soggy sole. Griffin had retired for the night, shortly after my arrival, and my godfather, in the middle of telling an outrageous story about a senior minister, a cat, a jar of marmalade, and an action that should be anatomically impossible, fell asleep. Fortunately, this was before he managed to explain the final part, which I am sure I would never have been able to put from my mind – he fell asleep mid-sentence, still clutching a glass of brandy.

It was close to three a.m., so I took a cover from his bedroom to throw over him, put a pillow behind his head, and with some difficulty prised the glass out of his hand. Then I went to see if the room I had slept in as a child, when I visited, was still a guest room. It was, and I tumbled happily into the extremely comfy bed and fell asleep – in his home, my godfather never compromised on the quality of his furnishings or linen.

The next morning, I found a shoebox at the end of my bed and a spare uniform, with boots. The shoebox contained footwear not unlike the pair I had been wearing the evening before, but considerably better made. I put on the uniform and went through to the kitchen. There I found Griffin making breakfast. Jack took one look at me and leapt from his basket, jumping up at me as if he was entirely made of manic rubber. I held the shoebox high above my head. 'You are not getting these,' I told him.

'Allow me, Miss Hope,' said Griffin. He took the shoes and placed them on a high shelf. 'I will see that these are delivered to your apartment this evening when you are home.'

'Thank you, Griffin,' I said. 'Is it terribly late? I forgot to wear a watch last night.'

'No, miss. If you'd like to eat breakfast,' he laid out an omelette with crispy bacon and a cup of black coffee. 'You should be able to catch a cab to arrive well in time for work. Lt-Col Fitzroy left an envelope with some coins to cover your fare.' He took a deep breath. 'He also asked me to apologise profusely for his behaviour last night.'

I was barely listening. I was staring at my plate.

'Is there anything wrong with breakfast? He said you'd like eggs. Can I do them a different way for you?'

I shook my head. 'Did he now?' I said.

Griffin's voice became most conciliatory. 'I don't know what Fitzroy did, Hope, but if you need anything or anyone to talk to . . .'

I raised my face to him. 'He fell asleep Griffin. He fell asleep in the middle of telling me a somewhat unsuitable story. Before that he had cooked me an excellent dinner. I threw a cover over him and went to sleep in my old room. What on earth did you think?'

'Oh nothing, Miss Hope. He's been in a rather jovial mood since his arrival home yesterday. He can be – er – difficult when he's like that.'

'You mean he often behaves like that?'

'Oh, no. He's most concerned at present. I think he rather hoped for a different outcome in this most recent operation. Of course, I don't know the details, but I believe he has rather a lot on his plate, and of course with your mother only being able to work from a distance now, there's more than usual falling on him.'

'Do you mean my mother often came up to London?'

'At least twice a month, if not more,' said Griffin. 'It made a massive difference to his load.'

'Of course,' I said. I looked down at my plate, so Griffin didn't see my astonishment. I had no idea my mother frequently came into London. She'd never tried to see me.

I managed to eat the eggs, but only by drinking a great deal of coffee. Griffin had to make me a second pot. 'Do you know when Fitzroy will be back?' I asked.

'Ah, yes, I almost forgot. He said to say to you . . .' Griffin looked up at the ceiling as he tried to recall the message. 'Let me see. He said that he had a delightful evening with you – did I say he sent profuse apologies too?' I nodded. 'Most unlike him. He also said he believes he will be up to his neck in it for the foreseeable future. He said don't contact him, he'll contact you.' Griffin looked directly at me. 'Although if there is anything I can do, Miss Hope, I am always at the end of that number.'

'Day or night?' I said jokingly.

'Oh, it can feel like it,' said Griffin, clenching his jaw for a second, 'No, I am sometimes allowed a few hours' sleep or a few minutes to walk Jack. Not that I can control the beast. We have two other persons who cover the telephone. Both trustworthy. Completely. You can ask them for help or ask them to get me to call you back. If it's the latter, please state how urgent it is. If the situation is desperate, I can generally call back pretty quickly. If you need help on the ground, it may take longer. But, generally, we can get someone to you within an hour or at most two. Unless the weather is terrible, or you're stuck on top of a cliff on one of the Scottish Isles. That might take us a little longer.'

'It's most impressive,' I said and meant it.

'I believe many of your godfather's peers were involved in

161

something of a scandal in Ireland in the twenties. Many careers were ended then. Fitzroy was never in Ireland. I believe that was somehow connected with you?' He looked at me hopefully. I shook my head. 'Anyway,' continued Griffin, 'it means that your godfather has a great deal more experience than his peers and that he has had longer to build up and strengthen his support network. He doesn't like the spotlight, but I believe nowadays he is becoming critical to Britain's survival. That troubles him a great deal.'

'How do you refer to Fitzroy when he's present?' I asked. 'You've used a variety of labels for him.'

Griffin straightened his tie, and dusted down his sleeves, 'When one has been working for someone for so many years – since before you were born, Miss Hope – one tends to get to know them very well. However, your godfather has always chosen to keep a separation between master and servant where I am concerned. Not that he isn't an excellent master. But your mother, I have been able to count as a friend.'

'You interest me a lot, Griffin. I've never heard you be so confessional before.'

'Well, you are no longer a child, and I suppose with the machines of war on our doorstep, I feel that both you and your mother should know, that however cavalier your godfather's treatment of me may seem, without his help I would be no more. Quite simply I owe him my life.'

'That sounds like a story,' I said.

'A very long one,' said Griffin. 'I believe you will have to hurry now if you are going to get to work on time.'

Chapter Twenty-one

June might have dragged as May had done, but I was one of the few people in Britain to know how much trouble the BEF was in. It struck me that the government's strategists had overplayed their hand. They had sent our forces off to Europe to finally stem what seemed an inevitable Nazi tide. The few soldiers who had been present digging in and waiting were suddenly reinforced by the majority of our fighting men. However, we were still desperate for arms, food, and supplies. Essentially, we were short on every-thing, including experienced men. Our raw recruits might be willing, but they had no experience of being in a war zone. Instead of being a well-oiled war machine – like the Nazis – we were a rag-tag bunch. I can also only think there were some severe lapses in Intelligence, because as the end of the month approached the better part of our army had been driven back towards the sea and was trapped on the beach at Dunkirk. There men desperately tried to shelter as the German air force strafed back and fore along the beach, killing men who had little more than sand to hide behind.

It was a total disaster. It honestly looked like Britain was finished.

I held onto hope by the slimmest threads. Neither my mother nor my godfather had told me to flee from London. At Christmas they had been serious that if invasion was coming, they would get me out of Britain. Now, even though I was only a typist, I knew

I wouldn't go. I might share the tribulations of those fighting only through the documents I typed, but my heart and soul was with every one of the men on the front line. I so much wanted to help, but I couldn't think of anything I could offer. I didn't call either my mother or Fitzroy because even though this wasn't their field, I knew they would be involved somewhere. I had no right to distract them.

I had realised now that my godfather had given me training to be a spy during peacetime. I excelled in observation and evasion. Counterintelligence when we weren't openly at war was where I could have helped. My mother on the other hand had been trained into the run-up to war and had been a servant of the Crown throughout the Great War until she became too heavily pregnant with me. Even then, I had been told, she insisted on reading and analysing papers right up to the moment she went into labour. I'd always allowed for a bit of exaggeration in that story, but now as I stood helpless while the enemy killed our people, I realised how strong the compulsion to help your country can become. If only I had better skills. Anything other than typing that would be useful.

Then I started to see the word *Dynamo* in some of the papers I typed. And, well, everyone knows what happened at Dunkirk. Operation Dynamo, the attempt to rescue our trapped army, was believed to have a chance of rescuing some 45,000 men at best. But then the British people did what they do best in times so dark there is barely any light, let alone hope. Every person in the British Isles who had a boat, or who had ever had a boat, made their way to the south coast, and despite the mines, the aircraft strafing, and the artillery waiting on the other side, went out to rescue our army, our boys; they brought back sons, fathers, uncles, brothers, and cousins. Civilians risked their lives to save people they didn't know, but who they knew were dying on the beaches of Dunkirk. Almost 350,000 men were saved. We lost so many, both soldier and civilian, but the evacuation showed what courage and, I think more than anything, a desire to help and to save those men who had been fighting for us, could do.

Dunkirk saw the very best of us. As a nation, but also as a collection of ordinary human beings, who for once were united in saving rather than killing. It almost makes me hope that one day humanity will outgrow war. The strongest motivation on that summer day, the one that united a nation, was to save our boys. The government was thinking of rescuing its army to give us a chance to fight on, but I don't think that was at the foremost of the minds of the men out in those tiny boats. I think one of the newspapers, I forget which, interviewed a man who had gone back and forth five times. He said, 'Well, someone had to go get those poor b**gers on the beach.' For once Bernie was home, Cedric tied up with secret things. Bernie and I held each other and cried as we listened to the radio, read the newspapers, and wept for all those who did not make it home that day. Both of us would have been a liability on a boat. Bernie had some idea of rushing down to the coast and offering people soup, but Cedric squashed it. I, being in uniform, had to stay where I was told.

It wasn't until several days after Operation Dynamo's success that I got a call from my mother.

'Hello, dear,' she said, 'are you well?'

My mother never enquired after my health. She had also stressed that if I was ill, I was to speak up at once. I suspect this was because she feared I might take after my father and develop a weak heart. However, I have always been disgustingly healthy.

'What's wrong?'

'It's your father, Hope!'

'No!' I cried loudly, bringing Bernie running into the room. I sank down, holding on to the phone. 'No, please no.'

'For heaven's sake pull yourself together!' My mother's voice cut through my sobs. 'Think, Hope. Do you think I am so unfeeling that I would calmly ask you how you are before revealing

165

your father, my wedded husband, whom I happen to love very much, was dead?'

The hiccupping sobs stopped. 'I suppose not,' I said. 'But you must have known . . .'

'That you would jump to that ridiculous conclusion? No, I didn't. Although I suppose the whole country is awash with emotion at present.' She paused.

'So, what is it about Father?'

I heard my mother take a deep breath. 'To put it bluntly, he's not at death's door but he is very unwell. I thought I should tell you in case any of those rags put it in the press. Apparently, he was photographed more than once. Although he hardly noticed. I mean, who would?'

'Mother, you're rambling. You never ramble.'

'I suppose I'm still a little astonished myself. Your father has never struck me as a man of deep cunning, but that is what it is.'

'What did he do? Could you please tell me before I conjure up any more nightmares?'

'He ran away.'

'With another woman?' I gasped.

'Really, Hope, you seem to have lost a vast amount of your intelligence while in London. You cannot be talking to the right people.'

'Who?'

'Of course he didn't run off with another woman. Your father adores me. No, he ran off to sea.'

She paused. My heart thudded loudly. 'You don't mean . . .'

'Yes, he has an old school friend who was looking for hands on his yacht. Apparently, your father sailed with him as a boy. And yes, before you ask, they took the yacht across to Dunkirk. Did three trips before the thing was so badly holed, they had to stop. Even then they didn't stop. Offered themselves as crew to other boats that had lost hands to the gunning.'

'But he made it back.'

'Yes, he did. His friend wasn't so lucky.' She paused for a

166

moment, and then said in a different tone, 'I am incredibly proud of your father. He is not a strong man, and he forced himself to his limit and beyond. He knows how proud I am of him, and he also knows how bloody angry I am. He didn't even leave me a note. I was going out of my mind with worry. It was Eric who cottoned on to what was happening. And he's made himself very sick.'

'Who? Fitzroy?'

'No, of course not. Eric doesn't get sick. He gets stabbed or shot instead. I mean your father. He's laid up in bed. Now, I don't want to bring on another storm of tears, but I think you should ask if you can get a pass home for a few days. Eric's off again or I'd ask him. I don't have the clout. A female. I'd be ruled far too emotional or some such rot.'

'I need to come now?'

'Look, my dear. Your father may live another five years, who knows, he may outlive me, if he does as his doctor asks and takes things slowly. But he's slipping. I can see it. His mind is as sharp as ever, thank goodness, but his health is failing in such a way that some things are now in the past. He'll never ride a horse again. God willing, never drive again. He's becoming less than he was and he's terribly aware of it. He'd want you to see him at his strongest. He would want you to remember him well, not as the invalid he's liable to become. Right now, he's a hero, and I think that would be a splendid memory for you to have, don't you? It would make him feel so much better about spending that last part of himself. He confessed, you see, he knew if he didn't get shot, he'd still have to give up his final strength.' My mother's voice finally broke, and I could hear her crying, very softly. 'He's always been so brave, your father. Irascible sometimes, but such a kind, generous soul. I don't know what I would have become if I hadn't met him. He's the best of us all, you know.' There was a final pause, and I knew she was still crying. 'Come if you can, my love. It would be more to him to see you than to be proclaimed a hero a thousand times. He misses you badly.'

167

She hung up. I cried so long and so hard, Bernie finally threatened to call an ambulance. Eventually, I managed to tell her the whole story. 'But I know what my supervisor is like. They can't give out passes at the moment to people who have actually lost a relative. It's all hands on deck for whatever is happening next.'

'But there are other girls who can type, aren't there? This isn't a metaphor, or is it an allegory, for you doing something spy-like?'

I shook my head miserably. 'I wish it was. I'm not doing anything useful.'

'Then they won't miss you,' said Bernie. She stood up and put her coat on. 'I'll be back in a little bit and I'll bring fish and chips. Go make yourself a cup of tea and wash your face.' She slammed the door on her way out.

She came back less than an hour later, smelling of food, and clutching two paper packets. 'That was rather fun. Do you know they actually wrap the food in newspaper? What are you doing?' she said.

I got up. 'I was cleaning the kitchen floor. I felt I had to do something.'

She threw the packets down on the side and pulled off her gloves, sniffing each one. 'Ruined. They smell of vinegar. Oh well. Now stop looking so morose, Hope. Auntie Bernie to the rescue.' She handed me an envelope. I opened it and saw a pass for four days, starting from tomorrow, in my name. There was also a train ticket for a departure first thing in the morning.

'How?' I managed to ask.

Bernie looked smug. 'Cedric,' she said. 'He has to be good for something.' She took off her coat and dropped it over the back of a chair. 'Come on. Let's eat while it's hot.'

'Cedric did this for me?'

Bernie tossed her hair. 'Actually, he wasn't there. I managed to get his tall, dark, glamorous assistant to do it for me. He's been flirting with me for ages. Anyway, we came to an agreement. I'm going for a sneaky dinner with him, and he got me the pass.'

'Is it a real one?'

'Oh, yes. Ian's Navy, but he has tie-ins with a load of people, all types, even some of your spy types. He pulled a few strings and here we are. And I was absolutely clear it was only dinner.' She tossed her hair back the other way, catching a chip which flew across the kitchen, but she didn't notice. 'Just dinner and maybe a teeny-weeny kiss,' she said and gave me the wickedest of grins.

Chapter Twenty-two

I arrived back home in time for tea. The trains had been busy and delayed due to troop movements. My mother, who had sent the ageing Merrit to fetch me from the station, came out into the forecourt at the sound of the car.

'Now that was smart work. You must be acquiring some decent contacts at last. Sadly, like most things that involve gentlemen, this job is as much about whom you know as what you know. Of course, when you can put them both together the world is your oyster.' She gave me a warm hug. 'You do look tired, my dear. Was the journey very bad?'

'No, busy, but not bad. How is Father?'

'Helping himself liberally to clotted cream on his scone now I'm not around to stop him. I haven't told him you're coming. It will be a lovely surprise. I really am amazed you got here so quickly. I suppose it's just as well. I don't think it will be long before most travel is stopped.'

'Is that because the government think we might be invaded?' I asked, following her up the steps to the front door.

'That, and they suspect the Germans would send in spies to get the lie of the land before they land.'

'Do you think they will?'

My mother shut the front door and leaned on the inside. 'Honestly, I don't know, Hope. We will need determination as well as all the luck in the world to stand against this. But no one dreamed that so many could be rescued from that accursed beach. It's amazing what can be achieved when people stand together.' She gave a small smile. 'I certainly have hope.'

We began to walk down the corridor to the library. I abandoned my bag in the hall, assuming someone would take it to my room. 'The house feels very quiet,' I said.

'The whole estate is quiet. It's as empty as last time. All the men have signed up, and of course some of the young women have gone to serve too. I only pray more come back than last time.'

'It's a different kind of war, this time, isn't it?'

My mother nodded. 'Yes, it will be fought as much on the home front as on the battlefield, in the air, or at sea. Now, hush, no more talk of anything but your father's heroism.'

I caught my mother's sleeve before she could open the library door. 'I saw my godfather. I don't think he's – all right.'

My mother nodded. 'Probably not. He loathes war and the pointless loss of life. I mean we all do, but he takes it rather hard. Thinks our business is all about preventing wars, which it largely is, but when a country determines on warfare then there is only so much that can be done by espionage. Our focus has to turn to other things, spies, information, signals, you know the kind of thing.'

'Not really. I'm sitting in a typing pool doing nothing but typing. I feel rather useless.'

'Your time will come,' said my mother. She added more quietly, 'Whether you want it or not.'

'I can hear women gossiping,' called out my father from inside. 'Are you talking about me? I'm not dead yet, you know. Why isn't there more jam!'

I walked into the room and my father leapt out of his Bath chair to hug me. He swayed a little as he embraced me and I took some of his weight without thinking.

'I hear you've been a hero,' I said.

'Tosh,' said my father, looking very pleased with himself. My mother helped him back to his chair. 'Shame about old Potters though. Mind you, man looked an absolute wreck. Never have believed he captained the First XI at cricket at school. On his last

171

legs, I reckon. Anyway, we got a number of our fellows back before he copped it – and it was quick. Reckon it was the way he wanted to go. I don't think he expected to come back. Not a bad end.' My father dropped his chin, looking down at the Bath chair he was sitting in. 'Bloody thing,' he said, picking up a cane from beside his chair and giving the chair a good whack. 'I can manage with my cane.'

My mother pushed me into a chair and sat down herself. With perfect composure she poured me a cup of tea and handed me a plate with a scone. Fortunately, she had thought to sit me by a tiny table. I've never had her knack for juggling crockery. 'Now, Bertie, you know the Bath chair is only for a little while. If you're good you'll be back to only using the cane in two weeks, three at the most.'

During these four days at White Orchards my father continued to be irascible and cantankerous towards my mother, who bore it all with unusual calm and even displays of physical affection. I had to pretend that I didn't notice they were holding hands under the table when we dined. My father had me wheel him outside when it was sunny, during which time he told me all about what he was reading. Then when I brought him in he showed me what he was reading, pointed out for the thousandth time the really good first editions – a number of which had been given to me at birthdays and Christmas by him and stood on their own shelf – and he produced book after book he thought I should take back to London.

'This one always puts me in good cheer,' he said, passing me *The Wind in the Willows*, 'Toad is such a funny old chap.'

'Father, I already have five books to take back. I don't have the time to read, and if I do there are bookshops in London.'

'Tommyrot,' said my father. 'All these books have been carefully selected by yours truly. No damn high street bookseller has my taste. Besides, these are mine, and I want my little girl to read them.'

This was the clincher, and he'd smile showing all his teeth like a lazy tiger in a basket, each time he used it and won.

In spirit he remained as alive as ever, but he tired easily, and it was now accepted in the household that between the hours of two and four thirty p.m., Mr Stapleford spent time in his room writing his memoirs, or as my mother explained, 'Sleeping. He often has dinner brought up on a tray, but with you here, he wants us to dine in style.' We were sitting in the sunny back parlour while my father dozed in his room.

'He is very unwell, isn't he?'

My mother sighed. 'I wouldn't say that. I don't believe he is in any discomfort. He's frail. He's always had times when he had to rest because of his heart. Do you remember when you were ten or so, and you had been out racing together? All of a sudden he had to stop. You sprinted calmly back to the house to get help, and as soon as Eric and Giles had gone out, you had a hysterical crying fit. I remember being rather taken by surprise.' I nodded. 'Well, that was when he realised he couldn't keep up with you any more, and decided to be your literary and geographic guide to the world.'

'Oh, how I hated that globe!'

'I agree. Learning from an object is no substitute for visiting foreign climes. But my point was that your father always had a reduced level of energy compared to the average man, but now it is more than that.'

'He's frail,' I said. 'So, he's not ailing, but you think he – his body might – might fail him soon.' I struggled with a catch in my throat.

My mother's eyes were bright with tears as she nodded. 'Very much that. His doctors, and he has seen the very best, say it's a wonder his heart has lasted this long.' She gave a short sharp shake of her head. 'Always was a bloody stubborn man.' One tear trickled down her cheek. She wiped it away with a quick angry gesture. 'Anyway, who's to say he won't rally again. There have been times when we thought he wouldn't pull through, even before you were born.'

'We?'

'Eric and I. He paid for the specialists. Don't tell your father, he thinks I managed somehow. He has no idea of the cost of . . .' At this point, she stood up, and turned away from me. 'I think I need a little fresh air. You won't mind me leaving you for a little while, will you, Hope, darling?'

'Of course not,' I said, standing up beside her. 'I'll come with you if you wish.'

She turned around then, and placed her palm against my cheek. I saw that more tears were falling silently. She sniffed. My mother never sniffs. 'Actually, I want to go into the woods and have a jolly good sob. I don't like your father to see me upset. It's the one thing about this situation that gets to him. Perhaps you might like to sit with him when he wakes and read him some Yeats? He does love that bloody awful poet.'

On the last word she turned swiftly away. Then, her head bent to conceal her face, she disappeared off towards the front door. I didn't see her again until just before tea. Something my father with uncanny accuracy always woke in good time for. She took me aside as I was going into the library.

'Thank you, darling,' she said. 'I won't make such a display of myself again. I'm doing perfectly fine now.' She gave me a brave smile. 'And, while I don't want to give you false hope, we don't know he won't rally again. Was the poetry too awful?'

I shook my head. 'He didn't wake until half past and I don't mind Yeats.'

'Rather you than me!'

'Mother, if you don't mind me asking – why did my godfather pay the expenses?'

'Other than him having more money than sense? Well, I think he feels partly responsible for getting your father involved.'

'How involved was he?'

'About as involved as you can get as an asset. We had a lot of fun together. I rather think it gave him something to live for. He enjoyed our work. Eric drew the line at him following me down the route of a full agent, because he believed that would be too much for him. If anything, your father hasn't forgiven him for that! He's said more than once that if he had to live his life over again, the only thing he'd change would be to ask me to marry him earlier.' My mother whipped a handkerchief out of her sleeve and dabbed at her eyes. 'I'm sorry, Hope. I really have become a milksop.'

I gave her a hug. She returned my embrace, but then gently eased me away. 'Your father's waiting. Besides, displays of affection will only set me off again.'

My mother took a deep breath, straightened her spine, and, head high, entered the library, saying, 'Don't even think of hiding extra scones down the side of your Bath chair! You know I'll search you before I leave the room!'

As I sat down next to my father he leaned over and whispered, 'That's half the fun.'

The rest of my visit passed in a relaxed and good-humoured way. My father continued to show no sign of illness except to tire easily, and thoroughly enjoyed all the attention he was getting. By the time I had to leave I was fairly confident that even his occasional show of irritation was more to ensure my mother's undivided attention than anything else.

Both my parents came out to the courtyard to see me off. My father had a ramp to negotiate rather than the steps. Giles wheeled him down, leaning backwards and panting and puffing as he stopped my father from rolling down too fast and away into the distance. My father waved his stick in the air, and yelled, 'Faster, Giles! Faster! Let's give Merrit a race to the station,' as his poor aged butler sweated under the strain. My mother stood behind them, a genuine smile on her face as she watched. Nothing, including world war, appeared to be enough to make those two like each other to the slightest degree.

When I hugged my father goodbye, he embraced me warmly. 'Would have come to the station, but Giles isn't game. Think the poor old chap's getting on a bit.' Behind, Giles stood staring straight ahead, unblinking, but a muscle in his jaw twitched.

'You shouldn't tease,' I said to him. 'It's been lovely to see you. You let everyone take care of you.'

My father nodded and gave an evil grin. 'I'll keep 'em all in shape,' he said. 'By the time you're back again, I'll be out of this ruddy thing,' he gave the Bath chair a whack with his cane, narrowly missing Giles. 'I'll be skipping around like a newborn lamb. You take care up in the big city and don't let that ruddy man put you into danger.'

'I'm typing confidential papers,' I said. 'The only danger is a paper cut.'

'Good,' said my father. 'You stay there until this bloody thing is over. I want to know my little girl is safe.'

'I promise to take care,' I repeated for the thousandth time since I had come home. I went to embrace my mother.

'Any time you have leave we would both be delighted to see you.'

'C'mon, Euphemia. Don't crowd the girl. She's a lady now. Out in the world. She doesn't want to spend time in the musty country with her old parents. Got to let her live a little. Like we did, hmm? If she has half the fun, she'll be doing it right.'

'I rather hope she doesn't do half the things we did,' said my mother. 'We were reckless.'

My father pointed his stick at my mother and said, 'She was a bit. I kept her on the straight and narrow. Always looked after her.' He paused. 'You'll look after her, won't you, Hope? I never should have . . . never mind.' He pulled me down and gave me a resounding kiss on the ear, half deafening me.

My mother ushered me into the car. 'I'll keep in touch,' she said. 'Be careful.' She lowered her voice, 'You can trust Eric, whatever your father thinks. Your godfather adores you, as do your father and I. We're so proud of you, darling.'

She closed the car door before I could reply. Merrit drove off. I watched them, waving, until they were no more than tiny dots. Then I put my head in my hands and sobbed my heart out.

176

Chapter Twenty-three

I had barely got through the front door of the flat before the phone started to ring. It was almost as if someone was watching. 'Hello,' I said, grabbing the receiver and trying to untangle myself from my coat at the same time.

'Hope,' said my godfather. 'I have some news.'

'About Father?' I said in alarm.

'No? Why? Where have you been?'

'White Orchards. Bernie got a pass for me via Navy Intelligence somehow.'

'I've always said that girl was trouble. How's your father doing?'

'Very frail,' I said, I could feel my lip trembling and was glad he couldn't see me.

'And your mother?'

'Desperately sad but determined not to let my father see.'

Fitzroy's voice became rather gruff. 'Hell of a time for her. But there, your mother's one of the bravest women I've ever known.'

'And Mother has always said you've known a lot of women,' I said, trying for a lighter tone.

There was a moment's silence, and then Fitzroy gave a bark of laughter. 'Sounds just like her. Always thinking the worst of me.'

'If you're not calling about Father . . .'

'Ah, yes, your friend Bernie. I heard through the grapevine that she took a tumble on some steps outside a club somewhere or other. She will wear those ridiculous shoes.'

'Oh, no!'

'I gather she's fine. A bit bashed up, but nothing major. Broken a bone, I think. So, she won't be back to the flat for a while. I doubted she'd have thought to contact you, so I thought I'd better let you know where she was. Expected you to have rung me, but if someone is giving out free passes . . .'

'Am I in trouble?'

'Not with me. Can't speak for anyone else. Glad you got away to see Alice and Bertie. I heard he'd done his bit down at Dunkirk. He can be such a fool!' He said the last words in a tone of pride rather than contempt. 'Your poor mother. Anyway, have to get back to work. I'll be in touch. Be a good girl, goddaughter.' He rang off before I could say another word, but my godfather never says goodbye. It used to upset me a great deal as a child, so eventually he gave in and would say farewell to my stuffed bear. He still refused to say it otherwise. When I think about it, growing up surrounded by spies and assets was an odd childhood.

I went into my bedroom, sat on the bed to take off my shoes, and only then realised Fitzroy hadn't said which hospital Bernie was in. I sighed and checked my watch. It was late and I had an early start. I decided I'd call first thing before I left tomorrow, and if I found her, spend my lunch break visiting.

Any hopes I might have had that either my job or the world would have changed while I was away were dispelled during my first morning at work, where I typed up page after page of instructions for Britain to prepare for invasion. At elevenses the normal chatter of the canteen had faded to no more than a whisper. Although no one discussed what was going on, eyes were wide with fear, and more than one girl dropped and broke her cup.

I found to my surprise that a number of the girls who had ignored me now gravitated back to my table. They gave me a quick nod and the slightest of smiles before sitting down. I ate the biscuits that no one seemed to want. One should never waste food in a war. None of the girls spoke to me, but they watched me eat with ill-concealed astonishment. Six biscuits, I felt, was the correct number for a healthy young woman who worked hard. I couldn't work out what the issue was until I realised that of all of them, I was the only person not visibly afraid. I don't know if they thought I knew something they didn't or merely wanted the company of someone who wasn't shaking like an autumn leaf in the wind, but before long I had collected enough that I might fancy myself as Mother Goose with a following of goslings.

I wasn't afraid for two reasons. Neither of which I wished to share. I was too worried about my father to spare the energy, and I knew Fitzroy would warn me long before any invasion happened. Prepare for the worst, hope for the best.

When I returned to finish the end of the morning I was followed by a flock of silent, pale girls. It would have made my father laugh.

When luncheon time came, having discovered where Bernie was berthed (she *was* engaged to a Navy man) I hurried off to the hospital which was reasonably close to my office. I managed to find a slightly scraggy bunch of flowers and bought a paper bag of mixed British fruit, grapes being far too much to hope for.

I found Bernie on the third floor of a terrible white hospital that smelled so violently of disinfectant it made the inside of my nose sting. She was sitting up in bed, flicking through a glossy magazine with her left hand. Her right was in a plaster cast from the edge of her palm to midway up her forearm. She wore a pretty, blue silk bed jacket and on the table beside her a glass jug burst with red roses. Next to it was a large card with a teddy bear on it.

'Darling!' she cried when I entered and threw open her arms. I put my far less impressive, and now wilting, bouquet down beside the jug and spotted a luxurious box of chocolates that certainly had not been bought with ration coupons. I dropped my apples and plums beside it and embraced Bernie.

'I'm afraid my offerings are below par compared to those of your admirers.

'Oh, sweetie, those aren't from admirers. Just Cedric, Mummy, and Harvey. Harvey's the chocs. I told Cedric it was from a dodgy cousin of mine. I really think otherwise he would have called in the cops! So, don't tell him it's our old friend!'

'I've never met Cedric,' I said, kissing her on the cheek. I sat down on the edge of the bed. 'I've only your word and that boulder on your ring finger to prove he exists.'

'Oh, come on. You must have!' Bernie screwed up her face; a sign she was thinking fast. Then she shook her. 'I thought you must have done. I've mentioned you so much. I've certainly suggested that we meet up dozens of times. Something always seems to come up. He's so busy with the war and all that. Did you have a good visit home? How is your father? Do say he's getting better. He's such a lovely old English gentleman. Much more knowledge about literature than me, and I'm the one who studied it!'

'He's frail,' I said. 'But carrying on going.'

'I wouldn't worry,' said Bernie, reaching for my hand and holding it. 'Your mother's not going to let him go anywhere yet. He'll be under orders to get completely better. And your mother isn't someone I would dare cross. I mean, she's lovely too, but steel inside, if you know what I mean. Does she know Fitzroy too?' She gave me a look I knew well, that bespoke a burgeoning curiosity.

'Of course, he's my godfather, isn't he?' I said. 'Never mind that now. But, Bernie, what on earth happened?' I checked my watch. 'Tell me all before I have to run.'

The corners of Bernie's mouth turned down. With her curly blonde hair, no make-up, and despite her sophisticated bed jacket, she looked absurdly young. Impulsively I leant forward and touched her other hand.

'Don't say a word if it upsets you. Just tell me what I can do to help?'

Bernie did smile at that. 'As you can see, I'm being well looked after. How did you know?'

'Fitzroy.'

'Goodness, he heard about me. What did he say?'

'Only that you were in hospital and had broken a bone. He didn't know which, but thought it wasn't serious.'

We both looked at each other for a moment and burst out laughing. 'He must have hated passing on incomplete information,' said Bernie, between giggles.

'Yep,' I said. 'He'd shout at anyone who did that to him.'

We laughed some more.

'Still, it was good of him to let you know. I did ask Cedric to do so, but I expect he got busy again.'

'Of course,' I said. 'He's very important to the war effort, isn't he?'

'That must be why Fitzroy knew,' said Bernie. 'Cedric has bodyguards. Sometimes he'll send one to see me home. Quite unnecessary, but sweet, don't you think?'

'What did you break?'

'Oh, some little bones in my wrist. Apparently, I was lucky not to break my collar bone. Fortunately, my wrist gave way first. I'd put my hand out to stop myself.' She demonstrated by flinging out an arm, and barely missing my head. 'Apparently there are hundreds of little bones in your wrist.' She leaned forward hovered the cast over my lap as if I could see through it. 'Well, maybe not hundreds, but quite a few. It turns out mine are all perfectly formed but on the frail side. Delicate, like me.' She pouted like a film star during a close up and then laughed again.

'So, you fell,' I said. 'Where and how?'

'Goodness, is this what you're like on official business?'

'Bernie!'

'Oh, all right. I fell down some steps. It was awfully silly. I stepped too far back and down I went over the edge. I hadn't even had one drink. No excuse except my awful clumsiness. Cedric tried to catch me, but I went down like a lead balloon. I don't remember too much. I hit my head too and I was awfully woozy in the ambulance. I don't remember the details.' She lifted her hair away from her forehead, and I saw that a dark black-blue bruise was blossoming around the side of her head. 'Beastly, isn't it?' she said, looking at my face. I did my best to hide my horror.

'It's not your best feature,' I said carefully.

'But I'm fine. They kept me in because of the bash on the head. Observation! But I haven't been sick once. I think they'll be letting me out tomorrow.'

'Oh, that's good. We can celebrate,' I said. 'What would you like me to ruin for dinner?'

She sat back against her pillows. 'I'm sorry, Hope. Cedric thinks it best if I go to stay with him for a while. He's hired a nurse.'

'But you said you were fine?'

'Well, the doctor here said I was rather underweight – as if a girl can be too slim – and he didn't like the look of . . . something or other. I mean, how rude? Anyway, he thinks I'm rather run down and recommended bed rest. It's not like you would be able to look after me with your work.'

'I'd much rather be looking after you. But no, we're not even related. They'd never let me off.'

Bernie gave a funny little laugh. 'I guess I get to see how well Cedric's house is run. After all, it won't be long till I'm in charge. I bet everyone will be as nice as pie to me! Get in good with the new wife!'

'Bernie, why were you walking backwards along the top of some steps if you weren't drunk?'

'Cedric and I were talking. I can't remember about what. He said I got rather animated and before he knew it the next thing that happened was me going over the top!'

'That must have been very frightening for him,' I said.

'Oh goodness, yes. He's been so lovely to me – and he's insisted on paying for everything. He even had two of these,' she plucked at the jacket, 'sent over from Harrods. They come with matching nightgowns, which are more like slinky ball dresses. I feel like a queen. Goodness knows how he managed it. Or maybe he didn't. Maybe he commandeered it for the war effort!' She gave a little laugh. 'He's so good to me. He really is.'

'So you keep saying,' I said with a smile. I checked my watch. 'I really have to go. I'll come back this evening after work. Maybe I'll even meet your Cedric.'

182

An expression of concern crossed Bernie's face, but it was gone so quickly I was unsure it had ever been there. I thought it likely her wrist pained her. 'Make sure they give you decent pain medication,' I said.

'Already on that,' said Bernie, giving me a beatific smile. 'And it's lovely.'

I half walked, half ran back to work. I must have looked like a scuttling mole. There was nothing flattering about my uniform or its colour. I knew it didn't suit me. In fact, it was so awful Bernie had never commented on it, which told me it looked very bad.

I arrived back in my seat exactly as the hour hand touched two p.m. I reached into my in-tray for my latest instalment on the decline of Britain, when my supervisor came over.

'You've an appointment,' she said. 'At four p.m. Don't be late. This tells you everything you need to know.'

She handed me a card. I read it and gaped. However, she had already moved on. It said,

Miss Hope Stapleford is invited to High Tea at the Ritz at 4 p.m. precisely.

Chapter Twenty-four

I don't know who I expected to be waiting for me. Possibly Fitz-roy. It was the kind of outrageous thing he might do. Or possibly Cole. I hadn't heard from him in a while, and I had things I wanted to ask him.

But when I surveyed the brilliant white linen covered tables with the dancing shadows of the palm leaves playing over them, I saw neither Cole nor Fitzroy. The Ritz, as ever, radiated calmness and serenity. The temperature of the room was perfect; a balance unachievable by English weather. The guests were all high-ranking officers, women displaying jewels larger than their eyes, and members of the Imperial elite who would never let something as mundane as war interfere with High Tea.

My eyes rested easily on pale pastel-coloured walls among the white plaster. The palm trees added a gentle scent of earthiness to the air that I didn't doubt would mix superbly with the taste of the teas on offer. (Except perhaps Orange Pekoe!) Somewhere a string quartet played something discreet, and melodic, but definitely music to hide one's whispered conversations rather than music to dance to.

The maître d' came over and enquired as to my name. With a slight bow, he asked me to follow him, and led me over to a secluded table at which sat a sandy-haired officer with a neat moustache. He stood up as I came closer and proved to be not much over five feet.

'Miss Stapleford? Delighted to meet you. Won't you have a

seat? Sorry, I can't introduce myself properly, but the war, you know.'

I nodded, having no idea what he meant, and more or less fell into the seat the maître d' had pulled out for me. I was quite the most gauche, most clumsy, and most ill attired person in the room. I tried not to feel it. The maître d' glided off. I didn't hear one footstep. I doubted the man even breathed.

The eyes of the officer opposite twinkled. 'Rather difficult interviewing a woman,' he said. 'Not that I don't enjoy the company of the gentler sex, but I usually conduct these kind of chats in gentlemen's clubs, and obviously today that was precluded.'

'Of course,' I said, not understanding at all.

'Though I should have thought about what you were wearing. Didn't. That's the thing. Officers are always dressed up like a carnival sideshow.'

I smiled at that. 'I think you look very smart, sir.'

The toothbrush moustache quivered slightly. 'Charming of you to say so,' he said. 'Though most cadets wouldn't dream of saying such a thing to an officer.'

'Really?' I said, deciding my only hope here was to be bold. 'Why not?'

'Why not indeed? A little civility can go a long way. Now, Miss Stapleton, before we select our teas, and I do hope you are someone who appreciates real Indian tea, may I ask, do you believe you could kill someone?'

I blinked once. 'If it was necessary, sir. I admit one never knows precisely what one might do in severe circumstances, but I would like to think I would be able to defend myself and others. I certainly have no moral objection to killing when it is necessary.'

'And what makes it necessary?'

'Generally, as I said, defence. Protection of civilians, those weaker than oneself, or to protect one's country.'

'Hmm,' he said. The waiter drifted over. 'Darjeeling for two, and we'll take the chicken and the cucumber for the sandwiches.' The man moved off. 'I'm not convinced about the potted shrimp

185

or the potted meat,' said my interviewer. 'Not at all sure it is what it says it is. But then, you know – the war.'

I nodded. I still felt completely at sea. The man opposite radiated a barely leashed-in energy. In fact, if he had suddenly sprung up and run across the top of the tables, I might have felt more comfortable. I got the impression he would have been more at home climbing a palm tree than sitting beneath one.

'Now, where were we? Ah yes, it was all very oneself and one, wasn't it? Could *you* kill someone, Hope?'

'Yes, I could, sir. I can.'

He nodded. 'Yes, I saw you had some skills already. Jujitsu? Beloved of the suffragettes? You're rather too young, aren't you?'

'To be in the women's movement? I don't think they are currently active.'

'Ah, yes, the war. Jolly decent of them. Oh look, here come our cake stands. I hope you're hungry. Can't waste food, can we?'

I watched as the waiter brought over two towers containing four plates. Two with sandwiches, one with scones, one with cream cakes. Individual pots of tea followed with the appropriate crockery. The waiter wafted noiselessly away.

'Rather good at moving silently, aren't they? Wonder if I should ask one of them to join us in training.'

'Good at moving silently in a tearoom,' I said, 'they might not be so accomplished out in the wild.'

The officer took a couple of sandwiches and placed them on his plate. 'Do you like the outdoors?'

'I was brought up in the Fens, as you probably know, sir, and I took full advantage of that. Admittedly I don't ride as well as my mother, who cannot understand why a saddle is required on a willing horse.'

'Can't she, by Jove? Quite the outdoors person herself?'

'She's at home in most environments.'

'Sounds fascinating,' said the officer. 'But we need to talk about you rather than your mother. How do you feel about getting into fights?'

'With anyone in particular?' He looked at me while chewing his sandwich, and I got the silent signal I was on the verge of being insubordinate. 'What I meant, sir, was that I would never seek out a fight. I don't enjoy violence, but neither do I object to it if there is a good enough reason. I have more than once had to deal with a difficult situation that required me to use the skills I have, and I am still here. However, in general, I believe my skills centre around observation and evasion. I can fight if I must, but it's not what I am best at.'

'Eat up,' said the officer. 'The War Office is paying. Salaries are small, so this is one way to get your money's worth out of 'em!'

I helped myself to some food. He waited until my mouth was full and then asked, 'Which would you rather do, shoot a man or kill him with your bare hands?'

I swallowed. 'Whichever was required. I wouldn't like either. But it might be necessary not to let off the sound of gunfire.'

He nodded. 'Some people do enjoy it. Killing. I don't mind if it's motivated by revenge against the people I want them to kill, but I don't want anyone in my unit who enjoys having the power over life and death. Rather obscene, that.'

I finished my sandwich. A mixture of chicken, cream, and spice, with something crunchy, it was close to being the best thing I had ever eaten.

'Do you know how long it takes to cook a rabbit over a campfire, or in a ditch stove?'

I told him. 'That's for an average size rabbit that's been prepared properly. I'd hope to find some wild garlic to add in as well.'

He nodded. 'It's food for the hungry unless you've got some wine to cook it in. How do you feel about the Germans?'

'The people?' I said, starting on the scones. 'I've nothing against the people. The Nazis and Mr Hitler are something quite else. I'd happily see them in hell.'

'Goodness, you can't say that word in here,' said the officer. 'You'll ruffle the dowagers' feathers.' He smiled. 'I quite agree.

187

Unfortunately, in war we do often end up killing those we don't have anything against. When you put on the uniform of the enemy, whether you opted willingly to do so or not, you become the enemy. Do you see what I mean?'

I nodded.

'What do you think of the situation in Europe?'

I glanced around nervously.

'Oh, it's fine. Keep your voice low. There's no one nearby who will hear anything they don't already know. Churchill is very fond of this place.'

It was with great difficulty I restrained myself from looking wildly around the room. The eyes opposite me twinkled again. 'I think Europe is on fire,' I said. 'I think the Germans are lining themselves up to invade.'

'And how do you think we are doing?'

'Honestly, not well,' I said very quietly.

He frowned at this. 'Do you believe Germany will conquer us?'

I thought back to what I had heard Fitzroy say. It seemed the perfect answer in this situation. 'No, sir, I don't think that. I can't think that.'

'Would you give your life to ensure that didn't happen?'

The rather lovely mouthful of lemon cake I had managed to get into my mouth – one that even rivalled the one I'd had at Buckingham Palace – turned to ashes in my mouth. 'I'd prefer not to die,' I said, 'but if my death was necessary to prevent Germany from capturing Britain, then like most people enlisted I would be prepared to die fighting.'

'Hmm,' he said again. 'No pun intended, but you sound as if no matter what, you would hold on to hope you would survive.'

I nodded.

'I appreciate your honesty,' said the officer. 'And I apologise if I'm ruining the taste of these excellent cakes, but I do need to ask these kinds of questions.' He ate another pastry, leaving the faintest trace of cream on his moustache. It was an oddly comic contrast to the chilling questions he asked. 'So, you're not the kind of person I should recruit to go on a suicide mission?' He said finally. 'Not something you'd volunteer for? Doing your country a great service, but knowing you had no chance of survival?'

'Is that what you're here to ask me?'

'If it was, what would you say?'

A wave of nausea swept through me. I kept my mouth firmly shut till it passed. He didn't say anything, but simply watched me. 'Honestly, if you asked me that – if you're asking me that – then I would want to ask two questions.'

'The Army doesn't generally encourage questions from the rank and file.'

I nodded. 'It breeds insubordination and it wastes time. You have to trust your senior officers. You have to trust the Army.'

'And you have only just met me,' said the officer, in a reasonable voice.

'But I can see you are of a senior rank,' I said, 'and I am a cadet. It is my duty to trust you.'

'I wouldn't put it quite as strongly as that. We do normally ask people to volunteer for suicide missions. Thing is, if you're with the right chaps, every hand in the room will go up.'

'I'm not the right kind of chap, am I?' I said.

'Well, you're not a chap at all, are you? But I've always felt women are somewhat underestimated by your average Army man. You have advantages that men do not – one of the main ones being that the enemy is unlikely to see you are a serious combatant until it is too late.' He picked up his napkin from his lap and wiped his moustache. To my relief he put it back down on his lap. It looked as if I would get another cake before I was sent off to die.

'I wonder where that leaves us,' he said. 'You strike me as a brave enough young woman, but not one who is ready to throw her life away. That's a good balance. However, with what is coming, it may be necessary for men, and women, to take on actions that they know will lead to their demise. Sadly, I don't mean in a quick and painless way, but rather the opposite.'

He poured himself a second cup of tea and topped up mine, which I had let go cold. I noticed his hands, although neatly maintained, had the calluses of someone who did more than sit behind his desk. His skin already had a patina that suggested he was used to being out in the sun. Not now, but later, it would age him. A career officer, I thought. A man who chose war from an early age, who saw every engagement as an opportunity to advance his career. Who saw soldiering as a profession rather than killing. I got the impression he could be kind to those around him. I suspected his men liked him, but he struck me as the kind of man who would consider the advancement of his side in terms of tactics and strategies. He wouldn't give in to any empathy for civilians killed on the other side, or even the deaths of soldiers who had never wanted to fight; his mind was filled with tactics and strategies. With any method necessary to let his side win. He struck me as the kind of man who would volunteer for a suicide mission only if no one else could do it, and even then, like me, he would hope until the end that he would come out the other side. I suspected we might be similar in a few ways, but it would have been totally out of order for me to say anything of the kind.

He drained his teacup. 'It has been delightful to share tea with you, Miss Stapleford. I would prefer it if you would keep this afternoon's activities between us. I need to go away and think. I am sure you will be of service to your country. What I need to decide is if you can be of service to the missions I will be overseeing.'

He stood up, and I did too. The maître d' rushed over to pull away my chair. I think he was terrified it would make a scraping sound against the floor. The officer walked with me to the one of the exits. Then he turned and said. 'I'll be in touch, one way or the other. You're very like him, you know.' Then he left me under a palm tree and exited in a different direction.

Chapter Twenty-five

By the time I left it was too late to reach work before the end of the day. The day was hot in a way that made both my hair and my clothes cling to my skin. If I had felt hot and uncomfortable in the Palm Court, by the time I reached home I felt like something any self-regarding cat would refuse to drag in.

The flat was empty. I had a slight hope that Fitzroy might have been waiting for me on the settee, ready to discuss my interview. I went over and opened the doors onto the balcony. A hot gust of air hit my face. This was not going to make me any cooler.

I wanted desperately to pick up the telephone and call Fitzroy. I wanted to ask him who that officer had been, and why he had asked to talk to me. The officer had said I was like him. Him who? It seemed most likely he'd meant Fitzroy as it had sounded as if they might be involved in similar projects. Or had he known my father at school? This option seemed less likely, but still possible. He'd asked me not to discuss the afternoon, but I would usually have ignored that when it came to my godfather. However, now we were at war, and things were becoming more serious by the hour, I didn't feel I could be as free with my confidences even with him.

I saw, and kept to myself, many facts that would have caused your average civilian to panic. It never occurred to me that Fitzroy might panic, but if he hadn't set up this interview, I might well distract him from more serious work. I believed, rightly or wrongly, that he would always look out for me. If the directive to meet with my interviewer hadn't come from him then there was every chance that learning of it would concern him. I couldn't see Fitzroy ever allowing me to go a suicide mission. I didn't want to go on a suicide mission. But then did anyone? I had no right to drag Fitzroy into this. I only hoped the Officer decided I was not suicide mission material.

I went through to the bathroom and began to fill the bath with cold water. I didn't even know if I would be asked to do such a thing. Hadn't he said I wasn't the right kind of chap? Or almost said?

I stripped off my sweaty uniform. I should at the very least wait until I had been asked to do something I didn't want to do. Besides, what made me so special? Whoever the officer had been he had known I was connected to Fitzroy, and unless he had a vendetta against my godfather, I couldn't see how he wouldn't have known Fitzroy would object to my death, and object in a decidedly militant manner.

I dipped a flannel in the bath and wiped it over my face. The best thing I could do was wait. In all likelihood it would turn out to be some kind of test cooked up by the pair of them. My keeping my mouth shut was undoubtedly one of the bigger parts of the test. Along with my not running to someone with more power than me and asking them to make everything better.

I dabbled my fingers in the bath. A touch too cold, but I hadn't lit the boiler. Still, they said a cold shock was good for the heart. I took off my underwear and taking a deep breath quickly lowered myself into the bath with a splash.

I don't know about it being good for the heart, but mine felt like it almost stopped. I sat up gasping and hugging myself. However, the late afternoon remained hot, and it wasn't long before the parts of me out of the water began to sweat. I started to wiggle and bathe, rather like an eel, cooling parts of myself as others heated and then reversing the procedure. It was rather fun. Normally, I couldn't have a bath of more than a couple of inches if I wanted to be conscientious about saving fuel. But with a cold bath I could really wallow. Best of all, there was no Bernie to bang on the door and demand I came out.

Thinking of Bernie, I remembered my promise I would go and see her tonight. Hospital dinners were generally very early, so I guessed I could pay a quick visit at seven o'clock. I would ring the hospital to check when I got out. I imagined Bernie, in her private hospital room, being brought lobster from a nearby hotel by her beau. Thinking of food reminded me about the chocolates she'd had. She'd said Harvey had sent them. But the last thing we'd heard, Harvey was in jail. Bernie must know something I didn't. I must remember to ask her—

My thoughts stopped mid-train and I froze. The water swished around me one last time. I had no way of stopping it. I waited. There it came again. Movement. Without a doubt, there was someone in our lounge.

I don't believe I am the kind of person who feels afraid very often, but there's something about being naked in the bath that sends one back to an almost child-like vulnerability. I'd left my uniform in my bedroom and dropped my underwear on the other side of the bathroom. I wasn't convinced that much less than full dress would make me confident enough to confront a burglar. There wasn't anything in the flat that I cared about. Apart from the ring around my neck on a chain, I hadn't brought anything from home but a few books. Even my father, I hoped, would think that my life was worth more than a few books. Bernie wasn't here. Confronting a man already high on adrenaline, whilst naked, and not winning the fight, would in all probability end in a nasty way. As I clung to the side of the bathtub, I realised that although the cold bath had once seemed a good idea, my limbs were now stiff with cold. If I stretched, I could possibly reach my towel, but the bath might creak. It was an old enamel one. The finish had been redone, but underneath it was still old. Bernie and I had thought about complaining to the landlord, but neither of us had ever got around to it. We'd thought, 'as long as it holds water . . .'

So, I made a decision. Burglars rarely bother with bathrooms unless they are looking for medicines, and I couldn't see why anyone would break into our flat looking for those. If I stayed still and made no noise, the chances were whoever my intruder was, he'd take what he wanted and leave.

I thought furiously. It was late afternoon edging into early evening. It was still light outside. Whoever this was, it must be someone who had taken a chance on seeing the open balcony doors. A big chance. This led me to two conclusions. Whoever it was would want in and out as quickly as possible. To take such a big risk they must be desperate.

Overall, the tactical choice was to stay here in my bath and wait for them to leave. I looked around the room for a weapon should I need one. Sadly, none of my jujitsu lessons had taught me the art of lethal soap-wielding. A half-empty bottle of shampoo completed my weapons supply. Bernie and I kept most of our stuff in wash bags, a habit from college, and we kept those in our rooms.

I sat, shivering now, and with my jaw clamped shut so my teeth didn't make a noise. The sounds from the lounge had moved to Bernie's room. Maybe it was one of her so-called chums down on his luck, and hunting for jewels to sell while she was in hospital? Maybe they didn't even know I existed. Or could it possibly be Harvey? If he was bringing Bernie chocolates he clearly wasn't in jail. Fitzroy must have got him out again. But no matter how desperate, I couldn't see Harvey robbing us – at least not without apologising for it and eventually returning our goods. Maybe it was Harvey and he thought of this as borrowing? Maybe he'd been on the way to see me and seen the balcony doors open – I couldn't deceive myself.

I heard footsteps in the hall. I held my breath. Not a sound came from me.

The door flew open and a male figure with a dark mask over his face rushed in. My instinct was to stand, back away, and ready myself, but he was too quick. He went towards the taps and grabbed my ankles. Before I knew what was happening, he'd hoisted my legs in the air.

194

Damn, I thought. This isn't the action of a normal burglar. Then I started to drown.

He held my ankles with an iron-hard grip. Water forced itself up my nostrils and he dragged my legs up. I slid along the bottom of the bath, scrabbling at the sides. There was no purchase to be had. I'd already been holding my breath and my lungs burned for air. My body was urging me to inhale deeply. My left hand found the chain on the plug. I pulled it and the plug came free.

It wasn't enough. I'd run myself a deep cold bath. Normally I'd only have filled it a few inches. Still enough to drown in, but at least I would have had a chance of it running out.

All this was happening in seconds. Any moment my body would force me to inhale and I'd swallow a lungful of water. Sitting up would do me no good, I couldn't fight his grip like that.

Grip. How do you break out of a strong grip, Hope? Fitzroy had taught me that when I was very young. You twist against the thumb. You put pressure on the weakest point.

With a last effort I twisted my legs, and my torso. Whatever he'd been expecting, this wasn't it. My killer loosened his grip slightly. I kicked my legs apart, and then kicked out as hard as I could. By pure luck I hit his nose. I felt the crunch of bone under my right heel. I pushed myself up and back. The shiny bath surface slid under my feet, but I hooked my arm over the side and rolled over.

My attacker was holding his nose, but when he saw me out and standing, he slammed into me, driving me back into the bath. I fell over the side, hitting my head in the process. Lights flashed before my eyes, and pain burst like fiery paint inside my head. Only my head and shoulders were in the bath. I was lying widthways across it. The man lay across me, forcing me down.

I pushed back against him, using his body as leverage. My left hand was caught underneath me, but my right hand was free. I grabbed for his face, but he'd had the sense to turn it away from me. I dug my fingers into his throat and squeezed his windpipe. I was still too cold to get a decent grip, but I managed to hurt him. I held on. He hooked his arm under my legs, lifting me, and swung me down into the bath. My other arm came free, and pushed up under his chin, forcing his head back as he leant over me. He caught my hand at his throat and peeled it off him, using the same trick I'd used on his grip. He kept hold of my wrist, twisting it into a lock that sent spikes of pain along my arm. I cried out. He kept the pressure on and I kept my hand pushing hard under his chin. He should have had all the advantage, but he hadn't been prepared for me to fight so hard. We were stuck like this – both straining to get a death hold on the other – when we heard heavy footsteps outside.

Were there two of them?

My attacker turned away from me, holding me only by the wrist lock. His body tensed. Whoever this was, he wasn't expecting anyone. I shook my head, struggling to think through the pain. Nausea swept over me, and I vomited. I pointed my head directly at my attacker. The better part of the Ritz's High Tea projected itself out of my stomach at considerable speed and splattered all over him.

This appeared to be more than he had bargained for. He released me, and opening the door, ran straight into a large fist. He went down with a satisfying thump.

I saw Cole enter the bathroom, and then I saw nothing.

Chapter Twenty-six

I awoke to find myself lying on the settee with a pillow under my head and a blanket over me. A cold cloth lay across my forehead. My eyesight blurred. My wrist was being held in a light hold. I immediately tried to pull it away and sit up.

'Easy. Easy,' said Cole's voice. 'You're safe. You took a whack on the head. I'm trying to decide if I need to take you to hospital.'

'How long was I out?'

'Minutes,' said Cole. 'Not long. How's your vision?'

'Clearing. Who was it?'

'I'm afraid I have no idea. I thought you might know. Made any enemies lately, Hope?'

'He got away?'

'I didn't hit him as hard as I thought. I was too busy checking you were all right. He must have got away while my back was turned. They way you'd fallen I was afraid you might have hurt your neck.'

I moved my head very carefully from side to side. 'Ow!' I said.

'You've got a bruise on the side of your head that's going to swell up nicely. Size of an orange, I should think.'

'I was sick over him, wasn't I?'

'Yes, are you going to do that again?'

'No,' I said, struggling to sit up. Cole got a cushion and tucked it behind me. 'I'm naked, aren't I?'

'Extremely,' said Cole, his dark blue eyes glittering. 'But then that is how one normally takes a bath.'

'I must have concussion,' I said sinking back in against the pillow. 'I don't particularly care right now.'

Cole sat down again on the kitchen chair he must have been using earlier. 'I think I should get you a doctor, but I don't want to make a fuss about this. If you have got a devoted enemy, then you don't want them to know you're weak. Even a military hospital isn't that safe, unless you put guards on it. Besides, I think it likely that this would be put down to an opportunistic burglar, no more.'

'That's what I thought,' I said, being careful not to nod. 'But as soon as he came into the bathroom, he went for me.'

'You think his intention was always to what, harm? Kill you?'

'Most definitely kill. Could I have some water please?'

Cole immediately got some from the kitchen. The glass felt cold and slippery in my hand, but I noticed my eyes could focus on the beads of moisture on the outside. 'You need to get me some ice for my bruise,' I said. 'There's tea towels under the sink. I can't have a large bruise.' I sipped the water. The first tiny mouthful made my bile rise. I closed my eyes. I took another sip, and another and my stomach settled. I felt the pillow being moved behind me.

'If you want to keep cold compresses on this, you're going to have to lie back down again.'

I complied and felt a glorious coldness encompass my head. 'Oh, that's nice.'

I opened my eyes to see Cole standing above me, looking down. 'I can't tell what you're thinking,' I said. 'You mask your thoughts and emotions well.'

'Thank you,' he said. 'I'm wondering what to do. I could call your godfather. He'd no doubt make a fuss, probably punch me, but I'm used to that. He could spirit you away somewhere safe.'

'Could you get a doctor to see me, discreetly?' I asked.

'I could, but you need to convince me I should.'

'Fitzroy's busy. Does he often punch you?'

'And I'm not? And no, not often. But he outranks me, so I don't generally get to punch him back.'

'You don't like each other?'

'Professional rivalry. Nothing more. You don't put two male lions in a cage and expect them to be friends. It's against nature.'

'Are you busy? If you find me a doctor, then you could leave. I think I'm about to be given something to do that matters to the war effort – rather than only typing.'

Cole frowned. 'That matters to you, doesn't it? Being of use?'

'Of course.'

'Sense of duty. Hmm. There's a lot of people who'd rather sit quietly in a corner and wait for it all to pass them by.'

'Also, if someone is trying to kill me, I need time to find out who it is, and I don't want them . . .'

'To know how badly you're hurt. I get that bit. Although as soon as you go back that typing pool, they are going to see those bruises. Even if we do manage to stop the swelling you're not going to be the colour of a normal girl for a while.'

I swore then.

'You have no idea who is after you?'

'No obvious suspects. I suppose it could be someone from my mother's past.'

'Or Fitzroy's.'

This time I frowned. 'They wouldn't know I was that important to him. I mean, I know he cares for me, but he will have ensured that's not common knowledge.'

'Hmm,' said Cole.

'Hmm?'

'I'd better go and find a telephone if I am going to get you a doctor. If he says you have to go to hospital, you go, no questions asked. That's the deal.'

'Agreed. There's a telephone in the hall.'

'Of course there is,' said Cole. He went off.

I lay back and closed my eyes. My thoughts were jumbled. I drifted off to sleep trying to make sense of it all.

Someone was shaking my shoulder. Strong fingers shook me from side to side. I opened my eyes. I was barely moving. Cole's concerned face was close to mine. 'Don't go to sleep. The doctor will be here in an hour. He said I'm to keep you awake till then. He's one of ours, so he'll be discreet. I found these in your bedroom. You should put them on.' He held out my pyjamas. 'I'll be checking the flat to see if your visitor disturbed anything. Call me when you're dressed. Or if you need any help.'

I nodded.

'I meant the last bit. You might find it hard. I've been concussed before. Can feel like your limbs have turned to jelly and are about as useful. It's not like I'd see anything I haven't already.' He said the last bit with a completely straight face, coldly professional.

'I will ask if I need help,' I said. I could feel heat in my cheeks. I really hoped I didn't have to ask. He might have seen me naked, but at least I hadn't been conscious.

It took me a while, but I managed to get into my pyjamas. Thank goodness he hadn't searched in Bernie's room. All he would have found was slinky nightdresses. Right now, the covering potential and totally unappealing cut of blue cotton made me feel much better.

'I managed,' I called out.

'Damnedest thing,' said Cole coming into the room. 'It doesn't look as if anything else was disturbed. Whoever this was, they were a professional.'

'I've been thinking about that,' I said, lying back down on the settee. 'I think someone has been watching me, planning to catch me unawares, and I think my foolishly leaving the balcony doors open was too good an invitation to be passed up.'

'Have you seen someone watching you? Had a feeling?'

'No, that's the worst bit. I thought I had once, but it turned out to be an old friend. I would have hoped I might have noticed, but it's been a strained few days.' I told him about Bernie.

'You don't think this is connected, do you?'

'I can't see how? Unless it's something to do with Bernie's engagement and nothing to do with me at all.'

'Who is she marrying?'

'Someone called Cedric. Quite high up in the Navy. Has an intelligence liaison called . . . Ian – I think. A bit tall, dark, and dashing.'

'Ian's the tall and dark one. Cedric's more middle-sized. Has a reputation of being a terrible to work for. That's why they brought in an assistant. Smooth the waters. He's strategically brilliant but doesn't play well with his department.'

'So, he's not a nice person?'

This made Cole laugh. His laugh was strangely similar to Fitzroy's, more of a bark rather than a belly laugh. He sat down next to me. 'I'm hardly one to judge. I have no idea how he might treat a woman. Who says your friend isn't being treated like a princess?'

'Oh no, I said I'd visit her again tonight. Could you please . . .?' I told him which hospital she was in.

'Be your secretary and call up the hospital to say you've been detained at work?'

I grimaced at that. 'Sorry, I shouldn't have asked that.'

Cole stood up again. 'It's not a problem.'

'Thank you. You're being very nice to me.'

'Yeah, something about unconscious, naked young women in baths that brings out the gentleman in me.' He patted me on the shoulder. 'Only teasing, I hope. You can't help who you are. I try to remember that.'

I opened my mouth to ask him what he'd meant, but he'd already left the room. He returned very quickly. 'She's not there. Apparently, her fiancé has hired a nurse and taken her home. I don't think you need to worry about her. The staff nurse said he ordered the best of everything for her.'

'Oh. You're sure?'

'Yes, I am sure. I managed to get the name right. I might be ageing but I can still manage simple missions. Do you want some more water? I can't give you anything else until the doctor has seen you.'

'I know,' I said. 'But please, yes.'

He went away and returned shortly with a jug of water. He refilled my glass and put the jug on the coffee table. His movements were neat, economical, and deft. No energy wasted.

'What did you mean I can't help who I am?'

He sat down on the chair. 'Nothing.'

'No, you're not someone to say nothing. What were you thinking?'

'Right now I'm thinking I shouldn't have said anything at all. I admit I was a bit thrown finding you as I did.'

'Deflection.'

'Are you positive you want to know what I meant? I don't think it's something you will want to hear.'

'Why? If it's about how badly the war is going, I know that.'

'Of course, working where you do, you'd see where we are heading long before the general population. But it's not that. This is much closer to home.'

'Please?'

'You've heard about curiosity and cats, I take it?'

'Does it have a bearing on who attacked me? And why?'

'It might,' admitted Cole. 'You might already know what I know.' He sighed. 'But if you don't it's going to be a shock. A big one.'

'Worse than a strange man bursting into your bathroom and trying to drown you.'

Cole gave me a level look. 'Far worse. If you don't know, it will mean the people you trust the most have been lying to you your whole life.'

'You can't not tell me now! I'll be left with doubts about everyone!'

'That's not a bad way for one in our profession to be. I'm serious Hope. You will regret asking me.'

'I won't blame you. Tell me.'

'Fitzroy isn't only your godfather. He is your father.'

Chapter Twenty-seven

I stared at him. 'You can't be serious?'

'That you're not throwing me out of your apartment at this moment means you've already been wondering.'

'I'm hardly in a state to throw anyone out, let alone you.'

'Ask me to leave. I'll go. The doctor is on his way. You can always call your father for help.'

'I don't believe you.'

He tilted his head on one side, 'And yet, you're still not asking me to leave.'

'I'm wondering why you would make up such a nasty and distressing rumour.'

'Most people will tell you I'm not nice. But that aside, I don't spread rumours. He told me so himself.'

'Why would he do that?'

Cole sighed. 'You think you know him, but you don't. He's an incredibly possessive man. Your mother and I had been practising. She had only then begun to learn how to fight, and so I'd been touching her. Nothing untoward. Locks and holds. Nothing more. He escorted her out to his car, came back alone, and punched me in the face. Out of the blue. He hit hard. I went down. He stood over me and said, "Lay off. She's mine." Then he stormed out.' Cole rubbed his hands over his face. 'I admit I admired your mother. She was, probably still is, very beautiful. But she was a colleague. I had no intention of ever crossing that line or trying to do so. Besides, I knew she was married, and I respect oaths.'

'But so does he! He says . . .'

'His oath is to the Crown only. His affairs are often with married women. Your mother's different. Others have come and gone, but she's always stayed.'

I gritted my teeth. 'I think you should leave.'

'You know I'm right, don't you? There's more. Worse. But maybe you'd rather forget this conversation.' He spread his hands wide. 'I understand, Hope. In the Service we lie for a living. It's uncomfortable when we realise others have been lying to us all along. It's his nature. But I understand you wanting to trust him. I'll go.'

He got up and, picking up his coat, said over his shoulder, 'I'll leave the door on the latch for the doctor. I don't think you should try standing up alone. I'll hang around outside until he comes. Don't want you getting any more unwanted visitors.' He turned and smiled. It wasn't a gleeful or gloating smile. If anything, he looked sad. 'Goodbye, Hope. Take care.' He put his hand on the lock.

I hated myself. 'Wait, you said there's worse. You can't leave me thinking about that.'

'Forget I said anything,' he said, latching the door.

'Oh no, you know I can't do that. Come back and tell me the rest. If there is anything more to say?' I sneered, baiting him. He gave a small, dry chuckle, but came back over to me.

'Your supposed father went on a mission during the Great War. It was a mission Fitzroy should have taken, but he'd conveniently hurt his shoulder. He sent your father instead. It was a trap. Your father was taken prisoner and they broke him. He'd never had a strong heart, but this broke both his spirit and his health. I imagine Fitzroy intended him to die over there. Certainly, the mission was one of those that get disavowed.'

'You're saying he knew it was a trap?'

Cole nodded. 'None of the contacts had ever met Fitzroy and

he needed someone who could pass as a French native. Your father, being half French and the right age, outwardly fitted the bill. Fitzroy convinced him to go, despite your mother's objections. Only it went wrong on him.'

'My father came back.'

Cole shook his head. 'No, your father was well on his way to a foreign grave, but your mother was losing her mind. Fitzroy is manipulative. He hooked her in, but she adored your father. So I'll say one thing for Fitzroy, he never could refuse your mother anything. He went and brought your father back.'

'This is only your version of the story. Told another way, it shows his friendship for my father more than anything else. You have no evidence to say *he* is my father.' I kept my voice level, but my heart was thumping so hard I thought it must be audible to the whole street. My thoughts went to that diamond necklace. The joyous embrace between them when he arrived at Christmas and they thought they were unobserved. A thousand other tiny things that had demonstrated their affection over the years. But it didn't mean they were lovers, had ever been lovers . . .

'I can see you thinking it over,' said Cole. 'I'll say this quickly. Your father becoming an invalid gave your mother a home and husband in name, but not so much in – putting it delicately – activity. Fitzroy saw he had someone to keep your mother so nothing would inconvenience him in the slightest if he needed to go off on a solo mission or had another woman in his eye. Then when your mother got pregnant, he had the perfect place to hide you. Like a cuckoo.'

'I hate you.' My head throbbed with pain. Angry tears rolled uncontrollably down my cheeks. 'I hate you. You're evil to say this. Why would you want to make me so unhappy? What have I ever done to you?'

Cole came and squatted by the edge of the settee. He had the sense not to try and take my hand. 'You've done nothing to me, Hope,' he said gently. 'Nothing at all. I thought I was doing the

205

right thing. I thought you needed to know. Fitzroy is possessive and controlling. You look so like her. I did nothing to prevent her getting caught up in his web. I saw you, and I saw her again. I thought this time I had a chance to do something.'

'But if he's my father . . .'

'Then he will love you. Loving your mother has never stopped him using her, ruining her life. He sentenced her to live in the Fens with an ailing man. He destroyed the love of her life. He picked her up and put her down as he wanted. She could have had a truly brilliant career, but that wouldn't have suited him. No, he wanted control. I fear he'll do the same to you. He's not the kind of man who loves selflessly.'

'I suppose you are?' I took refuge in attack.

'No, I'm not. But I make no bones about that. I'm a loner. I have no desire for a family. If I want sex I can find it, but I never leave my partners in any doubt that it is only about that.'

'What a horrible way to live!'

'My way? I find it rather restful. I prefer my own company. I have nothing to prove to anyone, unlike your father. I don't know who put that chip on his shoulder, but he always has to be the one in charge, the one those higher up notice. He's a maverick and proud of it. He's exactly what he has taught you from birth not to be – he lives to be noticed. Not by everyone, but by those he ranks as important.

I clung onto my last hope. 'Why would he tell you about me?'

'Isn't it obvious? He was warning me off. He said he'd kill me if I came near you. He's more protective of you than he ever was of your mother. So, I asked him outright if you were his, and he told me, yes. He added my death would be a long and painful one if I ever touched a hair on your head.'

I dropped my head into my hands. 'I can't think.'

The doorbell rang. Cole went away. I heard whispered voices. I couldn't stop sobbing. A man with a large black bag came over. 'Now, you are in a bad way, aren't you?' said a kind professional voice. 'I expect it's the shock. I'll give you something for that.

Let's have a look at you. I hear you don't want to go to hospital. Quite right. Lots of nasty diseases to catch there. I always avoid the places if I can.'

I felt his fingers gently probe my skull. He raised my head and looked into my eyes. He passed me a handkerchief, then asked me to look at a light. He peered at the side of my head. 'I think I should check the rest of you.'

'Is he still here?'

'No, your commander is waiting outside. I would have asked him to leave if he hadn't suggested it.'

The doctor completed the examination. Gave me a shot. Then he helped me get dressed. 'May I call him in? I think you had better both hear what I have to say.'

I nodded miserably. I closed my eyes. Shortly after I heard two sets of footsteps returning. 'She has a mild concussion. Definitely no field work for at least a week, and if the headaches get worse, her vision changes, or she is sick again, she's to go right to the hospital, no debate.'

'So she doesn't need to go now?'

'That depends. I've given her something to both help with the pain and calm her. However, she needs to be watched. Concussion is a tricky thing. It can turn bad very quickly. If she stays here, you'll need someone sleeping in the same room, who can check on her through the night. I could send a nurse?'

'There are reasons we need to keep this as low-key as possible,' said Cole. 'National security reasons. I'd rather keep it directly in the Service.'

'I have some most trustworthy people.'

'I'm sure you do, Doctor,' said Cole, 'but I'd prefer to involve as few people as possible.'

'As you wish. I'll leave you with some more medication for the pain. Read the instructions carefully, and don't let her eat anything before breakfast. She can get up tomorrow if all is going well, but nothing strenuous.'

'Thank you, Doctor.'

I heard the door close behind him. Cole walked over to the settee. 'Don't worry,' he said. 'I'll sleep on the floor.'

In a show of pettiness, I rolled on to my side, so my back was towards him. I regretted it immediately as it meant I leant on my bruise. I stayed there for as long as I could bear. When I turned back, I saw Cole, under a blanket on the floor, already asleep.

Chapter Twenty-eight

Day broke sharply and painfully across my vision. The wonderful smell of frying bacon tickled my nose. I sat up, forgetting how sore I was and gave a little involuntary squeal. Everything hurt. I could feel bruises blooming in places I didn't even know could bruise.

'Good morning,' said Cole. 'I thought perhaps a decent breakfast might go some way to putting us back on a better footing. Can you get up? Or do you need help?'

'I'll manage,' I said. I needed the bathroom and I'd rather have died than ask him to help me. I got to my feet slowly. The room swayed a little and then calmed. I walked carefully across the room to the bathroom. The floor had apparently become most uneven in the night, and I stumbled twice. I felt eyes on me, but decided if I didn't look, I could pretend he wasn't watching me walk to the loo. Goodness, but I felt embarrassed. I closed the bathroom door. The room rocked violently around me, and my heart tried to escape from my chest. I grabbed at the wall, unsuccessfully, but managed to lower myself against it rather than fall.

'Are you all right? Hope?'

'I'm fine,' I called. 'A bit dizzy.'

On the back of the door hung one of Bernie's house coats, a silky blue thing with embroidered doves on the back. I grabbed it after I had finished and wrapped it around me like armour. Cole's left eyebrow lifted when he saw what I was wearing, but he held out a chair for me and then placed a plate with bacon and fried bread in front of me. 'Not exactly the Ritz,' he said, 'but it should help.'

I did my best not to react to the word 'Ritz'. I hazily recalled I had been asked not to mention being there. For the life of me I couldn't remember the point of the interview, but then I wasn't sure I had ever known. I put my hand up to my forehead to cover half of my face, and the bewildered expression on it.

Cole handed me a fizzy glass of water. 'Drink this.'

As he could have murdered me a dozen times in my sleep, I took it from him and drank it. He sat down opposite me and started to eat his breakfast. The sound of my own chewing was overly loud in my head. I didn't speak, and neither did he. At one point the kettle shrieked, a sound so piercing I swore out loud. Cole grinned, but made us both tea. By the time I had finished eating my head had cleared a bit. My skull felt like it had been hollowed out with a spoon, and the everyday noises coming from the street were amplified tenfold, but the worst of the pain had ebbed. The curtains remained drawn, which my mother would have thought slovenly, but I was glad I didn't have to face the daylight yet. The dimness of the room was more than bright enough to for me.

Cole pushed his chair back, scraping it on the lino. It felt like needles being pushed into my eardrums.

'Like the worst hangover you've ever had?' asked Cole.

I nodded very slowly.

'Yeah, you've got concussion. Mild. I think. You weren't sick when you were in the bathroom, were you?'

Carefully, I shook my head.

'Good. We can move then. I don't like being here. We're too exposed. I've packed some stuff for you in that old kit bag you had. All you need to do is get dressed. There's no need to hurry. I have to arrange transport.'

'Where are we going?'

'It's better for you to be out of the way for a while. There's a farmhouse we use. Most likely empty. May be one or two of us

210

there. It'll do. I can fill in parts of your training while we're there. I'm going to register you as seconded to me. That should keep the typing pool happy.'

I rubbed the back of my hand across my right eye. Memories of last night's discussion poured back into my mind. What Cole had said about me, my mother, Fitzroy. I didn't want to believe a word he said, let alone disappear off into the countryside with him. But what options did I have? He had been nothing but kind to me in his actions. He had stayed with me and taken care of me. He must have a reason for this. I didn't buy it was because he thought of this as righting wrongs of the past. Whether or not what he had told me was true, or even partly true, which I still could not accept, he had something in mind. It was too much of a stretch to link him with the opportunistic burglar, but I was learning everyone who worked in espionage had their own secrets, and their own reasons for offering information. It seemed that being a spy soaked deep into the essence of who and what you were. None of them could ever bring themselves to speak straightforwardly. I found it infuriating. Still, this could be my best chance of discovering Cole's agenda. I felt pretty awful, but if I let him think I was even worse than I was, perhaps I would have the upper hand if I needed to surprise him.

I stood up using the back of the chair for support. 'Fine,' I said. 'Thank you.'

'All part of the service,' he said, leaving me to untangle the pun.

I managed to get dressed, but it gave me a new appreciation of how I had managed to dress myself from the age of four. Right now, getting a jumper over my head was so hard it felt like I should get a twenty-one-gun salute for managing. Fortunately, I felt ill enough not to be embarrassed by the thought of Cole packing for me. I didn't like it, but I'd had the sense not to keep anything precious at the flat. He'd already taken the bag, so all I had to do was get myself back to the lounge. I approached this with the same concentration I would have done for a ten-mile hike through the woods. It felt longer.

'I think I should go to hospital,' I said. Cole stood by the front door, a kit bag slung over either shoulder.

'You missed that boat, Hope. It's not safe.'

I tried to think through my options. Would he stop me if I made a break for it? I almost laughed out loud. A geriatric tortoise could wrestle me to the ground, the state I was in. At the back of my mind whispered the fear that I might be mortally injured. But if I was it didn't matter what I did, did it? I followed Cole slowly down the stairs. He kept turning to see if I was managing. 'You're small. I could carry you,' he offered.

But I didn't like the chances of not over-setting him if we tried that on the stairs, so I only shook my head. If he'd mentioned it earlier, I might have accepted. By the street door stood a car. Cole opened the back door, and I saw that it had already been laid out with a pillow and the foot wells had been blocked. 'Get in. I'll throw a blanket over you. You can sleep till we get there.'

I didn't need him to ask twice. I crawled in and flopped down on the makeshift bed. Cole threw a soft blanket over me. I'd expected a rough army one, but this was more like something Bernie would have used. I pulled it up to my chin, turned to rest on the least sore side of my head, and fell into a deep sleep. I barely noticed Cole get into the passenger seat. I turned my head and saw the back of the driver. It didn't look like Fitzroy. I knew I should be worried, but sleep kidnapped me.

I don't know how long it took to drive to the farmhouse. I slept the whole way. I only woke when Cole shook my shoulder and told me it was time to get out. 'I could pull you out by your feet,' he said. 'But I don't think you'd like that.'

I sat up expecting the nausea and dizziness to return. It didn't. I felt fragile, rather as if my head was a giant glass egg, teetering on a far too small egg cup underneath. I needed to move slowly, but this new sensation was an improvement. I scrambled out of the car and found myself standing in front of a large farmhouse. It wobbled up to four storeys high. The walls grew more and more wavy as it went up. Tudor-beamed, with panels of wattle and daub, it stood nestled in a forest glen without any other building in sight. Instead the trees gathered closer and closer the farther you looked. All that cut through them was the dirt track by which we had arrived. Light came from the moon, some of the buildings' upper windows, and the double oak doors that had been thrown wide. If you wanted to hold someone prisoner, it was an excellent location. Cole took our bags out of the trunk of the car and said goodbye to the driver. I heard a bit of his reply, no more than 'good luck', or some such thing. I noticed he had an odd lilt to his voice. A definite un-British twang, but I couldn't place it.

Cole led me into the building, and when I saw the old wooden staircase that I needed to climb, I forgot entirely about the driver. Fortunately, there was a thick wooden balustrade for me to haul myself up on. Cole carried my bag, but he said, 'Tomorrow either I stop treating you like an invalid or you're going to hospital.'

I couldn't blame him for that. If he genuinely had my well-being at heart, then it was my only choice. If he had more nefarious projects in mind, they would equally be scuppered by my becoming ill. For now, I was going with the former as his true intention. All the same, it was nice to know that there was a way out. I had no doubt I could feign illness on demand. Years of living with an ailing parent had tutored me in a variety of ways of being sick.

Cole left me on the top floor. I had a small attic room, with shutters that opened wide to the night sky. The room held no more than a bed, a chest, and a wardrobe. Not even a mirror. But the bedcover was soft blue cotton with stars scattered over it. Not entirely what you would expect in a military base. A short, but extremely slow, exploration took me to a large communal bathroom on the floor below. It was white, tiled, and spartan. There were two white enamel baths as well two shower cubicles. My overactive imagination immediately saw how very excellent those baths would be for either drowning someone or conducting water torture. They were free-standing, so more than one person

could work on the unfortunate occupant. I decided that shower-
ing was a far better way to keep clean. I inspected the door and
found it had a rudimentary bolt. Easy enough for someone to kick
in, but at least that would give some warning of an incomer.

I showered, changed, and unpacked, doing everything with
the slow carefulness of an octogenarian. Then I went downstairs,
all the way down the very long staircase to find the kitchen,
where Cole said he would be cooking dinner. As I passed through
the hallway, I saw the doors were not shut fast.

I wandered in to see him tucking a tray back into the oven.
'Smells like pheasant,' I said. 'Am I meant to call you sir now?'

He straightened and gave me a slow smile. 'I think that can wait
until the morning. Have a seat. It's almost ready. Glass of wine?'

I pulled out a chair from the large kitchen table. 'Goodness,' I
said. 'They do treat you well here.'

'Us,' he said. He put a bottle of wine and two glasses down on
the table. 'You do know that your . . .' he paused, 'your godfather
and I are rather the exceptions. It's unusual for field agents to
reach our age and still be in the service.'

I frowned. 'Do you mean people retire or do you mean they
are forcibly retired?'

He sat down opposite me, filled a glass and pushed it over.
'The latter.'

I took a sip. Rich, temperate, full-bodied wine slid across my
tongue. It reminded me of the wines Fitzroy brought to our
house rather than the ones my father habitually kept. 'So, a good
life, if a short life, is our reward?'

'It's like any other life,' he said. 'It's what you make of it.' He
raised his glass, 'To those lost in foreign fields.'

I raised my glass too and repeated his macabre toast. The oil
lamp above us made flickering shadows across his face. I could not
read his expression. I'm usually good at reading people, it's one of
my best skills, but I had no idea what this man was thinking. My
breathing became shallower, and I forced myself to take some
longer breaths. All the while he watched, occasionally sipping

from his glass, but making no attempt to engage me in further conversation. It struck me he might be trying to drive home the point that we were alone here, and I was in his power. Normally, I would have given myself a fair chance of escaping. Not in a direct confrontation, but in a more indirect way. Having no idea where I was, was unhelpful, but I could strike out until I hit a road or a river and follow that. It was my damned head that was the problem. I knew my energy levels were low. I needed good food and good sleep.

'This is your first lesson, Hope,' he said. His voice breaking the silence like a twig snapping on a forest floor. I started. 'In our line of work, you don't trust anyone. Not even friendly spies.'

'You consider yourself friendly,' I said, raising an eyebrow, and trying to act as if I wasn't as intimidated as I felt.

He gave a low chuckle. 'To be precise, I meant spies you have reason to believe are on the same side as you. I assume you think I am working for British Intelligence?'

I nodded. 'I had considered that the whole burglary might be some kind of set-up to make me trust you, but I cannot see how this has gained you anything except trouble. You've had more than one opportunity to kill me if you wanted, and I am handicapped by my injuries. You may be hoping for some kind of information from me. If that is the case, you are going to be disappointed. I don't know anything of interest.'

'Nothing coming across that little desk of yours an enemy agent might want to know?'

Very slowly I shook my head. 'Operation Dynamo would have been of interest, but currently, with the operations in the Scandinavian countries over, I haven't seen anything of any interest. It's like things have stalled. We're regrouping, preparing for the worst.'

Cole leaned back in his seat. 'You do know you've just this moment given me vital information? Information that in the wrong hands could be devastating.'

'I think any enemy who hadn't worked that out for themselves is no serious threat.'

'Do you have the experience, let alone the right, to make that call?'

'I thought that's what field agents did,' I said. I held his gaze, but my insides felt like they were free-falling.

'You know you're wrong, don't you?' said Cole. 'Not on having to make calls on your own, but you were wrong to tell me what you did know.'

'Yes,' I said, dropping my head. 'I do however honestly believe you are working for the British Service, even if you keep winding me up about my parentage.'

'I'm not winding you up, Hope. There's no love lost between Fitzroy and me, but I'm not the sort of man to use someone's child as a weapon of revenge. I warned you, that's all. I've no doubt you think he cares for you, and he probably does. Only not enough to own you as his. I suspect you're more of a project for him. He doubtless enjoyed training someone from such an early age. It's the kind of thing that would appeal to him.'

Cole had kept his voice low and calm. Fitzroy wouldn't have shouted at me for my mistake, but he would have been stern. I would have heard the steel in his voice, and possibly the disappointment. Cole's tone hadn't changed. It didn't matter. I could feel tears pricking behind my eyes. We were at war, and here I was crying over something that might or might not be a lie. I could whine about my concussion all I wanted, what Cole was showing me was that I wasn't strong enough. I could disassociate myself from the world around me, and most of its people, but when someone centred in on the three figures who had supported me through childhood, I was infinitely vulnerable.

'So why am I here?' I asked. I had to bite the inside of my cheek to keep my control. I tasted blood in my mouth.

'I read your file,' said Cole. 'I don't think I was meant to, but I did. You have remarkable potential, but your training is severely deficient in some ways. The opportunity to rectify that presented itself and I took it.'

'That's it?'

'That's it,' said Cole, rising and going over to the oven.

'And you just happened to be on my street when the attacker broke in?'

'Now that would be an enormous coincidence, wouldn't it?' He said. He brought over a bubbling dish and placed it on a trivet in the centre of the table. I could smell the gamy scent of pheasant, red wine, cinnamon, and some kind of berry. He looked down at the dish. 'I'm much more used to having to cook out of doors. It's a pleasure to have an oven and spices to hand. Wild garlic doesn't go with this.'

'An enormous coincidence,' I repeated, refusing to be distracted.

Cole went back to the dresser and returned with plates, cutlery and a jointing knife. 'I was tailing the fellow who broke in. I had no idea you lived on that street.'

'You said you read my file.'

'Fitzroy had redacted your address and, for that matter, your current mission.'

I gave a little shrug. 'What's the fruit in this?'

'Blueberries.'

He served both of us. We ate and drank, but he didn't start another conversation and I didn't ask anything. When we had finished. He said, 'Sink's there. Wash this up, will you? I'll see you here at six thirty a.m. tomorrow, and we can begin your proper training.'

I didn't object to washing up. The meal had been excellent, and it seemed fair. I did object to the thought of 'proper training'. I had no idea what he meant, and it worried me.

I made sure my door was both locked and bolted. I knew it wouldn't stop him, but I would hear it if he came for me. I had an impulse to take a knife to keep under my pillow. But as I only knew how to use a knife to eat, it would be rather like handing any intruder a weapon for free.

It took me some time to fall asleep.

Chapter Twenty-nine

The next morning Cole made us eggs and bacon. He was dressed for hiking, and as those had been the only kind of clothes he had packed for me, I was the same. I washed the dishes quickly, while he assembled cheese sandwiches, which I assumed would be for our lunch. He wasn't in the least bit talkative. Instead he directed to do things by jerking his head or gesturing. Fortunately, it was easy enough to tell what he wanted me to do.

Within half an hour we were setting out into the forest. The sun was up, but the light was thin. It filtered through the tall trees. Most of them were pines or firs, and so well-spaced that anyone who had ever been in a real forest would know they were planted by human hands. But whoever had done so, had done so a long time before I, or Cole, or possibly even my grandmother, had been around. The ground beneath our feet was uneven but scattered with layer upon layer of soft fir needles that moulded themselves to the landscape. The effect was akin to walking on a well-sprung dance floor.

Roots from the trees wove across between the trunks, half above ground, half below, in a wooden cobweb that lay across the forest floor. The trail Cole was leading us down was barely visible. If you looked very carefully you could see where people had walked before. I didn't give away that I could see it.

I was wary of Cole, but I didn't think I was in danger. As for the stories about Fitzroy being my father, they were either designed to keep me off balance, because he wanted me to say or do something for him – and would thus keep me alive. Or he genuinely believed what he had been told, and in some obscure, and possibly rather dark way, felt sorry for me and was trying to help. What I knew, and he didn't, was that even if I had been his daughter, Fitzroy would have told me long before he told Cole. Cole had no connection to my family, and he had admitted himself that Fitzroy was his superior. If my godfather had valued him, he would have told me about him, as he had told me places and people I could run to if I must. All of them were final options, people who owed him favours, and only to be approached if I needed to flee the country. They were the last resort, should he prove to be permanently out of contact – and I had known when he said that, he had meant if he died. At no point had he mentioned Cole's name and it hadn't been on the back of the card. Here was a man, clearly highly trained and competent, but not someone Fitzroy had ever recommended to me. There was no way he would confess my illegitimate birth to Cole, even if it had been true. What I didn't understand was, what game was Cole playing? What did he want from me?

We came to a clearing. Cole put his backpack down on the ground. He turned around and pointed a gun at me. I couldn't move. It was as if I had been frozen in time. My eyes focused in on the end of the gun. I knew I need to move. Either diving behind a tree, falling flat to the ground, or if I thought I could make it before he fired, running at Cole and knocking the gun aside. I did none of these. I behaved like a startled rabbit in the light of a poacher's lamp, obediently still and waiting to be shot.

Cole raised an eyebrow but made no immediate comment. Then he spun the gun around in his hand and offered me the handle. 'This is a Webley MkVI .455. I take it you haven't used one?'

I shook my head.

Cole thrust the gun towards me. 'Take it, Hope. It doesn't bite. The safety is on, but all the same I'd prefer it if you didn't point it at me.'

Gingerly I took the gun. It felt unexpectedly heavy. I kept my index finger well away from the trigger and pointed the barrel at the ground. Cole nodded approvingly. 'It's good to see you have respect for a weapon. I take it from your frightened expression you have never handled a gun.'

'No,' I managed to croak.

'Your godfather,' he placed too much emphasis on the first part of the word, 'used to be a crack shot. Supposedly he took part in the 1908 Olympics. I have no idea if that's true, but after what happened to his hand – well, he taught himself to shoot with his off hand, but he was never as good again. He wouldn't have wanted you to see that.'

I shook my head. It was true Fitzroy had never shown me anything that he hadn't proved to be a master in.

'Well, that's the gun we used in the Great War. Doesn't jam. Obviously, you should look after it, but it doesn't much care about mud or wet. I hear they're handing out Enfields to officers now, but I wouldn't swap my Webley. That's served me well. Sent a fair few to meet their maker.'

Revulsion washed over me. I wanted to drop it on the ground, but I didn't.

'Right then,' said Cole, and I could hear suppressed laughter in his voice. 'I'll set up some targets and we'll see how you do.'

The first time I fired the gun I both shut my eyes and dropped the gun. Cole swore at me. Then he picked up the gun and handed it back to me. 'Again. And do it properly. Don't take so long to aim, squeeze the trigger, don't jerk it. Or am I going to have to teach you to shoot like an amateur, where you shoot quickly from the hip without thought? A real marksman knows exactly where they are going to hit and the damage they will cause.'

'You mean because you think Fitzroy is my father, I should be able to shoot like him? I still think you have that wrong.' I was deeply impressed with myself that I had managed to speak two sentences. The thing in my hand felt wrong. It was a killer. 'I'm sorry I dropped the gun. I didn't expect it to be so loud.'

'So, it wasn't the recoil? If you have weak wrists that's an issue.'

'No, I don't.'

'Look at me, Hope. A gun is nothing to be afraid of – especially when you're the one holding it. I'm not trying to turn you into an assassin. A gun allows you to intimidate people and to hit things as well as people, but you need to know how to use it. One day you might have to shoot someone, but I suspect that your god-father is unlikely to utilise you in that way. However, the way things are going no one knows what any of us will be called on to do. This is a major hole in your training. If you can't use a gun, you're a liability to any partner. What if your mother was about to be shot and you had a gun but couldn't save her? How would that make you feel?'

I imagined exactly how I would feel. Although in my imagin-ation it was my gentle father who was in trouble. Even at the thought of this, I felt angry. I knew invasion was a possibility, and the thought of a German soldier pointing a gun at my father in his Bath chair made me both feel sick and fuelled a hot anger inside me that I hadn't even known I was capable of. I took a deep breath, let it out, aimed, and fired. By some fluke I hit the centre of the target.

'Better,' said Cole, 'Do it again.'

After half an hour's practice, I regularly hit the centre of the target. Once I'd mastered my fear, it seemed easy enough. You lined up the sight and fired. I couldn't particularly understand why anyone might miss.

'That'll do,' said Cole at the end of the half hour. He'd been moving the target further and further back. 'Next time I'll bring out a rifle and see how good you are at long-range shooting. But ammunition is short. It seems you can do this well enough. Lunch and then we'll move on to another part of your training.

Cole had assumed I didn't know how to fight properly. He'd seemed pleased that I knew jujitsu, but had thought I saw it as a game. When I showed him how I could coldly attack and defend he was clearly pleased. 'Pretty good, but there's a few tricks I can show you. Your style is too formal. What you're liable to be

221

involved with is more gutter fighting. Dirty tricks. Body dynamics too. Understanding the mechanics of the body can make up for lack of strength, as you know. There are also prime target areas that take down an opponent quickly – and also silently.'

We spent the next several hours in hand-to-hand combat. Cole struck me as someone who didn't suffer fools gladly. I expected him to be the hard-hitting kind of instructor, but he acted with the utmost professionalism and skill. He had excellent control and although I often felt the whipping by of a breeze as a blow came towards me, he never landed one. Similarly, when he was showing me methods for breaking out of various holds, I didn't acquire a single bruise. My control was good, but far from perfect, and I hit him more than once. He took this in remarkably good humour.

Finally, he led me on a circuitous run back to the farmhouse. I showered and took my turn to make dinner.

Over the next two weeks he played the role of instructor precisely. He wasn't too friendly, but he was never unkind. If I deserved a rebuke, I got it, and unlike Fitzroy he had no qualms about shouting at me. But he only did so when I did something truly stupid like dropping the gun. I never felt easy in his company, but I grew to be both respectful and to admit to a degree of admiration. Did I come to like him? I honestly don't know. He had rescued me, but he had also alleged the unforgivable about my mother. It's hard to like someone under those conditions. If he had never suggested that Fitzroy was my father, then I might have liked him very well, but I would still have been wary of him. Even at his most humorous there still lurked something in his eyes that reminded me this man was a self-admitted assassin. He worked for the good guys, but I couldn't help wondering if that was a matter of circumstance rather than choice.

Cole struck me as a born killer. When speaking, in discreet terms, of a past mission that emphasised his point, he showed the most enthusiasm I ever saw when describing the actual killing. Taking life made him feel powerful in exactly the way the Ritz officer had loathed. Cole took pride in doing the job well. He played by the set of rules the Secret Intelligent Service had given him, more or less, but I sensed this wasn't out of respect, but rather he knew that if he served well there would be more missions coming his way. Not that unlike a dog doing tricks for a biscuit.

But he was smart. Easily as quick as me, and I was no slouch. But while I might describe Fitzroy as morally flexible, I began to expect that Cole wouldn't know a moral if it came up and bit him. From a few things he said I got the impression that he'd had a hard childhood – possibly in an orphanage or with an abusive parent. The Army had saved him. It had made him. And for now, he was content to serve. But duty was not a word in his dictionary. It was Fitzroy's watchword for life, but for Cole it was no more than a strange and restrictive construct. But I got the oddest impression that not only did he enjoy training me, he was genuinely pleased when I did well. If he hadn't been so many years my senior I might have thought he liked me – more than a friendly like. But whatever he felt, he was far too professional to cross any lines.

However, our time at the farmhouse wasn't spent merely in practicing ways to exterminate our fellow human beings. I knew about dead letter boxes, but I'd only seen Harvey do a brush past. An exercise where two apparent strangers pass vital information, usually in the form of a note or a diagram, between each other in a public place. Cole got me to practise this again and again until it became second nature. It was a dull and tedious exercise, but it was far harder than I thought it would be. Once I was able to pass a small piece of paper discreetly without it blowing away across the forest floor, Cole graduated me to passing small objects. In our case these were acorns, the much more difficult pinecones, and then the utterly impossible handful of leaves.

We talked a little about surveillance and following others. All he said on this was, 'Yes, you've clearly got all that.'

A further discussion that came up over dinner one night was how to spot a lie.

'I look for signs of a person being uncomfortable first,' I said.

'Contradictions are the only way to be sure,' countered Cole. 'Perhaps a little sweat on the forehead if they are concentrating hard. It is unusual to find agents who are as highly skilled at lying as the two of us. Over time they will trip up.'

'I agree,' I said, although I had no idea about other agencies. I had learned that Cole was fixed in his belief that the British Secret Service gave the best training in the world. 'But long before someone makes a mistake they often give away that they are lying.'

Cole frowned. This was unusual. He rarely gave himself away through facial expressions. I could have taken it that he was becoming more comfortable with me, but I had the suspicion he was genuinely confused.

'Are you trying to suggest that some people find it unpleasant to lie?' he asked, much in the manner of someone being told the world was flat.

'Yes,' I said.

'The art of espionage,' said Cole, between chewing on a chicken drumstick, 'is based around the three principles of lying, cheating, deceiving, and stealing.'

'That's four,' I said.

'See principle one,' said Cole. 'Lying should be as instinctive to you as breathing.'

'Does that mean I should never trust another British spy, even if we're not on mission?'

'Honestly,' said Cole, putting down his drumstick and picking up another, 'no. Regardless of your speciality, a spy should be essentially a loner. Team-mates, single partners etc, they all come and go. You establish their parameters of behaviour as quickly as you can, but you never truly trust anyone. It makes you far too vulnerable.'

'To both deception and having someone you trust killed? I mean, if you completely trust someone, they're liable to be a good friend at least.'

Cole spat out a sliver of bone. 'A good spy, by which I mean one who is good at their job, doesn't have friends. You will have degrees of trust in the people you work with. You may even objectively enjoy the company of some more than others. But you need to be prepared to put a bullet in the back of the head of anyone who betrays you. That's extremely hard to do if you like them – or I imagine it is. I wouldn't know.'

'So, my mother and Fitzroy were an oddity.'

Cole poured us both another glass of wine. We hadn't opened a bottle since the first day we arrived, but for some reason Cole had got one out tonight. 'It depends who you ask. They were highly successful, but they were only active together in the field for a comparatively short amount of time. Both of them worked separately, and from what I've gathered them being on a joint mission for any length of time was the exception rather than the rule. One might run back-up for the other, but they weren't often together.'

'Does that matter?'

'Certainly, familiarity can form the basis of an efficient working relationship, but too much familiarity tends to distract. If for no other reason than many agents become overly worried about their partners or aren't prepared to put the mission above their team-mates. In short, a close team will take more risks than an unfamiliar one that is far more likely to stay focused.'

'Were they like that?'

Cole shook his head slowly. 'They should have been. But no, they were always acutely mission-focused – or they were in the reports I read. However, their whole relationship was frowned on by most of the Service. Certainly, Fitzroy became less of a maverick. Whether that was a good or a bad thing, I wasn't, and I'm not, in a position to say.'

'Did you ever work with them?'

'I came onside a couple of times, but I wouldn't stay I worked with them as a team. You know Fitzroy trained me.'

'That was as a sniper, wasn't it?'

'A lot of it, yes. But there's more to being an assassin than that.

He trained me in – well, a lot of things you don't need to know about.'

I gave him a slight smile. 'Are you protecting me?'

Cole shook his head. 'I don't like competition. You could be as good a shot as him if you worked at it. Must run in the family.'

'Oh,' I countered, 'was my mother a good shot?'

He gave a chuckle at that. 'Your mother was more than passable. Of course, she put in a lot of extra training after his injury. I think she always felt responsible.'

'What?'

'Do the dishes, please, Hope. Tomorrow will be different. You'll find your orders left on the table in the morning.'

I nodded. Questions tumbled through my mind, but I knew he was unlikely to answer any of them. He stood up. 'Good, no questions. How I like it. You've done well.'

Then he walked out of the door without a backward glance. Whether he was staying here tonight or whether he was about to leave, I had no idea. I went over and started running water into the sink. I felt suddenly very alone. Which, I thought to myself is ridiculous. Wouldn't I rather be alone than with a potentially sociopathic assassin?

I still hadn't come up with a firm answer by the time I fell asleep in bed. But I had remembered to lock and bolt my door.

Chapter Thirty

Morning came with such a brilliant sun that it even penetrated my starry curtains. I stretched, rolled over, and saw by my small travelling clock that I had slept in until eleven a.m. No wonder the sun was bright. It was practically noon. Cole and I were usually out the door by six a.m. But then I had never overslept here. I had always awakened well before my alarm, and this morning I had slept through it. I checked the alarm and saw it no longer registered.

Feeling somewhat muzzy headed from for once getting enough sleep, I picked up my wash bag and opened my door. I was halfway along the corridor to the bathroom when I realised my door hadn't been locked.

After a hasty wash, I hurried back to my room, dressed, and ran downstairs to the kitchen. To my relief the big doors weren't fully open. I had no actual way of knowing if anyone else was in the building, and I certainly hadn't been told how to lock and leave, but at least the main door was shut.

In the kitchen I found a note from Cole.

Left supplies in fridge and pantry for breakfast and lunch. I'm told there's a car coming to get you early afternoon. Envelope below contains your orders on leaving my secondment. Me. PS you look very sweet when you sleep.

There was a slim chance this was from Fitzroy, who had miraculously dropped by. But he never signed himself Me. He

227

used an F or more rarely an E; for some reason Cole hadn't wanted to sign himself as C. The thought that Cole had been in my room when I slept – had probably even turned off my alarm – made me feel sick. The message was clear. He or another person suitably trained could get to me even here in what was meant to be a safe space for spies. Was Cole trying to reinforce his message that even spies on the same side could not be trusted? Was he saying *he* could not be trusted? Was he telling me he could get to me whenever he wanted in some sort of alpha dominance display? Or was he rather trying to say that despite being able to get to me at any time he would never hurt me – hence the 'sweet' comment. The whole notion of Cole ever using the word 'sweet' was making my brain hurt. I'd spent several days in close proximity to the man and apart from his obvious skills, I hadn't got a clue how his mind worked. Fitzroy had taught me how to gauge a person's character and personality from observation and interaction. He'd spent a lot of time on that with me – years, in fact. But Cole was someone – something – quite out of my experience. The only aspect of him I was certain about was that he would make a highly dangerous enemy.

In the fridge I found half a dozen eggs, bacon, and a wedge of soft cheese I didn't recognise. There were also some red grapes, half frozen. In the pantry I found tea, sugar, and bread. I decided to make myself a breakfast of scrambled eggs, bacon, and fried bread, reserving the remaining eggs to boil for lunch, together with the cheese sandwiches from the rest of the loaf, and the grapes. That way I could take it with me if my lift arrived before I felt hungry. If I'd learned one thing working for the army so far, it was you didn't leave food behind. If it was available, you ate it or took it with you. I made myself a cup of tea and rinsed out the flask in the cupboard. I filled it full of sweet tea for later. I preferred tea without milk anyway. I felt a qualm about removing the flask from the house, but for all I knew one of the other rooms was packed with stores. I hadn't been encouraged to explore.

I found I was extremely hungry, and it was an effort not to eat the packed lunch as I made it. I stuffed it away in my kit bag to prevent accidental ingestion and made breakfast. It was only as I sat down at the table to eat that I saw the envelope. It was the usual dirty sand colour that the Army used, and it had been well camouflaged by the table's patina. There was no name on the front. I opened it.

Stapleford. Return to base and await further instruction.

Base? Did it mean my flat or the secretarial pool? I crunched down on the fried bread that I'd managed to thoroughly imbue with bacon fat. My mood lightened. Whatever would happen would happen. Cole's efforts had rounded out my training. I knew I had more to learn, but I felt somewhat more competent as a field agent. He'd even let me try his rifle. I'd realised quickly that one's breathing was the key to a good distance shot – that and the right position. Cole had grudgingly admitted that I had some aptitude for sniping. When he said it I had felt a welling up of pride inside. Later, though, when I thought about it, I realised I didn't want to kill people from so far away. I didn't want to kill anyone, but if I had to, I had some absurd idea that I would feel better about it if I looked them in the face. Cole loved being an angel of death from afar, but I knew I wouldn't sleep well doing that kind of work.

I had barely cleaned and put away my plate when I heard the sound of the main doors opening and a man's voice called, 'Halloo!' I picked up my kit bag and went out into the hall. Both doors had been opened wide, and I could see a car standing outside. Three figures were backlit by the sun. Two men and one woman. One man and the woman, both dressed in unremarkable dark clothes, merely nodded to me and headed up the stairs.

The remaining man came into the foyer and up to me at the kitchen door. 'You're my passenger, I take it? I need to take a wiz. Make us a cup of tea, will you, love? Should have time to gulp it down before we set off.'

The driver wore civilian clothes, so I didn't bother objecting to making him tea. Although I thought it would have been unlikely that he'd have asked my godfather to do the same. As for my mother, she would have said something very cutting about his ancestry if he'd asked her.

After making the tea I chose to sit in the back of the car and wait. At least I didn't have to worry about locking up. When my driver came back, he proved not to be the chatty type. He sighed frequently as his car jolted along the forest track and threw me vaguely accusatory looks in the mirror. Cole had actually packed a book in my kit bag when we'd left London, Dorothy L Sayers' *Busman's Honeymoon.* It might have been some kind of cryptic message. I'd searched it thoroughly when I'd found it in my kit bag and it appeared to simply be my book. Now I brought it out and read it. I'd read it before, but the story quickly engaged me. I pulled out my lunch packet and ate as I read, doing my best to make it last. I assumed at some point I would be dropped at a station. However, we had cleared the forest and had been riding through the rolling English countryside for some time. I checked my watch. An hour and a half. I thought about asking the driver but decided against it.

I know Fitzroy would have watched the journey to work out where we had been. Even Bernie would have done that, but my sense of direction and place has never been good. All the signposts and names of places had been removed, so I didn't even both to try.

Before I finished my book, but none too soon for my tea-filled bladder, the driver drew up outside my London flat. I hopped out. He didn't offer any assistance with my bag, so with a small wave I turned my back on him and headed indoors, carrying it myself. Need made me head straight for the bathroom, but I registered change as I rushed in.

When the urgency had been dealt with, I came out and inspected my newly painted flat. It was distinctly smarter and not one of the old pieces of furniture remained. Everything had been replaced with something smart and modern. Against the ceiling roses and general architecture of the flat none of it looked right. But it was the kind of thing Bernie might have done. For all she talked about how she loved the quaintness of England, she didn't much like living among it.

In my bedroom I found even my bed and my own linen had been changed. Fortunately, my books had been left alone, and the few personal things I had brought with me were still there. Even the bathroom had been updated, with the plain white fixtures having been replaced with white ones scattered with forget-me-nots. The tiles had all been replaced too. It would have taken time.

I checked Bernie's room. It was likewise new. Her bed was neatly made, and her same jewellery case was still on the dresser with her brush and comb. Her wash bag was in the top drawer. It was completely dry. I checked her sponge and found that it had begun to shrivel from lack of use. She hadn't been here in a while. Or at least she hadn't spent the night here.

I looked around for a message from her and found nothing. But then the last time I'd seen her I promised to visit. She'd been whisked away by her fiancé, but it shouldn't have been beyond me to track her new telephone number down.

I checked the kitchen. The new cupboards sparkled but were empty. I washed my face, brushed my hair, and went out to buy a few supplies from our local grocer and my dinner from our local fish and chip shop, which didn't stint on the mushy peas. I awoke several times during the night, and twice went and checked the doors and windows. Everything was always still securely locked, and eventually I realised my feeling of unease stemmed from Bernie's absence.

I sat down to a solitary breakfast. Suddenly sitting opposite her empty chair brought up a tidal wave of emotion, and I barely prevented myself from ruining a decent meal with sobbing. I missed Bernie a lot.

I had been in the flat alone before, but her absences had always been temporary. This time I feared she wasn't coming back. From what little I had gleaned from her, her fiancé struck me as a controlling man. It might well be what she wanted. Someone who could cure the insecurity she had previously assuaged with alcohol and late-night partying. But Bernie had never been in someone's power before. She had felt confined by security at the Embassy, but this was another situation entirely.

Cedric hadn't asked to meet me. Bernie had made various excuses, but it seemed clear that he didn't want to. I was Bernie's best friend. Possibly her only real friend in London. She knew a lot of people, but none of her partying acquaintances knew her like I did. I tried to pretend that I was overestimating my importance to her. That stung, but it was better than the thought that her new husband intended to sequester her in his world and remove her from all she had known before. She had said Fitzroy has asked her if she was sure about her marriage. He'd apparently done it in spite of strong governmental support for the Anglo-American wedding. Bernie hadn't taken him seriously and I feared that was a very great mistake.

My macabre thoughts were disturbed by the sound of the letterbox fluttering. On the mat lay another of those sand-coloured envelopes. This one had my name and address typed neatly on it. I peered a little closer; whoever had typed it hit the 'S' and 'N' keys particularly hard. The first line was slightly off-kilter too. Maureen, the freckle-nosed girl with the red hair, who insisted on wearing pink lipstick and had a boy she was walking out with who worked in a local chemist's. I felt rather proud of myself for working this out. Unfortunately, I had no one to tell, and no one who would want to hear it.

I took the letter into the kitchen and used a butter knife to slit it open. Inside it said, *three by five under vitreous feline of awful fame*

I turned the paper over. There was nothing else. I sat down. Well, a vitreous feline was literally a glass cat. I hadn't a clue what the three by five might mean. I made another cup of tea and thought about it. I knew I was to be assigned elsewhere. Last night I'd repacked my kit bag with clean clothes and two fresh books. Presumably the cat knew where I was going. Could there be a message on its base? Except if it was glass it would be transparent. Why was it of awful fame? I was sure there had been famous cats or cats belonging to famous people, but I couldn't think of a single one. I turned the paper over again, and realised it was less bumpy than Maureen's usual work. There were only two keystrokes that seemed to have been hit particularly hard. I turned the letter backwards and forward. It was the V of vitreous and the A of awful. Of course, the Victoria and Albert Museum. The V and A had closed last year, but then due to public pressure had reopened in November. A lot of the stock had been hidden in secret places, but larger pieces remained. It was some time since I had been there, and no glass cat stood out in my memories, but maybe it had been brought out of storage to take the place of some sent-away valuable? As for the three by five, I would have to work out what that was when I was there.

I decided not to take my kit bag, but to leave it downstairs with the porter. I didn't know if this was some kind of test or if the message left for me by the cat was highly classified. Erring on the side of caution, I dressed myself like a young housewife and did my best to look as much like anyone else as possible. I didn't wear lipstick or mascara and I slipped Fitzroy's ring onto the ring finger of my left hand. That would deter any man from paying me attention. I really needed a small child or baby in a carriage to explain why such a normal, plain woman wasn't at her work or her home, but I didn't feel I was of sufficient rank to impound one – and if I had, I wouldn't have had the faintest idea how to control it.

I adopted a brisk no-nonsense walk and decided to try for a maiden aunt-in-training sort of girl. I sat on the bus making up more about myself. I didn't have a boyfriend and didn't want one. My father had been the bane of my mother's life. I thought all women were better off without men. If I had been born before the Great War I would have been a suffragette, though not one of

233

the violent ones. I would have written long letters to everyone. As it was I contented myself with writing to the editor of the *Times* about the morals of young people today, and the partying that they had taken up – outrageous with war on our doorstep. I had a white-haired cat called Maurice and I worried that perhaps it was unpatriotic to keep a cat when food shortages abounded. But, on the other hand, I couldn't bear to be parted with my only friend. I was thinking of looking for somewhere to rent in the country where Maurice would be of use as a ratter. I decided he was a large cat of unknown pedigree, and that I was odd. Not eccentric, but one of those women who turn up at jumble sales and buy things that no one else can see the point of. I was also at least five years older than I actually was. I decided to try for the beginnings of a slight stoop brought on by much reading in bad light. I reflected I should have blacked out some of my teeth.

I admit I was quite enjoying myself. I had just pressed the bell for the bus to stop, when I realised that I had come straight from my flat and had made no attempt to conceal this. If anyone was watching the flat – and from my previous encounter in the bathroom I had every reason to suspect they were – I had given them every opportunity to follow me. Oh, I didn't look like my normal self, but anyone doing surveillance on me and the flat would have checked up on the other occupants. If they suspected what I really was then the idea I might come out in disguise would already have struck them. And even if they had been sloppy enough not to do due diligence on the other inhabitants, merely observing the comings and goings would have shown them that my 'maiden aunt' had never gone into the flats.

Still, there was little I could do now except check my reflection in shop fronts and any convenient mirror. I wished I had at least brought an umbrella. The unyielding tweed skirt and jacket I had chosen were too inhibiting for any violent action on my part. There was nothing for it, I would have to lead any potential followers a long and merry dance, and hopefully lose them before heading to the museum. The problem was, I had no idea how time-critical the message was. What I needed was a few crowds to lose myself in – only London wasn't particularly obliging at this time of day, on a weekday, during a war.

I walked off in the opposite direction to the V and A without a plan. I knew better than to take two left turns in case any followers were working in pairs – and therefore walked straight into one. In normal circumstances I might have like to do this and ask said follower a few pertinent questions, but I didn't have the time, the back-up to clear the scene after me, or the mobility in the clothes I had chosen.

I saw a sweet shop and popped in to buy a paper bag of humbugs. I told the shopkeeper all about Maurice and my worries for him, but underneath I had remembered another reason to kick myself. Other than Cole, I didn't know if anyone else knew about my attack. The flat had been refurbished, after the intruder it had probably needed it. I'd been too out of it to notice. So, someone knew. But was that someone part of Cole's team, like the doctor, or was it someone Fitzroy worked with? In the typing pool I had quickly begun to realise that the war effort had been divided up into separate groups and committees, some of whom overlapped, and all of whom squabbled amongst themselves to get their hands on our very limited resources. I had no reason to think Fitzroy would know anything about what had happened. In normal times I was sure he would have kept his eye on me, but he had more than enough to occupy his mind.

Besides, Cole had planted those horrible seeds of doubt in my mind. If I knew what Cole's motivation in training me truly was, then maybe I would have a better idea as to whether he had been telling the truth. The expensive jewellery and the way my godfather and my mother had behaved together when they thought they were unobserved lent credence to his suggestion. I walked out of the shop muttering under my breath about my shopping list. I should have greyed my hair if I intended on being this batty.

I would have disregarded the idea of my mother being an adulteress completely if it wasn't for two things. My father adored her.

He was a gentle and unpossessive man. He had been an invalid for a long time, even before my birth, and while no child likes to think of these things about their parents, why had there only been one child? Had I been an accident caused by my godfather? Could my father be incapable of fathering a child due to his disabilities? All three of them had essentially come together to be my parents. Was this some kind of Bohemian-like arrangement? I had no doubt they all loved me, and also that they had all done their best by me. I could imagine the three of them agreeing to raise me in such a manner. Though considering how everyone kept telling me how bad-tempered and/or possessive Fitzroy was, this seemed very unlikely.

I turned a sharp right into a street I didn't know. I checked briefly in a shop window, then putting the humbugs in my pocket I went across the road to a baker's to see if they had any cakes in the window. My maiden aunt clearly had a sweet tooth. The ring was back on the chain around my neck. My head throbbed. How could I think such things of my parents? Of my mother? Damn Cole, damn him to hell. Why had he put these doubts in my head?

Was it to disturb me? Was it to do with this upcoming mission whatever it was? Part of a test? Or a deadly earnest attempt to throw me off my game.

I stared blindly into the window. What did I do? I took a breath. Of the three of them Fitzroy would be most likely to give me answers if I demanded them. But he was a professional liar. Did it matter? If the truth was the worst then knowing it would upset everything – possibly causing the very distress they had conspired to avoid. I should let it be and accept I was loved.

Crossing the street, I caught sight of a ladies' clothing store. It was risky. I walked past the shop, around the corner, then doubled back and darted in. When I exited, I was a smart young secretary in a saucily split skirt and loose jacket. All traces of the maiden aunt were gone, including the humbugs, which I'd donated along with a large tip to the shopkeeper not to mention what I had done. I told her a story about being followed by an old suitor I needed to avoid. She quite understood, being herself the image of my maiden aunt and with similar opinions about men.

I weaved my way back to the V and A. By the time I reached the entrance I was as happy as I could be that I was not being followed. I walked through the doors and felt a weight lift off me. All I had to do now was find this blasted cat.

And then my brain, my always calculating brain, raised the question: what if Fitzroy was my real father and Father never knew? What if my mother and Fitzroy had conspired between them to raise me as a Stapleford for my safety and my mother's reputation? That would certainly explain the extraordinary interest he had had in me as a child.

I shoved the horrid thought to the back of my mind. Whether or not it was true didn't matter now. What mattered was finding the cat.

Chapter Thirty-one

The V and A is a gracious building built towards the end of the last century. Much of the elegance had been obliterated by the piling of sandbags both inside and out. It reminded me of a debutante in her presentation dress who had been forced to wear Wellington boots; still lovely, but made ugly by circumstances. Many of the normal exhibits being absent, it felt like a new, peculiar place. All my faintly known landmarks had been spirited away.

I wandered up and down flights of steps, turning corners, following vaguely familiar routes and yet still losing where I was. Until it occurred to me it didn't matter where I was. I only needed to know where the cat was. After that I could simply follow the exit signs. So instead of trying to work out where I was in the building, I worked my way in, noting the location of exit signs. Even doing this it was more than an hour later, when I was thirsty, tired, and footsore, and I had almost decided this was some obscure test, that I found sitting in a large glass case a six-inch tall, multi-coloured, rather smug-looking cat.

The cabinet was set back in an alcove slightly off the floor's main concourse. This meant one could retreat and not be easily seen if one was careful. I had the sense to walk past the case and on to look at another exhibit. It could have been anything in front me. I wasn't seeing it at all, but I stood in a studied attitude while my mind raced.

I couldn't be sure if anyone was still following me. Fitzroy had told me that in a serious surveillance operation on home ground he might use up to a dozen people to follow an individual. Most would be on foot, but some would also take buses or cars. The most important point was not to let the mark know they were being followed, and in particular to never allow them to suspect a particular face. He'd been the one who mentioned how useful were women with baby carriages, who frequently loitered unhindered around urban areas.

The only thing I could do was wait until the coast was completely clear and hope whatever I discovered was small enough to fit in my pocket. Now, I had to work out what three by five meant. I wandered around the gallery inspecting exhibits. Twenty minutes later the concourse was clear enough for me to enter the alcove with the cat without being seen. I darted in.

The plaque said it was from an island off Venice called Murano and an excellent example of handmade glass. It was by Maestri Vetrai Muranesi Cappellin. I couldn't imagine it sitting in anyone's home. The colours fairly vibrated, and all of them clashed. Perhaps that was what made it art?

I quickly ascertained the case around the cat was secure. I wouldn't be able to open it without smashing it. The pedestal below the case appeared to be completely smooth. It didn't make sense that I needed to get the cat. It would be far too noisy. Besides, even with the awful colours, the thing was transparent. If there had been a message in it or under it I would have seen it.

I heard voices in the corridor. I tucked myself back into the alcove. My stomach gurgled. It was a long time since breakfast and I always had a hearty appetite. I put my hands over my middle in a hope that would extinguish the noise. It didn't.

Fortunately, it proved to be a couple walking by. From the bits of the conversation I overheard they seemed far too wrapped up in each other to be interested in anyone else. Once they had passed, I began to examine the case once more. Could this all be some vengeful trick by Bernie for neglecting her for a week when she was injured? I couldn't see – and then I felt it. The back of the pedestal was made of small bricks. In a flash I knew what three by five meant. Reaching around the back of the case and using my fingers, as I couldn't see what was there, I counted three rows down and five across. When I reach the fifth small brick, I pushed it. Nothing. I pulled it. Nothing.

It wasn't until I had tried from both sides, counting the rows up and down, and become increasingly dusty, sweaty, and crumpled, that I found the loose brick. It wasn't even a brick, more of a tile, and it came away in my hand. By now my fingers were stiff, but I managed not to drop it. Bringing the tile out I found a train ticket tacked to the inside of it. I peeled it off. The train left in thirty-five minutes. I put it in my pocket. Then with a huge effort of will I carefully replaced the tile. With shaking hands, I took out my compact and, using the mirror, checked to see how busy the concourse was. There were a few people standing idly by. I didn't recognise any of them, and I didn't have time to wait. Taking a deep breath I emerged carefully from the alcove and walked smartly to the nearest exit. Every bone in my body shouted at me to run, but I knew that being seen running from the museum would draw the eye of every guard, and one might even take me for a thief.

I didn't have the time to be stealthy, so I took the quick and dirty solution and hailed a cab as soon as I left the museum. I got the taxi to wait while I fetched my kit bag, and then, waving a five-pound note in the driver's face, I told him it was his if I made my train.

So keen was he to win the prize that not only did three cyclists fall off their bicycles as we passed, but we narrowly avoided squashing a cat. When we arrived at the station the train was on the verge of leaving. My driver gallantly opened a door and threw the kit bag in after me, and I passed him the note from out of the window. He had to run alongside the train to get it and lost his cap in the process. However, it was a particularly nasty cap and he would now be able to buy himself a much nicer one.

I slid open the door to an empty compartment, dragging my kit bag behind me, and slumped onto a seat. I'd barely made contact with the upholstery when the guard appeared.

'This is a first-class carriage, miss.'

I handed him my ticket. 'I'll pay the extra,' I said. 'I'll pay even more if you can find me a cup of tea.'

'For the right price, miss. I may even be able to find you a biscuit,' said that fine fellow.

He did me proud, even producing some small cucumber sandwiches. I paid him handsomely and he left me alone after that. I knew I was heading into the countryside. The destination on the ticket was in Sussex, but otherwise the name meant nothing to me. I arranged my kit bag on the seat next to me, tucked my feet up, and fell asleep.

I awoke to the guard tapping at the door. 'Your stop is in fifteen minutes, miss. I thought you might fancy a last cup before you got off.' He set a cup of tea on the ledge by the window.

I thanked him nicely, tipped him, then once he had left rubbed the sleep from my eyes and did the best I could to straighten my hair without a mirror or easy access to a brush. It was at the bottom of the kit bag with my other wash things. I drank my tea and looked out the window. Fields, hedges, trees, and cows. Where on earth was I being sent?

I got off the train and refused the porter. I knew I made an odd sight in my city clothes, carrying an Army bag. Hopefully it would help whoever was directing me to the next phase pick me out. Only two other people got off the train. One was an elderly man who used a walking cane and the other a young man in a naval cadet's uniform. I didn't think it likely either of them would be going to the same place as me, so I hung back. For some unknown reason Fitzroy always tried to avoid working with the Navy. The old man limped his way off the platform. The train pulled out, sending a hot gust of air tugging at my skirt, and then everything was quiet. Insects buzzed, and although it was by now late afternoon the platform still had that hot tarry smell.

I made my way out. It was occurring to me that if I had taken my rightful seat, I might have found further instructions hidden on the train. There was nothing I could do about that now. I passed the little ticket office. The shutter was down. I walked on and came out into a gravelly area that served as the car park. There, leaning on a car, was the officer who had given me tea at the Ritz. This was so unexpected that I stopped in my tracks and stared. He gave me a friendly wave. 'Hello. Glad you made it, Hope. I don't normally pick up recruits, but seeing as I was down here anyway, I thought we might have a quick word. Throw your kit bag in the back and hop in. If you can in that skirt. Hop, that is.' His eyes twinkled with mischief.

Refreshed from my sleep on the train and now very much awake, I did as he asked, quickly. He started the car and drove off smoothly, just slightly on the wrong side of too fast. 'I wouldn't normally have arrived dressed like this . . .' I began.

'Oh, I know why,' he said. 'It wasn't a bad attempt at recovery after leading your tail straight from your flat.'

'So it was a test?'

'Think of it more of an initiation,' he said. 'Not everyone works out the clue or makes the train in time. But then we don't want everyone. We want the quick-witted and adaptive types.' He paused to negotiate a cow in the lane. He slapped the side of the animal as we drove past. 'Fine beast. You were brought up in the country, weren't you?'

'The Fens.'

'Ah, soggy countryside. Still, I assume you know your way around outdoors? Build a fire, find a shelter, catch your dinner and cook it? That sort of thing?'

'Yes, sir,' I said. The more time I spent in this man's company the clearer it became that he was used to command. He had the clipped accent of the well-polished and -heeled gentry, and a casual carelessness that showed he assumed most things would go his way, given time and effort. He also seemed relentlessly cheery, which I found refreshing after the long faces of the doomsayers in

London. I wouldn't be so cruel as to say he enjoyed war, but he delighted in being a soldier. The more I saw of him the more I noticed his cheeky charisma. I imagined that off duty he would always be game for a laugh. Unfortunately, our ranks were too disparate for it to be likely I would ever see him let his hair down.

'Well, that's good. You're late to training, but that couldn't be avoided. However, the thing is, I wanted to say it straight to you that despite this training, you won't be deployed,' he said casually.

'Sir?'

'Yes, I can see you thinking, "why would the silly so-and-so put me through this if I wasn't going to be utilised?". Well, frankly, I damn well hope none of you will be deployed. But if the auxis are, I'm not having women among them. I realise that sounds unreasonable to modern ears, but that's the way it is. It simply wouldn't work. So, you're here in case we go on to plan B – which I am very much hoping we will. In that case I'd be more than happy to employ both men and women for the job, but I need a bit of proof for the higher-ups that women can stomach it. That's where you come in. I'm hoping you'll be able to give me a bit of ammunition in that area.' He turned briefly to grin at me, 'I'm sure that's all as clear as mud, but it will make sense, I promise you. I wanted to tell you myself, so you'd know it's no slight that you won't pass to deployment. If it comes to that you're due to join up with another team.'

'Who are they, sir?'

'Can't tell you, I'm afraid. Typical Army. You have to trust the people above you. Though I shouldn't worry. The lot you're being put with are a good show. And if it doesn't work out you can always come and join my plan B. Provided, that is, you put on a decent show while you're here.'

'I'll do my best, sir,'

'Yes, well, that's all you can say, isn't it? Seeing as you haven't a clue what you're going into. Does that bother you?'

'Not as much as it should,' I said. 'I've been taught that

recognisance is next to godliness and I do appreciate its value. But today, not having a clue what was going to happen next . . .'

'Has been exciting?'

I nodded. 'Although I haven't had reason to think I was in any danger – or not much reason. That makes a big difference.'

The officer nodded. 'Exactly, it's all fun and games until the shooting starts. Still, that's no reason to lose your sense of adventure, is it?'

'Indeed not, sir.'

He turned the car through a gap in the hedge. At the end of a long track I saw a typical Elizabethan country house. 'Don't worry, I won't make you walk the whole way. About halfway up do?'

He actually took me to within a hundred yards of the house before he stopped the car. 'Hop out now. I want to be away before someone corners me.' He passed over my kit bag. 'Oh, and Hope, travelling first class is never discreet. Especially not when you're wearing a hat like that.' Before I could think of a suitable answer, he had turned the vehicle quickly in a shower of dust and driven off. It was only as I saw the car disappear through the gate I wondered if I should have saluted him. I wasn't entirely sure I could do it without feeling, and looking, silly. Naturally enough, Fitzroy, who hated all protocol, hadn't thought to tell me what to do about it before signing me into whatever Army division he had.

The afternoon was finally sliding into early evening. My stomach grumbled again. I slung my kit bag over my shoulder and started to walk up the drive. I saw sheep in fields to the left of the house. Someone had been mowing and I could smell the fresh tang of newly cut grass. The gravel of the drive made little puffs of dust under my feet. The last warm gasp of the day did its best to warm my back as I walked up to the house. Without the kit bag and at another time, I could have imagined myself walking to be received by a gracious host who might say, 'It's a bit late for tea, scones, and jam, but seeing as it's you why don't I have Cook send up a little something?' Then we'd settle down in the doubtless fine library and discuss books both old and new until the bell rang for us to go and dress for dinner.

This whole romantic image (and anything with jammy scones and books featuring in it I could see as romantic) broke apart as a man in plain khaki flew out of the main door and down the main steps. I couldn't see any insignia on him, but nor could I see any weapons. Clearly, he was in a terrible hurry. However, he had a strangely loping, staggering gait, which suggested that he had some kind of injury or handicap. I stepped over to the side of the drive, even though it was wide enough for a car and a half, to signal I had no intention of getting in his way.

To my surprise he lolloped straight up to me. Before I could see his face properly, I realised who it was.

'Harvey!'

'Bloody 'ell, Hope,' said my only convicted friend. 'What the 'ell you doin' 'ere?'

Chapter Thirty-two

I smiled up at him. 'I'm so pleased to see you,' I said. 'I didn't know how to get in touch with you after the incident at my flat, and before I could even try life got rather busy. So busy in fact I hardly know where or when I'm at.'

Harvey didn't return my smile. He frowned. 'I think there musta been a mix-up. It's only men 'ere. And some of them are pretty rough types too. Bernie said you were workin' in a typing pool. How did you get here?'

'I had to solve a puzzle, then catch a train, and a very nice officer picked me up at the station and drove me here. He said he'd been in already today and wouldn't put you lot out by coming back.'

Harvey's eyebrows shot up to his hairline. 'HE gave you a lift? Well, I suppose it has to be all right then. Course, 'e's not in charge proper, but if anyone would know what was going on, 'e would.'

'He gave me tea at the Ritz,' I said, trying to further strengthen my credentials. All that imagining of scones had awoken my appetite. I could already feel my stomach beginning its warm-up to a really good growl. 'Shall we go up?'

I started walking up the drive. Harvey followed. Moving slower, I could see he dragged his right leg slightly. The bullet he'd taken for Bernie had hit his right hip. He hadn't known then I was using him as an asset. He thought he'd been doing everything out of the goodness of his heart, and I suppose in a way, he had. He certainly hadn't been paid.

'So who is here?' I said. 'I don't know anything.'

Harvey scratched his chin. 'I don't know what to tell you, Hope. I had to sign the Official Secrets Act to be 'ere – oh, damn, I'm not meant to tell you that.'

'It's fine,' I said. 'I've signed it too.'

'I suppose I shouldn't be surprised. That godfather of yours is as odd a cove as I've ever met. Shifty. I never did quite get what 'e did. Or what you did for 'im. But now is not the time to ask. Besides, I'm supposed to be grateful.' He harrumphed.

'Is your leg very painful?'

'Actually, no,' said Harvey. 'Most of the time it's fine. Aches when it rains, which is odd, and of course I look like a clown when I try to run, but then the other fellows here all have their own issues. Wally Gibbs is deaf, and yet his team work together like a dream. Silent as the grave – as you'd expect.'

'So, what is this place?'

'It's a training site for the auxis.' I must have looked blank. 'The Auxiliary Units? No? Damn stupid name. Doesn't mean anything, but then we're not supposed to exist.'

'You're secret agents?'

'If only,' said Harvey. 'Workin' for the Secret Intelligence sounds exciting. This stuff . . . I suppose if you find terrifying exciting . . . anyway, why are you here? Clerical reports?'

'No, I'm to join you.'

'But you're a girl.'

'I had noticed.'

We had reached the bottom of the steps to the house now, and a quenching cup of tea within dangled tantalisingly in my imagination. Harvey stopped, crossed his arms, and barred my way.

'Well, I ain't letting you in. You know what our motto is? "To perish in the common ruin rather than to fail or falter in our duty".'

'What? I don't understand.'

'We're the last bastion, Hope.'

I was still trying to work out if he meant 'hope' as my name or

247

as a quality when he said, 'You do know we're about to be invaded, don't you?'

'No,' I said, shaking my head. 'I would have heard.'

'Really? You 'ave a telephone line to German High Command?'

No, I thought, but I've come straight from working with one of the SIS's head assassins, and I think he might have mentioned it. Besides, I'd have expected Fitzroy to have been in contact. This would have been what they had been talking about when they had mentioned getting me out of the country. Not that I would go, of course.

'Someone would have mentioned it,' I said firmly. 'Besides, if we were about to be invaded, I doubt they would still be training people to fight.'

'We are meant to disrupt the invasion,' said Harvey. 'Guerrilla tactics and the like. We're not expected to survive.'

'Oh,' I said, understanding dawning. 'That's why you're supposed to be grateful to Fitzroy. He's put you here rather than going to jail. Yes, I suppose several years' incarceration as opposed to a short-lived suicide mission doesn't sound an especially good swap.'

Harvey shook his head. 'I can't tell if you're barking mad or know something I don't. Hope, those bastards are lined up on the other side of the Channel. They're waiting to invade. They've supposedly got gas boats they're going to launch at the south coast.'

'I don't think there is any need for language like that,' I said. 'We are British. I'm no scientist, but the gas boat idea sounds very silly. If the wind was blowing the wrong way, they'd kill themselves.'

'Yes, well, there is that,' admittedly Harvey. 'But you're still not coming in.'

I thought about dodging round him, but I didn't feel up to a tussle. 'Harvey, if it helps, I am being sent here as an experiment to see how women might fare in the training. That officer who interviewed me made it quite clear I was not to be deployed. Which also, I think, rather adds to the idea of us not being invaded in the next week at least. And right now, you're probably disobeying several orders, and even if this is a more, er, unusual unit than normal, I'm fairly sure you can still get shot for disobeying orders.'

With reluctance in every line of his body, Harvey moved aside to let me up the steps. As I passed him, he said, 'I'd forgotten how much of a beast you could be, Hope.'

That stung. I thought we had always parted on good terms. I liked Harvey. I'd thought he liked me. Maybe he thought I should have made more of an effort to keep in touch. Bernie and he had. But it wasn't as if I'd been on holiday on the Riviera.

The main door was open and led into a reasonably sized hall. One of those typical Elizabethan ones. Dark panelling along all the walls, except for the window above the stairs that wound up. This was stained glass and several stories high. The effect was somewhat ruined by someone having taped crosses all over it to prevent flying shattered glass. I thought it was rather a shame. Obviously, an old piece of glass. I stood, looking up, while I waited for Harvey to catch up. Steps seemed to be difficult with his leg.

'Couldn't they have removed it and replaced it with clear glass for the duration?' I said, hearing Harvey finally approach behind me.

'I rather think people have other things on their mind at the moment, Miss Stapleford,' said a man's voice. I turned on the spot to see a middle-aged man of average height, slim, and with slightly over-long blond hair, in plain unmarked khaki. He had a pleasant enough face and might have been thought handsome if it wasn't for the scowl he wore. 'I'd been told you were the best candidate for the boss's experiment, but it seems you cannot even watch your own back.'

I bowed my head slightly. 'Yes, I apologise. Rookie error,' I said. 'Thinking I was in a secure site, but the door's wide open and we're close to the coast.' His frown deepened. 'No, I don't know where I am,' I continued, 'but I can smell the sea.'

'We don't use ranks here, but I am one of your instructors. My name is Hugh, but you will call me "sir". You will be referred to by your surname like the rest of the trainees, Stapleford. Do you have a problem with that?'

'No, sir.'

'Good. Now, we've been told to treat you exactly as we would treat one of the men, but I think they would be even more uncomfortable than you if I barracked you in with them. As you are the only woman you are receiving the luxury of being on the instructors' corridor. I trust you will not abuse that privilege?'

'No, sir.'

'Up the stairs to the first floor. Take the corridor immediately to your left. Your door has been left open and there is a uniform on your bed. Please change and come out to the grounds at the back of the building. As fast as you can.'

'Shall I help her with her kit bag, sir?' asked Harvey, who had finally arrived.

'Did anyone help you with yours, Cooper?'

'No, sir.'

'Then report back to Aubrey now!'

Harvey left quickly.

'You noticed we did not salute?' said Hugh.

I nodded.

'We do our best to preserve the discipline of the Army here, but most of the men are volunteers. Men who have somehow not been passed fit for duty. What about you?'

'I'm Army, sir.'

He raised an eyebrow, still managing to look stern, but at least he wasn't scowling. 'Clerical, isn't it? Hardly Army.'

'I'm a little more than that, sir,' I said, trying to keep calm under his scrutiny. 'I will do my best to exceed your expectations.'

He nodded and I trotted up the stairs. (The kit bag was too big to let me go faster. It wasn't much shorter than me.) Well, that won't be hard, I thought. Clearly, the man had a low opinion of the abilities of women. I determined to show him a thing or two.

I found my room easily enough. It had a proper bed, towels, a basin, a chair for clothes, a wash stand, and a rather pretty bed-cover and matching curtains. I wondered if this was the reason none of the other instructors had taken this room. There was even a small vase on the windowsill with bluebells in it. This rather cheered me up. It suggested there was a cleaning staff, and we wouldn't have to do the drudgery ourselves. I supposed if Harvey was right they wouldn't want their recruits to spend time on cleaning. Unless they learned how to defend themselves with mops. I considered the length of a mop, and how the wetted end might improve it, or whether it would be too unstable.

I got into my uniform. It was a bit of a struggle. I tied my hair back and regarded myself in the mirror over the sink. It didn't actually gape, but it was stretched tight over my bosom. At least the trousers weren't too long, and the waistband was snug but not painful. I stood away from the mirror and turned this way and that. An Army uniform is meant to be smart, but not meant to enhance one's female charms. Even I could see I looked rather too feminine in this. For the first time I could see what people said when they remarked on the resemblance to my mother. I sighed. I finally looked a bit pretty, and I was going to get into trouble for it. I washed my face to eradicate any last traces of make-up. Although, I confess, I did put a tiny, tiny bit of mascara back on. It had to be Bernie's influence, but I hated my lashes bare. I had to find a chance to corner Harvey and see if he had any more recent news about Bernie.

Elizabethan houses are generally laid out on the same lines, so after descending to the ground floor, I found my way out into the grounds easily enough. Immediately I heard the sound of stutter-ing gunfire. Not some kind of automatic weapon, more like a handgun that was being fired at irregular intervals. Weapons training. At least I should be all right with that after spending time with Cole, I reasoned.

As I came closer, I saw thirteen men, including Harvey, stand-ing behind some hay bales. Two were standing further forward.

One of them was firing in the erratic, annoying way. This had to be his second round. As I grew closer, I noticed that each time he fired his upper body flinched. But then I rather lost all interest in him. The instructor, Aubrey, was quite the most handsome man I had ever seen. Tall, dark-haired, early forties at the most, with broad shoulders, and as I was shortly to discover, the bluest eyes. He calmly reminded his student to aim, breathe, and squeeze the trigger. 'You'll have a chance at moving targets later, West. This is to gain you familiarity with the gun. It won't bite you, but before I let you loose in the forest I need to see you can handle it.'

I waited a few paces behind them and on the instructor's peripheral vision, while the unfortunate West continued his stuttering volley.

Aubrey squinted at the human-shaped target resting, I estimated, about twenty-five yards away. He took the gun away before slapping West on the back. 'Well done, old chap. You've hit the target. Won't be long before we have shooting the wings off flies.' There was a good-natured chuckle from the rest of the group. 'Cooper, go out and set up a fresh target for me.'

Then he turned to face me. 'Stapleford, your coming has been long anticipated.' The laugh this time from the group was less friendly. 'I understand you had some urgent business to attend to. But then I suppose filing won't do itself.'

What a shame, I thought, that such a good-looking man is an utter prat. I waited for him to tell me what he wanted me to do.

'I'd say the boys could all do with a good cuppa, but I've been told I'm to treat you like the men.'

I continued to wait for him to get either to a punchline or a point.

'So, what do you think of shooting, hmm? Do guns frighten you?'

'I'm not fond of having them pointed at me, sir,'

He checked the chambers of the gun were clear. 'Right, come here and hold it.' He winked at his audience behind my back. I could tell from their reaction. I took the gun from him. It was an Enfield 3 MkI. I weighed it in my hand and checked the sights, keeping the barrel pointed forward and at the ground.

'Shall I load it for you, Stapleford?' The query seemed genuine enough.

'I can manage, sir,' I said.

'I think for all our sakes I'll do it the first time.' He took the gun from me, loaded it, and handed it back. 'Just aim for anywhere on the target. If you hit it on your first time, you'll be doing better than this lot.' Now I was holding a live weapon, the mocking tone had vanished from his voice. Obviously, he had some sense.

'Free to fire?' I asked.

'Go right ahead, Stapleford.' I noticed he didn't step back but was clearly watching to see if I dropped the gun or swung round with it loaded.

'Two chest shots, one head,' I said. I stilled my mind as Cole had taught me, quickly but totally. Nothing existed but the target. I fired three times. Hitting exactly where I intended.

Aubrey stepped forward. 'I admire your confidence, but better luck next time.'

'I hit the target exactly where I intended, sir.' I didn't add, which you would have seen if you'd watched while I was shooting. 'Would you like me to do it again?'

He shrugged. 'Go for it. We'll get Cooper to bring us the target.'

I repeated the sequence. I would have liked to put the bullets through the same holes, and at this distance I probably could have done, but there's a difference between proving a point and making yourself loathed. When I had finished, I checked the gun and handed it back to him empty.

Once he had it, Aubrey nodded to Harvey to get the target. Harvey loped off with his odd stride. I wondered if he'd upset Aubrey somehow, or if he was being treated like anyone else. I waited patiently, taking the opportunity to look around at the grounds. Harvey returned with the proof that at this distance I could shoot where I said I would.

'Well, I'm blowed,' said Aubrey. 'I take it you've shot before?'

'My uncle taught me,' I lied. 'I grew up in the country.'

'I suppose you can fish, trap animals, and cook over a camp fire?'

'I'd use a covered oven in the earth, so as not to make smoke, but otherwise, yes, sir.'

'How charming,' said Aubrey. 'It looks like you won't wash out on your first day at least. Right, men, twice round the field, sixty sit-ups, and in for dinner. At twenty hundred hours you'll be having your first briefing on basic espionage skills that might be of use to you, codes and ciphers, dead letter boxes, tailing a mark. That sort of thing. Fergus will be leading the session.'

As one the men staggered to their feet and jogged off to the side of the field. Keeping my sigh internal I followed them. Today had been a wearing day, and while I hadn't been up at my normal pre-dawn hours, I had been hoping for a cup of tea and a slice of something. Ideally cake, but I would have taken bread and butter at a pinch. I was tired and hungry, but dinner was after this. Dinner presumably being made for hearty men's appetites. Something nourishing, full of butter and fat, with a bit of meat and a scrap of vegetable on the side, was my bet. I was more than happy with that.

A couple of the men sprinted off. I didn't. Aubrey wouldn't expect me to cope well with this, and I expected to suffer at the sit-ups, but I knew I needed to make an effort. I had hoped he might have cut my requirements in half, but as it turned out Aubrey tagged on at the back. He ran in an odd way that reminded me of Harvey's gait. Maybe he'd had a similar injury. He was around the right age to have gone into the Great War at the end. I ran behind them, but on the second time round my stomach was rumbling loudly and I picked up the pace. I got close enough that I could hear Harvey saying, 'She's all right, sir. Can handle herself. A damn sight brighter than me. Not that I think she should be in the auxis.'

254

'She's an excellent shot, but I agree with you, Cooper. What you're training for isn't a job for women.'

'She said they won't be deploying her.'

'Surprised she knows that, but yes, wouldn't be the thing at all. Can't ask a woman to do what we're asking you chaps to do.'

'What about you, sir?'

'What about me? Do you mean will I be hiding in a bunker somewhere?'

'I didn't mean it like that, sir.'

'I know, Cooper. Just my dark sense of humour. No, all the instructors are expected to go out in a blaze of glory. Don't know where we're being sent or what we'll be doing, but none of us are getting out of this alive.'

'Funny to think that, sir. I don't mean I'm not willing and all that. But can't get my head round this has been the last summer I'll see.'

Aubrey slapped him on the back. 'Never say die, that's my motto. You never know, we might all come out of this thing yet.'

'It's not likely though, is it, sir?'

'I'm afraid not, Cooper.'

I put on a burst of speed to overtake them. I'd heard quite enough to upset my appetite.

Chapter Thirty-three

Times might be hard but two hunks of sweet apple pie and custard for pudding inclined me to being an optimist.

The canteen had been set up in what must once, centuries ago, have been some kind of audience chamber. It had high wooden ceilings, tapestries, and panelling. The windows were long, thin, came in stained glass pairs, and let in little light. However, someone had strung up a makeshift spiderweb of cabling across the ceiling and brought electric light into the room. The bare bulbs against the Elizabethan setting with a couple of refectory tables and benches looked wrong, but at least we would see what we were eating. The instructors weren't present. Instead the men each took a tray, crockery, and cutlery from a stand near the door and then progressed down a series of metal trays of food. I can't say it was beautifully presented, but there was a generous amount and it tasted good.

I took a seat at the end of one of the benches. Some of the others had got there before me, and I let them be. If anyone wanted to come and join me, I wouldn't complain, but as far as I was concerned, I was still getting the lie of the land.

Several people had been at pains to tell me I was a prototype. Home-spun guerrilla of the female persuasion? I wasn't buying it. It was all too neat. Cole trains me to shoot just before I come to be assessed here. Either someone was loading the dice in the furthering of women's rights, or I was here for another reason. But what?

One thing I knew. I was not to get distracted trying to prove a woman was as good as any man at warfare. Was she, I wondered. I suppose it depended on how you measured it. I immediately started to wonder how my mother would match up to the modern-day soldier. She'd been outstanding in her day, apparently, but that was Fitzroy talking. He was biased. How biased I didn't know. I'd almost decided Cole was wrong about him and my mother – not that I thought Cole was necessarily lying, rather I thought Fitzroy might have lied to him – oh, damn it all! It was depressing and distracting. I did my best to push the whole ruddy issue from my mind.

'Right, Hope, budge up. This is my lot.' Harvey sat down beside me.

'Hello,' I said.

'This is Colin West. He's the one you saw getting to terms with his shooting,' said Harvey, indicating a man with a brown toothbrush of a moustache, and a weaselly face. 'But for sneaking, setting snares, and a bit of light burglary, there's no one better. Makes the best damn rabbit pie in England. Even catches his own rabbits.

West gave me a small smile, revealing yellow tobacco-stained teeth.

'And the other one is Dean Fordham. Dean's our brainbox. Anything electronic, wireless or explosive, he's the one.'

Although no older than Harvey or I, Fordham was already going bald. He wore round spectacles and looked like an old man in training. He gave me a slight nod, cocking his head on one side as if curious to see what I actually was. Rather unkindly, I imagined he hadn't had much to do with women before now. Except his mother. I imagined he wrote to her every night. He probably also drank cocoa.

'So, what are you?' I asked Harvey.

'I'm the gaffer,' said Harvey. 'Each team has to have one to co-ordinate things and, well, make difficult choices when it comes to, er . . . things.'

I nodded, keeping a serious expression on my face as if I knew what he was talking about.

'We thought we'd scoop you up to join us. Not sure 'ow you'd get on with some of the other fellows. And I could vouch for you to these two. We're the Owls. We're going to be specialising in night manoeuvres. Although we have to learn the other stuff too, obviously.'

'You're not going to be doing this for real, are you?' said Fordham suddenly, and very quickly.

'Are you worried working with me will spoil your team dynamics when this has to be done for real?' I said.

Fordham's eyes opened a bit wider. He nodded again.

'Oh come on, Fordham,' said Harvey. 'That's not cricket. We talked about this.'

'I didn't say anything,' said Fordham. 'I only answered truthfully. You remember what Hugh was saying about truth among fellows?'

I rather wanted to know what Hugh had said, but that had to wait. I suspected Hugh might be the one I had first met. He'd certainly been stuffy enough to talk about 'truth among fellows'.

'Look, chaps, I say it's up to you. Harvey said to me that invasion is imminent.' All three of them ducked their heads and made a shushing gesture. 'My point is, if it happens when I'm here then I'm ready to go all in. I'm not asking for any quarter because I'm female. I think it's a bit rich being told I can't do my bit. What am I meant to do, fix my hair and run around screaming? I can do better than that. Give me a gun and—'

'Hush,' said Fordham. 'I get the point. If it happens, you're on board. I'm happy with that. Anyone who can shoot like you has got to give us an edge.'

'I can use a sniper rifle too,' I said. 'I'm not bad.'

'Your uncle again?' said Harvey.

'Souvenir from the Great War,' I said. 'Used it to take out rabbits and voles.'

'Can't leave much of them,' said West.

'It doesn't,' I said. 'Uncle wanted them dead. He didn't care about eating them.'

West shook his head. 'Wasteful. Nob, is he?'

'Was,' I lied.

'Sorry,' said West. 'But some of us live off 'em rabbits.'

I nodded and made no further comment.

'Yeah, you're all right with me,' said West. 'As long as *I* get to trap our supper.'

'Hang on,' said Harvey. 'I'm not happy.'

'Harvey, if they come we're all in danger. I'd much rather stand in front of a group of mothers and kids fleeing away from the Nazis than hide behind them. You know me.'

'Damn it,' said Harvey. 'I don't like this.'

'Cooper, me old mate,' said West, 'I don't think any of us are meant to like this. Be a bit odd if we did. Now, eat yer food afore it gets cold.'

'I don't think you need to get to know everyone,' said Fordham, 'but it may help to know the other gaffers. Gilbert Eddington, the one at the far corner of the table. He's a bit of a snob. We're meant to be outwith class and rank, but everyone in his team speaks with plums in their mouths. I don't generally have a problem with the upper classes, but there are some . . . well, you know.'

'He's a right—' West swore particularly crudely. I ignored him.

'On the far table near the window, with the red beard, is Dominic Sykes. Answers to Dom. Says he'll shave just before we set off. It's some kind of personal ritual for him. Readying the inner and outer man.'

West said something equally foul and deprecating of Dom, but showed the width of his vocabulary by using another choice term.

'Dom's lot are good with explosives. We call them the BBs – short for Boom Boys. Then there's Wally Gibbs and his team. Deaf to a man, they are. But they move as silent as ghosts. They want to specialise in silent killing and demoralisation of the enemy. We're calling 'em Ghosts.'

'What do you call Eddington's lot?' I asked.

259

West made several equally creative and lewd suggestions.

'I don't think they have a name. Rest of us call them the Prigs.' said Fordham. His voice had taken on a new, confident tone speaking about the others.

'Were you a schoolmaster?' I asked.

Fordham nodded. 'Maths and general science at a minor boy's prep. Rather enjoyed it, until . . . well, that's all over now.'

'What are the instructors like?' I asked.

'Fairly decent bunch,' said Harvey. 'Aubrey's the best of them. He had his left leg below the knee amputated. It was at the end of the Great War. Bloody unlucky. But he doesn't let it hold him back. They wouldn't let him sign up for the BEF, but he'll be out there with us one way or another.'

I could tell from Harvey's tone that Aubrey had become something of a hero to him, so I didn't comment on the man's anti-female jibes. But then, why should I think any of the other instructors, or any of the other men, would be any different. The Owls – why the Owls? – were a crew of misfits. Harvey, their gaffer, an ex-con only here to prevent a term in jail. I thought that might apply to the others as well. West was clearly a poacher and Fordham had that faint aura about him of a man who wasn't interested in women in the usual way. I wasn't entirely sure, but if I watched how he unconsciously reacted to Aubrey next time they were in the same space, I would be able to tell.

'Right then, chaps. We're not on mess tonight, so bung your stuff on the table and we're off. I want to get Fordham a decent seat. Last time he couldn't make out all the diagrams, and that simply won't do when he's the one who ends up explaining it all to us afterwards!'

The table by the door where we had collected our crockery was now where we placed the dirty dishes. There was a slops bin underneath the table for scrapings. 'They've got pigs,' said Fordham. 'And I hear one of them is almost ready for eating.' He said this with a suppressed excitement that was somehow both endearing and a tad creepy.

260

Harvey led us off towards the evening lecture. When he wasn't running, he was able to walk fast. It wasn't long before we broke out ahead together. 'So, what do you think?' he whispered.

'Of what?'

'Everything!'

'I don't know anything,' I said, sounding even to my own ears rather pitiful. 'I can hardly be expected to comment on everything.'

Harvey stared at me.

'I like being the Owls,' I said. 'It sounds kind of predatory and ominous.'

Harvey gave a little shrug. 'We chose our code name first. West likes owls.'

'He's a poacher, isn't he? I've never met a gamekeeper who couldn't shoot.'

'We don't talk about anyone's past. But yes, a lot of them choose this rather than going to jail. I mean, if we're invaded, the talk is, they simply round up the men from the prisons and shoot them. This lets us get a bit of our own back first.'

'You're all on a suicide mission.' I said it bluntly, without any question in my voice.

'They don't like us using those kinds o' terms, but yeah, pretty much. I've been told that should I survive the first wave of the invasion, I'm to make my way back to London and harry them there. They mean, o' course, if West and Fordham are dead. They're both country men teamed with me because they know the land where we'll be sent.'

'And here's me being worried I'd sounded seditious,' I said. 'Looks like the government think it's all over bar a bit of shooting.'

'You don't sound convinced?'

'I'm hoping you're a fall-back plan,' I said. 'That there are other things going on we don't know about.'

'You're more likely to know about that than me,' said Harvey.

261

'Cooper's an alias, isn't it?'

'You're dodging my question,' said Harvey. I looked askance at him, and saw a mixture of fear, excitement, and hope on his face. I only wished I had better news.

'All I can tell you is, the people I think are most likely to be in the know are not acting as if invasion is imminent. No one has said as much to me, but I don't think we are at our last gasp yet.'

'You know Bernie has married her beau? She's still an American citizen though. That should keep her safe. From Germans at least.'

I stopped in my tracks. 'She's married!'

'Five days ago,' said Harvey. 'Keep movin' or the others will catch us up. She invited me to be a witness, but they wouldn't let me go. She couldn't find you. Cedric was insisting, and she'd only just recovered from her fall. She wrote to me she thought I'd 'ate her for it, but she needed something or someone. She was feeling lost. Stupid cow.' He said the last two words with sadness rather than anger.

'I've always thought Bernie pretty damn smart. She was out on some secret operation and washed out only when she met Cedric.'

This time it was Harvey that stopped. 'You do know he threw her down the stairs, don't you?'

That brought me up short. 'No,' I said. 'She would have told me.'

Harvey shook his head. 'Apparently, your godfather is a big deal in diplomatic or government circles or some such thing, and she knew our government wanted Cedric to marry her. All about improving Anglo-American relations. She thought if she told you that she was thinking of jilting him, he'd stop her.'

'But Fitzroy told her not to marry him! He went out of his way to find her at a function and warn her.'

Harvey shrugged. 'She didn't take it that way. She thought he was testing her. Said that was the kind of thing he did. Wasn't he?'

'No,' I said. 'He wasn't. My mother had looked into Cedric and she wanted me to stop the marriage. She didn't have a chance to tell me the details.'

'Yeah, well, she made a lot of bad decisions. I don't think either of us knew what a bad place she was in. We wrote,' he said, not meeting my gaze. 'I was someone she could say anything to.'

'Because she trusted you,' I said.

Harvey shook his head. 'Because I'm not anybody. It doesn't matter what I think.'

The others were almost on us. Harvey looked back at them. 'I was going to marry her,' he said. 'She was going to run away, and I would marry her so there would be nothing he could do. Then the silly cow goes out for a night on the town while he's away. Cedric finds out, throws her down the stairs, and then under the pretext of looking after her, takes her in to his home. The next thing I know I get a note from her inviting me to the wedding. That's how she told me it was all off. A wedding invitation. See now why this place holds an appeal for me?'

Chapter Thirty-four

Fortunately, we were expected to sit in our teams, so I could keep Harvey in sight. I needed to know more. He and Bernie in love? I couldn't imagine it. Or was he simply trying to rescue her because she was a friend? And Bernie marrying a lower-class ex-con – I couldn't imagine it. She might be wilful and a bit on the wild side, but she'd always been clear she'd never marry outwith her class and that she needed a rich husband. Besides, Harvey was here. One of His Majesty's suicide soldiers. How on earth did they think they could marry? Harvey would have had to desert and when they caught him, he would have been shot. Then Cedric would have been free to marry Bernie anyway – if he still wanted her.

The lecture must have been halfway through before I was thrown abruptly out of my thoughts by Harvey nudging me hard in the ribs.

'Miss Stapleford, are you finding my lecture irrelevant? Perhaps you'd like to give us a tip about how best to avoid being spotted when you're tailing someone?'

I focused in on the instructor. He must have been the youngest of all of them, scarcely older than me. Dark-haired, average height, but with what others, though obviously not me, might have considered 'a presence' or charisma. Behind him on a mobile blackboard was a mess of white chalk, sketchy diagrams he must have used to explain his talk. They were undecipherable to me.

'Stapleford is fine, sir,' I said. 'Avoiding being spotted following someone in an urban or a rural location, sir?'

The instructor, who I vaguely remembered Harvey saying when we arrived was named Fergus, pulled a spare chair from the front row and sat on it. 'Oh, both please, Stapleford. You clearly know enough not to listen to my talk.'

'In a rural setting, it is important to make use of natural camouflage, such as trees, shrubs, and dips in the ground. When walking one needs to pay attention to moving as silently as possible.'

'What do you do, if you do make a noise — other than get shot?' A rumble of amusement went around the room.

'It would be worth trying to either make more noise such as a burrowing animal might make, or even throw a small object into another bush at a distance, so your tail's attention was diverted, and you could attempt to move away.'

'And if neither of those options were available?'

I thought this a bit rich. It would be a funny sort of mission if neither of these could work.

'As a last resort, sir, you attack with full aggression,' I said.

'I can see Hugh is going to like you,' said Fergus. 'I might even come and watch him try to put you through your paces. I take it you will be paying more attention in the self-defence class than in mine?'

I didn't say anything. There was a lot I wanted to say, and I might even say some of it politely, but I was already noticeable as a woman, I didn't want to stand out in any other way. I needed to seem less knowledgeable if I was to discover whatever wrong thing was happening here. Assuming I had been sent here to pry out some secret fault, and that everything that had happened to me since the start of the war wasn't merely a combination of coincidence and Fitzroy trying to keep me out of harm's way.

And that was a big if. Was he merely a father trying to protect his daughter? I shunted the thought aside.

Fergus waited. I didn't know if he was hoping I would be insubordinate or, more likely, hoped I would flee in embarrassment or break down into feminine tears. I did neither.

265

After what seemed like an agonising wait, he said, 'Very well, and in town?'

'It's not that much different,' I said. 'You do your best to use the camouflage on offer and stay out of sight. Don't get too close unless you intend to intercept him or her.'

'Maybe I should let you take the lecture. You seem to be quite knowledgeable.'

'I am certain you know a great deal more than I, sir. The only things I know I've picked up from films. I like a good gangster flick!'

This did cause a ripple of laughter. Fergus eyed me with his head on one side. He clearly couldn't decide if I was making fun of him or not. Then he gave a little shrug. 'So you see, gentlemen, even movie producers have an understanding of how following someone works. Not that I would suggest that you copy your favourite western. Allow me to introduce you to the concept of being grey – although considering our circumstances, being green might be a better term in some cases.'

He went on then to speak, at some length, about the art of making yourself invisible in various settings. Not literally invisible. That would have been interesting. But rather how to be unremarkable in any setting. As far as I was concerned it was basic stuff, but Fergus inflated it by using, or inventing, a number of technical terms and theories, that could have been summed up by three words, 'don't stand out'. I tried to plaster a rapt expression across my face as internally I tried to make sense of what Harvey had told me about Bernie, and to avoid thinking about my parents

The clock on the wall behind Fergus read a quarter to nine by now. I reckoned he would finish on the hour, and we'd get an hour before lights out as rec. Certainly, Fergus seemed to be upping the energy a bit, like a horse on the final furlough. 'Finally, we come to how to pick a place where you, to quote Miss Stapleford, attack with maximum aggression and take down your target. Any thoughts, gentlemen?'

'Somewhere out of the way,' said a voice from the back.

'Somewhere where you can easily hide or dispose of the body,' said Harvey.

'Interesting, Cooper, but what if you want the body to be found? Isn't intimidation of the enemy one of our significant goals?'

Harvey blushed. 'Of course, sir.'

'Probably thinking about his old ways, sir,' yelled someone from the back. 'You're allowed to kill these ones, mate.'

Beside me, I felt Harvey quiver slightly, I knew that he was remembering the man we had seen die under interrogation last year. 'How do you stop the Germans from conducting local reprisals?' I asked to distract attention from him.

'You don't,' said Fergus. 'The only option you have is taking the Hun on. And if there's more of them than you, and that will almost certainly be the case, then you will see them taking reprisals.'

'You mean shooting women and children, like they did in Norway?' I said. 'How do you stand by and watch that?' The room went very quiet. 'I mean, if these men are going back to their local areas, then the chances are they'll know the people who are being shot. It would only be natural to want to help them.'

'You don't get to have a choice, Miss Stapleford. This is the war we are in.'

The mood of the room had dropped like a stone into a bottomless lake. Fergus went on to talk about how to hide and retrieve messages, supplies, and information through various dead letter drops, but despite his best efforts the room stayed sombre.

When nine o' clock came the men filled out of the room in order, but with a rapidity that reeked of them shaking the nastiness of the lecture off themselves. Harvey and I, as among the first there, were among the last out. As we waited, Fergus came up to me. 'A word, Miss Stapleford,' he said, and gestured for me to accompany him to the side of the room. I did so.

'I appreciate you are clearly a bright young woman, but you don't seem to understand what we are trying to do with these men. You're perfectly right we are asking them to undertake actions that may led to the death of their kith and kin, but that is what is required. Many of them will not engage in – or survive – more than one operation. In which case reprisals are not an issue that will concern them. These men are not in it for the long haul. They are all volunteers. They all know intellectually, even if they perhaps hold out some hope, that they will not survive. As such, we don't care to muddy the waters with matters that may confuse or distress them. We need to train them to do whatever is necessary for the job at hand – and sometimes that training entails keeping back, or certainly not emphasising certain pieces of information. Most people don't know what happened in Norway. It has been kept from the public in general for good reason.'

'To avoid panic,' I said. 'I understand. I worked in a typing pool for a while. I have a higher than usual security clearance.'

'And you saw a report about it. I assume you realise the material that passed across your desk was not to be discussed, or have you been merrily regaling your friends with anecdotes of highly classified material?'

'No,' I said. 'My slip is inexcusable. I understand you will report me.'

Fergus shook his head and moved slightly closer to me. I could smell his cologne, and feel the heat coming off his body. It took a supreme effort of will not to back away from him, but I needed to know what he intended. He leant in and whispered in my ear, 'Miss Stapleford, I suggest I let the matter rest for now, and in return you keep your moral qualms to yourself. If you need to question the operation, and I can see why perhaps a woman might feel more inclined to do so, then come and talk to me, or you will quickly find yourself in more hot water than is comfortable. The other instructors are not as tolerant as I have been.'

'Thank you, sir,' I said quietly.

He stepped back and gave me a wry smile. 'I'm glad they decided not to deploy women among us. This isn't the place for a female, no matter how clever. Women don't have the stomach for the kind of thing we must do. And that is more to the credit of the so-called weaker sex than it is to men like me.'

I had no idea what to say to this, so I waited. Eventually, Fergus said, 'Dismissed,' and I hightailed it out to find Harvey as quickly as I could without assuming the manner of a bolting rabbit.

I found Harvey in a rec room playing pool with Fordham. Despite Fordham's careful scientific consideration of each shot, Harvey was winning through sheer recklessness. Fordham's eyebrows were lowering more and more by the moment. His personal logic told him he should be the better player, but Harvey was beating him like milk in a butter churn. I wandered up and accidentally nudged Harvey, who missed his shot. He turned on me like a tiger, hurling verbal obscenities until he saw who he was talking to. Then he handed his cue to Fordham, and said to me, 'Hope, a word,' in what he clearly, and rather sweetly, thought were menacing tones.

I obediently went with him to the far corner of the large room, where there were two large armchairs. We sat. 'Honestly, Hope,' he snapped. 'Another man might have punched you out before he realised you were a girl. You have to be more careful.'

'So do you,' I said, 'Fordham was getting very distressed,'

'It's good for a leader to show who's boss,' said Harvey.

'Well, all you're convincing Fordham of is that better though his logic and accuracy may be, you can win by sheer recklessness. Not a trait I would have thought you wished to encourage in your team.'

'Damn it.' Harvey stopped and puffed out a huge gust of frustration. 'Of course, you're right,' he said. 'With what has happened to Bernie I'm all over the place.'

'Did you love her?' I asked. I felt a funny flutter in my stomach as I asked the question. Maybe I had enjoyed dinner too much.

Harvey shook his head. 'I don't think so. I liked her a lot. I liked her bravery and her forthrightness. She could be bloody infuriating too. I never imagined our life together would be a bed of roses, but it was the only way I could think of saving her.'

'It wouldn't have worked,' I said, without specifying if I meant the plan or the marriage. 'Besides, she's not dead. We can still get her away from this Cedric. Americans get divorced all the time. Provided we are not overrun by Germans, and I honestly don't believe we will be, we're learning all about concealment here.'

Harvey ground his teeth. 'I can't bear to think of her being hurt. He could be hitting her right now.'

'Their row was about her flirting – or him thinking she'd been doing so?'

Harvey nodded.

'That's all about control, isn't it? He's got her now. They are married. He has no reason to feel she is out of his control.'

'You condone what he did?'

'Good God, no. He's a brute and should be thrashed at the very least for hurting her. Bernie hasn't a notion of how to protect herself. I've tried to show her some things, but she's never wanted to know – too worried about her nails, or her hair or her frock. He knew she was completely defenceless.'

Harvey gave a little growl.

'I also,' I added, 'don't believe he won't hit her again. It's not a one-off kind of behaviour. But now, right now, in the honeymoon phase, is when he will behave his best. If we get her away from him as soon as we're done here, then she will be fine – and hopefully ready to leave!'

'But . . .' Harvey struggled for words and I knew he was thinking about Bernie, and the usual physical consequences of marriage.

'Harvey, she chose this. I raised objections a long time before he ever hit her. You've raised objections too. When she said "I do" I have to presume no one was actually holding a gun to her head. I agree she might have felt so frightened of Cedric that she went ahead with the wedding, but what I think is more likely is that she convinced herself it was all going to be all right. She wants his status. She wants the riches it brings. She wants security. She's made a terrible bargain, but she's made it. We can help her get free, when – if – she wants to.'

'It'll be that easy, will it?'

'It wouldn't be hard,' I said. 'I can think of half a dozen ways right now. Tell me, hand on heart, did you ever believe the plan she had of running away with you – did you ever believe she was serious?'

'What?' Harvey jumped up.

'I'm not saying she was lying to you precisely, but did it not strike you as – well – make-believe?'

I tugged on his sleeve. Harvey sat down. 'Had she done anything about arranging transport to meet you? Ever talked of packing, where you'd marry? Anything like that? Or was it all a bit "we'll be fine, walking into the sunset hand in hand"?'

Harvey went paler. He was quiet for what felt like a long time, but I knew better than to interrupt his thoughts. He had to work this out for himself. After a good five minutes, which is a long time to wait in a conversation, he said, 'You were at university with her, weren't you? What was she like?'

'She arranged to elope more than once,' I said. 'Each time she said she felt like it would have been rude to say no – or some such thing.'

'She never meant it,' said Harvey. He hung his head.

'I wouldn't say that. This was different. Before it was about not disappointing some silly boy she'd led on, but this time I think the fantasy was that she could get away. It must have been very bad for her to go this far. For what it's worth, I imagine she did really want to go through with your plan. She couldn't make it work. Why didn't she talk to me?'

'She said you'd talk to your godfather and put a stop to it.'

I shook my head. 'It's not like her to think the worst of me. Of course I would have helped her. I don't live in my godfather's pocket.'

'She said you were very close. That he talked about you to her all the time.'

271

I shrugged. 'The war changes things. Besides, I said my mother was against Cedric.'

'Why didn't she come to town to help?'

'My father is ill. She can't leave him. He's had health crises before, and we're hoping he'll pull through.'

'I didn't know,' said Harvey, looking at me more kindly. 'Don't you want to be at home?'

An unexpected lump rose up in my throat. I bit the inside of my cheek. 'Of course, but I'm Army personnel and this is a war. If it comes to a head, I might be able to ask for compassionate leave for twenty-four hours, but I don't know if I would get it. Besides, I think I have to hold that option in reserve if – if he takes a turn for the worse.' I stood up. 'I'm tired. I should go to bed. We can talk more tomorrow. Is there a bell or anything?'

'Six thirty a.m. out in the garden for a run before breakfast.'

'How jolly. Goodnight, Harvey.'

I left the room on the echo of his response. My emotions churned inside, and I knew I wouldn't be able to think straight until after I had slept. I headed up to my room, washed, and climbed into my bed. It was remarkably comfortable, but then it hadn't been meant for someone as junior as me.

I heard the door to the room next to me open. Then the sounds of male voices, low, urgent, and angry. I managed to make out the words, 'I tell you it doesn't need to come to that!' It sounded like Fergus. Then a door slammed hard enough to rattle my bed. I found I didn't care about any intrigues or plots. I didn't care who was my biological father. All I wanted to do was go home and be with my family – all three of them. I wept like a child, but I muffled the sound of my cries like a woman.

Chapter Thirty-five

'Everyone seems to have got the knack of the double shot,' said Aubrey, 'Even West. I should have known you'd be a rapid shooter with a name like that.' There was a rumble of laughter. Despite it still being the end of the summer, the day was overcast and drizzling with rain. During our early morning run, it had been torrential, and we had all ended up slipping and sliding in the muddy lanes until a collision with a large patch of dung had made Fergus call a halt to the run early so we could get back to fight over the hot water before breakfast.

Now, somewhat better clothed, we were standing at the edge of a wood, and had been practising the quick double pistol shot on sight of an enemy. We knew a target range had been set up inside the wood. For the first time I heard that not everyone was guaranteed to make it through. You could perform so poorly you were banished from the programme. I was surprised. I would have thought that if invasion was imminent, they would have taken anybody. I had yet to voice this thought. Right now, I was mostly aware of the icy water dripping down the back of my collar and slithering down to my underwear.

'First time through there will only be five targets. Each target will be at normal human height. Later we will have targets dropping down, springing up, and coming at you from every which way, but this time, while some of you are still learning how not to shoot each other, we're keeping it easy.'

No one replied. The group was miserable, cold, and

concerned. None of us had gloves, and while I had been trying to keep my fingers warm, tucking them into the sleeves of my over-sized camo jacket, the others hadn't that option.

'Sir,' I said. 'I appreciate that were this for real we would have to deal with whatever conditions were here, but as a first practice run, would it be possible for us to get a chance to warm our hands? I'd be happy to make a small smokeless fire. That's something we need to master, isn't it?'

Aubrey turned his gaze on me. I didn't expect him to be smiling at me, but his lack of expression as the rain ran down his handsome face made me shiver. Fortunately, I was also shivering with cold, so he couldn't know this. I squared up to him, polite, but meeting his gaze straight.

'Not all the men here are enlisted, but you are, aren't you, Stapleford?'

'Yes, sir,' I said, at a loss to know where he was going with this.

The men around me had started to shuffle from foot to foot. I sensed their agitation. None of us wanted to stand around in the cold.

'I would be interested to know,' Aubrey said in a casual voice, 'which part of the services exactly you are from?'

I opened my mouth to answer, but I didn't get a chance. Aubrey leant forward and bellowed in my face, 'Because I wasn't aware any part of it was a fucking democracy.'

I almost said, most competent commanders are not threatened by well-meaning suggestions from their inferiors. But I didn't. I stood there silently waiting to see or hear what he wanted from me.

'Are you deaf, Stapleford?'

'No, sir.'

'Then what part of the services now runs as a democracy?'

'None, sir,' I said, thankful I didn't have to reveal I didn't actually know which department I was assigned to.

'I am relieved to hear it,' said Aubrey. He paused, watching my face. I wondered if he thought I might cry. Certainly, Fitzroy had never shouted at me, but he could be far, far more intimidating with a quiet word. My challenge was not to show this man what an idiot I thought him.

Aubrey turned around. 'Even in this unofficial unit, we run strictly by the rule of hierarchy. In the field it is vital to have only one leader, one man, who makes the decisions. In wartime there is no time for discussion. There is no time to warm our little fingers. Cooper, into the forest. Stapleford, hold back.'

It transpired that by hold back he meant wait until everyone else has gone through the range. I watched as man after man disappeared into the undergrowth. After Harvey entered, I heard three rounds of two rapid-fire shots. He had only found three of the five targets. I counted the shots of the rest as they went through. It took my mind off how cold I was. I shifted my feet slightly from time to time. If I didn't, I was afraid I'd turn into one solid block.

As well as counting, I tried to puzzle out Aubrey. It seemed, so far, all the instructors had been less than keen on my joining the group. All of this appeared to be rooted in my being female. But if all I had experienced in the last few weeks had been leading up to this mission, then there had to be more to it than that. Or was I looking at the wrong people? Was I meant to be observing the whole group? At the end of my time here would Aubrey, Hugh, and Fergus ask me to sit down with them and profile all the men? If that was the case, I needed to get to know the others fast. But the teams were set up in a way that would make this awkward. It would show a real lack of planning to put a profiler in a segregated team. But then this training had been organised quickly. Yet the instructors seemed more than competent, and I'd been on my own now with all of them. None had shown any signs that I was anything other than mildly loathsome. For some reason the thought of being mildly loathsome made me smile. Aubrey noticed.

'Still want to try it, Stapleford? You must be frozen stiff by now. I've made my point.'

I shook my head. 'No, sir. I'd like to try it.'

Aubrey gave me a curious look. 'Think you can do better?'

'The most I heard was four double shots, and there are five targets, aren't there?'

Aubrey's eyebrows shot up in surprise, but he covered it quickly. 'There's nothing to say any of those shots hit their mark, is there?'

'Indeed not, sir,' I said. 'I'll give it a good go.' I waited for him to gesture me forward. It was a firing range after all.

Immediately I crossed into the tree line a target, or rather a stuffed dummy, swung out from behind a tree. I crouched and shot it twice. This whole double thing felt awkward to me, but it was supposed to make you more accurate. Three weeks ago, I'd never handled a gun, so what did I know? I could imagine Cole would call it a waste of ammunition.

I crept forward, crouching. I felt if I was shooting at people then, to make the exercise real, I should be wary of people shooting at me. A line of soggy blue string outlined the edge of the route. Various leaves and small branches unloaded more icy water on me, but I was fairly sure I couldn't actually get any wetter and I ignored it. Now the first shots had shown me I had kept my fingers warm enough in my sleeve to maintain a semblance of accuracy – the target had been large and close – I wanted to do well. There was the crack of a shot, and I slid behind a tree, ending up on my knees. Now this was more like it! It felt real. I darted to the next tree only for a target to spring up in front of me. I aimed and didn't fire. The target was child-sized. Thus, I assumed, not a threat. The target went back down now its spring was spent. I followed the string, and three more targets jumped out at me from various, but predictable angles.

After number four, I stopped to think. I wasn't counting the child, so there had to be another target. Had the others missed it because they had shot the child? Some of them would have – by accident rather than intent – automatically fired as it popped up, and of them how many would have actually registered it wasn't a proper target? Definitely some of them would have thought by

276

now they had hit five targets, but of the twelve men it seemed unlikely that one or more had got that right.

I took a couple of deep breaths. Weirdly, I was warming up. I hoped we got another go at this. It was rather fun. Now why would the others have missed the final target?

My brain whirled on empty air for a while, then I had a thought. What if the target had come from a different angle? We'd seen sideways, left, and right. In front of me and popping up from the ground. It had to be from above. Flying Nazis? I suppressed a giggle. Jumping out of a tree. That had to be it.

Another shot cracked, and I took it as a sign I needed to hurry. I used the trees and higher bushes as the best cover I could, but I kept an eye out for what was above me.

The string had almost run out, and I was beginning to believe I had been wrong, when I saw a shape swing out of the tree canopy. I shot at it and hit. As I did so, I felt something whistle past my ear. Probably a bee clearing the area in fright.

I crouched for the last few feet and crossed the last point. To my surprise I found quite a few of the men waiting for me. They all cheered. The instructors might be down on me, but it seemed the men didn't mind having me around. I gave them a big grin. 'Did I get the lot?' I asked.

Fergus emerged from the group. I saw that a lot of them had blankets around them and were holding mugs of tea. 'Someone get this soldier some hot tea,' he shouted as he approached me. 'She's practically blue in the face.'

'Thank you, sir,' I said, only slightly slurring my words, 'but that was such jolly fun I've started to warm up again.'

Fergus frowned. I heard him yell, 'Medic,' just before I felt my legs give from under me and everything went black.

A balding man with glasses was bending over me. He had dandruff and weak blue eyes. 'You must be the doctor,' I said.

'And you were on the edge of hypothermia. I thought part of

all this outdoor training nonsense was understanding your environment?'

I smiled sleepily at him. 'Thank you for not letting me die,' I said politely.

The doctor straightened up. 'Nothing to do with me. Your captain and another man wrapped you up in blankets and got warm fluids into you. My job was just about done before I got here. All I did was tell them to put you to bed with hot water bottles and let nature do its work. Wonderful cure-all, nature, and you're by the look of it normally a healthy young lady. Now, if you'd been one of those skinny girls that are all the rage, you'd have been dead before I got here.'

The door opened. The doctor turned. 'She'll be fine. Keep her in bed for the rest of the day, and if she feels like it, she can get up tomorrow. Nothing strenuous for the next forty-eight hours. Where shall I send my bill?'

I heard a low voice answer. The doctor walked out of my field of vision. There was a knock on my open door. 'May I come in? It's Aubrey.'

'Of course, sir,' I said, struggling to sit up a bit more.

Aubrey came in and sat down on the edge of the bed. I discovered then that my whole body ached like a rotten tooth. As his weight settled on the bed, it felt like an earthquake. I realised the ache was caused by all the shivering I'd done, and it had been part of what kept me alive. That, and, as the doctor had intuited, my love of cake.

'I owe you a huge apology, Stapleford,' he said, not quite looking me in the face. 'What I did was inexcusable. I've been told you almost died.'

'Shall we say, sir, that it was a slight miscalculation? I had been asked to be treated like the rest of the men,' I said. In fact, I hadn't, but there seemed to have been a consensus somehow that I should be, and I hadn't objected. 'I don't think a man would have got as cold as I did.'

Aubrey's eyes flickered towards me for a moment, and then

went back to staring at the curtain of the window to the side of my bed. 'I rather think West wouldn't have made it, if it had been him.'

'Just as well I like cake, then, isn't it, sir?' I said. 'Besides, I'm certain West wouldn't have spoken out of order as I did.'

Aubrey finally looked at me. 'You're being frightfully nice about this, Hope, but the truth is I got it very wrong and you almost died.'

'But I didn't,' I said. 'And perhaps if the Germans haven't invaded by the time I get up, you could persuade the cook to bake cake for tea for everyone. I like lemon best. Sounds like they all need feeding up.'

Aubrey tried hard not to smile and failed. 'This is very decent of you,' he said. 'And cheeky. But I'll give you a pass for that seeing as you are recovering.' He looked thoughtful for a moment. 'You're probably right, you know. These chaps are working harder than they ever have in their lives. We should be upping their intake while they're here. Goodness knows what will happen when . . .' He broke off. 'Dashed miserable subject. Do your lot have a plan for getting you out of here if the balloon goes up?'

'I haven't been told of one, but that doesn't mean there isn't one,' I said. 'Everything is compartmentalised now, don't you find?'

'Have you ever been in a regular Army unit, Hope Stapleford?' asked Aubrey.

'Does a typing pool count?'

'You're not actually a typist, are you?'

'I can use a typewriter. I can do shorthand too.'

'You're a grand shot.'

'A recently acquired skill, sir.'

'So not on your uncle's farm?'

Oops. 'I wanted to give the men a good reason why I was a fair shot,' I said.

'Evasion,' said Aubrey. 'I take it I'm not meant to know where you are actually from?'

'I went through the selection process like the rest, sir. If I hadn't solved the puzzle and caught the train I wouldn't be here.'

'I don't doubt your capability, Hope. I merely question why you're here.'

'I'm an experiment.'

'So I've heard. Well, you've got guts. I'll give you that. But you haven't a clue how to behave as a rank and file soldier. Or how to behave as if you're in the army at all, for that matter. I'd wager they even had trouble with you in the typing pool.'

I chose not to reply.

'Very well,' said Aubrey. 'You've every right not to confide in me. But do me one thing. If you get into trouble again, come to me. I'll sort it out. I owe you.'

I rather resented the implication that I got into trouble, but he seemed to mean well enough. So, I thanked him and he left.

I lay there wondering if Aubrey was all he seemed or if I needed to look for trouble in an entirely different direction. My cold-addled mind might have thought a bee passed me at speed in the forest, but my now rational brain knew full well it was a bullet that had come within an inch of my head. All the men had been there, as well as Aubrey, and Fergus too. Far too many suspects.

Chapter Thirty-six

I lay in bed deciding whether or not to get up. Part of me wanted to get up and on with the job, but I also knew that having suffered a concussion and near-hypothermia in under a month was not good for even the strongest constitution. Besides, if my opponent thought I was under par then they were more likely to underestimate me. However, the question remained, who was my opponent?

I heard doors opening on my corridor.

'Morning, Fergus,' said Hugh. 'Looks like a grand day for an invasion.'

'I do wish you'd stop that,' said Fergus. The lecturer sounded grouchy and tired.

'What?' said Hugh, sounding even more cheery. 'I didn't say the other thing.'

'Just as good as,' said Fergus.

'Hello,' said Aubrey, 'is there a meeting going on I don't know about? Only I quite fancied a bath this morning. Still feel as if I've got mud from that ruddy wood all over me.'

'Hugh's being his normal cheery self,' said Fergus, bitterly.

'Are you teasing him again, Hugh?' said Aubrey.

'I never said it. Ask him. I never said it was a good day to die,' said Hugh. I stuffed my fist in my mouth. This was far more humour and wit than I'd looked for from the rather stern man who had greeted me in the hall.

'Now, Hugh. I detect you're not being kind. Poor Fergus can't help it if he jumps every time a bell rings. He's . . .'

'What?' said Hugh. 'I can think of a few descriptors if you need a hand?'

'I was going to say,' said Aubrey, 'that he wasn't in the last scrap like we were. Imagining what's coming is far worse than knowing.'

'What rot!' said Hugh. 'You know damn well we went to hell and back. Just because we've agreed not to spell out the massacre of the last war to the recruits, doesn't mean you and I don't know what we face. And it doesn't mean we can't face it with a smile on our faces.'

'You're our head instructor,' said Aubrey. 'You need to keep up your staff's morale, as well as your men's.'

'If I'm in charge I shall do what I damn well please,' said Hugh. 'And that includes using the bathroom first.'

There was a sound of a door slamming.

'He doesn't mean it,' said Aubrey.

'Oh, he does,' said Fergus. 'He thinks I'm a coward. I'm not, you know. I'll face it out with the rest of them. It's just that when I wake on a bright day, I don't like my first thought to be how this might be my last morning on earth.'

Aubrey lowered his voice a bit. 'He's a funny sort, Hugh. Stern as a prison warden with the men, but a bit of a rotter with us. He looks for what upsets you and then goes for the spot. I suppose it's some kind of stress relief for him. I heard he had it pretty bad in the last show. Mind you, he came home whole in body at least.'

'Well, he's a useless commander,' said Fergus. 'I suppose I'm going to have to shave in that tiny basin in my room before he uses all the hot water. You can kiss your bath goodbye, Aubrey.'

'Do you think we should try and leave some for the girl? She was in a right state when we brought her in.'

'I don't know what they're thinking of, sending a girl in here. Have you seen how she fills out that uniform? We're lucky any of the men are paying attention to our instruction.'

My cheeks flamed, and I became overly conscious of the need not to make any sound.

'Can't say I have. She was in a flak jacket when she was out

282

with me. Besides, I was too busy paying attention to where the men were pointing their guns. In the normal way of things I wouldn't trust most of them with a pea shooter, let alone live ammo.'

'Is she any good with a gun? Or does she squeal when she shoots and shut her eyes?'

'Do you have something against women in general?' said Aubrey.

'I have nothing against them provided they stay in their place – and by that, I mean the kitchen or the bedroom.'

'How progressive of you,' said Aubrey, and I heard his voice grow colder. 'Actually, she's a top notch shot. Apparently, she's a bit of a sniper too. Can't say I care who's handling the weapon as long as they're taking down the enemy. I'll bid you a good morning.' I heard footsteps pad off down the hall. I wondered if that meant there were other bathrooms. I had only found the one, not wanting to roam the men's corridors at night.

I heard the sound of Fergus breathing deeply. It didn't sound like he was relaxed. Then I heard him move, a door slammed hard, and something fell to the floor. Fergus swore loudly. I decided that taking the lie-in the doctor had offered last night and waiting till the coast was clear before I got up would be the best course of action. I reached into my kit bag, pulled out a book, and settled down to read.

I woke up about an hour later feeling in great need of a trip to the bathroom. Happily, the others were long gone. I ran a bath of a few inches and had a good scrub. My skin seemed to appreciate the effort, and by the time I'd gone back to my room and put on a fresh uniform, I felt invigorated. My used uniform lay over a chair. I wondered if the men did their own laundry or if they had a service here. I rolled up my uniform and head off downstairs. I had an idea.

Instead of stopping at the ground floor, I managed to find a stone side stairway that led down from the entrance hall. As I'd hoped, it led to a swing door, and when I pushed through, I saw it had green baize on the other side. I had found the servants' quarters. After a small landing the steps continued for a short flight until I emerged into a narrow corridor. On both sides were wooden partitions. From the top of the steps I could see into both areas. One partly screened off the kitchen and the other partly screened off what appeared to be a makeshift laundry. The screens stopped some way short of the ceiling, also allowing me to see through several open doorways. Two giant copper kettles stood in the middle of the floor. One steamed as two mob-capped women pushed the clothes inside around with long poles. On the other side, a group of people, all dressed in civilian clothes, bustled around a large table. At the far end stood an enormous range cooker. I could feel the heat from where I stood.

I put my wrist to my head for a moment, as I considered whether I was still concussed and having visions of the past. Then one of the pole-wielders splashed herself and cursed. 'Bleedin' thing! Why can't they do their own washing?'

'Excuse me. Can we help you?'

I started slightly and looked down. A middle-aged woman in a neat black dress stood at the bottom of the steps. Yet again someone had crept up on me while my attention was elsewhere.

'I'm sorry to intrude,' I said. 'I've only been here a few days and I didn't know the procedure about laundry.'

The woman looked me up and down. 'Who are you?'

'Stapleford. Hope Stapleford. I am one of the recruits.'

At the sound of my voice, the complaining washer dropped her pole into the kettle and came out. Her exasperated workmate called out, 'Lucy!' But Lucy came straight into the hall.

'Who's she then, Mrs P?'

The middle-aged woman turned to say, 'She says she's a recruit.'

'Don't seem likely,' said Lucy. 'She probably stole that uniform. Barely fits over her . . .'

'That will be enough, Lucy.'

All the time I was standing on the top of the steps. It felt rather like being on trial. I came down quickly to their level.

'No, ladies. I really am a recruit. I'm part of an experiment. I can't tell you more than that. I can prove I've been active.' I unrolled my muddy uniform and flak jacket from the day before. 'As you can see, I had rather a day of it yesterday.'

'Well I'll be blowed,' said Lucy. 'Does that mean I can join up? I'd rather be shot at than cope with that ruddy kettle.'

I turned my attention to the housekeeper. 'But,' I said, 'Lucy does have it quite right. My uniform is barely decent. It was provided for me on arrival, and while it has been modified, it's clear whoever did it hadn't been told my measurements.'

'You mean that you've got big bosoms?' said the irrepressible Lucy.

'Hush!' said Mrs P. 'I don't know what you expect us to do about it.'

'Oh, nothing, of course,' I said. 'I can see you are all terribly busy. I was only wondering if I could borrow a pair of scissors and some thread. I could let out some of the seams myself. I'm not allowed to go into town and fetch anything, you see. None of us are.'

'Do you know anything about sewing?' asked Lucy.

'Not a great deal,' I admitted, 'but I don't want to do anything complicated. Just give me some more room.'

'Yeah, well, you'll probably end up with your doo-dahs hanging out. Your sort wouldn't know how to sew a handkerchief.'

Mrs P took the dirty uniform from me. 'I'll have this dealt with,' she said. 'Follow me and I'll see if I can find some things for you.'

I trotted along behind her. Lucy tagged along. 'Must be awfully hard doing all their washing,' I said. 'I've seen the state the men get themselves into.'

'You ain't kidding,' said Lucy. 'What are they doing out there? Making mud pies?'

'You're not far off,' I said.

By the time we reached Mrs P's office, Lucy had, as I had hoped, decided she liked me and was game for altering my uniforms. 'Anything other than the bleedin' copper.'

Mrs P wasn't too keen. 'If you could lend me an apron or smock, I could perhaps help in the kitchen, while she does it?' I offered. 'I might not be able to sew, but I can cook.'

After a bit of talk, in which I displayed not only appreciation of the below stairs staff, but admiration for them, we came to an agreement. Ten minutes later I was up to my elbows in flour making finger buns for lunch. Fortunately, iced finger buns are not complicated. You need to remember to put the eggs in the dough, and to wait for them to cool before icing. Our cook at White Orchards let me make my first batch at six years old. I didn't get much beyond cakes and buns, as I quickly lost interest in the kitchen once my godfather introduced me to riding.

I was engrossed in kneading the dough when a voice asked, 'So what do you lot do upstairs?'

I looked up and encountered a very young and freckled face with a pair of chocolate brown eyes, sparkling with curiosity. 'Lots of outdoor stuff,' I said. 'You must have heard the shooting?'

'Did you shoot too?'

I knew I shouldn't tell them much, but I was aware that everyone from Mrs P to the youngest maid had edged slightly closer to listen in.

'I'm not allowed to tell you much, but yes, I was shooting. My grandfather taught me to shoot rabbits when I was little. My grandmother loved nothing better than rabbit pie.'

'That's what we'll all be eating soon,' opined an older woman, stirring a pot on the range. 'The bleedin' Nazis will have taken everything else.'

'Well, that won't be too bad,' I said, 'If you throw in wild garlic, a few morels, and some pineapple weed you have a lovely dish. And if my grandfather's place is anything to go by, we won't run out of rabbits anytime soon.'

Mrs P crossed over the partition. 'That's the spirit,' she said. 'We're not beaten yet, are we?'

'Well said, Mrs P,' said the cook. 'Not hide nor hair of a Nazi on these fair isles, and I don't believe it'll happen myself.'

'But there's gas barges on the other side of the Channel,' said my brown-eyed inquisitor.

'We were lucky with Dunkirk,' I said. 'The English Channel is usually rough. If they try and get those things over here, they'd be just as likely to gas themselves. Besides, we have masks.'

'Well said,' said Mrs P. 'Whatever that lot are doing upstairs, at least they've got one sensible young woman among them.'

I smiled. 'It's mostly living off the land sort of training. As well as the shooting. The kind of thing all of us need to learn. I think the shooting is just in case the Germans try to drop a spy on us by parachute. It's not an important part of what we're doing. Most of the men will go on to train others, I expect.'

'Doesn't need to be a slimy little spy,' said the cook, tipping a handful of greenery into the pot, and filling the air with the smell of basil. 'I reckon any day one of those planes'll drop right in our back yard.'

'Planes?' I said.

'You know, the sky pilots in their little Firespits? Giving the Luftywatt hell.'

'Spitfires and Luftwaffe,' corrected Mrs P. 'There is something to that. Almost reminds me of the last time – seeing the odd dog-fight in the air again. Of course, these days they go much faster, and our boys are doing a good job of keeping them out.'

I realised that I had heard planes earlier in the day. Not know-ing anything about the brewing air battles I hadn't paid much attention to it. I sincerely hoped my godfather didn't take it into his head to fly into battle. He was far too old, although he would be the last man to admit it. I could see that kind of fast, high-risk action appealing to him. I needed to get a message to my mother to stop him. Short of Churchill or the King, I couldn't think of anyone else he would listen to.

'Here, don't worry, ducks,' said the cook to me. 'You've gone quite pale. Our boys in blue are blooming amazing.'

'The Spitfires are awfully smart,' said a small voice from the corner. I peered over the table to see a young lad shining shoes in the corner. 'They 'ave tremendous firepower too. The bullets from their guns go for miles!'

'You mind you stay out of the way of them planes,' said the cook.

'Yes, ma'am,' said the boy quickly. 'I'll be too busy scrubbing pots. It's a poor life I've got.'

Mrs P turned away, suppressing a smile. 'That's our little evacuee, Alfie,' said the brown-eyed girl. 'He got sent to us before the government took over the house. And he 'ardly does any work!' She directed her voice at him, 'I've told him if he'd pitched up at a farm he'd be up from the crack of dawn and clearing out the cowsheds.' She looked at me. ''E just don't like it that Mrs P makes him go to school.'

'So this hasn't always been a services base?' I said, taking care not to name which service. I formed the last bun into shape, ready for proving before going into the oven.

The cook came over. 'Not a bad job. Nancy can make up the icing later when they're cool. Well done. Fancy peeling some potatoes?'

'I do need to get back soon,' I said. The truth was I was feeling a bit wobbly on my feet. I also knew I had told a number of lies and I wasn't at optimal clear-headedness for keeping them all straight. 'I could help a bit.' Everyone else in the kitchen threw me a grateful look. The cook passed me a bucket of spuds. 'Put the peeled ones on the table and pile the scraps up for the pig bin. Have a seat. You're still a bit pale.'

'Looks like a bleedin' ghost,' said the brown-eyed girl, who I thought must be Nancy. Mrs P gave her a light clip round the ear.

'Language,' she said.

Nancy opened her mouth to get herself into more trouble. I cut her off, 'So did you all work here before?'

The cook, who had returned to stirring her pots, turned back again. 'Lord love you, yes. I came here as a scullery maid when Mr Hugh's father was still alive. Very old he was, but still very much a presence.'

'Mr Hugh?' I asked

'Hugh Davenport,' said Mrs P. 'This is his family home. He wasn't in the least bit happy that it was wanted. I think that's why they let him work here. He wanted to keep an eye on the place, and us.'

Could this be our instructor? 'Stern, middle-aged man?'

'That's him,' said Cook. 'Beautiful little boy, he was. All his worries got him down. Aged him faster than most.'

'You don't look old enough, Cook,' I said.

She chortled. 'I'll have you down here working with us any day,' she said.

Mrs P broke in, 'Poor Mr Hugh has had a lot on his plate. His father, a good man in his way, wasn't adept at farm management. He ran Home Farm into the ground.'

'Crying shame,' said Cook.

'And then the death duties were so high. He ended up selling the farm anyway. He didn't get a fraction of what it would have been worth when it was run properly though.'

'And his sister!' said Cook.

'I don't think we need to bore our visitor with family tales.'

Although I wanted to say, please do, I knew better. I lowered my head over the potatoes and applied myself to my task. Hopefully, Lucy would be back with my resewn uniform soon. After the rebuke, the kitchen went back to its normal routine. If anything, staff started moving more quickly. I glanced up at the clock and saw that the hour was closing on luncheon time.

'Who's on mess up today?' said Nancy.

'Cooper's lot,' said the lad. 'I like him. He gave me a shilling.'

'He's all right,' said Nancy. 'Makes his lads keep their hands to themselves.'

'Are some of them bad that way?' I asked.

'You haven't noticed? With your uniform looking like it did?'

'They wouldn't dare,' I said coldly, and Nancy laughed.

'Good for you,' she said.

'What's this about Mr Hugh's sister?' I asked.

'Oh, nothing really. Her mother died when she was young, and she was close to her father. When he died, she went a bit wild. Got into some trouble with the police, I think. Anyway, you know these old families, it was all hushed up. Sent her up to London to train as a nurse. But before they got her away, she led Mr Hugh a merry dance. Took after her dear old Pa and ran up a horde of debts. Expected her brother to pay them all off, she did. Nothing bothered Miss Evelyn. Any scolding Mr Hugh did — water off a duck's back.'

At this point Lucy returned with my uniform. I went into corridor and quickly tried it on. 'This is perfect,' I said.

'I'll do the other one once it's had a wash,' said Lucy. 'I'll get the lad to take it back up to your room when it's done. You should get up them stairs. Any minute now all hell will break loose when Cook realises how close we are to trough time. You'd be well out of it.'

I took this as a dismissal and went back through the baize door.

Chapter Thirty-seven

My stomach growled. It wanted luncheon. I agreed with it in principle. However, there were more important matters to attend to. Once upstairs, I managed to find a small study-like room that looked out over the gardens. There was a single three-sided window, not unlike an oversized oriel window. Most importantly the furniture in the room, an old desk, a captain's chair, a small two-seater sofa in front of a tiny blue-tiled hearth, and the surrounding bookshelves were all thick with dust. As soon as I closed the door behind me, I saw across the room the distant figures of people outside. I dropped to my knees and hid behind the sofa. They were coming in for luncheon. This meant the house would be the emptiest it got all day. I didn't know where the instructors dined, but I hoped I would hear them before I walked in on them. For now, I could hide in this unused room until everyone could be reasonably thought to be in one dining room or another.

I crawled away from the door, keeping low and well out of sight of the window. I found myself pulling ridiculous faces trying not to sneeze. Having met the downstairs staff, I was surprised they had let any of 'Mr Hugh's' estate get this bad. I paused by the side of a bookcase and read the spines on the lowest shelf. Ornithology. Fine in its way, but hardly riveting stuff. A little further on I found some Dickens and what looked like it might be a first edition Austen. Clearly, no one in the house understood either its value or their alphabet. The final lower shelf on that wall – the shelves were partitioned into threes – appeared to be books on gun dogs, their breeds and trainability. This was the typical study of a mild-mannered country gentleman. Hugh didn't strike me as the kind who watched birds – shot them and ate them, perhaps, but didn't admire them. This had to be the room of the last master of the house. Wiggling along on my belly I made my way to his desk.

I tugged gently at the handle of the lower drawer more out of curiosity than anything else. I still had time to wait before I could come out. I doubted there was anything to find, but it was good practice. Fitzroy had often talked casually about his occasional burglary exploits for the Crown, but he hadn't shared many of those skills with me. If a lock was simple, and I had time, luck, and lock-picks, I might be able to open it. I knew to wear gloves and how to move silently, but not much more than that. I had common sense, and I had thought to learn more of these skills from Harvey.

The drawer opened easily. Whoever had used this desk had taken the time, in their day, to wax the drawer runners or have them waxed. My fingers touched some papers. Carefully I lifted out a few sheaves and brought them down to the floor. Notes and drawings of birds. Most of them unfinished. The sketches weren't bad, but they were awkward, as if copied from books rather than life. I put them back and tried the other drawers. Pens, pen wipes, ink, coloured pencils, and assorted oddments filled them. The top drawer on this side was filled with blank writing paper headed *Davenport House* and likewise lettered envelopes. In the deep bottom drawer on the other side I found the earliest typewriter I had ever seen. I didn't lift this out but felt around it. Underneath lay typing paper. I risked peeping over the top. The very crown of my head would be in view from the window, but I doubted anyone would see it if they weren't looking for it.

The top piece of paper was blank. I pulled my finger along the sides of the pages, and as far as I could see it was all blank.

I hadn't been looking for anything in particular, but I felt strangely disappointed. I sat back, keeping my head below the top of the desk. Shouldn't there be something else here? The drawings now struck me as something that could be quickly placed on the desk as if one was in the process of doing them. They were so static because they hadn't been copied from life but from books – despite the fact the grounds here would have been excellent for sketching wildlife. I felt a slight shiver. There was something here, I knew it. But what?

Slowly, taking far too much time, and with a lot of effort, I got the typewriter out of the drawer. I pulled out the papers. They were indeed all blank. I felt around the bottom of the drawer looking for a false panel. Nothing.

Taking yet more time, I put the typewriter back. I checked for releases for secret drawers under the panel above the kneehole. I'd never seen a desk with a secret drawer, but I knew they existed. I didn't manage to trigger anything. It was only when I had almost given up that I noticed something was off. I had all the bird drawings on the floor, and the pile didn't seem anywhere near as high as the typewriter – yet the outsides of the two bottom drawers matched. I poked and prodded at the bottom of the drawer containing the drawings, to no avail. Then, taking a letter opener from the middle drawer, I partly prised up the base. There were papers beneath it. I couldn't find the trigger to open the secret panel, but I could break into it. It wasn't thick. Once I had I pulled out the papers therein, it didn't take me long to realise I was looking at Nazi propaganda.

I found one pamphlet that was written entirely in German. I recognised the word *Ubermensch*, but that was about all. However, the papers written in English, some typed, were all about the new world that fascism would usher in.

Feeling sick, I put the papers back into the drawer and did my best to cover them with the drawings. It was too risky to remove them from the room. My uniform might have been altered, but I still couldn't stuff a wad of papers anywhere that wouldn't significantly alter my figure. The significance of some of the pages being typed wasn't lost on me. I didn't imagine Hugh's father would have done the typing himself, but rather had had someone do it for him. His daughter, who he was so close to, perhaps? Asking a secretary to do such a thing would have been risky unless he was completely assured of her loyalty. No, it was more likely to have been the daughter. Loath as I was to admit it, women were better on these machines than men, and typing was seen as something a woman did. But then why had she been allowed to work as a nurse? Either she was being watched or I had it all wrong.

If both Hugh's father and his sister had been Nazi sympathisers, it didn't mean that Hugh definitely followed their beliefs, but it was problematic enough that he would never have been allowed to work with the auxis. Or indeed allowed anywhere near anything confidential. He wouldn't be assumed to be guilty without proof, but his connection with known Nazis would have earned him a back seat, where he could be closely watched and without access to anything of importance.

I didn't think a back seat role would suit Hugh. He was a man who liked being in control, but seemed to me also to be insecure in that role. Hence his intimidation of Fergus, a fellow instructor, who was simply, and quite reasonably, scared. Could this be because Hugh feared his father's affiliation would be discovered? But if so, why leave the material here? The obvious answer was he had no more idea how to get into the secret compartment than I did. Or perhaps he hadn't, for some reason, had time to get to it before the Army had moved in. There were few rooms ruled off limits to the Army. This was one. It appeared that the duties put on to the skeleton staff to wash, clean and cook for their khaki clad visitors, had meant these private rooms were abandoned. That would have given him unexpected breathing space, and then when nothing was discovered, it must have seemed safer and safer to let sleeping dogs, or in this case sleeping papers, lie. Breaking open a piece of furniture was bothersomely noisy and inconvenient.

Or, in fact, he might not know about the papers at all. Was he a double agent, or merely a man who was extremely unfortunate in his relatives? I could make a case for either.

I could imagine him as a bereaved son sorting through his late father's things and coming across some indication of this affiliation and being horrified. If he had then confronted his sister, I thought it likely she would have confirmed his fears. The staff thought she was difficult. I thought that perhaps she had been blackmailing Hugh, and that was why she expected him to pay her debts – but then the Army had swept in. One of the staff had said he had resisted it. Because he was a German sympathiser or because he feared discovery of his family's political leanings? I could imagine his sister running off to London and training as a nurse to look like a good citizen. Hugh was left to see the Army didn't find out any secrets from the house. I had found some papers in a dusty room, in a hidden drawer that perhaps only the old man had known about. He might not even have shown his daughter his secret cache. Wherever his loyalties lay, I didn't doubt that Hugh would have done everything he could to expunge his father's association with the Nazis. These few sheets, hidden away, had been overlooked – and they were damning. Even if he was only trying to protect his sister, he had been shielding a Nazi sympathiser. If he had even the vaguest suspicion I wasn't exactly what I seemed, a shooting accident would have removed a possible worry. I hadn't seen him at the range, but that didn't mean he hadn't been there. He would have been more likely to keep concealed if his intention had been to shoot me. Hugh couldn't afford to take risks. It was vital I got this information to Fitzroy's department.

I made my way back to my room. I needed to think about my escape carefully. We weren't exactly prisoners, but due to the sensitivity of the endeavour we weren't meant to go into town. When I'd been driven from the railway station, I'd had the impression the town must be nearby. Certainly, on our way here, I'd seen nothing but hedgerows, wide open spaces, and farm fields.

Would there be a map anywhere round here? That was, a map I could look at without anyone else noticing me doing so. The ideal thing would be to get to a telephone box, call Fitzroy's department, and then get back here undetected. With everything else going on, there was no guarantee they would be able to come at once. I needed to be able to stay on here without Hugh getting any suspicions that he had been rumbled. I also had what Fitzroy called my idiopathic sense of direction to contend with. Unless an absolute emergency happened, I needed to find good directions before I set off.

I washed my face in the sink and brushed my hair. It was long enough to tie back, so I stole a shoelace from one of my other shoes and did that. Without a scrap of make-up, I looked much more professional, but also rather younger. Never mind, I thought, that might garner me some sympathy. After all, I wouldn't have my youth for ever, so I might as well use it to my advantage while I had it. My stomach growled loudly. I had read many times that an army matches on its stomach, and if I was to beard a German sympathiser on his home ground, I needed to keep my strength up. Certainly, Fitzroy would tell me to take advantage of food while it was on hand. I checked my watch – there was the slimmest chance there were some people left in the dining area. I hurried out and down the stairs.

I heard voices coming from the room before I got there. 'Bleedin' hell, it's worse than clearing up at a ruddy zoo,' I heard Harvey say.

'You saw the way the others eat, Harvey,' said Fordham. 'To liken it to a bear pit would be unnecessarily denigrating to those of the ursine species.'

'Yer what?' said Harvey, sounding confused.

'Would be insulting to bears,' I said coming into the room. I looked around. Almost every available surface was dotted with some kind of food debris. 'Oh my! Was there a food fight?'

'Looks like it, don't it,' said West. 'Just everyone in a bit of a rush. Aubrey is setting up a Mark 1 – a Bren gun trial, and it seems nothing makes a man eat faster than the opportunity to get his hands on some real fire power.'

'I don't understand it,' said Fordham, as he started to wipe down one of the long tables with a wet rag of uncertain cleanliness. 'I heard it fires over five hundred bullets in a minute. What do we need that kind of firepower for? It's a weapon for massacres.'

'You'd be saying something different if it was only a Bren and you with a field full of Nazis bearing down on you,' said West, who was working away at cleaning one of the other long tables. 'You could defend an entire bloody village against a fu—' he stole a look at me, 'against a sodding battalion of the – er, rotters.'

'Gas operated, air cooled,' said Harvey, as he stopped stacking plates. 'Why can't people scrape their waste into the pig bucket? It's hardly a demandin' task.'

'How does the pig come into it?' I asked. 'I take it we're talking about a machine gun? Please don't tell me they're using a pig as target practice.'

'Dakka-dakka-dakka,' said West, using a dirty ladle he'd found as weapon, 'Even I couldn't miss with that. No pig, Hope. It'd be pig jam with a Bren. It's a .303.'

'I heard,' said Harvey scrapping a load of roast potatoes into the pail, 'that it's a Mark II.'

'Rubbish,' said West. 'There's only about two thousand or so of the guns in the army right now. They've not had time to mass produce the Mark II.'

'Harvey!' I cried, 'what are you doing with those potatoes? I haven't had any luncheon!'

'Right to the heart of the matter as usual,' said Harvey. 'There's another dish. Though they'll be cold by now I'd think.' He went to pick up the dish. I intercepted him with a speed that made me dizzy. I still wasn't quite right in the head. The thought made me giggle. Harvey looked at me oddly.

'Don't mind me,' I said. 'I love a cold potato. Especially a roast one.' I looked over the serving dishes that were piled up here. 'Anything else still edible?'

Harvey pointed to a covered dish. 'That had cheese and those wiggly things in it.'

'Wiggly?' I said, wrinkling my nose. I lifted the lid. 'Oh, pasta! Cold cheese sauce isn't a favourite though.'

'Pass what?'

I picked out one of the tubes on the end of a fork. 'Pasta, Harvey. It's made of oil, water, and flour. I add eggs too.'

'You're a cook?' said Harvey.

I shook my head. 'I *can* cook. My mother travelled a lot when she was young and brought back all kinds of ideas for food. It's always more interesting cooking something new.'

I burrowed further into the piled-up dishes, dislodging Harvey's best effort. Sadly, someone had put a custard spoon in with the end of a crusted meat dish, but I managed to salvage some slices of cold chicken, peas, and a chunk of raspberry crumble (without custard). I carried my treasures over to one of the newly cleaned tables. All three men stopped to protest. Before they could, I said, 'I'll clean up after myself. I won't be joining you for the machine gun training. Don't think I'm up to that yet. I was told to take a couple of days of rest. I'm hoping to be up and around properly tomorrow.'

'We've got a lecture tonight on camouflaging bases,' said Harvey. 'You should come to that if you can.'

I smiled. 'I'll try. I fancy going for a walk, but I don't know the area.'

'We're not allowed off base,' said Harvey flatly, giving me a stern look.

I sighed. 'Such a shame. I only saw the railway station, but there must be a little village round here?' I let my voice rise in a question and applied myself to the potatoes. They really needed salt, but Fordham had already got the salt and pepper on a tray ready to slide into the cupboard. I moved on to the chicken. I could get some when they were gone.

'It's nice,' said Fordham. 'My auntie lives there. I used to stay with her in the school holidays. She let me go anywhere I wanted. For a London boy it was amazing. Reckon I know every inch of this place.'

' 'Ere, don't let them here you say that,' said Harvey. 'They'll take you off training at once.'

Fordham shrugged. 'They must know I spent a lot of my childhood here. I don't know about you, but they investigated me thoroughly before allowing me to join up.'

'Odd that,' said West. 'Seeing as 'ow this is a one-way ticket kind of op.'

Fordham coloured slightly. 'Look, if we want any chance of seeing this wretched thing, we need to get the rest of the stuff down to the kitchen. The others will have been lining up for ages. At least we can get in the queue to use it.'

'Yeah,' said Harvey, 'Sorry, Hope. We'll have to love you and leave you.'

I waved a casual hand. 'I'll clear up, and put the dishes . . . where?'

Harvey directed me to a scullery near the kitchen. 'Now, if you've got any food left . . .'

'Don't be silly,' I said. 'Off you boys go and play with your toys.' I dearly wanted to question Fordham about the village, but Harvey was already wary, and I couldn't afford to raise his suspicions further. I needed to get a message out, but none of the men were about to be sent off on operations – or rather no one had yet rung the church bells to signal invasion – so on consideration I'd be better to wait and get the thing done cleanly than rush out and get caught or lost. The fact there were a considerable amount of potatoes left, and that when I finished them, I would want nothing more than to find a place in the grass and lie on my back, naturally had nothing to do with it.

Chapter Thirty-eight

I found a place outside screened away from general view by a hedge, and well away from both the sound of Bren gun fire and the woods where we had done our moving target training. So, there I was lying on a late summer's afternoon in the warmth of the sun and listening to what sounded like the maniacal tapping of a giant woodpecker. Five hundred bullets a minute. I thought of my careful shooting with Cole's sniper rifle at the end of my time at the farm. How deadly it had felt in my hands. How the importance of lining up a shot, getting your breathing and position right, could signify the end of a man's life. Cole had shown how care, professionalism, and skill were required to do the job. The Bren gun sounded like something you sprayed around yourself to kill everything in sight. How could such a thing require skill? Or even much thought? Was it West or Fordhàm who had called it a weapon of massacre? It didn't seem like a weapon that could allow you to sift the wheat from the chaff.

None of my mental metaphors were working. All I could think of as I heard the gun was of crowds of people, men, women, and children, falling in bloody heaps. There were times when I would rather not have an imagination at all.

I knew who we were fighting. I knew why we were fighting. I also knew that a significant number of the dead by the end of the fighting were likely to be civilians. I could get as caught up as any of them in patriotic fever, but when I thought what the real cost was likely to be I felt nauseous. Although no clouds had crossed my path I shivered. I understood the pacifists who refused to fight. It wasn't my way, but I took no pleasure in knowing I would have more blood on my hands in the future. Harvey had been wrong when he said I hadn't been moved by the man who had died under my mechanic's interrogation. I hadn't been distressed, but I *had* felt bad that my man had killed again on my orders. It must have brought back memories for him.

I was almost too lost in thought when I heard footsteps approaching. There was little chance anyone would spot me where I was, so I lay very still. My heart, wretched organ, decided to triple its normal beat — at least it felt like that, so the first few words of the conversation were lost to the blood thumping in my ears.

'So it's looking less and less likely by the day,' said a voice that sounded faintly familiar.

'What does that mean for us?' It took me less than a few moments to recognise Fergus' voice.

'Well,' continued the other man, 'I rather think we hang fire and wait. Carry on with what we're doing.'

'It doesn't put the end result in doubt, does it?'

'That, my friend, is a lethal thing to suggest.'

'I know. I know,' said Fergus. 'But you have to wonder. Things aren't going as . . .'

'Shhh, you never know who could be listening,' interrupted the other man.

'I doubt any local wildlife will betray us,' said Fergus mockingly.

'You never know who might be hiding behind a bush. One must take extraordinary care in these extra-ordinary times.'

The voices moved off. Fergus' had been easy enough to recognise, but I felt sure I had heard the other man's voice too. However, I had the unhelpful feeling that he didn't belong here. There was an itch at the back of my mind that suggested if I had heard him speak somewhere else I would have known him at once. Whoever he was, I had the strong suspicion he shouldn't be here. However, the conversation had been vague enough that I had no

301

grounds to accuse either man of – well, anything. They could have been talking about the effect of the weather on herbaceous borders as much as an attempt to assassinate the King.

I crawled on my belly to peek around the side of the hedge. I could see a distant image of two men walking away. So, while they had taken some care not to be overheard, it obviously struck neither of them that the other man could not be seen here. That meant he was either a straight-up fellow associated with the Service or a devious fellow who had infiltrated British Intelligence. In effect, I knew exactly nothing. I determined that I would definitely go to Fergus' lecture tonight. If I could I would needle him and see if I could draw a little blood.

The two men disappeared from my sight. I rolled onto my back and looked up at the sky. Clear blue with fluffy clouds. I had not yet seen a dogfight, and I can't say I wanted to. The idea of watching two men duel to the death, high above me, when I could help neither, made me feel sick to my stomach. But it seemed from what I had learned downstairs that some villagers regarded it as a form of aerial entertainment. When I'd mentioned this to Harvey, he'd told me some even took bets on how fast our pilots could shoot the enemy out of the sky.

I took a deep sigh and wished I'd had the willpower to resist that last potato. Lying there was achieving nothing and who was to say that the enigmatic duo might not be overcome with a sudden urge to check behind the hedge. I should move while the coast was clear. I got up and surveyed the ground. A splodgy, vaguely human outline disturbed the grass. I got down on my hands and knees and removed the indentation as I had been taught by both Fitzroy and more recently Cole. I found Cole's method more effective and quicker, but I had no intention of telling my godfather that whenever I saw him next. *If* he was merely my godfather, whispered a traitorous voice at the back of my mind.

I took a discreet way back to the house, using the mild undulations of that area of parkland to maximum effect. By the time I had reached the comparative safety of the interior of the building,

I felt comfortably sure that no one had seen me. I could still hear the Bren gun in the distance, but although the firing remained as rapid it was more infrequent. Could it be Aubrey was trying to teach them to use the weapon tactically?

Surely what they needed to work on was thinking tactically. If these guns were as scant as Harvey and his team thought, then the chances of any of these men having one, should the invasion happen, seemed remote. Unless, of course, it happened today. Then they'd have one weapon to fight over.

I recognised my thoughts were becoming somewhat grouchy. Fitzroy had always taught me that finding yourself with a strong inappropriate or distracting emotion meant something, and that if you had the time and space, you should stop and think. He had also said that quite often he found himself feeling enormously angry only to realise he'd been so busy he'd forgotten to eat for a day or two. This was not a problem I imagined having, but I was full of resentment.

I found a place in the shadows on the lower landing to sit and think. I could have gone to my room, but it was such a cosy and welcoming place, I felt it more likely I would settle down once again in a post-prandial stupor. I needed to be somewhere that I felt slightly unsafe. Where I needed to listen out for discovery. Somewhere that would give me an incentive to work out my problem quickly.

I sat and did the odd breathing exercise my godfather had taught me to induce calm. I breathed in slowly through my nose and imagined my breath as a golden string coiling down deep into my stomach and then rising up as I began to exhale, once more through my nose. It's a strange exercise that calms the heart and quietens the thoughts. I continued until the frantic mental flutter of worries and ideas had become a slow and steady stream. I asked myself, why am I so resentful? What has caused me to be like this? Then I did my best to sit back and see what my mind conjured for me. I felt that until I cleared this emotion, I wouldn't see anything clearly.

After breathing quietly for a few moments, I was hit in the stomach by a blow so hard I almost cried aloud. No one had touched me, but my mind had conjured up the single image of my mother and I walking back to White Orchards alone. My mother wore a black veil, and I knew my father was gone. I breathed through this. I had always known my father was frail – that he had survived to the age he had was hailed as a miracle by his doctors. And my mother, I now knew with Fitzroy's help, had always managed to get the finest doctors this country had to offer. His health crises this past year had frightened me badly. I saw that now. I hadn't truly accepted that one day he would be gone, and I would have to carry on without him. All the nonsense Cole had fed me about him not being my father had made my fears worse rather then lessened them. If he had known of my mother having an affair with Fitzroy and still stood by her, and me, he was an even more loving and generous man than I had supposed. I needed him to know that whatever the truth I loved him dearly. He would always be my father. Now that the troops were back in Britain and either bombing or invasion was expected on a daily basis, I had a sense that I was no longer alone in waiting for the death of a loved one. If I had hoped for some solace from this, I had not found it. Instead everything had become even worse. The feeling we were all in the same boat meant I was sinking under the fear of a grief that would reach from one end of the country to the other. How could we survive this? How could people send their sons and daughters, husbands and wives into danger? If I had my choice, I would scoop up my parents, Fitzroy, Bernie, and Harvey and put them somewhere safe for the duration. But then even if I could have done that, all of them would have hated me for it. And what was coming for my father was not something I could stop. Men might inflict death in war, and I might be able to defend some from it. Old age and fragility were different. They were insurmountable enemies – more dangerous by far than the invasion this island feared.

I saw death on the horizon, not only in my own family, but for so many others, and it horrified me. I could be stoic when necessary, but stoic about thousands, perhaps hundreds of thousands of deaths? I couldn't do that. I couldn't. I couldn't cope with what was coming. I knew I would be so consumed by my emotions I would be useless to everyone. Even now, only thinking my fears through, I was trembling, and I felt nauseous. I couldn't bear to lose my father.

And Bernie. I'd let her down so badly. If Harvey was right, and I suspected he was, she was in the hands of a controlling sadist. That should never have happened. Had I really had no time in between learning to type and shorthand to see how my friend was suffering so badly? I knew Bernie. I knew for all her wild ways how vulnerable she was.

It appeared I'd let Harvey down too. Without financial assistance from working for me, he'd gone back to his old ways to feed his family. I'd spent days, then weeks, thinking I should get in touch with him, and I had never even tried.

I had, quite simply, failed at everything – and failed everyone I held dear. I could save no one. That was my deepest fear. I was not up to the task.

All those I had relied upon for support had vanished from my life. There had been no malice. Instead they had been working, striving for the war effort, while I'd singly failed to show my worth. Neither my mother nor Fitzroy would send me on a dangerous mission unless they were sure of my ability to cope. They would use me, as they saw it, to the best of my abilities for the war effort. Fitzroy might have said he was building me a cover as a typist, but the truth was the Army was constantly short of good clerical officers who had a decent security clearance and could back up the various Army, Navy, or RAF officers who created vast amounts of paperwork – some of it even necessary. I would be of use, but I would not be what my godfather had hoped when he spent all these years training me as a child. But then he had been training me to be a peacetime operative. This was different.

As everyone remarked, I was not like my mother. I was not

305

averse to danger, but I would take the safer path where offered. My mother ran towards danger as if it called her by name. As did Fitzroy. I was much more like my father. Considering, cautious, and a natural observer. Occasionally a bit of my mother showed up in my blood, and I did something seemingly brave, but utterly stupid on reflection. I always knew what Fitzroy would have done – at least I had so far in my career – and why I wouldn't do the same. To be fair, it was usually because I wasn't as good at it as him, and more frequently because of his access to establishments and contacts I could only dream about. He also did everything with an air of *I don't care what anyone thinks*. A skill I was yet to acquire. I cared desperately what people thought of me. Perhaps, I thought, because I was brought up by three doting adults, who did their utmost to pass their skills on to me. I might have gone to the village primary school, but after that I was hot-housed by my supervising adults like a rare tropical flower. I had always been treated kindly, fairly, but with strict parameters in place.

Was that what was wrong now? I had no guide rails. Even when I had been working last year to uncover a murderer and a traitor, Fitzroy had always been in the background – on the end of a telephone or opposite me at supper. He'd given me a telephone number to call him at if I needed him, but I was well aware the Department needed him more than my insecurities required his presence. He wasn't mine anymore. My mother was caught up with my father's welfare and her own work. My father – my father was dying.

Was all my resentment about being alone? About facing the reality of my father's impending death?

No, I was not a spoilt child. Overprotected perhaps, but not spoilt. At the root of it all, I didn't like change. I did not want my world or anyone's to change for the worse and that was what Herr Hitler was promising us. The war threatened destruction of everything not only I, but so many others, held dear.

Was I simply scared?

There was only one way I knew to overcome my own fears – and that was to act.

306

Chapter Thirty-nine

I crept cautiously out of my hiding place. I couldn't hear anyone. Not a single footfall. The boys must still be playing with their toys. The staff I'd met had all been very much involved in the cooking process. They'd be cleaning up and preparing for the onslaught of tea and buns (very plain, barely sweet buns, you could count the currants on one hand, but filling.).

Across the corridor was the men's dormitory and beside it the day's programme was posted. It was posted on my corridor too, but it showed merely which of the tutors was meant to be on duty with few other details. Presumably they knew the programme we were all following. Although no one had said so, I got the impression there were other courses running somewhere else at the same time.

Still no sign of anyone. I went over to the notice board to check. After tea, instead of going back outside today, there was free time followed by dinner and an evening lecture, which took us up to lights out. I would be expected to attend the lecture. If I was too ill to sit in a chair, then one of the tutors would demand the doctor was called again and I didn't want that. I needed to be present for tea. It would be necessary to any plan for me to be seen. Eating two buns would definitely do that. I smiled inwardly. What a sacrifice to make for my country. Then, during free time, I would endeavour to make my way to a telephone box in the village and alert my godfather's department to my fears and my discovery of those papers. Then my part would be done. But how was I going to find my way to the village?

I thought it likely one of the tutors might have a village map in their room, but these were all seasoned men. They might not have booby-trapped their rooms, but I would be surprised if I could break into one. Even if I did, I wasn't aware of their movements. I had no idea what they did between teaching. Well, I now knew Fergus met his friends or contacts in the grounds, but that was it. The tutors hadn't specified which branch of the army or Intelligence services they were in, nor their specialities. I found this perfectly reasonable and not in the least suspicious. But it did make predicting their behaviour after a short acquaintance damnably hard.

Without conscious thought I opened the door to the men's dorm. It was empty. Two neat rows of cot beds faced each other. At the foot of each was a metal trunk. Laid on the end of each bed was the man's wash bag, a clean uniform, and a towel. Nothing else was visible. Obviously whichever tutor patrolled the dorm was a stickler for tidiness and inspections. Interestingly there were no visible locks on any of the trunks. Could this be some kind of trust exercise? I really hoped so.

At the start I was extremely careful how I laid out the items inside the trunks, but by the time I had reached the end of the first line, I knew the men would be bound to be back shortly to change out of their muddy clothes and make themselves presentable for the rest of the day indoors.

I had made a number of discoveries. Harvey had a large amount of cash in a pocketbook tucked down a side flap he had carved out of the trunk's cardboard lining. He'd had his initials stamped on the pocketbook and his name neatly written inside. Most of the other men weren't so obliging. I found a couple of collections of smutty photographs, which shouldn't have shocked me, but it did. I was even more grateful to the staff below for loosening my outfit. Several of the men had boiled sweets in paper bags. This led me to believe that someone might be sneaking down to the village for supplies. It didn't need to be one of the men. It could be one of the staff. They'd worked here a long time and must be familiar with the area. But then Harvey's stash of money suggested he was dealing something. I could imagine him acting as a go-between for the men and whoever was fetching the supplies and agreeing with his leg man to skim off profits between them. That was who he was.

Even though there was a potential Nazi sympathiser, or more than one, on site, it never crossed my mind that Harvey might have dealings of any kind with the enemy. He might have been crooked, but he was true-blue.

Eventually, halfway down the far side, I finally had some luck. I came across a postcard which had been sent to a prison and then redirected to 'Davenport House'. Other than the name of the house there was nothing else on the address, but amazingly the censor had overlooked, or simply not realised, that the curious black and white sketch on the front was the stylised map of a village. The postcard read,

My very dear Dean

You know I have always understood who you are, and that you cannot help the way you are made. You are a sweet and kind soul, and in my eyes so much the better man than any of the men in the local congregation. But now you are discovered and in circumstances even I cannot bear to think of, I think you should take the chance you have been offered. I know what they said about fearing for the boys was completely untrue. You may find companionship in a way out of the norm, but we both know you would never hurt a child. How cruel and judgemental they have been. What a waste of a life, or a bright mind like yours, if you stay where they have put you. Surely, anything is better than growing old in a cell. Besides, if we are invaded, I am told the Germans will go into the prisons and shoot everyone.

Your ever-loving Aunt Delia

Dean Fordham's aunt. Fordham, who said his aunt had lived around here. I tucked the postcard into my pocket and put everything else away carefully. I felt sorry for Fordham. I knew even Fitzroy thought that particular law archaic and irrelevant. Rife in the Civil Service, he used to say, rife.

I had barely closed the trunk when I heard the sound of voices in the corridor. I was halfway down the dorm. A quick look told me there was no other exit. I did the only thing I could think of and slid under Fordham's bed.

'I couldn't even see the bullets,' said a male voice. 'It was like watching a rush of air.'

'I saw them,' said another of men. This statement was greeted with a chorus of disbelief. I watched the sets of boots walk into the dorm. It had to be all of them. All of them between me and the door. The bed above me creaked.

'It was the vibrations that got me,' said Harvey. 'Went right through my bones. Like the Bren was trying to get me to dance.' I saw his legs as he jittered about in a mock dance. The men laughed.

'Dance of death,' said Fordham from above me. 'I reckon Stapleford had it right. It's a weapon that kills indiscriminately. Not something I thought the British Army would use outside a battlefield.'

'Isn't that the point?' said Harvey. 'The blighters are bringing the battlefield to our streets.'

'Yes, our streets with our women and children,' said Fordham.

'You've got to be careful,' said another man. 'If you go on talking like that, they'll think you're a conchie. You'll be locked up faster than you can say "how's yer father". Take it from one who has done a bit of time in his time. You wouldn't like it at all, mate.'

At this point Fordham's trousers slid to the floor. As I watched, a number of the men followed suit. Only a few of them bothered to take off their muddy boots first. Really, in so many ways men are so untidy!

Someone roared with laughter and I saw another pair of trousers land on the floor as if thrown. I was beginning to feel somewhat uncomfortable. I don't generally consider myself a prudish person, but I had no desire to see even the rather hairy naked ankles of these men. Unfortunately, they all seemed to have embarked on some kind of lark, and were kicking one another's trousers around the room as if each was a football. I saw more trousers rise and fall than a married woman might see in a year.

However, my view was limited and the worst I saw was a knobbly naked knee. Most of them had now taken off their boots, but these had simply been set aside, leaving me to enjoy both the sight and smell of socks they had worn through their active day. I honestly would have put on my gas mask if only I hadn't left it in my room. Another reason not to get caught and reported. I had little idea of what the punishments were here, but I had no desire to find out for myself.

I heard Harvey whoop with laughter, and then came the sound of him falling. All the air came out of him in a whoosh, and then he started laughing. I, on the other hand, turned my head away. Slightly too late as I had had full sight of his undershorts and even a glimpse of their contents. Only a glimpse. Nothing identifiable. But dear heavens, I thought, I must not get caught here. Surely the lure of buns would tear them away from their antics?

But I had not taken full account of how much the use of a machine gun can bring out the bravado in a man. Fordham was the only one to express concern. Someone jumped on his bed. The frame came down on my head. It hurt. My poor head had suffered too much of late. I pressed my lips together and managed not to vomit.

The person on the bed bounced. I turned my face against the floor to reduce contact. It helped a little. 'Get off my bed!' said Fordham. 'You'll break it.'

The only response was more bouncing. Then I heard Harvey gear up to make the sound of a machine gun. He was clearly the class fool. 'Dakka–dakka–dakka!' he yelled.

'Ah, man, that's not how I want to go!' shouted someone else. 'Shot by Harvey's . . .'

311

I put my hands over my ears and closed my eyes. I guessed Harvey was trying to distract whatever idiot was tormenting Fordham, but I did not want to imagine his method any more than I already had. It seemed that even Harvey, without the civilising presence of a woman, dropped to the lowest common denominator that marks the human male.

I could feel vibrations through the floor. Gradually they ceased. I peeked between my fingers and saw trousers going up – clean ones. Good grief, none of them had even got near water to wash. Fordham's boots were inches away from my nose. I saw him slip one foot in and then the other. At this point he realised someone had tied his laces together. He gave a shout of protest, but he also brought his head down low enough to see under his bed. Our eyes met. His eyebrows shot up.

I'm not proud of what I did next, but I couldn't think of any other way to prevent him giving me away.

I whipped the postcard out of my pocket, pointed at him and mouthed the words, 'I know'. Even bending over he paled. Then he continued unknotting and tying his laces without a word. I felt terrible. I'd never blackmailed anyone before. And to use this against him. I told myself that after I'd made my call to the Department, I would go straight to him and explain everything.

Chapter Forty

I didn't bother going to tea. Not only had I lost my appetite, but it would be easy enough to say I was lying down, still feeling a bit sub-par from yesterday. The men were in high enough spirits they might not even remember I existed. And the very last thing I wanted was to be caught in conversation with Fordham. I had no idea how he would react to my blackmail. Obviously, he'd be angry, but angry enough to privately confront me? I didn't know. All I knew was the nature of his secret meant he would not give me away, and for now that was all I needed.

Likewise, for a so-called secure base, it was all too easy for me to get out. I suppose as most of the men were volunteers, they were technically free to leave at any time. There was a guard on the gate, but no one parrolling the grounds – or at least I saw no one about as I squeezed through a gap in the hedgerow.

It was late afternoon. Mild rather than cold, and there were few people around. In an ideal world I'd have hidden a change of clothing in the hedgerow, but Fordham seeing me meant I had to take my chances in uniform. Hopefully, people would take less notice of me because I was in uniform. With luck they would not associate me with the base. If anyone asked, I decided to say I had a pass to visit a relative billeted here. That would give me a chance to ask for directions to the telephone box too. I could say I only had a number and not an address. I would have to say I had lost the address, I corrected mentally. When constructing a lie, one must always keep it as simple as possible, but not to the extent that it has an obvious flaw.

I had thought of running to the village, but I've never been much of a runner. Unlike my mother, who says it's the best way to get her brain working when she's stuck on a problem. It always seems like too much effort to me. Besides, not being one of the rail-like women who are all too popular, I had portions of anatomy that were adverse to running, and could be made exceedingly uncomfortable by my so doing.

I also realised that my time in the typing pool had significantly reduced any level of fitness I had had through my previous martial arts training. A fast walk was going to be the best I could do. I had memorised the sketch, but it seemed to be taking so long to get to the village I began to seriously wonder if I had had the wretched thing upside down and was going entirely the wrong way. It was, admittedly, the kind of thing that happened to me. I was useless with directions.

The country road I walked along was pleasant enough. Cows lowed in the fields. Hedges buzzed with insect life. Occasional trees overhung the road, and although I knew full well their shade would harbour clouds of gnats, I had already seen that the way was narrow and visibility bad. I had no desire to be run over by a passing motorist who hadn't taken pedestrians into account. I stuck to the side of the road.

By the time the village came into sight the backs of my hands, and my neck and face, itched horribly with bites. I'd done my best to batter the nasty things away, but without complete success. When I finally set foot past the painted-over signpost into the village, I was not in a good mood. I was hot and I was grumpy.

It was with profound relief that I saw the familiar red shape of a telephone box not far ahead. The road arced slightly to the left. I could see the village was comprised of a few shops; a butcher's, a baker's, a small post office, a tiny grocery, and a shop that appeared to sell jumble. All their glass panes were taped up. As were those of the houses that bookended them on that side of the road. On the other side was what looked like a local hostelry. As I walked past, I saw another short road that ended in a space with a market cross. Clearly the village had grown up around the market over the years. I could see no other reason for its existence. Unless Davenport House owned the land here. There was a bus stop towards the far end of the short stretch of road of the little high street. I could also see some chimneys and building behind this single street. It was a very small place.

There didn't seem to be anyone around. I walked quickly over to the telephone box, mentally rehearsing how to ask for a reverse charge call and the various passwords I would have to give. The telephone box sparkled in the late afternoon sun. Someone had recently polished it. This gave me hope the machine was in good order.

I opened the door and stepped inside. The telephone box was completely empty.

I stood there for a few moments, uncomprehending. My plan had dissolved before my eyes. I struggled to think of what I should do. A tapping on the glass made me jump. A hideous ogre peered in at me. I pressed back against the opposite side. Could I be dreaming? Was this whole thing a nightmare?

The ogre opened the door to reveal the face of small elderly lady wearing a blue headscarf. She was bent with age, and her face was heavily lined. Without the distortion of the glass she appeared entirely human. She smiled at me. 'I didn't mean to startle you, love, but there's been no telephone machine in here for a good few weeks now. It's been taken out on account of how Jerry might use it. They had talked about taking down the telephone line itself, but it took six years of arguing to get it installed, so the village council decided that the machine was the thing that had to go. I was at the meeting. "Who's he going to call?" I said to them. "It's not like Jerry's got any friends round here and Arlene on the switchboard knows better than to put a call through to Mr Hitler." But would they listen? Oh no. Come on out, dear, and we'll see if we can solve your problem.'

I let the woman guide me outside. She seemed friendly and harmless. I thought, if this was a fairy story, she'd turn out to be my fairy godmother and save the day. My real godmother was a mathematician with no hint of whimsy about her. The old woman prattled on. '"What if someone needs a doctor?" I asked them. If you ask me, Sheila Holden has the look of an appendicitis about her. Then there's that young couple who've taken the railway cottage. She's pretty as a picture and his call-up papers are due any day. I'll be a monkey's uncle, I said, if he doesn't go off to war leaving her with a bun in the oven. "No. No. No," I said. "We can't do without a telephonic machine."'

'You are quite right,' I said. 'It's a great pity no one listened to you.'

'Oh, they did in the end,' said the old lady. 'They left Bert in the pub with his one. Course he had to promise if the invasion came, he'd make it inoperable. But he keeps a big club behind the bar for the night before the market, so he said he'd use that. We all voted, and Bert kept his telephone. He's open now. You can pop in and ask him to use if it's an emergency. Nice enough bloke, Bert, always ready to help out a body. And there's you in your uniform. We've got to do our best for our fighting boys and girls. Everyone around here believes that.'

I could have kissed her. Instead I thanked her and said, 'You have been so helpful, Mrs?'

'Reed. Wilhelmina Reed.'

'Mrs Reed, thank you. I had better go now. I need to make the call. But you've done your country a service.'

'We're not being invaded today, are we? Only I've got my washing out and there's a nice bit of beef shank in the oven.'

'No, Mrs Reed. It's nothing like that. You're perfectly safe.'

'Oh, good. I'd better go see to my supper and you'd better go and save England. God bless you, dear!' She walked slowly away.

I jogged across the road and into the pub. I chose to go in through the lounge door. I was betting the telephone would be on the more refined side rather than in the bear-pit the standing bar could become on a market night.

Bert proved to be all Mrs Reed had promised. He emerged from behind a door in the middle of the wall. A big bear of a man, he was more than happy to let me use the telephone. Even happier when I said I would be reverse charging the call. 'It's just behind the bar, love. If you let me lift up the counter here, we'll have you at it in a jiffy. I'll make myself scarce in the snug. Knock on the door when you're done, and I'll come back through and see you out.'

I picked up the receiver and found I was trembling. The switchboard operator attempted to reverse the call to the number I gave. The woman who answered at the other end said, 'Longberry Tailoring,' but she instantly accepted my call.

I gave her my army ID number. There was silence for a few moments, then she said, 'What is the message, Stapleford?'

'I believe there is a German sympathiser at the base where I am. It is serious enough to warrant the Department's involvement.' I kept my voice as low as I could, but I wished Fitzroy had taught me some of the new codes – or Cole had – or Mother or anyone. I felt a fool having to say it straight, and I had no idea how thick the door between the lounge and the bar was.'

'Evidence?'

'Yes,' I said. 'Physical evidence.'

'Thank you for letting us know. Continue as ordered.'

She hung up. There had been no promise or offer of help. Perhaps I should have asked for Fitzroy by name. It was too late now. After all the tension I had carried today, it felt like a major let down.

I knocked on the door, and the landlord opened it wide. The standing bar had few customers, but the man at the bar looked up as the door opened. The landlord said something, but I didn't hear. With the door open I was looking straight into the eyes of Fergus, and he didn't look happy to see me.

'Bert,' said Fergus, 'could you show the young lady round. We need to talk.'

'I could let her through,' said Bert. Fergus shook his head. The barkeeper shut the door behind him. 'Sorry about this, miss. Mr Whitelaw brings a lot of business here. Friends of his from the city. I don't think he means you no harm. Always polite, but it'd be best for me and for you if you obliged him with a little conversation.'

'It's fine,' I said. 'I want to speak to him too.'

As we came round to the snug, a man shot out of the door before us. He kept his face turned away, but there was something familiar about him. 'One of Mr Whitelaw's London friends?' I asked.

Bert shrugged. 'They came in together. But you know, war time. Not the time to be asking questions, is it, miss? You and Mr Whitelaw both in uniform, you know the rules better than me.'

Bert showed me into the snug and then flipped open the counter on this side and went back behind the bar, clearly washing his hands of the whole situation.

'Hope,' said Fergus. 'What can I get you to drink?'

I realised the question was meant to put me off guard, but I was extremely thirsty. 'Whatever they have that doesn't have alcohol in it, please,' I said, with a polite smile.

'Lemonade, Bert. Make it a large one,' he turned back to me. 'It must have been thirsty work walking here. Don't worry, I can give you a lift back.'

'Thank you, sir. That would be much appreciated.'

Bert put a pint glass of cool liquid in front of me. If I could have climbed into the glass to drink I would have done so. Instead, I picked it up, said 'cheers' to Fergus, and allowed myself a couple of gulps before putting it down again.

'So,' said Fergus, 'would you like to tell me why you are off base? Were you given permission by someone? Or are we going to be holding a court-martial on grounds of desertion?'

'I had no intention of deserting,' I said hotly. 'I would never do that.'

'Even though if the worst happens while you're here you'll be expected to stay with us regardless of what the higher-ups might have said?'

'I was offended that they didn't want to deploy me. Shouldn't we be away from the main bar if we're talking about such matters, sir?'

'This is the local village, Hope. I'd be surprised if everyone here,' he looked around, 'well, the three of them plus Bert didn't know a fair amount of what we're up to. Little villages are like that.'

'I'm appalled.'

Fergus laughed. 'I haven't told anyone anything, but the bush telegraph works efficiently. They know how many of us are up there, and at least some of what we're doing. A Bren gun is loud, as you heard today. They're well aware we're an Army training ground.' He looked hard at me.

'I see,' I said. 'I suppose that's not surprising.'

'All Home Guards need training officers, don't they?'

He really didn't need to spell it out. I understood he was saying people knew only we were a training base and not what the auxis really were. The last thing the countryside needed was more fear about the invasion spread along their bush telegraph. Home Guard training was a good cover for the men at the house, especially as most of them weren't regular army. 'Absolutely,' I said. 'It's good for morale for the men who haven't been called up to think they are contributing in some way. Between them they must have a lot of experience from the Great War.'

'Exactly,' said Fergus. 'And you were off base, why?'

'I misunderstood,' I said. 'I thought I was exempt from the leaving base regulations because I was signed off duty by the doctor.'

'That won't wash, Hope. You were confined to the base over security issues.'

'But you are here, sir,' I said, looking him directly in the eye.

'I have a higher security clearance than you.'

'I doubt it, sir. Mine is unusually high.'

'And why would that be?'

'My mother, sir.'

'Your mother?' said Fergus, frowning.

'She is known in the Service as Alice,' I said. I watched his face closely to see any reaction. If he was a part of the Service, there was a chance he had heard of her. Especially if he had ever worked with counter-intelligence.'

'Good heavens,' said Fergus. '*The* Alice?'

I nodded. He sat down on the bar stool. 'No wonder you were more up on my lecture than the rest of the lads!'

I gave a slight shrug. 'I'm not up on all that much. It was never thought we'd have another war, but some of the skill set she possessed, that was relevant to civilian life, she taught me from childhood.'

'How very fortunate. I'm not sure it's enough to let you get away with being off base though. Who were you calling?'

'Her, actually,' I lied calmly. Fergus might be in the Service, but that didn't mean I needed to tell him everything. In fact, it was rather nice to know that for once I was dealing out the need to know policy.

'Reporting on us?' Fergus said with a thin smile.

'Not at all, sir. It's a purely personal matter. My father is very sick,' I blinked back genuine tears at the thought, 'and I thought to have some news of him.'

'How is he?' said Fergus in a kindlier tone.

'Still with us,' I said, 'but my mother doesn't think it will be much longer.' I gave a bit of a sniff. Again, entirely genuine.

'Did you get to speak to him?'

I shook my head. 'He sleeps a lot of the time now, and Mother doesn't like disturbing him.'

'I could petition for compassionate leave for you,' said Fergus.

'We had a good Christmas together,' I said, 'and he wanted me to remember him well. I'll need the compassionate leave to help my mother when – when it happens.'

Fergus laid a hand lightly on my shoulder. 'All a bit much, I should think, Hope. You being here, dealing with all this, while your father is so ill.'

'Not as bad as being at Dunkirk,' I said. 'That's what really pulled him down. He went out to help get the troops back. It sort of took the last of him.' I stood up a bit straighter. 'I'm enormously proud of him.'

'As you should be,' said Fergus. He still had his hand on my shoulder. He looked down at me with a much more friendly expression. 'You have been having a hard time. What say I drive you back up to the house and neither of us mention your outing?'

'Thank you, sir. That's very kind.'

He smiled. 'I think while we're off base you can call me Fergus. I can't be that much older than you – and I certainly haven't been in training as long as you have!' He gave a low laugh. 'You'll like my lecture this evening. It's all about hiding.'

'Hiding what, Fergus?' I asked.

'Everything and anything, Hope. Drink up. I need to get back and set up a few things.'

Fergus' car turned out not to be the Army car I was expecting, but a small two-seater. He must have seen my unguarded expression. 'Sometimes it's important I'm not driving an Army car,' he said. 'So they gave me this.'

This was as close an admission to being in the Service as he was liable to give – that and knowing of my mother. 'It's a nice car,' I said. 'I left mine at my parents'. I miss it.'

Fergus slipped behind the wheel. 'I can understand that. Driving is one of the few times one knows one is in control nowadays.' He started the car. 'Incidentally, Hope, I'm wondering if you knew the man I was meeting. David Danville? I'm guessing you must have done a London season?'

David Danville, the very man I suspected was behind the nasty business of a traitor in the Service last year but had been unable to prove. 'I've met him, yes,' I said.

Fergus accelerated away from the kerb. 'I thought so. He remembered you quite fondly, and your friend Bernadette. I believe she's married now – to someone in Navy Intelligence?'

'I haven't met her husband. It was something of a whirlwind romance.'

'War will do that to people,' said Fergus skilfully taking a corner at speed. 'No one knows if they will live to see tomorrow.'

'Is Danville an asset of yours?'

Fergus took his eyes off the road for a moment. 'You know I can't answer a question like that, Hope.'

'No, of course not.'

In my mind I replayed what I recalled of the conversation I had overheard. Yes, the almost familiar voice had been Danville. The question was, did Fergus know of the man's associations and was running an op, or did Fergus have such sympathies himself? Once I would have thought that impossible, but after last year I had learned not to trust easily. If Hugh was a Nazi sympathiser, was Fergus in on it? In fact, were all the instructors sympathisers?

'Penny for your thoughts, Hope?'

'I was thinking about my family,' I said.

Fergus nodded. 'I can imagine you have a lot on your mind.'

I hoped he didn't have any idea exactly how much.

Chapter Forty-one

Fergus drove fast, but he didn't take unnecessary risks. I might have enjoyed the ride if it hadn't been for my indecision. I couldn't get rid of the feeling that the operative I had spoken to on the Service switchboard hadn't take me seriously. If I had been right about Fitzroy putting me in the clerical pool, or at least leaving me there, for my own well-being, I thought, then it might be general knowledge in the Department that I wasn't well enough trained yet to be put on general deployment. Was it possible she could be so arrogant that she had dismissed the possibility of my having real intel?

'Do you think operatives in the Service tend towards arrogance?' I asked suddenly.

Fergus glanced briefly at me. 'Have you met any of them?' he asked.

I nodded.

'Then you have your answer.'

'Damn!' I said out loud.

'Problem?'

I could see Davenport House on the horizon. I made a decision I knew at least Cole would have strongly disapproved of, but I was desperate. 'I lied to you,' I said quickly. 'I wasn't calling my mother – though I would have liked to call home. I was calling in information to the counter-intelligence department. Only I don't think they took me seriously. The woman that answered the call was most dismissive.'

'Marjory,' said Fergus. 'She always comes across like that. I wouldn't worry. She's a good egg on the whole. I'm sure she'll pass it on.'

'You know her?'

Fergus didn't look at me, but he grinned. 'I cannot confirm or deny any knowledge of Marjory Dalrymple.'

'Oh, I see.' I sat looking down at my hands.

'I don't seem to have helped,' said Fergus. 'Do you want to tell me? I have a back channel. I won't be using it again until tomorrow, but I can see a message gets through.'

'I found some papers at the house which strongly suggest the late owner of the house and his daughter were Nazi sympathisers.'

Fergus took a sharp breath. 'I suppose I shouldn't be surprised. A lot of the aristocracy were taken in by Hitler. They liked some of his "world order" ideals. But why does it matter now?'

'Because his son is the instructor, Hugh.'

'Oh, hell,' said Fergus. 'I wondered about him. He seemed too familiar with the house.'

'You didn't know? The staff were the first to tell me.'

'Staff?'

'Below stairs.'

'Ah, yes, well they were far more likely to speak to you than one of the officers, I expect.' He paused. 'So you think Hugh is, what, a Nazi? A German sympathiser?'

I shook my head. 'I don't know. His sister was wild, according to the staff, and expected him to pay all her debts.'

'You're thinking blackmail?'.

'I don't know . . . I . . . I realise he might have asked to be assigned here to see whoever was billeted didn't tear up his house. However, it strikes me that the Germans having intelligence about where the auxi units are based before an invasion would be extremely useful to them. Useful enough to even precipitate an invasion.'

'Hell's teeth. That's a dreadful thought.' I saw Fergus bite his lip.

Fergus slowed the car and pulled over into the gap in front of a field gate. 'You do realise, Hope, that means I might be one too? All of us instructors could be in on it!'

I shook my head. 'I don't believe the country is filled with double agents. The service vets people too thoroughly. You knew Marjory.'

'I never said that.'

'Of course you did. You said her surname.'

'Clumsy of me,' said Fergus.

'No, I think you were trying to tell me I could trust you.'

'Perhaps,' admitted Fergus. 'Being Alice's daughter, you must know how full of shadows the espionage world is. It can be hard knowing where to turn. Especially when you are new to the actual business end of the work.'

'I'm realising that,' I said. 'I haven't had much to do with Hugh. I'd love it if he was loyal, but even shielding his family, however natural a thing to do, isn't on.'

Fergus nodded. 'Would you leave this with me, Hope? I'll talk to him. The best thing for him would be to turn himself in and plead family loyalty. They might give him the benefit of the doubt if he owns up. If he doesn't, then . . .' He shook his head.

'What?'

'He'll be shot for treason like as not. He's an officer in the King's army, shielding a sympathiser — if that's what his sister turns out to be, if not an operative of our enemy or actually being one himself.' He shook his head. 'There's no love lost between Hugh and I, but I can't believe he's a Nazi.'

I thought for a moment. 'The staff think well of him. That says something. I think you should talk to him and give him the chance to hand himself in. It would be easier for everyone. The only thing is, can you handle him alone.'

Fergus laughed out loud at that. 'Don't worry, Hope. I've had some of the best hand-to-hand combat training the Army can offer.' He offered me his hand. 'So, we have a deal.'

I leaned forward to shake his hand. He pulled me towards him with a quick gesture and kissed my cheek. 'Never trust a spy, my dear,' he said, drawing back and winked at me. I was surprised, but it struck me this was exactly the kind of thing Fitzroy might have done when he was a young spy. According to my mother he'd had what is politely termed 'a roving eye'.

Fergus eased the car out of the dip and drove on towards the house. Neither of us spoke, but I, at least, felt a sensation of lightness that I was no longer alone responsible for ensuring that Britain's plans and locations didn't fall into the hands of the enemy.

We pulled up outside the house, and to my surprise Fergus parked in full view of the building. 'I must have hit my head very hard,' I said, 'I never noticed your car when I arrived.'

'I'm often out and about,' said Fergus. 'Swift of wit and fleet of foot.' He gave me a grin. 'Now, get inside before anyone sees us together. And remember while we're on the base it's sir, not Fergus.' He winked at me.

I felt myself blush, so I quickly scrambled out of the car and headed upstairs. When I appeared to rejoin the men in the common room the tea urn was entirely empty. Harvey and his team were clearing up the rest of the mess. It looked rather as if there had been a bun fight.

'Where the hell have you been?' said Harvey. 'Look at this ruddy mess.'

'Headache,' I said. 'I went to lie down. I want to hear the lecture.'

'Yes, well,' grumbled Harvey. 'Can you help us out a bit? Wally Gibbs started a food fight.'

'Wally?' I said, finding a fallen, largely undamaged bun under a chair. 'He didn't strike me as the type.' I sat down, picked the small amount of fluff off the bun, and bit into it. 'See,' I said. 'Helping. Less to clear up.'

'Sometimes, Hope Stapleford,' said Harvey, 'you are truly disgusting. You have no idea where that bun has been.'

'I doubt it was placed here by a master poisoner,' I said. A

326

ridiculous concern flitted across my mind. 'The instructors didn't come down here during tea break, did they?'

'Yes, Hugh did. Even threw a bun, when he thought no one was looking, on the way out. Made no attempt to stop the fight. I guess he thought we were blowing off steam. But then he's not the one who had to clear up the mess.'

I put the bun in the pig bin. 'On second thoughts,' I said, 'where are we meeting for the talk? Usual room?'

Harvey shook his head. 'Outside by the edge of the forest. I assume we're going to be taught how to climb trees. Sure you want to join in? You could still plead illness. It'll be dark and colder by then.'

'No, it's all good,' I said. 'I am more than capable of climbing a tree without falling. I learnt as a child. I'll go and rest before dinner. What are the rest of you doing?'

'There's going to be a cricket match,' said West, his eyes bright. 'They have no idea how good a bowler I am.'

'I'm done,' said Fordham abruptly. He threw a hard glance in my direction and stormed out.

'What on earth was that about?' said Harvey.

'Maybe he doesn't like cricket?' suggested West.

'I'll have a word,' said Harvey.

For the rest of the free time until dinner I went and lay on my bed and thought. I still had an uneasy feeling. I was uneasy about Fordham, and I was uneasy that at any moment Hugh might reveal top secret plans to the enemy. Did anyone even know if he had access to a crystal set? Had the instructors' rooms ever been searched? Did the staff clean them? Would they even know . . . I fell asleep still fretting.

My stomach woke me up. I was surprised it didn't wake up the whole house. Obviously worrying made me very hungry. My Aunt Richenda always turned to cake in times of stress, but my tooth wasn't so sweet. Although I did appreciate a good bun. I checked myself in the mirror and made myself as presentable as possible. I also took a jacket down with me. I'd hang it somewhere in the hall. The men could fetch them from the dorm in seconds. It took me minutes and I didn't want to miss any of the lecture after dinner.

I was already sitting in the hall when I realised, I should have been down in the kitchens helping to mess up. I was not going to be a favourite with any of Harvey's team. Still, it was probably better if I left Fordham alone until I got a chance to explain to him properly and privately. Yes, I reasoned, while I was waiting for matters to unfold it was better if I kept my head down. Consequently, I wrapped myself around a large quantity of meat and two vegetables without paying that much attention to what I was eating. Twenty minutes later I was standing on the edge of the forest with most of the rest of the men. Harvey and West arrived last. I raised an eyebrow at Harvey, but he simply shrugged. Of Fergus there was no sign.

The men started shifting their feet. The conversation stayed reasonably civil. I couldn't help suspecting that was because I was there. My father's accent wasn't especially posh, but both my mother and Fitzroy, when they relaxed, had voices which could cut glass, and unfortunately no one had given me any voice training. Consequently, I sounded like I spent my free time at Buck House, when in fact nothing could be further from the truth. I'd much rather be in a field. This gave me an idea.

'Our instructor appears to be missing,' I said. 'I'll have a quick look around.' Then, before anyone could stop me, I climbed up the nearest stout tree as fast as I could. The men looked on in stunned surprise. When I reached the highest part of the trunk it was safe to climb – about fifteen feet or so up – I spotted Fergus at once. He was taking advantage of a hollow in the land to conceal himself from view, not very far from the group at all. This was clearly the first part of his lecture.

'North-west, four yards!' I called down.

The men swung round, looking into the forest. 'I mean south-east!' I hurried down the tree.

Fergus stood up and sauntered over to the group. 'Good idea to climb the tree, but that would have been more impressive, Stapleford, if you had got the direction right. Sun sets in the west most nights.' There was a rumble of amusement from among the men. Fergus caught my eye and winked so swiftly I also missed it.

'There will be times,' said Fergus, 'when you are evading the enemy and there appears to be nowhere to run. What I want you to learn this evening is the essence of concealment. We've covered the other main elements of fieldcraft. You should all now be confident in how to find your way in woods and close country. In England, what side of the tree does moss generally grow?'

'The west,' I said.

'And which way do trees generally tilt?'

'East.'

He shook his head. 'You appear to have some knowledge, but yet you called out the wrong direction.'

I didn't answer. There wasn't much I could say.

'To continue, you should all know how to make a shelter, catch wild animals and forage for food, construct a trench oven, and cook. Although the jury is still out on whether what you produce, Sykes, is actually edible.'

Another rumble of laughter. Big Dom Sykes blushed red and hung his head.

'We've also done some work on laying false trails, and we've alerted you to the reactions of animals to strangers which might betray your presence, or even the enemy's. What should you remember when approaching a village, Cooper?'

'Always approach village dogs upwind. Both domestic and wild animals will look the same way if a stranger approaches. Cows can start mooing and sheep bleat. Givin' your presence away or announcing the approach of the enemy – dependin' on where you are. I mean what country you're in – whether you or they are the stranger. Not that I'm saying cows are strange . . .' He broke off.

'That's all right, Cooper. Your field skills are clearly better than your ability to describe them. Now someone else. If you must live in the open where are your best options?'

'The tree line, sir,' called out someone

'Edge of a wood,' corrected Fergus. 'If you camp on a tree line on the horizon you'll stick out like a sore thumb. You can also use to effect disused quarries, chalk or gravel pits, and, if you're especially lucky, find an old lime kiln. By now you should be thinking of the countryside as another tool in your kit to overcome the enemy. We have more work on codes and ciphers to do in the coming week, but we will be rolling a lot of your learning into a treasure hunt and later, a more serious subversive organisational exercise.'

'Will we get a prize, sir?' called out West.

'I'll see what I can do, West, but there's a war on, you know!'

This last sally caused gales of laughter. It must have been some kind of in-joke that I wasn't in on.

'Right, back to today's topic. How to hide by day – this shouldn't tax your intellect. In a hollow tree. An evergreen bush. By night, you should consider haystacks. From May to September in a hay or corn field, but remember to enter from the correct direction so as not to leave signs of your passage. Then we come to dips in the land, bracken, heather and any such low undergrowth. Come on out and look at this field with me. Stapleford spotted where I was hiding from above. One thing to remember is there is never a hiding space that is one hundred per cent foolproof. Though I did manage to fool the rest of you!'

This was greeted with some jocular male noises, not wholly unlike those produced by pigs when they hear the sound of the swill bucket approaching. 'Right, I want you to divide into your teams and take some time hiding from each other on the edge of the forest and across the fields here. Reassemble in thirty minutes. I expect you all to have learning to share.'

Harvey, Colin West, and I came together. 'Where's Dean?' I asked.

Harvey shrugged. 'No idea, and I'm beginning to get rather cross about it.'

'He told me he had to talk to one of the instructors,' said West.

'Didn't want me to mention it. Said he'd catch up with us quickly. Wanted to know which of them was the C.O.'

'That's a bit odd,' I said. 'Is there a C.O.?'

'I think technically it's Hugh,' said Harvey, 'but they pretty much muck in together. The chap who was here just before you arrived, I rather think he's behind all this, but he visits the base rather than stays on it. Does that make him a C.O.? I'm not up on all the Army stuff yet.'

'Come on. We'd better start lying down in muddy puddles or whatever we need to do,' said West.

'This is a clean uniform,' protested Harvey.

'It's about camouflage,' I said. 'These uniforms are pretty good, but we have to tell Fergus that if we were in other colours, we'd take the time to change the colour of our clothing. Mud is often the first and easiest choice.'

'All right,' said Harvey. 'What else?'

'It's not that complicated really,' I said. 'Most kids are good at hiding. You probably were. Where it changes is the level of risk. If you're found under the circumstances you're training for, you'll be shot. The natural anxiety that provokes in all of us makes us over-think how we might hide, but it's no different to the kids' game. We're more experienced now. It should be easier. The hardest thing is to have confidence in your hiding skills. If someone approaches and you're in as good a position as you think you can be, the last thing to do is bolt – and yet, some people do just that.'

'Giving a talk to the troops,' said Fergus, coming up behind me. 'Perhaps I should get you to lecture the men?' His tone was more amused than critical. 'Did she make any good points, lads?'

'Nothing that I didn't know,' said West. 'But I agree with her, it's as much about holding your nerve as it is about finding the right place. I've seen a lot of bolters. Up before the magistrate before you could say "Jack Quick!"'

Fergus' smile broadened. 'I believe you will be an excellent addition to your team. Good sneaking, good trapping, and I'm hearing your shooting is coming on.'

331

'I believe it is, sir,' said West, puffing out his chest. 'I do believe I can now hit the proverbial barn door.'

Fergus tapped him lightly on the shoulder. 'Good man. Keep working on it. Back to the tree line, please. You've given me your fact.' He walked off to see Dom and his group, who seemed absorbed in poking bits of leaves through their beards.

'I hope he's finishing up soon,' said West. 'I've got a lot of dinner in my stomach and it wants me to be lying down.'

'Been an odd day,' said Harvey. 'I'm more tired than usual.'

'It'll be all the excitement of using the Bren gun,' I said. 'Got you all worked up.'

'How do you know that, Hope?' said Harvey.

'The bun fight,' I said, quickly covering my tracks. 'And the way Fordham was behaving. He hates the idea of using a machine gun. He stormed off, and that's not like him at all.'

We reached the tree line. Harvey leant back against a tree and lit a cigarette. He offered me one, but I refused.

'You're allowed to smoke when you're not actually being trained,' he said. 'It's fine.'

'No thanks,' I said. 'Besides, I think you're taking the "not being trained" a bit too literally.' I gave him a smile to show I wasn't trying to be rude to him. In reality, I was beginning to worry about Fordham. Did his trying to find the C.O. have anything to do with him seeing me under his bed? Surely, he had too much to lose if the men found out about him. The instructors would know, and men like my godfather wouldn't care, but this group? Some of them were distinctly rough around the edges.

I found a tree to lean against and looked out at the groups in the grounds beyond, and Fergus casually walking between them. He seemed very relaxed, almost too much so. As if he was putting on an act. He hadn't struck me a man who would be intimidated by this group when I had met him in the village. I didn't know what would worry him. He reminded me of Fitzroy in his devil-may-care attitude. That was what had made me decide to trust him. To believe he must be running Danville rather than

332

working with him. Actively befriending the seemingly untouch-able Nazi sympathiser to get enough information to get him locked up or shot. I'm not inclined to bloodthirstiness. I wanted him off the streets of London, away from the soirées, dinners, and home parties that were still happening to some extent. I wanted him away from the world that Bernie inhabited and locked up somewhere safe where he could do no more harm. Though if it was decided to execute him, I wouldn't be shedding any tears.

'You're looking rather fearsome,' said Harvey. 'A moment ago I looked over to say something and you looked all dreamy-eyed and distanced. Now you're scowling like an 'arpy.'

'All dreamy-eyed,' said West. 'Do you have a thing for Fergus? I suppose he's about as far from an Aryan as you could get. Seems to fancy you.'

Harvey looked from West to me. 'Is that true? Do you have a thing going on with him?'

'Of course not,' I said, feeling treacherous heat rise into my face, 'I hardly know him.'

Harvey raised an eyebrow at me. 'No wonder you weren't looking for me, if you were off chasing men in uniform.'

'Harvey!'

But the others were arriving back now, and all further conversation ceased. Fergus walked up to us and through the group, who parted quickly to let him pass. 'This way,' he said, as he walked further into the forest. Quite quickly we came upon a small clearing. It looked as if some of the trees had been felled, possibly due to disaster or merely for firewood. Fergus sat down on a tree stump, while the rest of us tried to position ourselves in this small place without getting a branch in an uncomfortably intimate position. It was a squeeze. Fergus watched us. His eyes flickering from one man to another. 'So, what do you see?' he asked. 'Please look carefully.'

There was a general shuffling and grunting. A few exclama-tions as various people bumped various parts of themselves into both blunt and sharper points of the trees. After a few minutes

333

Fergus called a halt and demanded we watch. He stood up and kicked at the tree trunk which unhinged, revealing an entrance.

'I believe this one was once a badger sett. It should hold two men comfortably. Three at a pinch. We've been having them built up and down Britain. It is likely you will all be assigned to one of these underground bases if, and when, you graduate from here. Right, who wants to see down there? Orderly queue please.'

The Owls proved to be one of the more surprised teams, so we ended up mid-queue. The first man disappeared down, while Fergus stayed at the top. Then another, and finally the third. It was like watching a conjurer's trick. When they were all in Fergus kicked the stump closed. There were some startled cries from underground.

'Of course, it opens from the inside, but I imagine it will take them a bit of time to find the mechanism in the dark. All these bases are light-proofed, but as you heard, not entirely sound-proofed. Once you're in there's no telescope or similar gadget to let you see out. Maybe one of you will be clever enough to invent something. But what I want to impress upon you is that you may have a radio below, but you are blind above unless you leave someone on watch – and that might not always be possible.'

The top of the tree trunk folded back, and a worried face peeked out. Everyone laughed. 'Even in the dark, you can still find your way out,' said Fergus. 'Everything that can be done to add all amenities to these subterranean dwellings has been done.'

'I am sorry to interrupt,' said Aubrey from behind us. 'But I need your instructor and Stapleford to accompany me back to base.' He caught sight of Harvey. 'Cooper, you had better come too.'

I turned to see he was escorted by two other men in uniform, who Bernie would have referred to as 'muscle'. It looked like I was in trouble.

Chapter Forty-two

I stood in front of Hugh's desk. We were all in a large room that I hadn't seen before. It seemed to be more than an office. Plans and charts were spread all over the wall, and folders were stacked up in one corner. One of the charts showed the position of the enemy across the channel. This wasn't the sort of thing I should be seeing. That worried me. Either my security clearance had been upgraded again, or Hugh didn't think I would be in any position to tell anyone of what I had seen once this interview was over.

'Do you know why you're here, Stapleford?'

I shook my head. 'No, sir.'

'Not the faintest idea?'

'Did I take too much time off?'

Hugh lowered his eyebrows in an ugly frown. 'It would be the best course of action for you, Miss Stapleford, if you told us the truth. I do not like falsities.'

Fergus, Aubrey, and Harvey stood behind me. I couldn't catch their attention. At what point did I announce this man was a Nazi sympathiser and most likely a German informant? The proof was in the house, but not in this room. Would Hugh overrule my request to have the desk searched – of course he would. I had to take this carefully.

'I do not know why you wish to question me, sir. I am not aware of having done anything wrong.'

'Indeed,' said Hugh angrily. 'Fordham, get in here, now.'

The door opened behind me and Dean came to stand next to

me. He looked white and a little frightened. 'Dean?' I said. He didn't even glance in my direction.

'Kindly repeat what you reported to me earlier today.'

'I saw Stapleford hiding underneath my bed in the men's dorm when we came back from using the Bren gun. I was going to tell the others, but she held up a postcard from my aunt that had been in my trunk. She blackmailed me into silence.'

'In what way?' said Hugh.

'Must I say?' said Dean.

'Yes,' said Hugh flatly.

'The postcard refers to my preference – albeit obliquely – in the matters of love. It was clear that Stapleford had deciphered its meaning.'

'You mean that before being here you were residing at His Majesty's pleasure on charges of being a homosexual?'

Fordham swallowed and nodded.

'How could this be considered blackmail? All the instructors are aware of your background.'

'But the men are not,' said Dean softly.

'You feared their derision?'

'Or worse,' said Dean. 'I've been beaten before for my – my particularity.'

'Very good, Fordham. You may go.'

Dean finally looked at me, and his eyes were full of hatred. I shook my head, but his expression didn't change. I think if no one else had been there to witness it, he would have spat on me.

'Is what Fordham saying true, Stapleford? Were you under his bed and did you attempt to use this postcard to blackmail him?' said Hugh.

'Yes,' I said. 'But it's not . . .'

'Enough,' said Hugh.

'Sir, if she did what he said she must have had a good . . .' said Harvey, before Hugh told him to be silent.

'Fergus, you have told me you came upon the girl in the village. Is this correct?'

336

'Yes,' said Fergus.

'Did she give you a reason?'

'She gave me two,' said Fergus. 'I have no idea if either was true.'

At this I did turn around to look at him. He returned my gaze with a blank expression. 'I do regret this, Stapleford,' he said. 'I thought you showed promise. But my loyalty is to my country.'

And then I understood all of it. I also understood I would get no justice here.

'You also informed me that this girl had alleged that my family were Nazi sympathisers and that my late father and sister had been working as German informants.'

'She did,' said Fergus.

I had turned away by now. I was checking the desk for any options. A paperweight, a swagger stick, a letter opener, too far away – and besides I didn't want to stab anyone. Well, I wouldn't have minded stabbing Fergus.

The voices continued. I didn't listen again until Fergus began explaining the desk I had mentioned had been searched and found empty.

'Might there have been a secret compartment?' said Fergus. 'Not that your family could be – but Stapleford might have misunderstood. Especially if it was in German.'

'For all we know, the girl reads German fluently. No, there were no papers. There is a secret compartment. This was also checked and found empty.'

'You played your cards badly, Stapleford,' said Hugh. 'You didn't know that Fergus was my father's secretary. He's been a loyal member of staff for many years.'

'Oh, I had worked that out by now,' I said. 'A lot of things have become suddenly much clearer.'

'Don't take that tone of voice with me, young woman!' said Hugh, rising to his feet. I took my chance. I grabbed the swagger stick and lunged at his sternum. Taken off guard, he swayed and sat down again. In the meantime, I had turned and struck hard and widely with the stick. The men's instinctive reaction was to get out of the way. I made it to the door, but I had two toughs out there to get past.

I flung the door open, and yelled, 'Help! Help! He's having a fit! I'll get a doctor,' I said to the surprised guards who rushed up.

No one expects a small young woman to be a fighter. Or even a wrongdoer, if she speaks with the right accent. The guards hesitated a fraction of a second until the others poured through the door. One went after me, but I smacked him hard across his face and he went backwards and down. The whole group of them had been huddled together like a group of ninepins and the inevitable happened.

I ran.

Of course, they were not far behind me. Once they'd picked themselves up I would have practically a whole company chasing me. Or at least that was what it felt like hearing the shouts and the scrambling. I hurtled down the corridor and ran through the next door, leaving it swinging behind me. Another door lay ahead. I spotted what I thought might be a broom cupboard. I pushed the exit door to make it swing and dived into the cupboard shutting it tightly behind me.

A tiny crack of light showed round the edge of the door. Several shelves dug into my back, and I only just managed to catch something I dislodged. It was too dark to see what it was but, it was heavy, bottle-shaped and went slosh. Chances were it was cleaning fluid. I kept it in my hand. I didn't want to douse anyone with disinfectant, but I would if I had to. The swagger stick and I had parted company somewhere along my immediate escape route. Survive, make do, and get the job done. Fergus' behaviour had proved his loyalties in my mind. Whether Hugh was in on the whole thing I had no idea. For all I knew the Intelligence branch had taken its eye so far off the ball that even Aubrey was a traitor. Maybe all the auxi instructors were. My heart beat faster, and I could feel panic welling up. I deliberately slowed my breath, breathing in for a count of four, holding my breath for a count of four and then quietly breathing out for four. It was one of Fitzroy's tricks for calming anxiety while you waited to go on an operation. He'd tried to teach me meditation as well, but my mind wouldn't stop wandering and chattering at me. Right now, I wished I'd put more effort in. I could feel sweat pooling in my back, and it was an effort to stop fidgeting with my fingers. I was now completely at one with Colin West on the difficulties of being confident in your ability to hide. I'd known the theory, but actually suppressing the stress invoked by not fleeing, is rather hard.

I heard them come through the door. Fergus was first, and he had taken slightly longer than I expected. Fortunately, the door must have still had some vestige of movement as he cried out, 'She went this way.' Although to any observer it should have been clear there was nowhere else to go. Gentlemen in general, I have found, are unaware of cleaning cupboards.

Now came the hardest part. I hadn't enjoyed the idea of them passing me by, but I knew the view from the front of the house would quickly make it clear to even the dullest mind that unless I was crawling through ditches – a possibility I hoped they would investigate thoroughly – I hadn't gone that way.

Whatever else Fergus might be, he was thorough – I heard him shouting instructions to the guards to search outside. Then I heard the sound of some feet coming back towards me. This was the danger moment. If any of the men had some kind of brainstorm and remembered they were real people who cleared up after them then they might, just might, think of opening a cupboard.

I heard Harvey say, 'This has to be a misunderstanding. Hope's true blue if ever anyone was.' My eyes teared up momentarily. I mentally shook off the sentiment. There would be time for things like that later. What I needed to do now was hang on until Marjory got someone down here. I no longer believed Fergus' story that no one was coming. I had to believe. On this base, with instructors with these kinds of skills, I'd be lucky if I held out for an afternoon, let alone a few days. Going to the village would now only get me spotted. My best chance would be to get on a train. I didn't have a travel warrant, nor enough money in cash, but it was always possible to insinuate yourself onto a busy train. Except that would mean lurking in the vicinity until I saw such a one. Also, it would be hard to get the right train. Even I knew that I needed to go in the reverse direction to the one I had arrived on. So I knew which side of the track to wait, but how to tell if something was a local train or a London train? Signs, timetables, and announcements were all now banned.

I stopped making circular plans and listened. I couldn't hear anyone. That introspective episode must have taken up a minute or two. Being mentally busy had kept me physically still. It seemed I'd got away with this bit. But what next?

Where would be the last place they looked? When the thought struck me, I almost laughed out loud. It was daring enough that hopefully they wouldn't associate it with me. The only question was, did I have time to get any supplies? I turned it over in my mind. Ideally, I wanted everyone out of the house and grounds hurrying to the train station to stop me fleeing, but I couldn't count on that. There was an example first aid kit in the main lecture room. If I went out those doors, and didn't turn on any lights, I might manage to swipe it. I was going to have to be very, very quiet and, more difficult, I would need to be both cautious and quick. When it came to actual action caution was not my middle name. I preferred to get that kind of stuff over with quickly. I could take the time and patience to observe and plan, but I liked my action swift and dirty.

Chapter Forty-three

The manor had proved to be largely empty. I didn't know if the rest of the men had been roused to help find me, or if the original six men had decided to keep it between themselves. Whatever side the instructors were on, they wouldn't want to draw any attention to the base. So hopefully, the men were all tucked up in bed. If they had been set to comb the grounds, I had little chance.

Now it was going into dusk, the blackout was in effect. The staff in the manor had been well trained. The house was in almost total darkness. It would certainly leave no light showing outside. Strangely, although I have the worst sense of direction in the world, I am not bad in finding my way through empty buildings in the dark. I put this down to growing up in a rambling manor on the Fens when it was not unheard of for the lights to go out with little warning. The problems of preventing my father from trying to fix things himself, and waiting for a good tradesman to be found, meant that we'd all had to learn to circumvent the house in near pitch darkness. Once Fitzroy had pounced on me in a corridor and picked me up, I must have been no more than seven, and whispered in my ear, 'Do you know what the scariest thing in the dark is?' I think I probably only whimpered a reply. He said, 'Me!', put me down, and chased me through the house roaring like a tiger. By the end of it, when there was another tiger pounce and tickle, I had realised my senses did allow me to run in the dark as long as I paid attention.

I did so wish he were here now to pounce on me again and rescue me. I ran light-footed, as if being chased, down to the lecture room that opened out on to the grounds at the back. As I entered I felt the edge of the display table on my right. A cursory feel over the contents located the first aid kit. It was an open satchel. I managed to replace the surrounding contents that had been on display, close the flap, and slip the tab through the buckle. Then I went over to the back door and opened it, carefully.

An owl hooted. I pulled the blackout curtains tight behind me and slipped through the door, pushing it to until the latch clicked softly. From here the grounds sloped gently towards the woods on the left. To the right lay the firing range, and beyond that, well protected by hedging and fences, was the Home Farm. Directly opposite, the ground rose to a ridge at the skyline. The final part of the rise was craggy, rising to a steep, sharp-looking edge. I hadn't been up there and had no idea what lay beyond. Instead I started running towards the woods. I was about halfway when, in my peripheral vision, I saw a light. It was small and red. Some kind of filter over a torch? A cigarette being smoked? Whatever it was it wasn't floating on its own. Someone was carrying it. The road inside the manor grounds continued in that direction. It was too slow to be a car. It could be members of my search party. I dropped to the ground. Where I was there was a remote chance that anyone tall enough to see over the hedge might make out not only that something was moving in the ground beyond, but that it had a human shape.

I began to crawl along on my belly, pulling myself forward with my elbows. As well as being uncomfortable it was also slow. The ground beneath still held a faint trace of warmth from the day, but the closer I got to the wood, the rougher the terrain became. It would be even slower going.

My heart beat loud in my ears. I listened as the beat got faster and faster. My heart pounded in my chest. My breath became shallower. Now came a roaring in my head. I felt sick. I stopped and flopped forward into the earth. Breathe in for four, hold for four, breathe out for four. Breathe in for four, hold for four, breathe out for four. Repeat and repeat until you're in control.

I don't know how long it took to calm my panic. More time than I had to spare, no doubt, but I knew I had come within a hair's breadth of simply bolting across that field. I might have got away with it. Or I might have been seen by a pursuer, or for all I knew shot by a guard on duty. We hardly ever saw them, but this was a military establishment in time of war. There would be security precautions – precautions students would not be privy to.

Finally, I crawled forward again. I didn't look to see if the light that had caused my panic was still there. It didn't matter. When the slope rose enough that the trees obscured the road I got to my feet and ran.

I should have checked behind me, but I didn't. I was lucky I reached the clearing with the tree stump without anyone behind me shouting out. I kicked it where I had seen Fergus hit it. Nothing happened. I kicked again and again, but still got nothing. Finally, I got down on my hands and knees and felt around the tree stump until I found the indentation. I had been close. I got up again and kicked it hard. The tree stump opened. My feet and then my hands found a ladder. Without hesitation I stepped down onto the rungs and went lower and lower, until I was forced to pull the stump back into place.

It closed with a soft click. I had thought that the night outside with its waning moon was dark, but that was nothing to where I was now. This was as pitch darkness as I had ever known. More so. It fell like velvet around me. A smell like damp mushrooms or old leaves rose up from below me. There was also a musty animal-like scent. I wondered if this really had been an old badger sett that had been enlarged. I climbed down a couple more rungs. How far could it go?

Was that my imagination or did I hear something move? If it had been a sett, I only hoped that the badgers had been safely evicted. I didn't much like the idea of coming upon the creature in its own lair. Badgers are fierce animals that will bite and claw

343

in self-defence. I didn't like the idea of running into one in the dark.

However, the idea of running into the instructors was worse. I continued to climb down. Although it was already pitch black it felt like it became even darker as I went downwards. Darker, mustier, and all-encompassing. Looking up I could no longer make out where I had come in. Then I stepped off the ladder onto a hard floor. I stepped back and my hair brushed the top of the cavern. Carefully I got to my knees. I pulled the satchel round to my front and fumbled as I undid the tab. Then I carefully felt inside for the one thing I knew I needed: matches.

I found the box. My fingers trembled annoyingly as I lit my first match. A hiss then an orange flare as bright as the sun. My vision blurred white in shock, but I got the impression of a round-ish cavern with various box shapes at the edge. I closed my eyes to try and recapture what I had seen. The image didn't improve much.

This was a training site, but I had to believe it was laid out as an actual site would be. In which case candles or lanterns or whatever light source was there would be near at hand. I shuffled back towards the ladder, stood up, and felt around. I found a niche by the side of the left-hand side of the ladder, and a candle in it. It didn't budge when I gently pulled at it. I took out another match and lit it. I then lit the candle. The candlelight seemed as bright as a star, and although reason told me it would not be seen outside, it was hard to believe. The light didn't even reach the back of the cavern, but it did illuminate an oil lantern. This too was fixed in place on the wall, but further in. I lit this and blew out the candle by the ladder. Then I turned the lantern down as low as it would go without guttering. Tree roots arched through the earth of the roof. Small tendrils of plantlife hung down. When I traced my finger against the roof, earth, dry as dust, fell in tiny clouds. A stem of some vegetation poked out in the far wall. This reassured me that there was enough oxygen down here — unless the plant got that through the roots. I'd never been any good at botany. I could only hope that this practice den allowed occupants to breath.

I started to make an inventory of what was here. I found ammunition, but no guns. I assumed the idea was the men using this place kept the guns on them at all times. In a biscuit tin I found some kind of dried strips of meat that you would need to be very hungry to eat. I didn't find any water. There were other bits and pieces that would be useful in sabotage and setting snares, and what I was fairly certain were dummy grenades. Essentially the place was stocked as a real hideout would be, but anything perishable and any actual weapons were not included. I opened an ammo box and found it too was empty. Supplies of Bren guns I knew were limited. At dinner the men had still been talking endlessly of their luck at having a shot. Could it be that even guns and knives were also in short supply, or was it simply a reluctance to leave such useful things lying idle?

I emptied out the first aid satchel by the low light. I could now see there were two boxes of matches, some practice bandages that showed signs of frequent re-rolling, three safety pins, some cotton wool, an actual bottle of iodine, and a small pair of rather blunt scissors. There was also a large bottle of what claimed to be saline solution. If I was lucky this was filled with water. If I was unlucky it was a real bottle of saline. Either way, if I became desperate, I could drink it.

Now I had taken stock of my surroundings I could think of little else I could do. Coming here was taking a chance. If I was found there was no way out but the ladder. I would be trapped. On the positive side I was still breathing. I'd left an urgent message for aide. There was nothing more I could do, while they actively hunted me above. I found two blankets under an oil skin. I rolled one up for a pillow and wrapped the other around me. There would be no chance I would sleep, but I could take the chance to rest. I placed my matches back in the satchel and put that beside my pillow. Then I extinguished the lantern and lay my head down on my pillow. I lay staring into the dark, and rather than my mind forming images in the blackness, as it is so easy to do, I saw nothing. The den hadn't been cold, but now my body heat was warming the air about me. With three men in here it would be uncomfortably hot. With only me, it had a comforting warmth. That and the dry earthy smell reassured me. It reminded me of making dens in our own woods at White Orchards. I felt my eyelids flutter and within moments I was fast asleep.

Chapter Forty-four

I was dreaming about playing hide and seek in the woods at home. Harvey was there, as were Fitzroy and Bernie. My mother kept appearing in the most unlikely spots and complaining that tea was getting cold. It was all quite jolly, and we were determined not to go for tea until we had finished our game. Then everything changed, and instead of hiding from each other, we were being pursued by something. Something that snorted and grunted in the undergrowth. I came upon my godfather crouching down, peering into a bush. He turned to me and said, 'Whatever you do, don't look it in the eyes.' I heard my childish voice say, 'I'm not afraid,' and then I looked at the bush. Bright yellow eyes stared back at me and I was suddenly filled with terror.

I woke up sweating. For a moment I was utterly confused, then I remembered where I was. I was wearing my watch and thought about lighting a match to see the time, but the darker it got, the more chance there would be of light seeping out from the hideaway. I had a great appreciation of whoever had designed and built this hideout, but there were always limits, even to genius.

I sat up carefully and reached my hand towards the ceiling, touching it easily. In my sleep I had moved further away from the ladder. My blanket was tangled around my legs and I pulled it off me. I felt warm and drowsy. A man's voice shouted from somewhere in the woods. I stiffened in every muscle, like a gundog when he sees his master raise his gun. The voice came again. It was shouting, 'Hope'!

I moved towards the ladder to hear better. Again, and quite distinctly, the voice shouted, 'Hope!'

It didn't sound like my godfather. He would have known I would come here, and I couldn't imagine anyone else would think like that. Of course, I could have been asleep for a long time, and it might have been a matter of deduction as all else was ruled out.

This time the shout came from almost directly above. It was Harvey! Of course, he knew me better than anyone else at the manor. He might realise I would come here. I stood up and put my left foot on the bottom rung of the ladder, reaching up to grab another.

I stopped. He was calling my name and wasn't being discreet. I stepped back and scrabbled to find a match. Shielding the light as much as possible I struck it and checked my watch. I'd been asleep for around two hours. That wasn't enough time for anyone to come to my rescue. So, either Fergus had been exposed by someone else, or Harvey – Harvey was what? He'd never betray me.

I came back to the ladder. Looking up, I saw the top hinge open and a light shone directly down in my face. 'It's all right. She's here. I told you she would be,' said Harvey.

Then the bright light was gone, and when my vision recovered enough to see again, all I could spy were stars above. I heard a startled noise from Harvey, an exclamation perhaps, and there was the sound of boots shifting on the forest floor. Oh, Harvey, I thought. Who did you bring with you? Please let it be Aubrey.

'Hello, my dear,' called Fergus. 'I do believe Harvey would like you to come out now. He's having a bit of trouble speaking. I'm sure you understand.'

I understood only too well. Harvey had unknowingly put himself into a hostage situation.

'Do come out, dear girl. He's positively dying to see you,' said Fergus. His voice had a tone of amusement in it which made me feel sick.

If he wanted to get away with this, he'd have to kill both of us. He'd probably try and make it look like I killed Harvey.

'Don't think she cares about you as much as you might have thought, Harvey. Never mind, it'll all be over soon.'

I made my decision and swiftly climbed the ladder. I had no doubts that Fergus could fight and fight well. But right now, he was dealing with Harvey. He couldn't risk a gunshot, so he must be restraining him somehow. Had he stuffed something in Harvey's mouth to stop him calling out for help?

I climbed swiftly up and jumped over the side of the trunk. I wasn't going to risk Fergus following me down and shooting me like a rat in a barrel.

A shaft of moonlight illuminated the scene. I gasped. Fergus stood behind Harvey, his left arm around Harvey's neck, with his forearm bearing down on his Adam's apple. The back of his other arm was on Harvey's right shoulder. Fergus gripped his own right arm with his left hand, and I knew, without seeing, that his right hand would be on the back of Harvey's head. This was a stranglehold. I'd never seen it before, but I remembered Fitzroy talking about something he'd seen when in Asia. I recalled all too well him describing it and warning me never to let someone hold me like that because there was no way out. As Fergus pulled backwards with his left arm and pressed Harvey's head forward with his right, all oxygen would be cut off. Harvey would die quickly and silently. It was an assassin's move.

'Harvey has been saying such nice things about you,' said Fergus. 'Unfortunately, he seems a bit sleepy now. If you're a good girl, maybe I'll let your boyfriend wake up.'

'What do you want me to do?'

'Over there by the tree you'll find a stub of a pencil and a sheet of paper. I need you to write your confession. Believe me, the pencil is far too short to be of use as a weapon. I shaved it down specially for you.'

'Then you'll let Harvey go?' Harvey started to slump. If Fergus didn't let him go soon, he would die. The move he was using was designed primarily for a quick kill, not for holding someone between life and death.

I had to do something now.

Fergus smiled. 'It's the best chance he has. It's not like he's going to remember what's happened, is it?'

'And then what? You kill me?'

'I'm afraid so, Hope. I'll make it swift.'

'You don't think I can defend myself?'

'Possibly, but even if you try, I'll still beat you. I suppose something of a struggle would appear more convincing. Should I give you first go?'

Harvey's face grew whiter. I saw a flutter of movement under his eyelids indicating he was still alive, but only barely. Then whatever trick of the night had let me see him, was gone.

I turned and fled toward the manor as fast as I could. The only chance Harvey had was if Fergus released him to chase me.

'Help!' I called as I ran. Better to be locked up in a cell than dead out here.

I heard the sound of Harvey's body fall to the ground as Fergus let him go. I prayed it wasn't too late.

'Help!' I was too far away for anyone at the manor to hear me yet, but they were supposed to be out searching for me. Where were they? Ruddy useless search party!

I broke out of the tree line. I could hear Fergus closing in behind me. My heart pumped adrenaline, giving me speed, but I had slept in a curled-up position and my muscles were knotted. I caught my foot on something and stumbled. My arms flailed. I flung them out to steady myself. Thankfully I didn't go down, but I lost a few precious moments. Fergus caught me.

He threw his arms around my torso in a crushing bear hug, lifting me clean off my feet and into the air. I felt his strength as his arms tightened around my ribs. All the air burst out of my lungs. I heard him give a grunt of satisfaction.

I kicked as hard as I could at his right knee. He cried out in pain and staggered back slightly, but his hold didn't loosen. I whipped my head backwards, connecting with his nose. It made a thoroughly satisfying crunching noise and he finally released me.

I landed on my feet and went to make a break for it. A broken nose makes your eyes tear up, you simply can't help it, and as he wouldn't be able to see me, if I could just . . .

I had underestimated his resolution. His hand grasped the top of my head, grabbing a handful of my hair. I immediately put my hands up to the top of my head, one clasping his wrist, the other his arm. I didn't need to think about it. I knew this move so well. I turned, breaking his grip and bringing his arm away from my head, moving it down into an arm lock in front of me, but as I shifted my weight onto my left side, my ankle twisted, and I stumbled. I didn't let go, but neither did I see him swinging his other arm around. The punch landed full force on the side of my face.

A searing pain exploded along my jawline. The world swum around me. Letting go, I fell to the ground. I groggily turned on my side to see him raise his boot high above my face, ready to stomp it down in what would undoubtedly be a killing blow. Knowing the underside of his boot would be the last thing I saw, I was about to close my eyes, when I saw a fast-moving object in the night sky. I thought I was hallucinating until, with it, came the sound of propellers.

The noise became deafening. Fergus looked up, and with the last of my strength, I grabbed at the bottom of his boot and, levering myself up, propelled him backwards as hard as I could.

The plane passed directly over us and the noise diminished. I watched Fergus topple and fall to the ground, hard.

I shuffled backwards, trying to put some distance between myself and him. My head still screamed with pain, but I was alive. I waited for his next move.

It never came. Fergus didn't move.

Aware this could be a trick, I approached him slowly. Within a few feet I could see a dark stain spreading out among the grass around his head. Coming closer, I saw his head was impaled on a sharp stick jutting out of the ground. It was what I had caught my foot on when trying to run away from him. A wire snare was attached to it. West. Colin West, ex-poacher, who loved a bit of jugged rabbit. If he'd been there at that moment, I would have kissed him.

I stood up, swaying, wondering if my skull had been cracked. It wasn't possible for your head to hurt this much and live, was it?

Then I heard the sound of the plane again as it banked and turned. As I watched it approach the grounds, the wings were dipping this way and that. The course was erratic.

I was going to be really angry if, after fighting off the traitorous Fergus, I was going to be done in by a plane landing on me. It came down, bouncing two or three times in the process, before it came to a halt. I could see now it wasn't a military aircraft.

The pilot sprang out of the cabin, landing neatly on the ground, far better than he had landed his plane. He was wearing a long coat, and I could see by the way it moved that he walked with a distinct swagger.

I stumbled forward. 'Fitzroy,' I shouted. 'Help. Harvey . . . Harvey is . . .'

I collapsed onto the ground. The next thing I remember was my godfather leaning over me and gently running his fingers down the side of my face. He was wearing a flying cap and goggles pushed back on his head, and the starlight made them shine like moons

'Good heavens, Hope! What have you been doing? This is most inconvenient.' He might have said more, but knowing he was there I allowed unconsciousness to claim me.

Chapter Forty-five

I came to lying on a settee in an office I didn't recognise. The grouchy, frowning face of the base's long-suffering doctor hovered above me. 'Ah, you're awake. Most people enjoy having a head on their shoulders, young woman. Can I suggest, if you wish to keep yours, you take more care of your skull.' He stood up. 'As far as I can tell, she'll be all right. Terrible headache. At least you're not flying an open cockpit. De Havilland Moth, isn't it? Used to fly one myself, before the war.'

'Leopard Moth,' said my godfather. 'That's right. So, she can travel?'

'If it's essential.'

'It is,' said Fitzroy.

I tried sitting up. A thunderclap went off in my brain. I paused and tried again. This time I felt hands helping me. Fitzroy sat down on a chair next to me.

'Harvey?' I said.

'He's fine.'

'Court-martial?' Words made my head hurt.

'You?' said Fitzroy with genuine amusement in his voice. 'No, not this time.'

Aubrey and Hugh came into view. 'Hello,' I said. Then added, 'Sirs'.

Both of them drew up chairs. I propped myself up on the cushions and looked at the three senior officers surrounding me.

'I am so sorry this happened,' said Aubrey. 'Fergus was excellent at his job. None of us had any idea.'

353

'I don't understand . . .' I said, looking at Hugh.

'It's complicated,' said Hugh. 'It's true my father was a fan of the Nazis. I informed on him a long time ago. I trusted Fergus though. He and I watched my father and sister together. As my father's private secretary, he had access to all his communications. I think you will understand when I say my father and I didn't see eye to eye. Fergus passed information to me, and I passed it on to the authorities. Now, of course, I'll have to let them know it's all suspect. What a mess.' He passed a hand over his face. 'When you said you'd found some papers, I didn't think it possible. Fergus was always so careful and tidy. But no one's perfect, he must have forgotten those – or kept them for some reason.'

'My people will sweep the place,' said Fitzroy, 'but I imagine that once Hope found them, he would have burned them.'

'Why did you blackmail Dean Fordham?' said Aubrey.

'Didn't want to be found,' I said. 'Wanted help finding the village and searching for information. His aunt lived there. Censor missed the village map. Very stylised. Hate blackmail. Like Dean,' I ended somewhat forlornly.

'Tut tut, Hope,' said my godfather enigmatically.

'He showed some real gumption, coming to me the way he did,' said Hugh. 'I mean, all of us instructors knew, but he wanted my permission to tell the men – rather than let you do it.'

'Yes, yes,' said my godfather. 'Terribly brave and all that. I've never understood why people are so bothered by . . . oh, but I digress. Are you satisfied? Can I take my goddaughter away? I'd rather fly by night. There are no guns on that plane, you know. I'm not interested in dancing with the Luftwaffe. Pretty awful pilot at the best of times, and if we die up there, I'll be the first ghost to be haunted by a vengeful human.' He looked down at me. 'Your mother, in case it isn't obvious.'

'He met Danville in the village,' I said.

I heard Fitzroy take a short breath. He swore obscenely, making both Hugh and Aubrey start.

'You didn't know?' I said.

'This is going to be . . . well, anyway, gentlemen, this has been interesting. I doubt we'll meet again, as my goddaughter has done the necessary and rooted out the double agent. Awfully rare, an Englishman turning on his own country. Makes it harder to spot.'

'I do think it would be best if you called in your flight plan, just in case any young blood decides to take pot shots at you.'

Fitzroy got up. 'Oh, very well. If it was only me . . .' and stalked out of the room.

Hugh rose and shook my hand. 'Thank you very much, Miss Stapleford or do I address you by rank?'

'Hope is fine,' I said.

Hugh gave me a nod and left.

'I'll wait till your godfather comes back,' said Aubrey. 'He's a smart man. He put it all together from the bits and pieces we were able to tell him.'

'He was trying to get information on the auxis to the Germans, for the invasion, wasn't he?' I said. My head was becoming clearer and less painful. I rubbed at an injection mark on my arm. I'd been given something. I wondered how long it would last.

Aubrey nodded.

'I heard them,' I said. 'They were talking about things not going as expected and what they should do. Danville was telling him to sit tight.'

'You didn't report that?'

'Fergus had me convinced he was an intelligence operative,' I said. 'Please don't tell Fitzroy that. He'll think I'm such a fool.'

'You had better tell him yourself. Those few comments you overheard might be significant.'

'How?' I said.

'Goodness, Hope,' said Aubrey. 'You must have been hit in the head awfully hard. He might have been talking about the Germans cancelling their invasion plan. Our boys in the RAF have been putting up a hell of a fight.'

'Oh, gosh,' I said. 'That never occurred to me.'

'What didn't,' said Fitzroy re-entering the room.

355

I told him.

He shrugged. 'My people can look into that too. Mind you, fits with what I thought all along. It's bloody hard to invade an island. Even harder when that island is Britain.'

Aubrey stood up. He offered me a hand. 'Do you want some help getting up . . . What *is* her rank?' he asked Fitzroy.

'Lieutenant. Can't remember if I made her a first or a second one. Mind you, people get promoted quick as lightning during a war. Does it matter?'

'It would have been nice to know,' I said.

'Bah,' said Fitzroy. 'I don't have the time to tell you every little thing.' Then he bent down and picked me up in his arms. 'Hmm, not as light as a bird, but then you do like your cakes. Rather too much like your aunt. Never mind.'

He walked towards the door as Aubrey ran forward to work the blackout curtains for him.

'I'm sure I can walk,' I said.

'I'm sure you can't,' said Fitzroy. 'We've wasted too much time already.'

He carried me out into the cold night air. Aubrey opened the door of the passenger side of the plane and Fitzroy more or less hoisted me up. Even the act of hauling myself into the seat sent my head spinning. I closed my eyes.

I heard Fitzroy get in beside me. 'There are bags in the door pocket if you're going to be sick but do try not to be. The smell will linger.'

The propellers whirred into action.

I leaned back in my seat and looked out at the stars scattered across the night sky. It was, as ever, a breathtaking sight.

'That's a thought,' said Fitzroy. 'Maybe I should teach you how to find your way by the stars. I don't believe you will ever acquire a sense of direction now.'

The plane bumped along the grass as Fitzroy turned it around, paused for a moment, then with an intense expression set off across the fields gathering speed. I thought it would be very rude of me to close my eyes, so I held on tight to the sides of my seat. At least we were going towards the fields and not the trees.

We went faster and faster, then there was a sudden weightless feeling and we were aloft. We rose into the air, and the intense expression on my godfather's face relaxed. 'Well, that went well,' he said. I tried not to hear the tone of surprise in his voice.

'Where are we going?'

'Ah,' said my godfather. 'We're going to White Orchards. Your mother needs us.'

'We're flying home?'

'Hmm, yes. I would have thought was obvious,' said my godfather tapping at one of the dials in front of him. 'Wonder why it's doing that? Probably not important.' He looked at me for a moment. 'I must remember to give this plane back.'

'It's not yours?'

'Commandeered it. Privilege of rank. Colonel.'

'Lieutenant-Colonel,' I corrected him.

He shrugged. 'No one keeps track of these things during wartime. The longer you survive, the more you get promoted. Ridiculous really.'

'Why does my mother need us?'

'I was hoping you wouldn't ask that – not yet anyway. This is an excellent opportunity for me to teach you about the stars. Even you must know where Orion's Belt is. We can start with the North Star.'

'Orion's what? Oh, never mind. Tell me, why are we going home?'

Fitzroy kept looking forward, but I saw his shoulders move as he gave a big sigh. 'I'm sorry, Hope. It's your father.'

Epilogue

'On your knees.'

The first light of day broke across the forest sending out rays of gold between the trees. Night began to slide away in hues of purple and blue. At the centre of a small clearing a man slowly knelt down on the uneven ground.

'Come on! I was following orders,' he said. His tone somewhere between jocular disbelief and pleading. 'I only did what I was told.'

'Which was?' said Cole. He stood behind his prisoner, pistol levelled.

'To frighten her.'

'What was it? A blood-rush of excitement in terrorising a young woman that made you go too far? Or was it that she was naked in her bath?'

'Well, that was unforeseen, but my good luck. She's a looker. I like them curvy . . .' The kneeling man smiled and tried to turn his head.

'Eyes forward,' snapped Cole. 'The timing of your mission?'

'Like I told you, pure chance. I'd been keeping an eye on her place for the previous couple of weeks, but this time she came home alone, and she left the balcony windows open. I mean, I'd been told she was good, but that was a rookie mistake. The way I got to her, too easy. She hid. Stayed frozen in her bath, like a pretty little piglet waiting for the slaughter.'

'I see.'

'Fought like a tiger though, when I went for her. No screaming. She's a survivor. I'll give her that. Thinks on her feet too.
When you grab their legs and pull them under, ninety-nine
people out of a hundred drown. They don't have the guts to do
what's needed.'

'So, you did mean to kill her?'

'Nah, I was going to let her up. I told you. I keep telling you.
I only meant to rough her up a bit. Of course, her being naked,
there were temptations . . .'

'I see.'

'She got no more than a few bruises from me. You came charging in like a white knight. Hit me like a bloody horse you did. I
don't think my face will ever be quite right again.'

'Shame.'

'So, can I get up now? You've made your point.'

'No,' said Cole. 'I don't believe I have.'

The morning chorus broke as a single shot rang out, and the
birds of the forest weaved in alarm between the trees.

Cole walked out of the forest and back towards the farmhouse.

We hope you have enjoyed reading *Hope to Survive*.

Don't miss *Hope for the Innocent*!

With war approaching, innocence is the first casualty. Hope soon finds herself thrust into a web of political intrigue that threatens the very heart of the nation . . .

For further information about the Hope Stapleford series as well as the Euphemia Martins mysteries and to read exclusive extracts from Fitzroy's private diary visit: caroline-dunford.squarespace.com.

And if you'd like to receive the Euphemia and Hope monthly newsletter please email carolinedunfordauthor@gmail.com with your request.